THE HUNTED

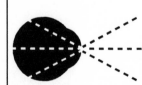

This Large Print Book carries the
Seal of Approval of N.A.V.H.

THE HUNTED

BRIAN HAIG

THORNDIKE PRESS

A part of Gale, Cengage Learning

GALE
CENGAGE Learning·

Detroit • New York • San Francisco • New Haven, Conn • Waterville, Maine • London

BOCA RATON PUBLIC LIBRARY
BOCA RATON, FLORIDA

GALE
CENGAGE Learning™

Copyright © 2009 by Brian Haig.
Thorndike Press, a part of Gale, Cengage Learning.

Thorndike Press® Large Print Basic.
The text of this Large Print edition is unabridged.
Other aspects of the book may vary from the original edition.
Set in 16 pt. Plantin.
Printed on permanent paper.

LIBRARY OF CONGRESS CATALOGING-IN-PUBLICATION DATA

Haig, Brian.
   The hunted / by Brian Haig.
     p. cm. — (Thorndike Press large print basic)
    ISBN-13: 978-1-4104-2166-1 (alk. paper)
    ISBN-10: 1-4104-2166-X (alk. paper)
    1. Large type books. I. Title.
   PS3608.A54H86 2009b
   813'.6—dc22   2009031134

Published in 2009 by arrangement with Grand Central Publishing, a division of Hachette Book Group, Inc.

Printed in the United States of America
1 2 3 4 5 6 7 13 12 11 10 09

For Lisa, Brian, Pat, Donnie, and Annie.
Dedicated to Elena.

ACKNOWLEDGMENTS

There are always very many people to thank when a book is finally slapped on the shelves for sale. Certainly my family: Lisa, Brian, Paddie, Donnie, and Annie, who are always my inspiration, especially since the kids are all facing college, and I have to pay the bills. Also my parents, Al and Pat Haig — they are in every way absolutely wonderful parents, and I love them both.

And of course everybody at Grand Central Publishing, from top to bottom, a remarkable collection of talented people who couldn't be more helpful or exquisitely professional: Jamie Raab, the lovely, warmhearted publisher; my overwhelmingly gifted and understanding editor, Mitch Hoffman; the very forgiving pair of Mari Okuda and Roland Ottewell, who do the too-necessary patchwork of repairing the horribly flawed drafts I send and somehow, remarkably, make them readable; and Anne Twomey and George Cornell, who designed this stunning cover.

Most especially I want to thank my trusted agent and dear friend, Luke Janklow, and his family. Every writer should have an agent like Luke.

Last, I want to thank my friend and favorite writer, Nelson DeMille, who in addition to being — in my view — America's best and most entertaining author, does more to help and encourage aspiring writers get a start than anybody. When I first met Nelson he generously offered this great advice: "You will only write so many books, so do your best to make each one as perfect as you can."

He does, I try to, and I very much hope you enjoy this latest effort.

■ ■ ■ ■

BOOK ONE:
THE HEIST

■ ■ ■ ■

1

November 1991

In the final days of an empire that was wheezing and lurching toward death, the aide watched his boss stare out the window into the darkness. Time was running out. The fate of the entire nation hinged on the next move at this juncture; the entire planet, possibly.

Any minute, his boss was due to pop upstairs and see Mikhail Gorbachev to deliver either a path to salvation or a verdict of damnation.

But exactly what advice do you offer the doctor who has just poisoned his own patient?

Only three short miles away, he knew, Boris Yeltsin had just uncorked and was slurping down his third bottle of champagne. Totally looped, the man was getting even more utterly hammered. A celebration of some sort, or so it appeared, though the aide had not a clue what lay behind it. A KGB operative dressed as a waiter was hauling the hooch, keeping a watchful eye on ol' Boris and, between refills, calling in the latest updates.

After seventy years of struggle and turmoil, it all came down to this; the fate of the world's last great empire hinged on a titanic struggle between two men — one ordained to go down as the most pathetically naïve general secretary ever; the other an obnoxious, loudmouthed lush.

Gorbachev was frustrated and humiliated, both men knew. He had inherited a kingdom founded on a catechism of bad ideas and constructed on a mountain of corpses. What was supposed to be a worker's paradise now looked with unrequited envy at third world countries and pondered how it had all gone so horribly wrong. How ironic.

Pitiful, really.

For all its fearsome power — the world's largest nuclear arsenal, the world's biggest army, colonies and "client" nations sprinkled willy-nilly around the globe — the homeland itself was a festering pile of human misery and material junk.

Two floors above them in his expansive office, Gorbachev was racking his brain, wondering how to coax the genie back into the bottle. Little late for that, they both knew. He had unleashed his woolly-headed liberalizing ideas — first, that asinine glasnost, then the slam dunk of them all, perestroika — thinking a blitzkrieg of truth and fresh ideas would stave off a collapse that seemed all but

12

inevitable; inevitable to him, anyway. What was he thinking?

The history of the Soviet Union was so thoroughly shameful — so pockmarked with murders, genocide, treachery, corruption, egomania — it needed to rest on a mattress of lies to be even moderately palatable. Fear, flummery, and fairy tales — the three F's — those were the glue that held things together.

Now everything was coming apart at the seams: the Soviet republics were threatening to sprint from the union, the Eastern Bloc countries had already made tracks, and communism itself was teetering into a sad folly.

Way to go, Gorby.

On the streets below them a speaker with windmilling arms and megaphones for tonsils was working up a huge rabble that was growing rowdier and more rambunctious by the second. The bulletproof thickened windows smeared out his exact words; as if they needed to hear; as if they wanted to hear. Same thing street-corner preachers were howling and exhorting from Petersburg to Vladivostok: time for democracy; long past time for capitalism. Communism was an embarrassing failure that needed to be flushed down the toilet of history with all the other old faulty ideas. Just rally around Boris. Let's send Gorby and the last of his wrinkly old apparatchiks packing.

His boss cracked a wrinkled knuckle and

asked softly, "So what do I tell Gorbachev?"

"Tell him he's an idiot. Tell him he ruined everything."

"He already knows that."

Then tell him to eat a bullet, Ivan Yutskoi wanted to say. Better yet, do us all a big favor, shove him out the window and have that spot-headed idiot produce a big red splat in the middle of Red Square. Future historians would adore that punctuation point.

Sergei Golitsin, deputy director of the KGB, glowered and cracked another knuckle. He cared less for what this idiot thought. "Tell me you've finally found where Yeltsin's money's coming from."

"Okay. We have."

"About time. Where?"

"It's a little hard to believe."

"I'll believe anything these days. Try me."

"Alex Konevitch."

The deputy director gave him a mean look. After a full year of shrugged shoulders, wasted effort, and lame excuses, the triumphant tone in his aide's voice annoyed him. "And am I supposed to know this name?" he snapped.

"Well, no . . . you're not . . . really."

"Then tell me about . . . what's this name?"

"Alex Konevitch." Yutskoi stuffed his nose into the thick folder, shuffled a few papers, and withdrew and fixated on one typed sheet. "Young. Only twenty-two. Born and raised in an obscure village in the Ural Mountains you've never heard of. Both parents are educators, mother dead, father formerly the head of a small, unimportant college. Alex was a physics student at Moscow University."

Yutskoi paused for the reaction he knew was coming. "Only twenty-two," his boss commented with a furious scowl. "He ran circles around you idiots."

"I've got photographs," said Yutskoi, ignoring that outburst. He withdrew a few blown-up eight-by-ten color photos from his thick file and splayed them like a deck of cards before his boss. Golitsin walked across the room, bent forward, adjusted his rimless glasses, and squinted.

The shots were taken, close up, by a breathtakingly attractive female agent who had entered Konevitch's office only the day before on the pretext of looking for a job. Olga's specialty was honeypot operations, the luring of victims into the sack for entrapment or the value of their pillow talk. She could do shy Japanese schoolgirls, a kittenish vixen, the frosty teacher in need of a role reversal, a doctor, a nurse, a wild cowgirl — whatever men lusted after in their most flamboyant yearnings, Olga could be it, and then some.

Olga had never been turned down. Not once, ever.

A top-to-bottom white blonde, she had gone in attired in an aggressively short skirt, low-cut blouse — not too low, though — and braless. Olga had pitch-perfect intuition about these things: no reason to doubt her instincts now. Demure, not slutty, she had artfully suggested. A few tactful hints, but sledgehammers were to be avoided.

Alex Konevitch was a successful business-man, after all; office games were the play of the day.

A miniature broadcasting device had been hidden in her purse, and every chance she had she snapped pictures of him with the miniature camera concealed inside her brace-let. Yutskoi reached into his folder and withdrew a tape recorder. The cassette was preloaded and ready to roll. "Olga," he mentioned casually, requiring no further introduction. "She was instructed merely to get a job and learn more about him. If something else developed, well, all the bet-ter."

Golitsin jerked his head in approval, and Yutskoi set the device down on the desk and pushed play.

Golitsin craned forward and strained to hear every word, every nuance.

First came the sounds of Alex Konevitch's homely middle-aged secretary ushering Olga into his office, followed by the usual nice-to-meet-you, nice-to-meet-you-too claptrap before the game began.

Very businesslike, Konevitch: "Why do you

16

want to work here?"

Olga: "Who wouldn't? The old system's rotten to its core and ready to collapse. The corpse just hasn't yet recognized it's dead. We all know that. This is the best of the new. I'll learn a lot."

"Previous work experience?"

"Secretarial and statistical work, mostly. There were the two years I spent working at the State Transportation Bureau, helping estimate how many bus axles we would need next year. Bus axles? . . . Can you believe it? I nearly died of boredom. Then the Farm Statistics Bureau, where I'm stuck now. Do you know what it's like spending a whole month trying to project the demand for imported kumquats?"

"I can't imagine."

"Don't even try." She laughed and he joined her.

Back to business, Konevitch: "Okay, now why should I want you?"

A long and interesting pause. Stupid question — open your eyes, Alex, and use a little imagination.

Olga, sounding perfectly earnest: "I type eighty words a minute, take dictation, have good phone manners, and am very, very loyal to my boss."

Another interesting pause.

Then, as if Konevitch missed the point: "I have a very capable secretary already."

"Not like me, you don't."

"Meaning what?"

"I will make you very happy."

Apparently not, because Konevitch asked quite seriously, "What do you know about finance?"

"Not much. But I'm a fast study."

"Do you have a university degree?"

"No, and neither do you."

Another pause, this one long and unfortunate.

Konevitch, in a suddenly wary voice: "How do you know that?"

"I . . . your receptionist . . ." Long pause, then with uncharacteristic hesitance, "Yes, I believe she mentioned it."

"He. His name is Dmetri."

"All right . . . he. I misspoke. Who cares who told me?"

Konevitch, sounding surprisingly blasé: "What gave you the idea I'm looking to hire?"

"Maybe you're not. I'm fishing. My mother is desperately ill. Throat and lung cancer. Soviet medicine will kill her, and I need money for private treatments. Her life depends on it."

Nice touch, Yutskoi thought, admiring Olga's spontaneous shift of tack. Among the few details they *had* gleaned about Alex Konevitch was that his mother had passed away, at the young age of thirty-two, of bone cancer in a state sanitarium. Like everything in this country, Soviet medicine was dreadful. Yutskoi pictured Mrs. Konevitch in a lumpy bed with filthy sheets, writhing and screaming as her bone sores oozed and burned and her young son looked on in helpless agony.

Surely that pathetic memory rushed into Alex's head as he considered this poor girl and her ailing mother. Have a heart, Alex; you have the power to save her mama from an excruciating, all but certain death. She'll twitch and suffer and cough her lungs out, and it will be all your fault.

"I'm sorry, I don't think you'll fit in."

She had been instructed to get the job, whatever it took, and she had given it her best shot and then some. Olga's perfect record was in ruins.

Yutskoi slid forward in his seat and flipped off the recorder. A low grunt escaped Golitsin's lips, part disappointment, part awe. They leaned forward together and studied with greater intensity the top photograph of Alex Konevitch taken by Olga. The face in the photo was lean, dark-haired and dark-eyed, handsome but slightly babyfaced, and he was smiling, though it seemed distant and distinctly forced.

Nobody had to coerce a smile when Olga was in the room. Nobody. Golitsin growled, "Maybe you should've sent in a cute boy instead."

19

"No evidence of that," his aide countered. "We interviewed some of his former college classmates. He likes the ladies. Nothing against one-night stands, either."

"Maybe he subsequently experienced an industrial accident. Maybe he was castrated," Golitsin suggested, which really was the one explanation that made the most sense.

Or maybe he suspected Olga.

"Look at him, dressed like an American yuppie," Golitsin snorted, thumping a derisive finger on a picture. It was true, Konevitch looked anything but Russian in his tan slacks and light blue, obviously imported cotton button-down dress shirt, without tie, and with his sleeves rolled up to the elbows. The picture was grainy and slightly off-center. He looked, though, like he just stepped out of one of those American catalogues: a young spoiled prototypical capitalist in the making. Golitsin instantly hated him.

He had been followed around the clock for the past three days. The observers were thoroughly impressed. A working animal, the trackers characterized him, plainly exhausted from trying to keep up with his pace. The man put in hundred-hour workweeks without pause. He seemed to sprint through every minute of it.

Broad-shouldered, with a flat stomach, he obviously worked hard to stay in tip-top shape. Olga had learned from the receptionist that he had a black belt, third degree, in some obscure Asian killing art. He did an hour of heavy conditioning in the gym every day. Before work, too. Since he arrived in the office at six sharp and usually kicked off after midnight, sleep was not a priority. Olga had also remarked on his height, about six and a half feet, that she found him ridiculously sexy, and for once, the target was one *she* would enjoy boinking.

Yutskoi quickly handed his boss a brief fact sheet that summarized everything known to date about Alex Konevitch. Not much.

"So he's smart," Golitsin said with a scowl after a cursory glance. That was all the paucity of information seemed to show.

"Very smart. Moscow University, physics major. Second highest score in the country his year on the university entrance exam."

Alex had been uncovered only three days before, and so far only a sketchy bureaucratic background check had been possible. They would dig deeper and learn more later. A lot more.

But Moscow University was for the elite of the elite, and the best of those were bunched and prodded into the hard sciences, mathematics, chemistry, or physics. In the worker's paradise, books, poetry, and art were useless tripe and frowned upon, barely worth wasting an ounce of IQ over. The real eggheads were drafted for more socially progressive purposes, like designing bigger atomic warheads and longer-range, more accurate missiles.

Golitsin backed away from the photo and moved to the window. He was rotund with short squatty legs and a massive bulge under a recessed chin that looked like he'd swallowed a million flies. He had a bald, glistening head and dark eyes that bulged whenever he was angry, which happened to be most of the time. "And where has Konevitch been getting all this money from?" he asked.

"Would you care to guess?"

"Okay, the CIA? The Americans always use money."

Yutskoi shook his head.

Another knuckle cracked. "Stop wasting my time."

"Right, well, it's his. All of it."

Golitsin's thick eyebrows shot up. "Tell me about that."

"Turned out he was already in our files. In 1986, Konevitch was caught running a private construction company out of his university dorm room. Quite remarkable. He employed six architects and over a hundred workers of assorted skills."

"That would be impossible to hide, a criminal operation of such size and scale," the general noted, accurately it turned out.

"You're right," his aide confirmed. "As

usual, somebody snitched. A jealous class-mate."

"So this Konevitch was always a greedy criminal deviant."

"So it seems. We reported this to the dean at Moscow University, with the usual directive that the capitalist thief Konevitch be marched across a stage in front of his fellow students, disgraced, and immediately booted out."

"Of course."

"Turns out we did him a big favor. Konevitch dove full-time into construction work, expanded his workforce, and spread his projects all over Moscow. People are willing to pay under the table for quality, and Konevitch established a reputation for reliability and value. Word spread, and customers lined up at his door. When perestroika and free-market reforms were put in place, he cleaned up."

"From construction work?"

"That was only the start. Do you know what arbitrage is?"

"No, tell me."

"Well . . . it's a tool capitalists employ. When there are price differences for similar goods, an arbitrager can buy low, sell it all off at a higher price, and pocket the difference. Like gambling, he more or less bets on the margins in between. Konevitch's work gave him intimate familiarity with the market for

23

construction materials, so this was the sector he first concentrated in."

"And this is . . . successful?"

"Like you wouldn't believe. A price vacuum was created when Gorbachev encouraged free-market economics. The perfect condition for an arbitrager, and Konevitch swooped in. There's a lot of construction and no pricing mechanism for anything."

"Okay."

That okay aside, Yutskoi suspected this was going over his boss's head. "Say, for example, a factory manager in Moscow prices a ton of steel nails at a thousand rubles. A different factory manager in Irkutsk might charge ten thousand rubles. They were all pulling numbers out of thin air. Nobody had a clue what a nail was worth."

"And our friend would buy the cheaper nails?" Golitsin suggested, maybe getting it after all.

"Yes, like that. By the truckload. He would pay one thousand rubles for a ton in Moscow, find a buyer in Irkutsk willing to pay five thousand, then pocket the difference."

Golitsin scrunched his face with disgust. "So this is about nails?" He snorted.

"Nails, precut timber, steel beams, wall board, concrete, roofing tiles, heavy construction equipment . . . he gets a piece of everything. A big piece. His business swelled from piddling to gigantic in nothing flat."

24

Sergei Golitsin had spent thirty years in the KGB, but not one of those outside the Soviet empire and the impoverishing embrace of communism. Domestic security was his bread and butter, an entire career spent crushing and torturing his fellow citizens. He had barely a clue what arbitrage was, didn't really care to know, but he nodded anyway and concluded, "So the arbitrager is a cheat."

"That's a way of looking at it."

"He produces nothing."

"You're right, absolutely nothing."

"He sucks the cream from other people's sweat and labor. A big fat leech."

"Essentially, he exploits an opening in a free-market system. It's a common practice in the West. Highly regarded, even. Nobody on Wall Street ever produced a thing. Most of the richest people in America couldn't build a wheel, much less run a factory if their lives depended on it."

Golitsin still wasn't sure how it worked, but he was damned sure he didn't like it. He asked, "And how much has he . . . this Konevitch character . . . how much has he given Yeltsin?"

"Who knows? A lot. In American currency, maybe ten million, maybe twenty million dollars."

"He had that much?"

"And then some. Perhaps fifty million dollars altogether. But this is merely a rough estimate on our part. Could be more."

Golitsin stared at Yutskoi in disbelief. "You're saying at twenty-two, he's the richest man in the Soviet Union."

"No, probably not. A lot of people are making a ton of money right now." Yutskoi looked down and toyed with his fingers a moment. "It would be fair to say, though, he's in the top ten."

The two men stared down at their shoes and shared the same depressing thought neither felt the slightest desire to verbalize. If communism went up in flames, their beloved KGB would be the first thing tossed onto the bonfire. In a vast nation with more than forty languages and dialects, and nearly as many different ethnic groups, there was only one unifying factor, one common thread — nearly every citizen in the Soviet Union had been scorched by their bureau in one way or another. Not directly, perhaps. But somebody dear, or at least close: grandfathers purged by Stalin; fathers who had disappeared and rotted in the camps under Brezhnev; aunts and uncles brought in for a little rough questioning under Andropov. Something. Nearly every family tree had at least one branch crippled or lopped off by the boys from the Lubyanka. The list of grudges was endless and bitter.

Yutskoi was tempted to smile at his boss and say: I hope it all does fall apart. Five years being your bootlicker, I've hated every minute of it. You'll be totally screwed, you nasty old relic.

Golitsin knew exactly what the younger man was thinking, and was ready to reply: You're a replaceable, third-rate lackey today, and you'll be a starving lackey tomorrow. Only in this system could a suck-up loser like you survive. The only thing you're good at is plucking fingernails from helpless victims. And you're not even that good at that.

Yutskoi: I'm young and frisky; I'll adapt. You're a starched lizard, a wrinkled old toad, an icy anachronism. Your own grandchildren fill their diapers at the sight of you. I'll hire you to shine my shoes.

Golitsin: I cheated and backstabbed and ass-kissed my way up to three-star general in this system, and I'll find a way in the next one, whatever that turns out to be. You, on the other hand, will always be a suck-up loser.

"Why?" asked Golitsin. As in, why would Alex Konevitch give Yeltsin that much money?

"Revenge could be a factor, I suppose."

"To get back at the system that tried to ruin him. How pedestrian."

"But, I think," Yutskoi continued, trying to look thoughtful, "mostly influence. If the union disintegrates, Yeltsin will wind up president of the newly independent Russia. He'll owe this guy a boatload of favors. A lot of state enterprises are going to be privatized

27

and put on the auction block. Konevitch will have his pick — oil, gas, airlines, banks, car companies — whatever his greedy heart desires. He could end up as rich as Bill Gates. Probably richer."

Golitsin leaned back and stared up at the ceiling. It was too horrible to contemplate. Seventy years of blood, strain, and sweat was about to be ladled out, first come, first served — the biggest estate sale the world had ever witnessed. The carcass of the world's largest empire carved up and bitterly fought over. The winners would end up rich beyond all imagination. What an ugly, chaotic scramble that was going to be.

"So why didn't we find out about this Alex Konevitch sooner?" Golitsin snapped. Good question. When, three years before, Boris Yeltsin first began openly shooting the bird at Gorbachev and the Communist Party, the KGB hadn't worried overly much. Yeltsin was back then just another windbag malcontent: enough of those around to be sure.

But Yeltsin was a whiner with a big difference; he had once been a Politburo member, so he understood firsthand exactly how decrepit, dim-witted, incompetent, and scared the old boys at the top were.

That alone made him more dangerous than the typical blow-hard.

And when he announced he was running for the presidency of Russia — the largest, most powerful republic in the union — the KGB instantly changed its mind and decided to take him dreadfully seriously indeed.

His offices and home were watched by an elite squad of nosy agents 24/7. His phones were tapped, his offices and home stuffed with enough bugs and listening gadgets to hear a fly fart. Several agents insinuated themselves inside his campaign organization and kept the boys at the center up to date on every scrap and rumor they overheard. Anybody who entered or left Yeltsin's offices was shadowed and, later, approached by a team of thugs who looked fierce and talked even fiercer. Give Boris a single ruble, they were warned, and you'll win the national lotto — a one-way ticket to the most barren, isolated, ice-laden camp in Siberia.

Concern, not worry, was the prevailing mood among the big boys in the KGB. This was their game. After seventy years of undermining democracy around the world, they knew exactly how to squeeze and strangle Yeltsin. An election takes money, lots of it; cash for travel and aides and people to carry and spread the message across the bulging, diverse breadth of a nation nearly three times the size of America.

Boris wasn't getting a ruble. Not a single ruble. He would rail and flail to his heart's content in empty halls and be roundly ignored. After being thoroughly shellacked in the polls, he would crawl under a rock and drink himself into the grave. So long, Boris, you idiot.

It was the inside boys who first raised the alarm. Hard cash was being ladled out by the fistful to campaign employees, to travel agencies, to advertisers, to political organizers. The conclusion was disquieting and inescapable: somewhere in the shadows a white knight was shoveling money at Yeltsin, gobs of it. Boris was spending a fortune flying across Russia in a rented jet, staying in high-class hotels, and to be taken more seriously, he had even traveled overseas to America, to introduce himself to the American president; Gorby was forced to call in a big favor, but he got Boris stiffed by a low-level White House flunky before he got within sniffing distance of the Oval Office. Boris's liquor bills alone were staggering.

Millions were being spent, tens of millions. Where was the mysterious cash coming from?

A task force was hastily formed, experts in finance and banking who peeked and prodded under all the usual rocks.

Nothing.

A team of computer forensics experts burgled Boris's campaign offices and combed the deepest crevices of every hard drive.

Not a trace.

Long, raucous meetings were held about what to do, with the usual backbiting, finger-pointing, and evasion of responsibility. This sneaky white knight, whoever he was, knew how to hide his fingerprints. Whatever he was doing to evade their most advanced techniques of snooping and detection had to be enormously clever. That level of sophistication raised interesting questions and dark misgivings. After much heated discussion, inevitably the preponderance of suspicion fell on foreign intelligence agencies. Surveillance of selected foreign embassies and known intelligence operatives was kicked up a notch and the squad of watchers increased threefold. Most of the foreign embassies were wired for sound anyway. And after seventy years of foreign spies lurking and sneaking around its capital, the KGB had a tight grip on every drop site and clandestine meeting place in Moscow.

More nada.

As Yeltsin's poll numbers climbed, frustration grew. The KGB was averse to mysteries — unsolved too long they turned into career problems. So the KGB chief of residency in Washington was ordered to kick the tires of his vast web of moles, leakers, and traitors in the CIA, DIA, FBI, NSA, and any other alphabet-soup agency he had his devious fingers in. Money, cash, lucre — that was America's preferred weapon. And even if America wasn't the culprit, the CIA or NSA, with their massive, sophisticated arsenals of electronic snoops, probably knew who was.

More nada, nada, nada. More wasted time, more wasted effort, more millions of dollars flooding out of nowhere, with more supporters flocking to Yeltsin's banner.

Yutskoi observed, "Actually, it's a miracle we found out at all. Konevitch is very, very clever."

"How clever?"

"In the private construction business, nearly everything's done in cash. And nearly all of it under the table. Compounding matters, right now, we're a mix of two economies: communist and free-market. The free-market guys know we don't have a good handle on them. They're inventing all kinds of fancy new games we don't know how to play yet. It's —"

"And what game did he play?" Golitsin interrupted in a nasty tone, tired of excuses.

"Everything was done offshore. It was smuggled out in cash, laundered under phony names at Caribbean banks, and from there turned electronic. He moved it around through a lot of banks — Swiss, African, American — divided it up, brought it back together, and just kept it moving until it became untraceable and impossible to follow."

"And how did he hand it over to Yeltsin's people?"

"That's the beauty of it. Not a single ruble

ever touched the Soviet banking system. That's why we never saw it." He smiled and tried to appear confident. "What we now hypothesize was that he smuggled it back in as cash and handed it over in large suitcases." The truth was, they still had no idea, though he wasn't about to confess to that.

"Then who helped him?" Golitsin immediately barked, with a sizzling stare. Another good, unanswerable question. Soviet citizens knew zilch about international banking, money laundering, electronic transactions, or how to elude detection. The Soviet banking system was backward and shockingly unsophisticated. Besides, nobody had enough money to dream of getting fancy.

Or almost nobody — the Mafiya had money by the boatload. And they were masterminds at financial shenanigans; they had tried and perfected all kinds of underhanded tricks and scams. In the most oppressive state on earth, their survival depended on keeping their cash invisible. Golitsin waved a finger at his aide's folder. "Any evidence of that?"

"None. Not yet, anyway. It doesn't mean their crooked fingers aren't in it, just that we haven't found it."

"Keep looking. It has to be there."

After a moment, and totally out of the blue, Yutskoi mentioned, "I read a term paper he wrote as a freshman, something to do with Einstein's theory of relativity."

His boss had moved back to the window, restlessly watching the loud, angry crowd down on the street. Only a few years before the whole lot would already be in windowless wagons, trembling with fear on their way to Dzerzhinsky Square. They'd be worked over for a while, then shipped off to a uranium mine in the Urals where their hair and teeth would fall out.

The old days: he missed them already.

Yutskoi interrupted the pleasant reverie. "At least I *tried* to read his paper, I should say. I barely understood a word," he mumbled. "And all those complicated equations . . ." He trailed off, sounding a little stunned.

"What about it?" Golitsin asked absently. The crowd below was now dancing and chanting and growing larger by the minute. He felt weary.

"I sent it off to the director of the thermonuclear laboratory at the Kurchatov Institute. He said it was one of the most brilliant treatises he had read in years. Wanted to get it published in a few very prestigious international journals. You know, show the international community Soviet science still has what it takes. When I told him an eighteen-year-old college freshman wrote it, he called me a liar."

His boss glanced back over his shoulder. "You already told me he's smart."

"I know I did. Now I'm saying he's more than smart."

They stared at each other a moment. Golitsin said, "He's only twenty-two."

"Yes, and that's the whole point. He's not hamstrung by old ideas. Nor has he lived long enough to have his brains and ambitions squeezed into radish pulp like everybody over thirty in this country."

Lost on neither of them was the ugly irony that they and their thuggish organ had done that squeezing. The average Russian could barely haul himself out of bed in the morning. The only social superlatives their nation boasted were the world's highest rate of alcoholism and the shortest life span of any developed nation. What a fitting tribute.

Yutskoi cleared his throat and asked, "So what will you advise Gorbachev?" He began stuffing documents and photos back into his expandable file.

Golitsin acted preoccupied and pretended he didn't hear that question. Yutskoi was an inveterate snoop and world-class gossip; if he let the cat out of the bag now, the news would be roaring around Moscow by midnight. Then again, Golitsin thought, so what? This news was too big to contain anyway. One way or another, it would be on the tip of every tongue in the world by morning. What difference would a few hours make?

He moved away from the window and

ambled back in the direction of his aide. "On Gorbachev's desk is a document abolishing the Soviet Union. That jerk Yeltsin had the Congress vote on it this afternoon."

"And it passed?"

"By a landslide. If Gorbachev signs it, the Soviet Union is toast. History. Kaput."

"And if he doesn't?" asked Yutskoi, fully enlightened now about the cause of Yeltsin's drunken celebration that night: this was bound to be a bender of historic proportions. His tenders would have to pour Boris into bed. "What then?" he asked.

"What do you think will happen, idiot? We'll disband the mutinous Congress and crack down." He pointed a crooked, veiny finger through the window in the direction of the unruly crowd below. "We'll collect a few million malcontents and dissidents. Throw a million or so into the gulags. Shoot or hang a hundred or two hundred thousand to get everybody's attention."

"Won't that be fun," the aide blurted.

Golitsin shrugged. "Leave that file on Konevitch. I'll want to study him further."

Yutskoi stood and started to leave when he felt the old man's grip on his arm. "And keep me informed of what you learn about Konevitch. Spare no resources. I want to know *everything* about this young wunderkind. Everything."

2

August 1993

The first team picked him up the moment he and his wife raced out the metal gate of their housing compound and stepped on the gas toward Sheremetyevo Airport. As usual, whenever the couple traveled around Moscow, a car with flashing blue lights rode in front, the shiny black armored Mercedes sedan was tucked securely in the middle, and a third car filled with heavily armed guards brought up the rear.

They followed at a discreet distance in a beaten-up rusted Lada sedan that blended in wonderfully, since it looked like all the other wretched junkheaps roaring around the streets of Moscow.

A totally excessive precaution, really. The plane tickets for the couple had been booked electronically; they knew the flight number, the departure time, his and her seat numbers, where they were going, and how long they planned to stay.

Why he was going wasn't in their briefing; nor did it matter, nor did they care. They knew why they were following him.

That's what mattered; all that mattered.

He and the Mrs. were booked in first-class side-by-side seats, and were picked up by a fresh team the instant they cleared customs and stepped onto the plane. Within moments after falling into their plush reclining seats, they ordered two flutes of bubbly and held hands as they sipped and chatted. A lovely couple, the second trail team agreed.

This new team, one male, one female, was positioned ten rows back, squished into cramped economy seats selected for the excellent view it gave them of their target. Nobody in first class ever glanced back at the deprived unfortunates in cattle class. Detection really wasn't an issue, but they worried about it anyway, and took every precaution possible. They munched on dried-out prunes, sipped bottled water, stayed quiet, and watched.

Another precaution that was totally useless, really. Wasn't like their targets could escape, flying twenty thousand feet above the earth, racing along at five hundred miles per hour.

Besides, a third team, much larger, about eight or ten people, would be in position an hour before landing at Ferihegy Airport outside Budapest.

Tedious work, but the watchers were professionals and never relaxed. They patiently spent their time hoarding mental notes that might come in handy later. Despite all the careful planning, rehearsals, and precautions, you never knew.

He, Alex Konevitch, was dressed in a superbly cut two-piece blue wool suit, obviously imported, probably from England, and just as obviously expensive. She, his wife, Elena, wore a lovely black wool pantsuit, also superbly tailored and definitely more expensive than his. From one of those faggy, ladi-da European design houses, they guessed, but the his-and-hers fancy rags were a big tactical mistake on their part. Russians and East Europeans in general are notoriously awful dressers and it set the couple apart.

After studying countless photographs of him, they agreed his likeness was a perfect match; he would be impossible to lose or misplace. His unusual height also worked heavily in their favor; even in the densest crowd, he would stick out.

No pictures of her were included in their file — a sloppy oversight in their professional judgment. What if the couple split up? What if they took separate cabs, he to his business meeting, and she maybe to a local plaza for a little noodling through stores?

They therefore focused mostly on her, collecting useful mental notes of her appearance, her distinguishing features. About his age, they estimated — possibly twenty-two, more likely twenty-four — though vastly shorter than him. Shoulder-length blonde hair, casually brushed, light on the makeup, and she really didn't need any, they both agreed. Delicious blue eyes, large, innocently doelike, with a slightly upturned nose, and nice figure, but a little on the skinny side, in their view. All in all, though, a sweet number, very pretty, very sexy — and best of all, very difficult to miss.

They had been told little about her. Perhaps because little was known or maybe because her background was irrelevant. Why did they care?

She was with him.

That was the key.

Thirty minutes into the flight, he extended his lounger chair, unbuttoned his collar, loosened his tie, then dozed off. She handed the stewardess a few American dollars, plugged in her earphones, and intently watched a subtitled American action movie about an airplane hijacking, of all things.

He awoke from the siesta an hour later, refreshed, ready to dig in. He turned down an offer for a meal, withdrew a thick ream of papers from his briefcase, and got down to work. The file said he was a workaholic, driven, focused, and greedy. Looked about right.

But somewhere on this flight, they were

almost certain, lurked a bodyguard. Possibly two, but no more than two: of this they were nearly certain. Alex Konevitch's life was in perpetual danger in Moscow, where it was open season on bankers, entrepreneurs, and rich businessmen. Nearly seven hundred had been whacked, bombed, or kidnapped that year alone, and there were still four months to go.

But the Wild East was behind him now; or so he believed. He would relax his precautions, as he always did when he left Mother Russia in the dust. And besides, Alex Konevitch, they had been confidently informed by their employer, regarded large bodyguard detachments as distasteful, ostentatious, and worse — bad for business. A large flock of elephant-necked thugs tended to upset the Western investors and corporate types he dealt with.

But somewhere on this flight, they were quite sure, a bodyguard or bodyguards were seated, like them, calm and unobtrusive, waiting and watching. They held out little hope of detecting them, at least during the flight; these boys came from a well-heeled foreign private outfit with a first-class reputation, mostly former intelligence and police types who got paid big bucks not to make stupid mistakes. But the dismal odds aside, they were ordered to give it their best shot anyway; maybe they'd catch a lucky break. They agreed beforehand to look for anybody staring a little too possessively at Alex and his pretty little Mrs.

So the couple traded turns making idle passes through the cabin, trolling back and forth, mostly to the toilets. There were a few young men with tough faces and thick, muscular builds, but that seemed abnormally conspicuous for an elite security firm that loudly advertised its discreetness and invisibility.

At least the bodyguards wouldn't be armed; they were sure of this. Smuggling a weapon through a Russian airport was absurdly difficult. And detection would cause a public mess, the last thing a prestigious, supposedly ethical firm needed or wanted. No, they wouldn't be that stupid.

Besides, why risk getting caught when a better alternative was available?

Far easier to have somebody meet them in Budapest and discreetly hand over the heavy artillery.

On August 19, 1991, the old boys had their last desperate fling at preserving an empire hanging by its fingernails. Gorby, who had wrought so much damage with his flailing attempts at reform, was vacationing at his Black Sea resort when a clutch of rough-looking KGB officers stormed the building and took him hostage. In Moscow, a cabal including his chief of staff, vice president, prime minister, minister of defense, and KGB chairman promptly seized the organs of government.

A few thousand troops were rushed to the capital, the state television stations were seized, and water reservoirs secured; heavily armed guards were posted in front of food distribution centers to ensure a stranglehold on the city population. Tanks were littered at strategic intersections around the government section of the city — the usual signs of a beer-hall putsch in progress.

Next, the cabal convened a hasty televised press conference to introduce themselves as the saviors of communism and the union. It was a disaster. They were wrinkled, sclerotic old men, unpleasant, nasty, and afraid. And it showed. Their hands trembled, their voices quivered and shook, no facial expression registered above a fierce scowl.

Never before had they smiled at their people: why start now?

Worst of all, they appeared disorganized, feeble, nervous, and ancient — as impressions go, at that precarious, decisive moment, the wrong one to convey to a fractious, anxious nation.

To say it was a glorious gift to Boris Yeltsin, a born opportunist and addicted rabble-rouser, would be an understatement. He rallied a band of fellow flamethrowers and is-

43

sued a call for all Russians to join together and battle for their freedom. A large, unruly mob flocked to the Russian Congress building, heckling and chanting and daring the men who led the coup to do something about them. The cabal had been supremely confident their good citizens would respond in the best Soviet tradition — like scared, obedient sheep. The combative show of opposition caught the old boys totally by surprise.

Half argued strenuously to slaughter the whole bunch and hang their bodies from lampposts. A fine example, a paternal warning and long overdue, too. That wet noodle Gorby had been a sorry mollycoddler. The nation had grown soft and spoiled, they insisted; a good massacre was exactly the paternal medicine needed to whip it back in shape. The more dead wimps the better.

The other half wondered if a bloody spectacle might incite a larger rebellion. They weren't morally opposed by any means. In Lenin's hallowed words, as one of them kept repeating, as if anybody needed to hear it, omelets required broken eggs. But the nation had grown a little moody toward tyrants, they cautioned. The wrong move at this brittle time and they, too, might end up swinging on lampposts. Ignore the mob, they argued; in a day or two, at the outside, the crowd would grow bored and hungry and melt into the night.

Agreement proved impossible. Kill them or ignore them? Stomp them like rodents or wait them out? The old men were cleanly divided in their opinions, so they sat and squabbled in their gilded Kremlin offices, brawling and cursing one another, drinking heavily, collectively overwhelmed by the power they had stolen.

For two sleepless days the world held its breath and watched. Boris's protestors turned rowdier and more daring by the hour. They constructed signs. They howled protest chants and hurled nasty taunts at the security guards sent to control them. They erected camps, stockpiled food, heckled and sang, and prepared to stay for the duration; the coup leaders argued more tumultuously and drank more heavily.

Despite serious attempts to scare away the press, a small pesky army of reporters had infiltrated the mob and was broadcasting the whole infuriating standoff via satellite, smuggling out photographs and earning Pulitzers by the carton. The whole mess was on display, in living color for the entire globe to see.

Yeltsin adored the spotlight, and was almost giddy at having all the world as his stage. Televisions were kept on in the Kremlin offices 24/7. The old boys were forced to sit and watch as Boris — miraculously sober for once — pranced repeatedly in front of the cameras, calling them all has-beens and wannabe tyrants, threatening to run them out of town. That clown was thumbing his nose and shooting the bird at them.

For an empire in which terror was oxygen, it was humiliating; worse, it was dangerous.

On the third day the old men had had enough. They ordered the tanks to move, scatter the rabble, and crush ol' Boris. But after three hapless protestors were mowed down, the army lost its stomach. As miscalculations go, it was a horrible one. Should've sent in the ruffians from the KGB, they realized, a little sad, a little late. Need a few bones snapped, a little blood spilled, the boys from the Lubyanka were only too happy to oblige. Soldiers, on the other hand, had no appetite for flattening their own defenseless citizens. A handful of disgusted generals threw their support behind Yeltsin. A full stampede ensued.

The coup leaders were marched off in handcuffs, tired, defeated, disgruntled old men who had bungled their last chance. And Yeltsin, caught in the flush of victory, sprinted to the cameras and declared a ban on the Communist Party: a bold gesture, the last rite for a rotten old system that had run its course. The crowd roared its approval. It was also insane, and shortly thereafter was followed by an equally shortsighted act: the complete dissolution of the Soviet Union.

With a few swipes of ink the immense

empire fractured into more than a dozen different nations.

For seventy years, communism had been the ingrained order — the legal system, the governing system, the economic apparatus of the world's largest nation. Lazy, wonderfully corrupt, and spitefully inefficient as they were, its millions of servants and functionaries were the veins and arteries that braided the country together. They kept it functioning. They doled out the food and miserly paychecks, assigned housing, mismanaged the factories and farms, maintained public order, distributed goods and services, kept the trains running. A terrible, horribly flawed system, for sure. Nonetheless, it was, at least, a system.

Yeltsin had given little serious thought to what would replace it, or them. A few vague notions about democracy and a thriving free market rattled around his brain, nothing more. Apparently he assumed they would sprout helter-skelter from the fertile vacuum he created.

Worse, it quickly became apparent that Yeltsin, so brilliant at blasting the system to pieces, was clueless about gluing the wreckage back together. He was a revolutionary, a radical, a demolitionist extraordinaire. Like most of the breed, he had no talent for what came after the big bang.

But Alex Konevitch definitely did. By this

point, Alex already had built a massive construction business, a sprawling network of brokerage houses to administer an arbitrage business that began with construction materials and swelled to the whole range of national commodities, and a Russian exchange bank to manage the exploding finances of his hungry businesses. Amazingly, every bit of it was accomplished under the repressive nose of the communist apparatus. Dodging the KGB and working in the shadows, somehow he had self-mastered the alchemy of finance and banking, of international business.

The nation was not at all prepared for its overnight lunge into capitalism. But Alex was not only ready he was hungry.

With killer instinct, he rushed in and applied for a license to exchange foreign currency. The existing licenses had been granted by the government of the Soviet Union; whatever permissions or licenses had been endowed by that bad memory were insolvent, not worth spit. Anyway, the spirit of the day was to privatize everything, to disassemble the suffocating state bureaucracy, to mimic the West.

After a swift investigation, it turned out Alex's banks were the only functioning institutions with adequate experience and trained executives, and with ample security to safeguard what promised to be billions in transactions. Not only was the license granted, Alex ended up with a monopoly — every dollar, every yen, every franc that came or left Russia moved through his exchange bank. Cash flooded through his vaults. Trainloads from every direction, from Western companies scrambling to set up businesses in the newly capitalist country, and from wealthy Russians pushing cash out, trying to dodge the tax collector and hide their illicit fortunes overseas.

Millions of fearful Russians lined up at the doors to park their savings in Alex's bank, which happily exchanged their shrinking rubles for stable dollars or yen or deutsche marks, whatever currency their heart desired, and let them ride out the storm.

Overnight, Alex and his senior executives were setting the national exchange rates for all foreign currencies. Heady power for a young man, not yet twenty-five years old. Also, quite happily, a gold mine.

Alex took a slice of every ruble shuttled one way or the other, only two percent, but as the mountain of cash approached billions, he scraped off millions. Then tens of millions.

He saw another rich possibility and promised twenty percent interest to any Russian willing to park their savings at his bank for one year. Reams of advertisements flooded every TV station in Russia. A striking female model was used for certain pitches. She wiggled her pliant shoulders and gyrated her sinewy hips, and in a seductive whisper purred that her boyfriend was a sexy genius: his money was earning interest. Who knew it only took a little interest to get laid? To appeal to a different segment, a handsomely aged couple stood against the backdrop of a decrepit wooden cottage and in tearful voices thanked Alex's bank for ensuring their retirement funds were not only safe but actually growing by the day. Then, flash a year forward in time, and the same old couple were shown climbing sprightly into their gleaming Mercedes sedan parked in front of a charming seaside dacha.

It was unheard of. No Soviet bank ever advertised. None offered interest, not a single kopeck. Wasn't it enough that they protected their customers' money? Why should any bank dish out the bucks for its own generosity?

The commercials were vulgar and the promise of interest bordered on criminal negligence, the Soviet-era bankers growled among themselves and to whatever reporter would listen to their gripes. But twenty percent? Okay, one or two percent, maybe; but twenty? Konevitch would pay dearly for his bluster — he'd be bankrupt before a month was out.

Millions more investors lined up at the door. Billions more rubles flooded in. Alex took the deluge and hedged and bet it all against the unstable ruble, then watched as inflation soared above a thousand percent. At the end of a year, the investors took their twenty percent cut and considered themselves lucky indeed; at least their life savings hadn't melted into half a kopeck as happened to millions of miserable others. The remainder of the spread went to Alex. Nearly ninety percent of every ruble in his savings bank was his to keep. He cleaned up.

And as the economy limped from one catastrophe to another, as the disasters piled up, Boris reached out desperately for help. At the president's insistence, a telephonic hotline was installed between Boris and his trusted whiz kid, who seemed to have this whole capitalism thing figured out. Late-night calls became routine. A single push of the red button and the president would rail about this problem or that, long, whiny diatribes fueled by staggering amounts of liquor. Alex was a cool, sober listener; also a quick study with a mathematician's lust for numbers.

Yeltsin had little background and even less appetite for financial matters; all the economic prattle bored him to tears. Alex would talk him through the latest disaster — boil it all down to simple language — propose a reasonable solution, and Boris would pounce on his cabinet the next morning, issue a few brusque instructions, and a total meltdown would be avoided, or at least postponed for another day.

One night after a long rambling conversation about the evaporating foreign currency reserves, Yeltsin paused to catch his breath, then, seemingly out of the blue, asked Alex, "By the way, how's your house?"

"Nice. Very nice."

"Is it big?"

"Fairly large, yes. Why do you ask?"

"I heard it's huge."

"Okay, it is. Very, very big."

"How many bedrooms?"

"Six, I think. Maybe seven. Why?"

"Which is it, six or seven?"

"I honestly don't know. Could be ten for all I know. I've wandered through most of it, but there are rooms I've never seen. It was a wreck when I bought it, an old brick mansion constructed before 1917. According to local lore, it was built for a baron or maybe a wealthy factory owner to house his ten children. Poor guy. He was dragged out and executed by a Bolshevik firing squad three days after the last stud went in."

"Are you pulling my leg?"

"The bullet scars are still visible on the west side of the house. That adds a certain charm."

"And after that?"

"Well, I don't know about the early years. But the Ministry of Education owned it for decades. Occasionally it was used as a school for children of the elite, sometimes as a training center for school principals. Of course they neglected it disgracefully. The electrical wiring, even the plumbing had not been updated since it was built. The pipes were made of cast iron. Turn the spigot and chunky brown slush poured out."

"But you like it?"

Alex chuckled. "What's not to like?"

"You tell me," Boris replied.

"Not a thing. I used my own construction company to gut and rebuild with the best of everything. Voice-activated lighting, saunas in every bathroom, two mahogany-paneled elevators, the works. I even had an indoor pool installed, and a well-equipped gym. The attic is now a movie theater, twenty seats, with real popcorn machines and a ten-foot screen. A French chef and three servants live in the basement and take care of everything."

After a long moment, Yeltsin asked, in a suspiciously knowing tone, "And your wife, does she like it?"

"There are a few things she might like to change," Alex admitted, a loud understatement. Elena detested the house. He had bought and refurbished it before they met, a gift to himself after he made his first hundred million and regarded it as a neat way to pat himself on the back. A gay Paris decorator had been flown in and instructed to spare no expense. He did his best. He chartered a plane, flew around the world, slept in five-star hotels, loaded up on antiques from Asia, the Middle East, and Europe. He had drapes hand-sewn in Egypt, and furniture hand-manufactured by the best craftsmen in Korea.

As the bills piled up, Alex convinced himself that he wasn't being wasteful; it was a business expense, an unavoidable cost he couldn't do without. The big moneymen from Wall Street and Fleet Street and Frankfurt did not talk business with anybody not like themselves, prosperous enough to show it off.

The house was cavernous and every nook and cranny was saturated with grandeur. But Elena liked things simple and small enough that you didn't have to shout across the room at each other. She didn't care for servants, either; she was reared to do things herself, and that's how she preferred it. If she even thought about a cup of coffee, a silver urn appeared out of nowhere. The flock of hired help violated their privacy. They made her feel guilty and spoiled.

The mansion sat on the corner of two furiously busy Moscow streets, for another thing. Traffic and pedestrians were always pausing to gawk at the impressive old home, and occasionally littered the property with letters strewn with vile curses and filthy threats. In a city populated largely with impoverished former communists — their families and few belongings suffocating in six-hundred-square-foot apartments — the newly rich and their expansive indulgences were not viewed fondly.

Any day, Elena expected a flotilla of Molotov cocktails to sail through her window.

After enough hateful letters, Alex built a small guard shack out front and posted guards around the clock to chase away disgruntled tourists. But it was, quite spectacularly, a mansion and thus a magnet for the growing breed of Moscow criminals. After two attempted break-ins, another guard shack was erected, more guards were added to the rear of the house, one was posted on the roof, and enough state-of-the-art surveillance systems were sprinkled around to give a porn studio fits of envy.

Elena began calling their home "The Fortress," without affection. Still, there was no doubt the house continued to pose serious security issues and little could be done about it.

They had had discussions, Alex and Elena. Not arguments, but mild disputes that were never settled. Elena was increasingly distressed about Alex's safety. He was famous now — more truthfully, infamous — a poster child of the gold-digging opportunists who were raking it in while most Russians slapped extra locks on their doors to keep the bill collectors at bay.

And their house was right there, on the

street! A bazooka fired from a passing car could blast them all to pieces.

But the place was perfect for Alex. His office was only five minutes away, on foot. He was working twenty-hour days, seven days a week. Seconds were precious, minutes priceless. And everything he needed was right here, a floor or two above, or a floor or two below: a gourmet feast at the snap of a finger, that superb gym for his morning conditioning, the heated pool to unwind in after a long day of shoving millions around.

Elena had been raised in the country. She loathed the city and all its appendages — senseless crime, roaring traffic, the ever-present noise, the reeking smell and pollution. Most of all, she hated that disgruntled people walked by and spat angry hawkers on her property. She longed for clean air, lush forests, long, private walks around her property.

Long walks without a squadron of beefy guards shepherding her every step.

"Why do you ask?" Alex finally said.

"I want you closer," Boris replied. "No, I *need* you closer."

"I'm only forty minutes away. Call and I'll drop everything."

"Nope, that won't work. One minute I worry about foreign currency reserves, the next I'm dreaming of ways to get my nuclear missiles back from Kazakhstan. I'm a very spontaneous person, Alex. I have the attention span of a horny Cossack. I think you know that."

"Yes, I know that. So send a fast helicopter for me, Mr. President. The army's not doing anything these days. I think they have enough of them, and their pilots need a workout. I'll even foot the gas bill. Twenty minutes flat from my doorstep to yours."

"Not fast enough."

"Then describe fast enough."

"I want to reach out and touch you. Besides, you've been very good to me. I owe you more than I can express. Do me a favor, let me pay some of it back."

"Just fix this damned country. Finish what you started. Believe me, I'll be more than delighted."

Yeltsin chuckled. "You'll be old and senile before anything works in this land. I'll be dead and buried, with throngs of people lining up to pee on my grave for causing all this chaos. I'm giving you a house, Alex."

"I have a house already. Didn't we just go over that?"

Yeltsin ignored him. "Not quite as garish as yours. But big, and believe me, you'll love this place. It's out here, in the country, inside the presidential compound. A mere two-minute walk from my quarters — one minute if you sprint, which I expect you to do if I call. A gym and indoor pool. Six servants, a chef, and — hey, you'll love this part — they have separate quarters outside the house."

The president paused to let his sales pitch sink in, then threw out a little more ammunition. "Here's the kicker, Alex. My presidential security detail guards the entire compound. Even with your money, you couldn't touch the kind of security these goons provide."

Alex chuckled. "Is that a challenge?" He could not say it, but he abhorred the idea of living in walking, or even sprinting, distance of Boris. The man drank and partied until four every morning, frothy bacchanalias that consumed enormous amounts of liquor. He was notoriously social by nature and regarded it as sinful to get tanked alone. The idea of being dragged into those late-night orgies was appalling.

Yeltsin chuckled as well, then a loud belly laugh. What was he saying? With all that wealth, Alex could probably buy half the Russian army; maybe all of it. After a moment the laughing stopped. "I'm serious, Alex. My economic advisors are all boring idiots. Even that bunch of Harvard professors who've camped out here to tell me how to build a capitalist paradise — just stuffier idiots."

"All right, replace them."

"You're not listening. I'm trying to."

But Alex was listening, very closely. A week before he and Elena had attended a dull state dinner to honor the visiting potentate of some country where, apparently, everybody was short and squat, with bad teeth, horrible breath, and nauseating table manners. After the usual tedious speeches about eternal brotherhood and blah, blah, blah — along with a seriously overcooked meal — the party shifted to the ballroom, where Yeltsin promptly invited Elena to dance.

Boris had an eye for the ladies and Elena in a baggy sweatsuit could snap necks. But attired as she was, in a gold-embossed scarlet gown, she nearly sucked the male air out of the ballroom. And of course, three-quarters of a lifetime of ballet training had made her a splendid dancer who knew how to make her partner look graceful and better than he was. Yeltsin and Elena laughed and chatted and whirled gaily around the floor. All eyes were on them — Fred and Ginger, cutting the rug. One dance turned into two, then three.

Alex was sure he was listening to the echo of that third dance. Clearly Elena had whispered into Yeltsin's ear her growing concerns about Alex's safety. If her husband wouldn't heed her warnings, she would take matters over his head. He admired the effort and adored her for trying. He had absolutely no intention of humoring her.

He would just litter a few more guards around the property and hope it settled her nerves.

"Oh, one other thing," Yeltsin added, an

afterthought, an insignificant little note to round out the pitch. "It happens to be Gorbachev's old house. The official quarters of the general secretary himself. I had him booted out the day after I took over. Didn't even give him time to clear the clothes from the closets. Ha, ha, ha. Had those shipped to him, later, with a nice personal note. 'I got the country, you keep the rags.' "

Alex suddenly went speechless. Had he heard that right? Yes! Gorbachev's home! Sure, his own mansion was grand, perhaps larger and more loaded with extravagances than the general secretary's residence — money, after all, was the great leveler. But some things money can't buy. Yeltsin was offering him the most storied home in Russia.

The thought of living in that home — How may bedrooms did Yeltsin mention? Who cared? — the thought of him and Elena basking in the general secretary's hot tub, making love in that bedroom, taking long, leisurely strolls around a property where legions of presidents and world leaders had stepped and stumbled, was simply exhilarating. Flushing the toilets would be a thrill.

It wouldn't hurt business, either. Alex could picture the amazed expressions of the Western investors he invited over for a light business dinner. Please don't chip the general secretary's china, he would tell them and watch their faces.

And so what if it was forty-five minutes from the office? The big Mercedes 600 was equipped with an office in the rear, a pull-down desk made of mahogany, a satellite car-phone, enough gadgets that not one of the forty-five minutes would be idle or wasted. It might even be better, he thought: forty-five minutes of solitude, each way. Organize his thoughts on the way in; unwind from the daily turmoil on the way out.

And it was safe. Plus, it was in the country; Elena would love it.

Mistaking Alex's prolonged silence for indecision, Yeltsin prattled on. Like the politician he was, he couldn't stop selling. "Let me tell you, my boy, hell, I'd dearly love to live in it myself. Sometimes, at night, Naina and I wander around that house and dream of moving in. The chandeliers alone cost more than I make in a year. Of course, word would inevitably leak out to all these poor folk scraping by on a hundred rubles a month. There'd be another revolution. You know what, though? I don't think I'd enjoy this one as much as the last."

"My moving van will be there first thing in the morning," Alex blurted. He was too stunned to say "thanks."

Matching his speed, Yeltsin snapped, "Good, glad that's settled."

"It's definitely settled. Don't you dare make this offer to anyone else before nine o'clock tomorrow. By then, Elena and I will be seated on the front porch with shotguns to drive off the interlopers."

"Oh, one other thing. From now on, I want you along when I travel overseas. Russia needs as much money and foreign investors as we can get. I'm miserable at making that happen. You don't seem to have any problems in that department."

"Sure, whatever," Alex mumbled, dreaming of who to invite over first. Would they need furniture? Where would they get groceries? In his mind he was already moved in.

The instant they signed off, he rushed upstairs, awoke Elena, and broke the news about their incredible new home.

"Oh, isn't that wonderful," she replied, even managing to make the pretense of making her surprise look sincere.

At one o'clock, Bernie Lutcher crunched hard on his third NoDoz tablet and quickly washed it down with the bottled water he had carried onto the plane.

After twenty-five years as a successful cop in the NYPD intelligence bureau, retiring as a highly regarded lieutenant, he was now five years into his second life, five years that were nearly everything he hoped they would be.

The English security firm that employed him, Malcolm Street Associates, paid him one hundred grand a year, plus housing, plus car, *and* the chance for a twenty thousand annual bonus. Four for four in the bonus department, thus far. And the way this year was going, next year's was already in the bag and mentally spent. Supplemented by his NYPD pension, he was finally and faithfully putting away a little nest egg.

But not *exactly* as he always dreamed it would be. Cancer had struck five years before, had stolen his beloved Ellie, and only after it wiped out the paltry savings they had managed to scrimp from a meager cop's salary. His medical insurance had handled the prescribed treatments, but in the final months and weeks, as Ellie stubbornly wasted away, Bernie had thrown good money after bad, desperately investing in a plethora of unorthodox treatments and quackery, from Mexican miracle pills to an oddball dentist who swore that removing Elle's silver and mercury fillings would incite a complete remission. To no avail, it turned out. In the end, Elle had passed away, stuffed with all manner of phony cures and big holes in her teeth.

So now Bernie was rebuilding his life. No longer surviving one miserable day at a time, he was again viewing life as a promising future rather than a sad past. Both kids were grown, out of college, out on their own; the first grandkid was in the oven, and Bernie looked forward to many more.

Plus, he was living in Europe. Europe! He

had acquired this dream in his late teens when Uncle Sam borrowed a few years of his life, making him a military policeman in Heidelberg, a gorgeous city in a lovely country that captured his heart. Other NYPD types had Florida fever; they dreamed of sweating out their idle years in tropical heat, blasting little white spheres around manicured lawns. Bernie hated golf, hated heat, and desperately hated the idea of spending his sunset years reliving the good old days — what was so good about them, anyway? — in a community saturated with retired cops. He had always yearned to return to Europe: the slower pace, the opportunity to travel, sip exotic coffees, and of course, the money was fantastic.

He hunched forward in his seat and noted, once again, the same wrinkled old biddy lurching and waddling down the aisle toward the lavatory. He had long ago learned not to ignore anything — not the innocuous, not the apparently innocent. The stakeout king, the boys in the NYPD had nicknamed him, with good reason — he had put more than a few banditos in the slammer by paying unusual attention to cars and pedestrians that appeared a little too often, often stickup artists and bank robbers reconning their targets. Pattern observation, it was called in the trade. Bernie wrote the book on it.

This was her fifth potty trip, by his count.

A little suspicious: she did look old, though, and faulty kidneys couldn't be ruled out; or doctor's orders to keep her blood circulating; or just plain old-age restlessness.

In preparation for this job, the firm's experts had produced a thick folder detailing all known and presumed threats to the client. It was a wealthy firm with a big ego that could afford to be comprehensive and took it to the hilt.

Background checks were de rigueur for all prospective clients; unlike other firms, however, this was accomplished *before* a contract was signed. The client's ability to pay the firm's impressive bills was the principal topic of curiosity, of course. Also the nature of the client's business, types of threat, known enemies, special circumstances, and bothersome vulnerabilities.

British snobbery definitely weighed in. Unsavory clients were blackballed no matter how much they pleaded or offered.

But in a ferociously competitive business, reputation counted for everything. It all boiled down to two simple questions: How many lived? How many died?

The firm had dodged more than a few bullets by politely and firmly snubbing clients whose chance of survival was deemed subpar; in over thirty percent of those cases, the clients had been dead within a year, a striking piece of guesswork. A clutch of actuarial wizards lured from top insurance firms were paid a small fortune to be finicky. A computer model was produced, a maze of complex algorithms that ate gobs of information and spit out a dizzying spread of percentages and odds.

A client or two were lost every year, a better than average record for work of this nature, one the firm loudly advertised.

Regarding his current client, at the top of the threat chain were the usual suspects for a Russian tycoon: Mafiya thugs, hit men, and various forms of independent crooks or assassins intent on blackmail, or fulfilling a contract from a third party. They were effective and often lethal. They were also crude, obnoxiously brutal, notoriously indiscreet, and with their clownish affectation for black jeans and black leather jackets, usually ridiculously easy to spot. Bernie had already swept the cabin twice. No likely suspects of that ilk.

Next came business competitors who stood to benefit by eliminating an entrepreneurial juggernaut like Konevitch, followed closely by investors disgruntled for any number of reasons. His business was privately owned. Two limited partners, that was it. He owned eighty percent of the shares and neither partner was dissatisfied, as best the firm could tell. Really, how could they be? Konevitch had made them both millionaires many times over.

His estimated worth — a combination of cash and stock — now hovered around 350 million dollars — in all likelihood a lowball estimate — and growing by the hour, despite generous and frequent contributions to local charities and political causes. He had his fingers deeply into four or five mammoth businesses, was contemplating a move into two or three more, and his personal fortune was multiplying by the day. The construction firm he began had given birth to an arbitrage business — initially for construction materials only, then for all sorts of things — that bred a prosperous bank, then a sizable investment firm, part ownership in several oil firms, a car importing company, a real estate empire, ownership of two national newspaper chains, several restaurant chains, and myriad smaller enterprises that were expected to balloon exponentially as Russia fully morphed into a full-blown consumer society.

As fast as Alex made money, he poured it into the next project, the next acquisition, the next promising idea. Whatever he touched spewed profit, it seemed. In the estimation of the firm, that remarkable growth rested firmly on his own deft brilliance, his own impeccable instincts, his golden touch.

Take him out and Konevitch Associates would fold. Maybe not immediately, maybe it would limp along for a few anguished years.

But with the brain dead, the body would atrophy. Eventually the pieces would shrivel and be sold off for a fraction of a pittance. Alex was a money-printing machine; surely his partners knew this.

Next came possible political enemies, and last, though not insignificantly, the obligatory threat for anyone with heaps of money — family members who might hunger for an inheritance and/or an insurance windfall.

Nearly all rich people dabbled in politics to a greater or lesser degree; this client was in it up to his neck. According to the dossier, Konevitch was very close to Yeltsin, had apparently backed his rise to the presidency, and he continued to throw cash by the boatload at Yeltsin's hungry political machine and a few of the reformist parties ambling in his wake.

The old commie holdovers were resentful, angry, and plentiful. Konevitch had played it smart and hid in the background — the mint behind the throne, an underground well of money — going to great lengths to keep his contributions invisible, or at the very least anonymous. But there were those who knew. And among them, it was assumed, were some powerful people who might wish to settle a historical score. A nasty political grudge couldn't be ruled out.

He had a serious ten million dollar term life policy with Carroythers & Smythe, a financially plump, highly regarded insurance company. That firm shared Malcolm Street Associates' intense concern for Alex's health and secretly informed its partner agency that his wife was the sole beneficiary. No brothers, no sisters, and his few cousins were distant, angry, avid communists, and unfriendly. His mother was long dead, leaving just a father, a former educator with few apparent wants and needs, who was wiling away his retirement from academia reading books that were formerly banned to Soviet readers.

Using his vast riches, the son set the old man up in a nice dacha in a resort town on the Black Sea with a tidy trust fund that would allow him to comfortably live out his life in pleasant surroundings. A bribe to the local hospital revealed the old man had incurable pancreatic cancer that was expected, shortly, to kill him. He was being treated with the best medicines imported from the States, but few had ever survived pancreatic cancer and time was not on his side. So what would the old man want with his son's fortune? Wasn't like he could take it with him.

Alex dutifully visited every few months. He and the old man spent hours in the garage, tinkering on old jalopies and knocking back imported beers. An odd relationship, given the wild differences between father and son. But they were close.

So it all boiled down to one intimate threat

— his wife, Elena.

The firm had quietly observed their marriage: happy, healthy, and loving, or so it appeared. No indications of affairs or dalliances or even one-night regrets. Not for her, not for him. They had met a year and a half earlier. And from the best they could tell, from the opening instant, the couple could barely keep their hands off each other. A surface background check revealed that she had been a dancer, Bolshoi-trained. And though marvelously talented, with a technique that was deemed technically flawless, at only five foot and one inch she lacked the long limbs and extended torso demanded by audiences. She was offered a position as a full-time instructor, teaching giraffes with half her talent to prance and pirouette; she opted, instead, to retire her tutu. She put dance in the rearview mirror and majored in economics at Moscow University, graduating five down from the top of her class. Bright girl.

A month after they met he had asked and she agreed, he suggesting a quick and efficient civil rite, she arguing vehemently for a traditional church wedding. She won and they were joined together, till death do they part, in a quiet ceremony by a hairy, bearded patriarch at a small, lovely Orthodox chapel in the pastoral countryside.

The firm regarded her fierce insistence on

a church wedding as a hopeful sign — she had apparently been raised a closet Christian during the long years of godless communism; presumably, the sixth commandment meant something to her.

Her tastes were neither extravagant nor excessive. Some expensive clothing and a few costly baubles, though not by choice and definitely not by inclination: an outwardly prosperous image was necessary for business, he insisted, and he encouraged her to buy half of Paris. Day to day, she preferred tight American Levi's and baggy sweatshirts, limiting herself to a few elegant outfits that were mothballed except for social and business occasions. The couple never bickered, never fought. They enjoyed sex, with each other, nothing kinky, nothing weird, and it was frequent. The firm knew this for a fact.

The Konevitch apartment had been wired and loaded with enough bugs to fill an opera house, surreptitiously, of course, the day after Alex first contacted Malcolm Street Associates. All married applicants were electronically surveilled, at least during the opening weeks or months of a contract — this was never divulged to the clients, and the firm's prurience had never been discovered. Since part of its service was to sweep for listening and electronic devices, it would never be caught.

Statistically, the firm knew, a high number

of rich men were murdered by their own wives, concubines, and mistresses. The reasons were mostly obvious: marital neglect, sexual jealousy, and, more often, outright greed. Nothing was harder to protect against, and the actuarial boys demanded a thorough investigation. The firm's gumshoes enthusiastically obliged; snooping in the bedrooms of the rich and famous, after all, was definitely more entertaining work than the normal tedium of tailing and watching.

But all evidence indicated that the marriage was strong. And Elena Konevitch, for now and for the foreseeable future, was rated low risk.

In January 1992, the first of what soon became a flood of newspaper stories about the amazing and mysterious Alex Konevitch appeared in the *Moscow Times*. Though other newly minted Moscow tycoons begged to be noticed, pleaded for publicity, actually, Alex had prodigiously tried his best to remain a complete nobody. Other fat cats blustered and bribed their way into every hot nightspot in town, rolling up in their flashy, newly acquired Mercedes and BMW sedans, a stunning model or two hanging on their arm — typically rented for the occasion — only too hungrily enthusiastic to strut the fruits of their newfound success, to show off their sudden importance.

Publicity management firms sprang up all over Moscow. Moguls and wannabe moguls lined up outside their doors, throwing cash and favors at anybody who could get them noticed, a few seconds of limelight, the briefest mention in the local rags. Under the old system everybody was impoverished, with little to brag about, and even less to show off; in any event, sticking one's head up was an invitation to have it lopped off. Now a whole new world was emerging from the ashes; old desires that had been cruelly repressed were suddenly unchained, flagrantly indulged. A thousand egos swelled and flourished, giddy with the impulse to show off. Donald Trump was their icon; they longed to live his life, to emulate his oversized image, to become famous simply for being obnoxiously famous.

Alex lived like a hermit, a man few knew and nobody knew well. He avoided parties and nightclubs, was rarely observed in public, and adamantly refused any and all requests for interviews. In his quest to remain anonymous, every employee of Konevitch Associates and its sprawling web of companies was required to sign a serious legal vow never to whisper a word about their reclusive employer. This only made the search for his story all the more irresistible. One of the richest men in the country, the kid millionaire they naturally called him. And he wanted to remain anonymous?

After several unfruitful attempts, a midlevel employee at his investment bank was secretly approached by a Moscow weekly and offered five thousand easy American dollars to chat a little about his employer. The employee confessed that he not only did not know Alex personally, he had actually seen him only twice in person — two fleeting glimpses of Alex speeding through the trading floor on his way to his office upstairs. Didn't matter, they assured him. Surely Alex's companies were rife with rumors, gossip, and anecdotes, concocted or otherwise. The price was kicked up to seven thousand and the employee was suddenly too eager to cough up a few confidences — as long as the check was good and, for sure, his name stayed out of it.

"Kid Midas" was the predictable headline that outed Alex, and it said it all and then some. It was rumored that Alex was Russia's richest man, its first fat-cat billionaire; he owned an armada of towering yachts; two hundred rare and exotic sports cars housed in a temperature-controlled underground garage and spitshined daily; a fleet of sleek private jets to ferry him to his sprawling estates in Paris, London, Rome, New York, and Hong Kong. The chatty employee had recently finished a spicy, newly translated, unauthorized biography about the marvelously perverse life of Howard Hughes, and he plagiarized liberally and imaginatively from that intoxicating tale to earn his seven grand.

Alex was a total schizoid paranoid, he'd said; he sat around his office nude, counting his rubles and hatching new businesses in between watching old black-and-white Katharine Hepburn flicks. He collected beautiful women by the carton, renamed them all Katharine, and was so germophobic that he boiled them before he slept with them. He was anti-Semitic, antisocial, ate only raw vegetables, drank only boiled water, was left-handed, was rumored to go both ways sexually, and had to be chloroformed by a squad of brawny assistants to get haircuts and his fingernails trimmed.

The resulting article was ridiculous, packed with bizarre lies, and viciously fascinating.

Fictitious or not, it incited an all-out frenzy and induced scores of Moscow reporters to join in the hunt. Sensationalized stories about Alex quickly became daily fare, more often than not outrageously fabricated nonsense. One enterprising weekly magazine initiated a column dubbed "Kid Midas Sightings" so the whole city could join in the fun: a five hundred dollar reward was offered to anybody who could produce a photograph of Alex, five thousand if he was nude, purportedly his normal state.

Alex's attorneys begged him to sue, promising to terrorize the publishing industry, as only lawyers can do. A flat, persistent refusal was his stubborn response. It would only generate more unwanted publicity, he insisted. And anyway, it was a novelty that would quickly wear off, he assured them, but he promptly hired his first security people. Six private bodyguards. All former Spetsnaz special forces warriors, who looked fierce and swore they would be loyal to the end.

Alex was still scribbling notes and poring over thick business files when, two hours later, the pilot's nasal voice launched the usual preparatory steps for landing. Seat backs were jolted forward, eating trays shoved back into position, a few people got up and stretched. The pair of watchers exchanged knowing winks.

Time for the fun to begin.

They followed Mr. and Mrs. Konevitch as they deplaned, he hauling their leather overnight bags casually slung over his broad shoulders; both of them totally clueless. Light packing for what the couple obviously assumed would be a brief and enjoyable business trip, in and out, a single night at most. Guess again, Alex.

The carry-on luggage was a welcome relief, nonetheless. Their instructions were stern and clear: avoid loose ends, anything that might make the authorities suspicious. The Hungarian police weren't known for nosiness or efficiency. Interference seemed unlikely. Still, unclaimed bags that were tagged with contact information might cause an unwanted problem or two.

At customs, Mr. and Mrs. Konevitch offered polite smiles to the green-uniformed customs guard, flashed their Russian passports, no problems there. Then they went directly through the sliding glass doors into the expansive lobby.

Midday. The foot traffic was sparse, which made the targets easy to track, but also made it harder for the reception team to blend in and hide.

Their briefing was unequivocal on this point — stay with the Konevitches every second of every minute. No respite until the arrival-and-reception team had matters firmly in hand. Same kind of job they had done hundreds or possibly thousands of times during the past fifty years, always successfully. Old age had slowed them down a few steps, but in their line of work the trade-off was more than equitable; nobody suspected a pair of doddering old geezers.

The customs agent barely gave them or their passports a glance as he waved them through. What possible threat could these wrinkled old wrecks pose to the Republic of Hungary? they were sure he was thinking. If only he knew. They had thirty confirmed kills to their credit, with six more they stubbornly claimed, though the corpses had been incinerated into ashes or fallen into deep rivers and washed away.

Mr. and Mrs. Konevitch were walking briskly through the lobby, straight for the taxi stand outside. The tail team followed at a safe distance, hobbling and creaking with every step.

At the taxi stand, three people were already lined up ahead of the Konevitches — a hatchet-faced lady struggling with her over-sized luggage, and two faces the tails instantly recognized, Vladimir and Katya.

Vladimir was the boss of the arrival-and-reception team, a man they all thoroughly feared and deeply loathed. Katya, like the rest of them, was vicious, cold-blooded, and unemotional, a veteran killer with a long and enviable list of hits — but always just business. Vladimir was a sadistic bastard with freakish appetites. He would've done this work for free; paid to do it, probably. Even the toughest killers in the unit felt a wash of pity for his victims.

The tail team from the airplane backed off, ignoring the Konevitches and redirecting their attention to trying to spot the private bodyguards. They had memorized as many faces from their flight as they could. Now they separated from each other, about twenty yards apart, stopped, pretended to fumble with their luggage, and watched for familiar faces.

The call came in at 2:37 p.m. and the secretary put it right through.

Sergei Golitsin checked his watch, right on time. He lifted the phone and barked, "Well?"

"Good news, they're here," the voice informed him. "Everything's under control."

"So you have them?"

"No, not yet. They're at the taxi stand two feet from Vladimir and Katya. Everything's on schedule, everything's in place. I'll call you in a few minutes when we do."

"Don't mess this up." Golitsin snorted.

"Relax. We won't."

There was a long pause. Golitsin, with barely suppressed excitement, asked, "Are the communications set up?"

"They are. The listening devices are state of the art. You'll get a crystal-clear feed into the phone lines and through your speakerphone. I tested it with your secretary an hour ago. Everything's fine." After a pause, the voice added, "Vladimir's going to handle this. It's going to be loud and ugly."

"It better be." Golitsin closed his eyes and smiled. "I want to hear every sound."

3

The old lady at the front of the line shoved two bags at a cabbie and crawled painfully into a blue BMW with TAXI splashed in bold letters across the side.

The couple directly in front of Alex and Elena stepped forward, and a black Mercedes sedan that had been idling by the far curb suddenly swerved in front of the other taxis and screeched to a noisy halt half a foot from the taxi stop. Vladimir, wearing the garb and collar of a Catholic priest, made a fast survey of the surroundings, then quickly threw open the rear door. The same instant, Katya, dressed as a nun, pushed out an ugly black pistol hidden inside the folds of her baggy sleeve and pointed it in Alex's face.

Her partner turned around. Coldly and in Russian he said to Alex, "It's a simple choice. Get into the car or die right here and right now."

Alex looked into his eyes. He had not the slightest doubt he meant every word. After a moment, he said, "Fine, I'll go. This young lady, however, you will leave alone. I don't know her. She's not with me."

"Don't be stupid, Konevitch. Katya will kill you, or your wife, or both of you. Doesn't matter to us."

Alex's face froze. His *name.* The man had used his name, and he *knew* Elena was his wife. For three years he had prepared himself for a moment like this. Dreamed about it. Dreaded it. Now it was actually happening, and he couldn't think or react.

Vladimir's thick hands shot out and grabbed Elena by the neck. He spun her around like a puppet; one hand slipped under her chin, the other against the back of her head. Elena squirmed and fought at first, but Vladimir was too large and strong. He tightened his grip, and she yelped with pain.

Vladimir said to Alex, "You have a black belt, I hear. Surely you recognize this stance. A quick shift of my weight and her neck will snap like a rotten twig. Now, will you *please* get into the cab?"

As they were sure he would, without hesitation or another word, Alex climbed inside. A moment later, Elena was shoved in beside him and landed awkwardly against his side. The man knew what he was doing; he was using her as a buffer from Alex's hands, and he squeezed into the backseat to her right. The woman in the nun's outfit, obviously anything but one of God's saintly servants, slipped into the front passenger seat with her pistol in Alex's face.

The driver, a trusted cohort and a skilled getaway man, gunned the engine, popped the clutch, and off they sped with a noisy screech. Nobody said a word. As if on cue, the lady in the front shifted her gun at Elena's face. The man in priest's garb said to Alex, "Hold up your hands, together."

Alex did as he was told. The man bent across Elena and efficiently slapped thick plastic cuffs on Alex's wrists, then with a show of equal dexterity, Elena's.

After a moment, Alex asked, "What do you want?"

"Be quiet," came the reply from Vladimir. He withdrew two black hoods and clumsily covered their heads.

In March 1992, two months after the press frenzy over Alex Konevitch began, the initial attacks on his companies were detected.

Somebody was making repeated highly sophisticated attempts to break into Konevitch Associates' computer networks. Quite successfully, or so it appeared. The Russian Internet backbone, like everything inherited from communism, was shockingly backward and inefficient. Alex had therefore hired an American company that specialized in these things and plowed millions into creating his own corporate network, a closed maze of servers, switches, and privately owned fiber-optic cable that connected his companies. The only vulnerabilities were in the interfaces between his private network and the Russian phone companies, interfaces that were, regrettably, unavoidable. Naturally this was precisely where the attacks occurred.

That discovery was made minutes after a new American anti-virus software program was installed, a magical sifter that sorted gold from fool's gold. Tens of thousands of spyware programs were detected — like small tracking devices — that had penetrated and riddled the entire network. The programs were sophisticated little things, impossible to detect with homegrown software. They not only tracked the flow of Internet traffic, they caused each message to replicate and then forwarded copies to an outside Internet address.

Private investigators easily tracked the Internet address to a small apartment on the outer ring of Moscow and burgled their way into the flat. It was completely empty and wiped clean. Nothing, except a small table and dusty computer. The plug was pulled out. The hard disk had been removed.

What was going on? Alex had anxiously queried his technical specialists. Somebody is mapping your businesses and transactions, came the answer. For how long? he asked.

Maybe weeks, more probably months, and it seemed fair to conclude that whoever launched this attack now had an avalanche of information regarding how his rapidly expanding empire came together, how one piece interfaced with the next, how and where the money flowed, even the identities of the key people who pushed the buttons. The computers in the human resources department, particularly, were riddled with enough spyware to feed a software convention.

The programs were wiped clean, gobs of money were thrown at more protective software — all imported from America, all state of the art, all breathtakingly expensive — and nothing was heard from the originator of the attack. Corporate extortion or any of several forms of embezzlement had been anticipated — pay us off, the intercepted traffic will be destroyed, the attacks will stop. But after long weeks during which Alex's hired computer wizards held their breath and nobody approached the firm, a new, more hopeful scenario was reached. It was probably one of the expanding army of nettlesome computer nerds, his technical people speculated — nothing to be overly concerned with. This was an everyday problem in the United States, Alex was told, where hackers sat up all night and thought up ways to be bothersome for no greater reason than the idiotic satisfaction of imagining it made them something more than the insignificant little twits they were.

In fact, Alex was warned, it could have been much worse; the sneaks could've hacked in, crashed the entire system, and demolished mounds of irreplaceable information. A helpful and timely warning, actually — take better precautions, spend whatever it takes, and then some. Stay alert. Be thankful we detected the problem early and eliminated it, Alex was told by his head technician, an American imported and paid a small fortune for his erudition in these matters.

4

The old lady was merely daft, Bernie Lutcher concluded, at first.

She had jumped in front of him, repeating something loudly in Russian. At least it sounded like Russian. He understood not a word and shrugged his shoulders, and she switched to a different tongue, more quick bursts of incomprehensible gibberish — possibly Hungarian now — while he continued to shrug and tried to brush past her. To his rising impatience, she clutched his arm harder and ratcheted up the incoherent babble.

He recalled her from the plane, the old lady with apparent incontinence issues who made trip after trip to the potty. Maybe she was seeking directions to the air terminal ladies' room, he guessed. Or maybe she was a certified loony, a lonely human nuisance of the type found in every city in the world.

He tried to tug his arm away again and noticed how surprisingly strong she was.

Ahead, he watched Alex and Elena pass through the electronic doors, and felt a sudden clutch of alarm. Depending on the length of the line outside, it might take only a few seconds for them to climb into a taxi and disappear into the vast, winding labyrinth of Budapest streets.

He knew their schedule and the name of their hotel: he could always catch up with them there. Unfortunately, he was pathologically honest and duty-bound to enter any coverage lapses in the report he assiduously completed and turned in after each job. In his mind he had already spent his annual bonus on a nice holiday in Greece, on a luxurious slow cruise through the sunbaked islands, sipping ouzo and ogling Scandanavian tourist girls in their Lilliputian bikinis; he now was watching it all go up in smoke.

He tried to recall any fragment of every language he knew and quickly blurted at the old lady, "Excuse me . . . *entschuldigen* . . . *excusez-moi . . . por favor?* . . ." Nothing, no relief.

A large crowd began catching up to him, impatient travelers who had just cleared customs and now were plowing ahead and jostling for choice spots in the taxi line. He could hear their voices, but kept one eye on the old lady — who clutched his arm harder and acted increasingly distressed — and the other on the glass door Alex and Elena had just exited. He never turned around, never observed the old man who quickly approached his back.

The old lady continued prattling about something, more loudly frantic now, more mysteriously insistent, still stubbornly clasping his arm. Firm procedures were unequivocal about such situations: public scenes and embarrassments, indeed public attention in any form, were to be avoided at all costs. He reached down and gently tried to pry his arm loose from the old hag's grip, even as an old man approached from his rear aggressively swinging his arms with each step. Gripped tightly in the old man's right hand, and mostly obscured by an overly long coat sleeve, was a razor-thin, specially made thirteen-inch dagger.

One step back from the bodyguard's rear, it swung up. The blade entered Bernie Lutcher's back nearly six inches below his left shoulder blade, grazed off one rib, then immediately penetrated his heart.

The old man gave it a hard grind and twist, a signature technique honed decades before, one he was quite proud of, tearing open at least two heart chambers, ensuring an almost immediate death. In any event, the blade was coated with a dissolvable poison primed to instantly decrystallize and rush straight into Bernie's bloodstream. One way or another, he'd be dead.

Bernie's eyes widened and his lips flew open. At the same instant, the old lady gave him a hard punch — an expertly aimed blow to the solar plexus to knock the wind out of his lungs — and he landed heavily on his back, gasping for air and grasping his chest, as though he was suffering a heart attack, which he surely was.

The two assassins immediately scattered, moving swiftly to the departure area for a flight to Zurich that left thirty minutes later.

The first assassinations happened in the last three days of August 1992. The Summer Massacres, they were called afterward by the thoroughly cowed employees of Konevitch Associates.

Andri Kelinichetski, bachelor, bon vivant, and very popular vice president for investor relations, ended up first in the queue. A lifelong insomniac, he left his cramped apartment at two in the morning for a brisk walk in the cool Moscow air to clear the demons from his head. He had made it three blocks from his apartment when three bullets, fired from thirty feet behind his skull, cleared his head, literally. Andri stopped breathing before he hit the cement.

Five hours later, Tanya Nadysheva, divorced mother of two and a specialist in distressed companies, started up her newly purchased red Volkswagen sedan for the drive to work, triggering a powerful bomb. Her head landed half a block away; she had been operating her fancy new sunroof at the precise instant of detonation.

By ten o'clock that morning, six employees of Konevitch Associates lay in the morgue — one long-distance shooting, one short-distance, a hand grenade attack, one car bombing, one very grisly slit throat, and a notably devout employee who was literally fed a poisoned wafer as he stopped off at his local church for his habitual morning Communion.

Six victims. Six different types of murder. No failed attempts, no survivors, no witnesses. With the exception of the sliced throat and the fatal Communion wafer, the killers — obviously more than one — had struck from a distance, safely and anonymously. No forensic traces were found beyond spent bullets and bomb residue. The particles from the explosive devices were analyzed on the spot by a veteran field technician. In his opinion, the devices were so coarse and simple, virtually any criminal idiot could've built them.

A few hours later, a pair of special police investigators showed up, unannounced, at the headquarters of Konevitch Associates. They flashed badges, announced their purpose with a show of grim expressions, and were ushered hurriedly upstairs. They marched into Alex's office, where they found him and several of his more senior executives assembled, making hasty arrangements for the families of their dead friends and employees, plainly in shock over what had just happened. One executive, Nadia Pleshinko, was blowing snot into a white tissue, unable to stop weeping.

One officer was fat, mustachioed, and late-middle-aged, the other surprisingly young, runway skinny, with a face that looked glum even when he smiled. Laurel and Hardy, they were inevitably nicknamed by the boys at the precinct, a resemblance so glaring that even they celebrated the epithet.

They were both lieutenants with the municipal police, they informed the gathering, here to discuss what had been learned or not about the morning butchery.

"The Mafiya," the fat senior one opened his briefing. "That's who's behind this. It's not just you, it's happening all over Moscow. There have been over sixty murders in the city just this past month. Sixty!" he said, rolling his bloodshot eyes with wearied disgust. "Nearly all were businesspeople, bankers, and one or two news reporters who were getting too close to one of the mobs or to a corrupt politician on their payroll."

Skinny picked up where his partner left off. "Under the old system, the city averaged maybe three murders a month. And that was a bad month. Nearly always angry wives or husbands getting even for an affair or some marital slight or squabble."

"And the Mafiya is behind all these murders?" Alex asked, totally uninterested in a prolonged recounting of Moscow murderography. All that mattered was what happened to *his* people *that* morning. And what might happen tomorrow. Were the killers finished, or just warming up? Were these six the final toll? Or should Alex buy bulletproof vests and begin building thick bunkers for his employees?

A serious nod from both officers and Skinny said, "In the old days they were into drugs, prostitution, the black market, that kind of funny stuff. Capitalism has given them a whole new lease. The big money these days is companies like yours. It's —"

"What do they want?" Alex interrupted.

"Hard to say," Fatty replied with a sad frown. "Usually it's a shakedown. Some variation of a protection or extortion racket. 'Pay us a few million, or give us a cut of the monthly profit, and we'll stop killing your people.' I'm afraid that's the optimistic scenario."

Alex paused for a moment, then reluctantly asked, "And what's the pessimistic one?"

Skinny took over and said, "It could also be that somebody — a competitor perhaps — is paying them to wipe you out. Or maybe to soften you up for an attempted takeover.

Either way, they'll keep killing until you're out of business, or until they believe you're ready to meet their terms. These people are ambitious, creative, and vicious." He looked over at Fatty, who offered an approving nod. "For instance," he continued, "they hit a banking company two months ago. Before you could say turnip soup, twelve executives were dead."

"The Mafiya," Alex said, rolling that ugly sound off his lips. "Aren't they organized into families or groups? It's not just one big mob, is it?"

"No, you're right," Skinny told him, warming to the subject. "Only two years ago we could've told you which syndicate was behind this, who headed the group, with an accurate, up-to-date, well-detailed manning and organization chart. These days there are so many mobs . . ." He trailed off.

He paused for a quick look at their beleaguered faces. "Even the ones we do know about multiply, merge, and divide so fast, we've lost count. They outnumber us, outgun us, and, worse, frankly, they're now smarter than we are."

"Can you protect us?" one of Alex's executives nervously asked, clearly speaking for them all.

It was a good question and the two officers looked at each other. Eventually, and with matched, timid expressions they turned back to Alex and his people. Fatty cleared his throat once or twice. "We can certainly give it our best try. Add more people to the investigation, make inquiries to local stoolies, throw a few uniformed guards outside your headquarters, that sort of thing. We're not in the bodyguard business, though. And frankly, you have too many employees to protect. That bank I mentioned a moment ago, we were doing our best to protect it." He rolled his eyes and sighed. "Twelve dead."

Before they could dwell on that, Skinny looked at Alex and asked, "Have you received any threats? Direct communications in any form from the killers?"

"No, not a word."

This was apparently a bad omen, as both policemen seemed to frown at the same time. As if by hidden cue, Fatty eventually shook his head and spoke up. "Not good. Typically they warn you beforehand. You do this, or we'll do that."

"Sometimes it's Chinese water torture," Skinny threw in, showing off his own mastery of the subject. "Other times it's a sledgehammer, and, to be perfectly frank, this has all the hallmarks of the latter. These people are professionals. They choose how and when to make their approach."

If they were trying to scare Alex and his employees, they were succeeding nicely. A few chairs were pushed back. One or two executives uttered loud groans.

After another quiet pause, Fatty said, "Here's the pattern we're seeing. Number one, they knew the names of your employees, their addresses, and their personal habits. I don't need to tell you what this implies. Your company has been under their eye for a long time, maybe even penetrated from the inside. Who knows how many of your people are on their payroll, or how many of you are targeted for hits. Number two, the potpourri of killing methods is a carefully scripted message in itself — they can kill you however and whenever they want, wherever you are, whatever you're doing."

The two officers continued batting around theories and chilling speculations, oblivious to the sheer horror they were inciting. Alex and his underlings exchanged piercing looks before Alex, with a discomfited shrug, looked away and contemplated a white wall. Nobody needed to say it: resentment cut like a knife through the room. Alex had all those layers of personal protection — those six beefy bodyguards, a private home with the best security systems money could buy, an armored Mercedes limousine, and a lifestyle that kept him off the streets, out of harm's way.

The four senior executives in the room, just like the rest of the employees of Konevitch Associates, were sitting ducks. Totally defenseless. Morgue meat, all of them.

And the cops were right. It took less than a year after the disintegration of the Soviet Union for Moscow to descend into chaos. Brutal murders were a daily event, soldiers were hawking their weapons and ammunition on street corners for a few measly rubles, unemployment had shot through the ceiling. In the clumsy rush to privatize, prices had climbed to dizzying heights, and public services, which had never been decent, deteriorated, then collapsed altogether. A long, fierce winter of misery set in. Hundreds of thousands of Muscovites couldn't afford oil to heat their homes, to buy decent food or clothing, and were turning to crime to make ends meet.

The newspapers were loaded with stories about the self-ennobling extravagances of the newly rich and famous, while hundreds starved or froze to death in Russia's arctic winter. Nobody was going to feel sorry for Konevitch Associates. No matter how many of its well-fed executives were shot, bombed, or chopped up, nobody would waste an ounce of pity. And the drumbeat of news stories about the shining toys and refurbished palaces of the newly rich worked like a tantalizing announcement to the criminals: "Here it is, boys! Come and get it."

When the two officers finished batting around the possibilities, Alex said, in an accusatory tone, "So you can't protect us?"

"To be honest, no," Fatty replied with a sad shake of the head and an earthquake of chin wobbles. "These days, we barely have enough manpower to haul the bodies to the morgue."

"What do you suggest, then?" Alex asked, avoiding the eyes of his executives, who looked ready to dodge from the room and flee for their lives.

"What we tell everybody who asks. Private security, Mr. Konevitch. You have a rich company. You can afford to hire the best."

Skinny looked like he wanted to say more and Alex glanced in his direction. "If you have something to add, we'd like to hear it."

"All right. Off the record. Between us. And just us, please. These are Mafiya people we're talking about. In case you haven't already gotten the message, they're tough, ruthless, and stubborn. But there is somebody who scares the shit out of these guys."

"Go on."

"KGB people. Former KGB people. They and the Mafiya have been at war for fifty years. Remember the old saying 'it takes one to know one'? A lot of highly trained former operatives are now out on the streets, unemployed, desperate for jobs and willing to work hard. Talented people, a lot of them. They have skills, experience, and attitude. To be blunt, the KGB people are even worse than the Mafiya types."

Alex spent a quiet, troubled moment thinking about the officer's suggestion. He had nothing but rotten memories of the KGB and was privately delighted that he had helped put them out of business. They had booted him out of college and nearly destroyed his life. They very nearly destroyed his country. Under communism, the Mafiya were nothing but a nasty irritant, two-bit gangsters engaged in shadowy enterprises that barely made a dent. The real mob was the KGB. It turned itself into the world's greatest extortion racket, a mass of faceless thugs who abused their power endlessly, living like spoiled princes while their people suffered in an asylum of terrified poverty.

No, he decided on the spot: not today, not tomorrow, not ever. No matter how bad it got, he would never employ a former KGB person to work in his company.

Fatty read his disapproving expression and withdrew a business card from his pocket that he smoothly slid across the table. "In the event you change your mind, Sergei Golitsin is the man to call. He was the number two in the KGB, a retired three-star general. Whatever you need, believe me, he can take care of."

The next morning, after four more dead employees of Konevitch Associates were scraped off the cement and hauled to the morgue, Alex called Sergei Golitsin.

■ ■ ■ ■

The door opened loudly and the room filled with noisy voices, a number of people, one or two women and several men, speaking crudely in Russian. Alex had no idea where he was — the car ride had lasted nearly half an hour — a fast trip filled with abrupt, jarring turns probably intended as much to disorient Alex and Elena as to elude any followers. He and Elena were pulled and shoved out of the backseat, then pushed and tugged through a doorway into a building that smelled cloyingly of oil and kerosene. The floor was hard concrete. By the loud echoes of their footsteps, the room was large, cavernous, and mostly empty.

A vacant warehouse, Alex guessed. Or possibly an abandoned garage.

From there, he and Elena were immediately split up and forced into separate rooms. Alex was rushed inside another, smaller room, laid out on what he guessed was a hard table or medical gurney, and the work began. A pair of strong hands untied his shoes, yanked them off his feet, and they landed with a noisy *clumpf* on the floor. A knife skillfully carved off his pants and shirt, leaving him naked except for his Jockeys.

A different pair of stronger hands efficiently clamped his arms and legs tightly with leather straps attached to the sides of the table. Because of the blindfold, he had not a clue what they had done with Elena, where they had taken her. The only thing Alex was sure of was this: it was no coincidence the kidnapping had taken place on one of the few occasions when they traveled together outside Russia, man and wife, on a business trip. This, more than anything, terrified him.

But he squeezed shut his eyes and somehow forced himself to think. Whoever these people were, they had somehow breached, then eliminated his security. Further, the simple yet elaborate kidnapping indicated they had advance knowledge, somehow, that he and Elena were traveling to Budapest. They were waiting for him. They knew his schedule and movements to a tee. And they were professionals — he was sure of this, for whatever it meant, for whatever it was worth.

What kind of professionals, though? Kidnappers out for a fat ransom? Or assassins? That was the urgent question.

They knew he was wondering and left him alone on the gurney to stew and suffer in isolation for nearly half an hour.

Then he heard two sets of footsteps approach, one pair moving lightly, the other heavy, making loud clumps. Probably hard-soled boots. Through the blindfold, he sensed somebody looking down on him, still not speaking, barely breathing. Alex's own breaths were pouring out heavily, his heart racing, his nightmares growing by the second. His mind told him they were allowing the terror to build and he should fight it. His heart would not allow it; he was utterly terrorized.

Without a word or warning, a fist struck him in the midsection; every bit of oxygen in his lungs exploded out of his mouth with a noisy *ooompf.* He sucked for air and tried to say, "What do —" when the fist struck again, this time in his groin. He couldn't even double over or writhe in agony. He screamed, and the beating continued, methodically, without pause, only the sounds of the fists striking against flesh and bone, and Alex howling and groaning in agony.

Vladimir stepped out of the room and slipped off the leather gloves that now were nearly saturated with blood, Alex's blood. He lifted the phone, and Golitsin, sounding like he was next door and experiencing an orgasm, said, "That was wonderful. Just wonderful. Thank you."

"You heard it all?"

"Every punch, every groan. What a treat. How did he look?"

"In shock, at first. He had not a clue why he was being beaten. Now he is merely miserable and confused. You heard him."

"I certainly did. Any broken bones?" he

asked, sounding hopeful.

"A few ribs, I would think. Possibly the leg I banged with a chair. And I tore his left shoulder out of the socket. You must've heard the pop. It was certainly loud enough."

"Ah . . . I wondered what that was." Golitsin laughed. "As long as you didn't damage his precious right hand."

"No, no, of course not," Vladimir assured him, then waited, knowing Golitsin was calling the shots. If it was another beating, fine, though Vladimir needed at least ten minutes to catch his wind and rest his muscles.

After a moment, Golitsin asked, "Is he still conscious?"

"A little bit less than more. We had to revive him a few times. In twenty minutes or so the bruises will be swollen and his nerve endings will resensitize." He sounded like he'd done this many times.

"Good. Give him twenty minutes to recover, then mark him." There was a long pause before Golitsin stressed, "Slowly, stretch it out for all it's worth."

They were not going to kill him, Alex, in his moments of groggy consciousness, kept telling himself. Between the sounds of his own beating, he heard a voice, a woman's, deep and scornful, issuing occasionally stern reminders to the man torturing him. Soften the blows, she warned. Avoid damaging important organs, she reminded him. Twice she had loudly snarled that he had better stop choking Alex before their precious hostage had to be hauled out in a box.

So they needed him alive. They wouldn't kill him. They wanted something from him, and they would keep him breathing until they had it; whatever it was.

Then they might kill him.

The door opened loudly again, and two sets of footsteps approached. Same two pairs of feet, Alex thought, one light, one heavy. Were they going to beat him again? He totally forgot his earlier reasoning and wondered, maybe they *were* going to kill him?

The blindfold was ripped from his head. He blinked a few times. "What do you want?" he croaked, throat parched. No answer, not a peep. He tried to focus his eyes, which were blurry and unfocused though he was positive the hazy shapes before him were the same man and woman from the taxi. And probably the same pair who had inflicted the brutal beating.

"Please. Just tell me what you want."

The man, Vladimir, he had heard him called, bent down over his face, smiled, squeezed open his lids, and studied his pupils a moment. Vladimir then took two thick leather straps and, one at a time, stretched them across Alex's chest, strung them underneath the table, fastened them as he would a belt, and tightened them enough that they bit painfully into Alex's skin. Next he held something before his face — a handheld device. A machine of some sort. Oddly enough, it looked like a compact traveling iron for pressing clothes. "See this?" he asked Alex.

"Yes . . . what is it?"

"You'll learn in a moment."

"Where's Elena?" Alex demanded.

Vladimir laughed.

"Please," Alex pleaded. "Leave her out of this. She's done nothing to you."

"But you have," Vladimir informed him with a mean smile.

"I don't even know you." Sensing it was the wrong thing to say, Alex suggested, a little hopefully, "If it's money, let's agree on a price. Let her go. Keep me. She'll make sure you get paid."

"Are you proud of what you did?" Vladimir asked, backing away. He spit on the iron and enjoyed the angry hiss.

"I don't know what you're talking about."

The woman spoke up and said, "Most of us are former KGB. Career people, patriotic servants who protected Mother Russia. You ruined our lives."

"How?" Alex asked.

"You know how. You fed millions to Yeltsin and destroyed our homeland."

"How do you know about this?"

"We know all about you, Alex Konevitch. We've watched you for years. Watched you undermine our country. Watched you become rich off the spoils. Now it's time to return the favor."

Alex closed his eyes. Things had just gone from bad to worse. Not only did they know him, they knew *about* him. A simple kidnapping was bad enough. This was revenge on top of it, and both Vladimir and Katya allowed Alex a few moments to contemplate how bad this was going to get.

Vladimir held up the iron so they could jointly inspect it; the metal undertray was red-hot, glowing fiercely in the dimly lit room. He held it before Alex's face. "American cowboys branded their cattle. I hope you don't mind, but now we will brand you."

Without another word, Vladimir slipped a pair of industrial earphones over his head, thick black rubber gloves over his hands, then with a steady hand lowered the iron slowly toward Alex's chest. Watching it move closer, Alex squirmed and tried to evade it with all his might; the new belts totally immobilized him. The first hot prick of the iron seared the tender flesh above his left nipple — Vladimir used the recently sharpened edges of the iron and glided it slowly and skillfully around his skin.

Alex screamed and Vladimir pressed down firmly, though not too hard, etching a careful pattern: a long curve first, then another curve, meticulously connecting them into the shape of a sickle. The stench of burning flesh filled the room. Next, he began drawing a squarish shape — completing the hammer and sickle, the symbol of the once feared and mighty, now historically expired Soviet Union. Vladimir had done this before; this was obvious. Just as obviously, he was the kind of artisan who reveled in his work. The entire process lasted thirty minutes. Alex screamed until he went hoarse, piercing shrieks that echoed and bounced around the warehouse.

Katya stood and tried to watch, then, after two minutes, horrified, she gave up and fled.

5

By 3:30, Eugene Daniels was quaffing down the final dregs of his third Bavarian brew, a special, thick dunkel beer produced seasonally without preservatives that was totally unavailable in the States. Across the table, his wife, Maria, was stingily nursing her second wine, a Georgian pinot she had just explained, for the second time, with an excellent bouquet, overly subtle perhaps, but with fine, lingering legs and other insufferable claptrap she had obviously lifted from one of those snobbish wine books. How could anybody make so much of squished grapes? An attractive Hungarian waitress approached the table and, while Eugene wasn't looking, Maria quietly waved her off.

She toyed with the stem of her wineglass and reminded her husband, "Business meetings are best conducted sober."

"If Alex wanted me sober, he'd be here on time."

"Maybe he has something up his sleeve.

Hundreds of millions are at stake, Eugene. Maybe he wants you loaded and stupid before he arrives." And maybe he's succeeding beyond his wildest dream, she thought and smiled coldly.

"You don't know Alex, obviously."

Rather than risk another squabble, Maria lifted a finely plucked eyebrow and insisted with a disapproving frown, "All the same, switch to coffee."

Eugene ignored this and took a long sip of beer. He checked his watch for the thirtieth time, then repeated the same thing he had said at least twenty times. "I've never known Alex to be late. He's punctual to a fault. Always."

"Maybe he has a Russian watch. I know for a fact, their craftsmanship is awful."

He was tempted to say: How would you know, you stupid spoiled twit? but swallowed the sentiment and instead noted, "No, something's wrong. I smell it."

"Yes, you're right. This whole thing is dreadfully wrong. We flew all the way from New York, he only had to come from Moscow, we're here, and he's not. This is rude and unprofessional. We should leave."

Eugene stared hard at his wife and fought the urge to stuff a napkin down her throat. Wife number four, actually — and without question, the biggest mistake of all. He was still on his third wife and making a decent go of it when Maria, a buxom brunette half his age and with a penchant for tight leather miniskirts, became his secretary. He'd chased her around the desk a few times, but not too many before she hit the brakes and made the pursuit pay off.

When it got out — with more than a little assistance from Maria, he only belatedly and after the fact realized — Wife Three stomped off into the sunset with a fifty million settlement and that big, ostentatious mansion in the Hamptons to quell her hurt pride. Word was she now had a shiny new red Rolls and a good-looking cabana boy to help her through the emotional relapses.

The house and money had been bad enough. What Eugene most sorely regretted was losing the one really capable secretary he ever had. Maria was pushy, curt, and anal, keeping him organized and punctual, and cleaning up behind him — qualities that now made her insufferable as a wife.

And now that she was bound to his money by a marriage license, any pretense of pleasantry had worn off. Even the sex had turned infrequent and limp.

He whipped out his cell and punched the preset for Alex's office in Moscow. The call went straight through to Alex's warm and efficient secretary, Sonja, who picked up on the second ring. Eugene and Alex had done a few very profitable deals together, he lining up American backers and bringing in the American greenbacks, while Alex plowed them into Russian enterprises that minted gold. Though he and Alex's secretary had never met face-to-face, Sonja never forgot a voice. She called him Mr. Daniels before he finished hello.

Eugene quickly explained his problem — Alex had scheduled a meeting with him, here, in the restaurant of the Aquincum Hotel for two hours before. "I know that," replied Sonja, who instantly turned equally perplexed and talkative. Alex was never tardy, she replied with considerable pride. Yes, she had made the travel arrangements herself, and no, Alex had not contacted her regarding delays or problems. They quickly exhausted the possibilities, and she eventually transferred Eugene to Alex's head of security, a former KGB general named Sergei Golitsin.

"What may I do for you?" Golitsin asked in heavily accented, stilted English.

Eugene slammed down his beer and came directly to the point. "Have you heard from Alex?"

"No."

"He's over two hours late for a meeting."

"Two hours?" he asked, only mildly interested.

"Yes, that's what I said."

"So what?"

"Alex is never late. That's the *what.*"

"So maybe he makes an exception this time."

"Maybe he did. But wouldn't you know if he was diverted, or missed his flight, or had a car accident? Maybe he fell down a rabbit hole."

"Probably not."

"But shouldn't you *know?*"

"No, I should not. At Mr. Konevitch's insistence he employs an outside security company for foreign travel. I have strongly advised him against this dangerous practice many, many times. Outside Mother Russia, his itinerary and security . . . well, they are out of my hands."

Eugene was dismayed by the too-bored-who-gives-a-damn tone at the other end of the line. If this guy was his chief of security, he thought, Alex better invest in plenty of body armor. He tried to swallow his exasperation and said, "Look, Alex and Elena are supposed to meet me here for a late lunch to discuss a pressing business deal. This deal has to close by tonight. Millions might be lost."

"I believe this is your problem."

"According to your job title, Alex's personal security is your problem."

"No," Golitsin replied with a nasty laugh, "that is Konevitch's problem."

"Can't you at least call the outside firm that handles Alex's security? Better yet, give me the number. I'll call."

"This is inside confidential information that cannot be divulged."

"All right, fine. Surely you won't mind if I call the local police and report Alex's disappearance."

The general's voice suddenly changed from a gruff blow-off to conciliatory. "No . . . there is no need to do that. Let me handle this."

"I don't think I trust you to handle it."

"I will. Give me your number. I will call the moment I have something."

"Call me even if you don't. I've got twenty million riding, my own cash, and four greedy partners who are throwing in another seventy mil each." He glanced at his watch. "If the deal's not going through, I'll have to cancel the bank order by five at the latest."

"Yes . . . of course."

Eugene gave him his number and the line went dead.

They let him rest for an hour after the branding was finished. A large industrial fan had been brought in and locked into high gear to push out the stench of roasted flesh. The iron had been pressed down hard enough that the best plastic surgeon in the world could not totally eliminate or disguise Vladimir's handiwork. Alex would spend the rest of his life tattooed with the symbol he had done so much to destroy.

At exactly 4:05, Vladimir and Katya reentered the room, herding a harried-looking doctor and a plump, greasy-haired lawyer who reputedly specialized in the rapidly changing Russian business legal codes. Vladimir and Katya stood and waited with indifferent expressions at the end of the gurney. The doctor checked Alex's pulse and monitored his breathing, then spent a while poking and prodding various body parts.

Eventually the doctor looked up and in high native Russian informed Vladimir, "Pulse count's a little high, no doubt the result of the trauma and fear. At least two ribs are broken and there's a terrible contusion on his leg. Without an X-ray I can't determine if it's broken."

The room was unheated and cold, and as nightfall moved in was becoming colder by the minute. Naked but for his underpants, Alex's teeth were chattering. His arms and legs would've been shivering except for the tight restraints. The doctor glanced again at the broken, bleeding body on the gurney, then, after wasting a horrified grimace at Vladimir, scuttled swiftly from the room.

Vladimir and Katya pulled over a long wooden bench and sat beside Alex. They had agreed beforehand they would play out their best imitation of the old good-cop/bad-cop routine.

Vladimir had already done a thoroughly

credible job of establishing his credentials as the bad cop. Acting good wasn't exactly Katya's strong suit, either; as long as she sat beside Vladimir, though, she'd look like an angel. Vladimir slowly lit a foul-smelling French cigarette, exhaled loudly, and in his most blasé tone said to Alex, "You're probably wondering what this is about."

After toying with the idea of answering him, Alex decided against it. Finally they were getting down to business. They had beaten him to a pulp, branded him, had nearly killed him — at last they were going to tell him how much it would cost not to finish the job.

No use beating around the bush, and Vladimir in a commanding voice came right out with it. "You're going to sign over your money and businesses to us."

"What?" Alex was sure he hadn't heard right. A demand for money had been expected. In fact, given the scale of this operation and the brutal professionalism of his kidnappers, Alex had fully anticipated the initial demand to be huge: in all likelihood preposterous. They would threaten and insist, he would tell them whom to talk with, then the negotiations would begin in earnest. Eventually, the ransom experts at Alex's expensive English security firm would be brought into the game, there would be some haggling, a little give, a little take, threats and counterthreats, but sooner or later a reasonable price would be agreed upon and promptly paid. But sign over his businesses? Ludicrous.

These people were either stupid or crazy. Or both.

"You heard right," Vladimir insisted, very calmly, very seriously. He stood, bent over, and lowered his face within twelve inches of Alex's eyes. "It's simple. You sign a letter we've already prepared. Nothing fancy — you're tired, worn out, and frustrated from the crushing work and responsibilities. Then you sign a simple contract with a blank space for the name of the person we will designate as your successor. You don't touch that — we will later. All you do is sign the bottom of the page."

"That simple?"

"Yes, that's it. My lawyer friend here will notarize it, and you and your wife are free to go." The shyster stood quietly in the corner, and he nodded and smiled energetically, so damned pleased to be of service to both parties.

"And if I say no?" Alex asked.

"Then you and your wife are dead. Think about it. You lose your businesses either way."

Katya butted in and, taking her best stab at playing the good cop, informed him, "Vladimir will happily kill you and your wife. Believe me, he'll enjoy it. Don't be stupid, don't give him the excuse."

Alex took a long look at the dark ceiling. So this was what it was all about. His money *and* his businesses and his properties, the works — the greedy bastards were demanding everything he'd spent six years creating and building. He drew a heavy breath and, as firmly as he could, insisted, "Money you can have. Plenty of it, enough to live happily ever after. But no, you can't have my businesses."

Vladimir had expected this, in fact was fully prepared for it. He smiled and then turned around and looked at Katya. "Get the wife," he told her.

Katya rushed off. Vladimir sat back down on the wood bench and blew lazy smoke rings while Alex pondered his options. At least now he knew what they wanted. But what would they do to Elena? Had they already harmed her? He had been unconscious for a while and his imagination began playing with all the horrible things they might already have done during that interlude. The man on the bench was a monster, utterly without conscience. Maybe Elena had also been branded. Had she been molested? Tortured? Raped?

Moscow was filled with Vladimirs these days, murderous scum whose depravity and cruelty knew no limits. In the old days they were employed by the state as instruments for spreading terror and submission; they were now as much a part of Russia's free-market economy as potatoes and vodka. They wouldn't think twice about punishing a rich man's wife — they would *enjoy* it, in fact. Alex's mind filled with the ugly possibilities.

Eventually the door opened and Elena was led in by Katya, dragged along like a dog by a rope tied to her wrists. She was frightened out of her wits, and looked it. But on the surface, at least, she appeared healthy and unmarked. Then she took one long look at Alex on the gurney and lost it. She screamed, "You bastards!" at Vladimir and Katya. She yanked on her rope, trying to break free and move toward her battered husband.

Katya grabbed a large knot of her hair, gave it a hard jerk, and yanked her backward, nearly off her feet. So much for good cop.

Vladimir stood and moved toward Elena. He placed a gag in her mouth and tied it off behind her head.

"Leave her alone," Alex protested weakly.

"After I kill you," Vladimir informed him with cruel nonchalance, "I'll give her to the boys waiting outside. She's a very attractive lady. Imagine how much fun they'll have with her."

Eugene, halfway through his seventh beer, took the cell phone call at 4:10. It was Golitsin and he opened in a very reassuring tone, saying, "Good news, I've located Alex."

"Have you?"

"Yes, and he's fine."

"Glad to hear it. Where is he?"

"Apparently a more critically important meeting came up. He asked me to inform you that he needs to reschedule."

"Reschedule?"

"Yes, that's what he said. He suggested tomorrow afternoon. What do you think about tomorrow?"

"Out of the question. He knows that. Are you sure you spoke with Alex?"

"He's my boss. I believe I know his voice."

Eugene studied his fingers a moment. This made no sense. If this deal didn't close by five o'clock, the financing evaporated — by 5:01, there was no deal. Back in New York, a cluster of lawyers and accountants were huddled around a long conference table on a high floor of a massive tower, waiting impatiently for Eugene's call. They had been there all night, drinking stale coffee, munching stale pastries, telling stale jokes, drumming their fingers — and turning surlier with each passing moment.

Three months of sweat and hard work. Three long months of Eugene assuring and reassuring his anxious investors that it was safe to dive into Russia's crooked and rigged markets with Alex Konevitch as their guide. It was the Wild, Wild East, perilous and unruly for sure; but for those audacious few willing to jump in on the ground floor, colossal fortunes were waiting to be plucked.

Three months of lengthy business plans, proposals, risk assessments, long boring briefings, and all the other tedious twaddle entailed in due diligence had taken place before this deal could be cobbled together.

Three insufferable months of sucking up to some of the biggest egos in New York.

All about to go down the drain. The thought of it was nauseating. This couldn't be happening. Over three hundred million electronic dollars were loaded and waiting to be fired into Alex's vaults. The investors were anxious and mistrustful, their commitments precarious at best. If one thing went wrong, they had collectively whispered in Eugene's ear — just one infinitesimally tiny thing — they would withdraw their dough and never take another call from him.

"I don't believe Alex told you to reschedule," Eugene spit into his phone in his best New York accusatory tone. "You're lying. I don't know why, but Alex is well aware this deal closes by five or it never closes."

A long silence followed while Golitsin recognized he had clumsily misplayed his hand. This pushy American on the other end was proving to be a big problem. If he alerted the Budapest police about the mysterious disappearance of Alex Konevitch, this whole operation could come unglued. There was the dead bodyguard at the airport to be factored in. The locals had already initiated an investigation, Golitsin had been informed by his well-placed sources. But the Hungarians had no idea of its relevance. And corpses don't complain or become impatient.

Once they learned, though, that Alex had disappeared from Ferihegy Airport at around the same time as the murder, they might put two and two together.

Alex was a rich, seriously important man, a celebrity back home, a big-time FOB — Friend of Boris. For sure, the Hungarians would not welcome the diplomatic noise and ugly publicity his disappearance would almost certainly ignite. A citywide manhunt would undoubtedly be initiated. The police would scour the airport for any witnesses who might have noticed anything. The Konevitches were an attractive couple and quite noticeable. Who knew what the cops might turn up?

His last report from that sicko freak Vladimir indicated he would need another hour to close the deal. Then another hour or two after that to tie up the nasty details like disposing of Alex's and Elena's corpses somewhere they would never be found. They would simply disappear and Golitsin would fuel rumors around Moscow that Konevitch had embezzled money from his own bank and eloped with it into nowhere. A brilliant plan, really, since Golitsin would embezzle the money himself, many, many millions, with dead Alex as his foolproof cover.

His bluff had been called, though. Americans! The greediest, pushiest bastards on earth. No, the one on the other end wasn't going to let him off the hook. And too much was at stake for this to be mishandled at this stage.

"Do not call me a liar," Golitsin pushed back in his most threatening voice. "I am merely telling you what Alex told me. I'll call him again if you insist."

Eugene thought to himself: This guy is trying to jerk me off. He suggested, "Don't bother. Give me the number, I'll call and I'll speak with him."

"He told me he was not to be disturbed. He was very firm on this. No matter what."

"Fine. Why don't I just call the cops?"

"Don't. It would cause a public mess, an embarrassment. Alex would be most upset."

"Then have him call me. Five minutes or I'm on the phone to the locals." Without waiting for a reply, Eugene punched off, checked his watch, and ordered another beer from the buxom young waitress with the comely smile.

Maria was upstairs in the hotel suite, pouting and packing. Sometime during the middle of his sixth beer, Eugene had lost his temper and poured out his resentment on her. She had gotten fired up, replied in kind, and stormed off in a huff, threatening a divorce that would make the last three look like pleasant skirmishes.

Vladimir was just getting ready to hand Mrs. Konevitch over to the boys in the back when the clunky satellite phone on his waist began bleating. Every step that would lead to Konevitch's capitulation had been plotted well in advance by Vladimir, personally. He was quite proud of his plan. He intended to let the boys have her as a plaything for an hour, and had encouraged them to do whatever they liked, as long as it produced plenty of screams and was not fatal. Konevitch would be forced to suffer the anguish of blindly listening to her shrieks and howls, knowing his own stubbornness was the cause; then she would be brought back in and tortured before his own eyes.

Vladimir hated to have his work interrupted, but the obnoxious satphone on his waist wouldn't quit. He uttered a loud curse, answered, listened for a moment, then stepped out of the room, away from prying ears, for this conversation.

"No," he told Golitsin in a reproachful tone, "not yet. Just say we're at the critical stage. You're interrupting progress."

"How long?" Golitsin hissed.

"Hard to say. He was really shaken when I told him we wanted everything. He thought it was only money. What a shock. You would've loved the look in his eyes when I told him what this was really about."

Golitsin was indeed very sorry he missed it. "Are we talking hours or minutes?"

Vladimir paused to consider this delicate question. Alex Konevitch had been horribly beaten, branded, and put under mind-crushing stress. With his considerable experience in these matters Vladimir prided himself on knowing his victims and their breaking points. Konevitch was tougher than most — probably too stubborn for his own good. Given five hours Vladimir could break anybody — make them plead and beg and roll over like dogs. That now was out of the question.

Then so be it; time to skip a few steps and accelerate the action. The boys in the back would have to wait their turn; his pretty little wife was about to get her leading role in the drama. Vladimir relished that thought, but her treatment would have to be paced just right. Too fast, and Alex would become enraged and dig in his heels. The emotional line between fury and surrender was brittle, and Vladimir had to calibrate, nudge, and terrorize Konevitch in just the right direction, at just the right speed. Of course he would be angry, initially. He would put up his best front, would threaten and spit and yell profanities. But this was his wife's pain and degradation; ultimately, he would end up desperate, utterly helpless, and would cave in to every demand Vladimir imposed on him.

Yes, it had to be slow and quite horrible.

Then Alex would confront his only real choice: what was left of his wife, or his fortune and companies. "Three hours," Vladimir replied, very firmly. "With luck, two."

Golitsin exploded into the phone, calling Vladimir everything from incompetent to a moron. Vladimir pushed the phone away from his ear and let him vent and fume and spew whatever filthy invective he wanted. For a year now he had had to put up with the old man's abuse and derision. He was sorely tired of it and tried his best to ignore this latest diatribe. How tempted he was to just tell the old man to screw off. He eventually placed the phone back to his ear, smiled to himself, and said, "Maybe you want to come here and do it yourself."

"I don't like your impertinence," Golitsin barked back.

"Nobody ever does." He paused for a moment, then insisted, "Two, maybe three hours."

"That won't do."

"Fine. What will do?"

Golitsin explained the problem in rapid-fire fashion and Vladimir listened. Golitsin eventually asked, "Can you have him call this Eugene man and make up an excuse? He's a dangerous pest. Get rid of him."

"Give me the number," Vladimir confidently replied, then wrote it down. "If Konevitch says one wrong word, his wife dies. You understand the risks, though."

"No, tell me."

"If I have to kill her, we lose an irreplaceable leverage."

"I'm sure you'll find a way without her."

"Right now his mind is on one thing, and one thing only. His own misery. Relieve him of that thought, even for a brief moment, and I might have to start over."

"You mean . . . beat and torture him again?"

"Almost from the beginning."

"So what's wrong with that?"

The straps and belts were quickly unfastened, Alex was helped to sit up, and Katya positioned the cell phone by his ear; her forefinger hovered tensely over the disconnect button. His instructions and options had been explicitly and cruelly explained. "Make this man go away, or else," Vladimir had informed him. To help him comprehend the "or else," Vladimir placed a big knife against Elena's throat, poised on her jugular for a lethal slice.

Eugene answered on the second ring. Struggling to sound apologetic rather than terrified, Alex told him, "It's me, Alex. Sorry I'm late, Eugene. It was unexpected and, believe me, absolutely couldn't be helped."

Eugene replied in a simmering tone, "Check your damn watch, Alex. I've got a briefcase packed with contracts for your signature. In thirty minutes this deal goes through or I'm screwed."

"I understand, Eugene."

"Do you? Then what are you doing about it?"

"There's nothing I can do," Alex replied. "I'm tied up right now," he explained, speaking the unvarnished truth.

"In Budapest?"

"Yes."

"Fine. I'll come to you."

"No. Even if it were possible, it's not advisable."

"Make it possible, Alex. If this deal collapses I have to pay the partners a penalty of ten million. It was the only way I could get them to pony up. You know this."

"This isn't my call, Eugene. Believe me, I would help if I could."

"My last wife took me for fifty mil, Alex, and my mansion and even my dog. And Maria's upstairs right now scheming and counting how much she can make. I'm desperate here. I can't afford to lose *one* million right now. Ten will ruin me."

There was a long pause while both men considered their options. Eugene was brilliant and talented, and, like many of his ilk, his skill at business was matched only by his incredible ineptitude at romance. Three ex-wives, with now possibly a fourth in the making. But three already: three hefty alimony payments and seven needy children, four in obscenely expensive private colleges and three in equally rapacious private schools. And there was his own luxurious lifestyle to be considered. Not to mention Maria's, who thought designer clothes grew on trees. Eugene was burning through the cash faster than he could make it — almost faster than the U.S. Treasury could print it. This deal was make or break for him.

Alex glanced at Elena with the knife at her neck; she stared back, wide-eyed, plainly terrified. He felt a stab of gut-wrenching guilt that he had gotten her into this mess, and he tried with limited success to push that aside and figure out what was going on here. When he hadn't shown up for the scheduled meeting, Eugene had obviously called his office in Moscow, probably tossed around a threat or two, and gotten a concerned response. And then — somehow — somebody in Konevitch Associates had passed this news to Vladimir, who was now brandishing a knife at Elena's throat. With a blinding flash of the obvious he understood what this meant: an inside job. Somebody in his employ was a traitor.

No wonder they knew what flight he was on, that he was traveling with Elena, and how to bypass his security.

It dawned on him for the first time that definitely they intended to kill him and Elena. He could sign over his businesses and every last penny of his millions, the deeds to his homes, the titles to his cars, even the clothes off his back. Or he could refuse and tell them to go pound sand, they weren't getting a single penny.

It would make no difference. Absolutely none. He and Elena were dead either way.

Alex drew a long, deep breath. "All right, here's the deal," he blurted into the phone. "You remember the special clause? If Elena and I aren't in the restaurant in thirty minutes, invoke it. Both of us, or —"

A moment too late, Katya jerked the phone from his ear and with an angry forefinger punched the disconnect button.

"What was that about?" she hissed with a stare meant to kill.

Alex ignored her and looked at Vladimir and the knife at Elena's throat. He yelled, "Oh God . . . wait!" to Vladimir, then yelled at anyone who would listen, "Kill her, spill one drop of her blood, and you'll get nothing. I swear. Not a penny."

Vladimir played with carving a deep gash across her throat, but Katya barked, "Don't. Not yet." Obviously the smarter of the two — at least the less instinctively sociopathic — she awarded Alex a hard look and demanded, "What was that you told him?"

"It's very simple. Eugene is an American investor with three or four very wealthy backers in New York. It's called a joint venture. They are pooling hundreds of millions for this deal. They put up the cash, and I invest it for them, keeping a fair share of the profits for my trouble. In return I had to put up collateral."

Vladimir and Katya were in the wrong line of work to comprehend the meaning of this word, "collateral," and Vladimir snapped, "What are you talking about?"

"It's a common business term. In return for their trust and capital risk, I put my companies on the line. It's all stipulated in the contracts inside Eugene's briefcase. Every one of my businesses, right down to the final nail. If I fail to do my part, title to every business I own reverts to them."

"He's lying," Vladimir hissed at Katya.

"Am I?" Alex asked, definitely lying. He turned to the legal shyster who was hiding in the corner, watching this scene with nervous fascination. Alex asked him, "Have you ever heard of a business deal that did not involve collateral?"

The man frowned, stroked his chin, and tried to look thoughtful. He had small, crowded features and they pinched together; like a pug with hemorrhoids. And he was totally, irrevocably lost. He had been a criminal lawyer under the old Soviet system where the extent of his legal expertise was not lifting a finger or raising a squawk as his clients were ramrodded through the politically corrupt courts and crushed by the state. These days the big money was in corporate law, so he had hung out a new shingle and was avidly trying to cash in. Everything was crooked and rigged in Moscow anyway and the shyster knew as well as anybody who needed to be bribed and/or threatened for a deal to go through.

In short, the man on the gurney had just tossed a pebble down an empty well. The thoughtful pause dragged on.

Well, he might not know squat about contracts, but he had a firm grasp on survival, he told himself. If he said no, this man is clearly a liar, and it turned out the shyster guessed wrong, everything would be lost — all those hundreds of millions of dollars. Naturally, they would hold him responsible. For well over an hour he had stood out in the warehouse, hearing Alex's anguished howls and shrieks echoing through the walls. He felt a sudden shiver as he considered how they might punish him.

But if he said Alex was telling the truth, well, whatever happened afterward — good, bad, or worse — they couldn't blame him.

Feeling quite Solomonic, and with a tone of utter conviction, he offered his best professional opinion. "No, never. As he says, it is typical to arrange collateral in these matters."

"And this is the special clause you referred to?" Katya asked Alex.

"That's right. In forty minutes, everything I own will revert to Eugene and his group of New York investors."

The lawyer walked over to the gurney and leaned in toward Alex. "But there is a way to void this clause, am I right?"

"I'd be an idiot if there weren't."

"Good. Tell me about it," the lawyer demanded, enjoying his sudden moment of importance.

"Put me through to whoever you work for. I'll tell him about it."

"Not a chance," Vladimir answered for all of them, sneering and sliding the knife back and forth against Elena's throat.

"Fine, your call," Alex replied, trying his best to look confident rather than terrified. He had done hundreds of high-pressure business negotiations, tense parleys upon which many millions of dollars hinged. They always involved a fair amount of posturing and bluffing, and Alex had become a master at it. This time, though, he was bargaining for Elena's life, and his own. He took a hard swallow, then forced a smile and said to Vladimir, "In forty minutes, everything will be gone. These are New Yorkers. Greedy bastards, every one of them. If they get their fingers on my properties, you can beat and torture me all you want. You'll never pry them back."

"Maybe we'll just go to the hotel and kill this Eugene man," Vladimir suggested, his preferred course for solving problems.

"That would be stupid. It won't make a difference," Alex told him. "Copies of all the contracts are with his partners in New York. In fact, they'll appreciate it. One less partner means more for them."

Vladimir nodded. Made sense.

"Also," Alex confided, sounding like an afterthought, a small, insignificant detail that meant nothing, "once I sign Eugene's contracts another three hundred million dollars will be electronically transferred to my investment bank."

"What?" Katya asked, suddenly hanging on every word.

"You heard me. When I sign the contract, Eugene and his investors will immediately wire-transfer their funds into my investment bank. Three hundred million American dollars. Cold cash."

Vladimir licked his lips and looked at Katya. Both were struggling to maintain the pretense that they were still in control. And both were clearly rattled and looking for a way out. When Golitsin learned about this, he would throw a tantrum of monumental proportions. But if they didn't call him and Konevitch's companies and properties slipped out of their fingers — much less losing the possibility of three hundred million more, in cash — well, neither of them wanted to think about what he would do to them. It would be horrible and slow, they both knew.

An unspoken signal passed, Vladimir removed the knife from Elena's throat, stepped out of the room, flipped open his clunky satphone, and dialed Golitsin.

"Why are you calling?" Golitsin asked with a ring of hope in his voice. "Is it done? Did he sign over the properties?"

"No. And now there is a new glitch," Vladimir replied, then quickly recounted the problem.

The moment he finished, Golitsin asked, "Is he telling the truth?"

"How would I know? The lawyer says it makes sense. Capitalists don't trust each other. What's new?"

Vladimir stopped talking and allowed this to sink in. He had done the smart thing, he decided; he had booted the problem upstairs. They would get only one chance at this, one shot at becoming unimaginably rich; just one shot at the biggest heist in Russian history. And Golitsin had done excruciating planning for every eventuality, had plotted and surmised and second-guessed every conceivable scenario — except this.

Golitsin knew what Vladimir was doing. But he wasn't at all sure what Konevitch was up to. Was this a trick? Did Konevitch have something up his sleeve?

On the other hand, another cool three hundred million in cash was there for the taking. Three hundred million!

Golitsin rolled that delicious number around his head. He spent a long moment relishing the new possibilities. In one swift swoop the overall take would nearly double. Better yet, this was cold cash, fluid money available for spending on fast cars, big homes, a sumptuous yacht, even a private jet — whatever his heart desired.

And the idea of ripping off a horde of greedy New Yorkers appealed to him mightily. He could hear their anguished howls when they learned their money was gone, stolen. Suddenly he could think of little else.

Eventually Golitsin said what needed to be said. "Take him to the hotel. And make sure he signs the contract." He thought about the extra three hundred million, and with palpable excitement added, "This is better. Much better. I can badly use that much cash."

"Yes, couldn't we all."

Golitsin didn't like the message but he absorbed it. "Pull this off, it will also mean another two hundred thousand for you. How many people do you and Katya have available?"

"Eight here, more than enough."

"He's a financial genius," Golitsin reasoned, as much to his listener as himself. "But he can't spell escape and evasion. A complete amateur."

"He doesn't worry me," Vladimir replied, bubbling with confidence. "Nabbing him was child's play. Besides, after his beating, he can barely walk."

"Still, if he does one thing wrong . . . if he even looks suspicious, kill the wife."

The doctor was rushed back into the room to hastily clean up Alex and make him presentable for the rich boy from New York. A relative term, of course — though Vladimir's blows had mostly been spent on Alex's body, there was a nasty open gash on his forehead, a broken nose, various welts, and some ugly swelling on his face. Six swiftly applied butterfly sutures took care of the nasty gash and a bandage was slapped on to hide it. The other wounds were wiped with medicinal alcohol and, where necessary, also bandaged. "Tell him you were in a car accident," Katya ordered Alex, again proving she was the smart one, the one to be watched. "You've been in the hospital getting checked out."

"All right."

Vladimir leaned in close and warned, "We'll be in the restaurant watching, close and personal. One false move . . . if I just become slightly bothered by the look in your eyes, your pretty wife dies."

"But if I sign the contract and everything

goes fine, Elena and I will live. We're free to go. Right?"

"Yes, that's the deal," Vladimir said, dripping phony sincerity.

"How do I know you're telling the truth?" asked Alex. Of course, they were lying. They would take his money, his companies, his homes and cars, then kill the both of them.

"What choice do you have?"

The doctor was slathering a gooey yellow ointment on Alex's chest, a light analgesic. The burn went deep and covered nearly his whole upper left chest. It was raw, already blistering. It would be days before the wound scabbed over and the open nerve tissue was protected. Once they put a shirt on Alex, the material would rub and the pain would be serious. The doctor ordered Alex, "Stand up. Let's see if your leg works."

Alex slowly pushed himself off the gurney. He emitted a sharp yelp as he moved his dislocated left shoulder and stretched the tender skin around the burn. He put his left foot down on the hard floor, followed, more gingerly, by his right. A spike of pain from his right leg, where Vladimir had pounded it with a wooden chair, shot like a thousand-volt current instantly to his brain. A strangled gasp and he nearly collapsed. He would've collapsed except he focused on one overriding thought, one unyielding imperative: there would be no second chance, no do-overs.

This was it. Get through it, whatever it took. Swallow the pain, don't let this opportunity slip away, he repeated to himself, over and over.

A man hauled in Alex's overnight bag, unzipped it, withdrew the spare fresh shirt and suit Alex had packed, and lazily tossed them on the gurney. "Get dressed," Vladimir ordered. "Hurry."

The doctor handed Alex a fistful of ibuprofen along with a bottled water, then instructed Alex to swallow them, all of them. Vladimir informed Alex, "Your wife will stay in the car in front of the hotel. She's our insurance. If I give the word, the boys will give her a Bulgarian necktie. Know what that is?"

Alex shook his head. It didn't sound pleasant.

Vladimir answered with a wicked laugh, "They'll slice her throat open and pull her tongue through the hole."

"That would be a big mistake," Alex said, swallowing his anger and carefully slipping a white dress shirt over his damaged shoulder. "I mean separating us. She has to be with me."

"Do you think we're stupid?" Katya asked.

Yes, he most certainly did. Stupid, crude, and impossibly cruel. But also, as he had just learned, afraid to make a move without instructions from their boss, who presumably was back in Moscow. But instead of saying that, Alex replied, "No, you're obviously quite smart. You're overlooking something, though."

"Are we?" Vladimir snarled.

"Think about it. Eugene's expecting Elena to accompany me. If I walk in, looking like I look — without Elena — he'll know something's wrong."

"So what?"

"A legally binding contract depends on both parties being of sound mind and operating of their own free will. People don't get rich being sloppy or stupid. And Eugene is a very, very shrewd and rich man. A flawed contract is worthless. If he suspects I'm under duress, or that something's not right, he'll balk." Alex looked pointedly at Katya, the good cop. "Three hundred million dollars will go out the door with him."

"Just tell him she was also injured and still in the hospital," said the lawyer, deciding to throw in his two cents. Suddenly, he was Mr. Big Shot, brimming with brilliance.

"What an idiotic suggestion," Alex said with a withering stare in the direction of the shyster. "I'd leave Elena seriously injured, in a hospital, just to attend to a business deal?"

"Sure," Vladimir replied, totally clueless. Why not? What husband wouldn't neglect his wife for money? "I don't see the problem."

"Because he'll know I'm lying. And he'll naturally ask why I didn't just invite him to join me at the hospital to sign these contracts."

They were all looking at one another. Nobody liked this idea. Really, though, what difference did it make? On second thought, it might in fact be even better. Just as easy to grease her in the restaurant as carve her throat in a car idling outside: it simplified things, really. With only eight gunmen, far easier to keep an eye on the couple together than split up.

Besides, with his beloved wife beside him, Konevitch would remember exactly what was at stake in the event he was tempted to try any funny business. Reminders were always helpful.

"And we need to carry our bags with us," Alex added, awkwardly knotting his tie with his one usable arm.

Vladimir kicked the base of the table. "Not happening," he snorted.

"Think again. Eugene knows we haven't checked into the hotel yet. I assume you want this to work. We need to look like we've just arrived."

"Think you're smart, don't you?" Vladimir replied, with a mean grin as he held up two tiny red booklets. "Go ahead, bring the bags. I've got your passports and your wallets. You won't escape, and you can't get out of Hungary, no matter what. But even if you do, we'll hunt you down and there won't be a second chance."

"I want this to work just as much as you. Probably more. I want to live," Alex assured him. "And three hundred million is a lot of money," he reminded him, as if anybody had forgotten, as if anybody could.

"We can live without it," Katya said, trying to sound indifferent and failing miserably. "But you're going to perform one small service before we set foot in that restaurant."

"Am I?"

"You definitely are. You're going to sign the letter of resignation and the contract that reassigns your businesses and properties to a new owner."

The show of confidence Alex had shown a moment earlier drained away. Now he looked crestfallen. "And if I say no?"

"That's your choice," Katya informed him. She looked over at Vladimir. "Count to five," she said, motioning her chin at Elena. "Then kill her."

"One . . . Two? . . ."

Before he got to three, the lawyer was holding a sheaf of documents in front of Alex's nose and helpfully pointing out where to sign.

6

The black Mercedes, trailed by a pair of matching rental Ford Fiestas, pulled up to the entrance of the Aquincum Hotel. Two thugs hustled out of the nearest Fiesta, walked quickly through the entrance, strutted through the expansive lobby, and moved directly to the Apicius Restaurant located on the ground floor.

With a show of deliberate rudeness, they brushed past the attentive maître d', occupied the closest table to the exit, withdrew their pistols, placed them under the napkins on their laps, snapped at a waitress to bring them two bowls of steaming goulash, and waited.

After three minutes, Katya stepped out of the Mercedes, looked around to make sure the coast was clear, then signaled for Alex and Elena to get out, Elena first. Then Alex painfully hobbled out onto the curb. He slung their matched his-and-hers overnight bags over his good shoulder and waited. A moment later, Vladimir got out as well, taking a moment to stretch and slip the gun he had held at Elena's head into the belt behind his back.

A storm had moved in; thick, angry clouds covered the skies, and it was prematurely dark. With Katya leading, Alex and Elena in the middle, and Vladimir bringing up the rear, the parade entered the hotel and marched directly to the fancy restaurant on the ground floor.

Katya entered a little ahead of them and brusquely instructed the maître d' that a table for four was required, definitely in the middle of the room, make it quick. No problem. Hungarians are rigorously late sleepers and late eaters, and the crowd was subsequently sparse, mostly foreign guests of the hotel who didn't get the local customs.

Katya followed the maître d' to the table and sat. A moment later, Alex and Elena entered. Alex looked around, then spotted Eugene at the far-right corner table beside a plate-glass window where he could kill the boredom watching the pedestrians wander by. Alex took Elena's hand. They walked slowly across the room. With each step, his chest and leg radiated pain. He slowed his walk to a near crawl, shuffling like an old man.

It was their first chance to talk. He whispered to Elena, "They're going to kill us, no matter what."

"I know. It's not your fault," she replied.

Oh yes, it definitely was his fault, but this wasn't the time or situation to discuss it. At this stage, fault or fate or serendipity made no difference. Don't waste time; think quickly, he told himself. He squeezed her hand and said, "This is an opportunity — probably our only chance. We have to use it."

"Do you have a plan?"

"I'm thinking." He tried to smile re-assuringly but it came across weakly. "If you think of anything, let me know." She squeezed his hand back, and made no reply.

Eugene had spotted them and jumped from his seat. He took in the gallery of bruises and abrasions on Alex's face, noted the severe limp, and his face turned instantly into a mass of concerned wrinkles. "My God, Alex, what happened to you?"

"Car accident," Alex replied with pretended indifference, slipping the overnight bags off his shoulder and placing them on the floor to free his one good arm for a lame handshake. His leg was killing him. His left arm hung limp and useless. The yellow ointment cover-ing the burn was seeping through his white dress shirt. He forced a smile and said a little lamely, "You should see the other guy."

After a polite chuckle, Eugene asked, "That's why you're late?" It was a dumb question. Why ask? The answer was right before his eyes. He suggested, "It looks like the accident was damned serious," suddenly swimming in guilt that he had insisted on Alex coming here.

Elena explained, "Well, first there were the police reports. That took nearly an hour. Our taxi driver ran a red light, two other cars were involved, a complete mess. We went to the hospital afterward."

"The hospital?" Eugene echoed, still stunned by the condition of his friend. Elena looked fine; on the surface she appeared unharmed, anyway. Nervous and distressed, for sure — but considering the dreadful state of her husband, that was easily understandable.

"It's not as bad as it looks," Alex assured him. "I was lucky. A few cuts, some nasty bruises, a few broken ribs, I think."

Eugene stared at the floor, torn between empathy for his friend and sympathy for himself if he didn't get Alex's signatures on the contracts. Cuts and bruises heal. Ten million bucks are forever.

Only thirty minutes before, Maria had stormed back downstairs, suitcase in hand, and announced that she had booked a flight back to New York and scheduled a meeting with the most venomous East Coast divorce lawyer money can rent. A real loudmouthed cutthroat with sterling references. Among those references, Eugene well knew, were wives two and three, whose divorces the lawyer had handled with appalling effectiveness. Practice makes perfect — how sadly true. Wife Three had walked away with twice what Wife Two got. Eugene shuddered to think how much Number Four might cost.

Alex stole a glance over his shoulder, took in the two boys by the exit, and noted that Vladimir had slipped in and joined Katya at her table in the center of the room. Vladimir and Katya were partially blocking the views of their pals by the exit.

Not that it mattered; they were arranged perfectly to keep him and Elena bottled up.

He needed time, and Alex looked at Eugene and said, "Incidentally, please call your friends in New York. Tell them I require another thirty minutes."

"Not possible, Alex."

"Please make it possible."

"You know the stakes. If this deal's not locked down by five tonight, I'm deeply, deeply screwed."

Alex and Eugene stared across the table at each other, frustration hanging in the air like mist. Alex eventually noted, "Surely your contract with them has an Act of God provision. Am I right?"

"Do I look stupid?"

"So use it, Eugene. I was an innocent victim, a hapless passenger in a taxi accident. That's a shining example of an Act of God." He pointed at his own face. Eugene needed no reminder.

"Alex, these contracts have been months in the making."

"I think I know that."

"I faxed copies to your office a week ago."

"And I can't tell you how much I appreciate it."

"Seven whole days. Surely you've had more than enough time to study them."

"I'm a slow reader."

"Damn it, Alex, I —"

"Look, Eugene, let me be honest. I once signed a contract my lawyers and I had examined only the day before. During the interim, without mentioning it, the other party slipped in a few clauses, a few very expensive clauses. I trusted them, Eugene. I signed the contract without noticing the changes. That little stunt cost me two million dollars."

"You're kidding."

No, not kidding; lying, definitely, though he offered a regretful shrug and lied again. "I swore I would never sign another contract I haven't read on the spot. Please get on the phone and buy me some time."

"This is me, Alex. Eugene Daniels."

Alex bent forward, inspected him closely. "Yes, no doubt about it."

"How many deals have we done together? Five? Six?"

"Four."

"All right, four. Have I ever cheated you? I'm telling you, nothing, not a word has been added or subtracted from the contracts I faxed you." He awarded Alex a look of complete bewilderment. "It's the same paper, Alex, identical, down to the commas. Don't you trust me?"

"Of course I do."

"Good. Then it's settled."

A brief pause. "You trust me, too, don't you, Eugene?"

"I'm here, aren't I?"

"Good. Then let's just dispense with those contracts. A useless waste of time. What's paper between friends? Let's just swap a few hundred million on a handshake."

Eugene lowered his head in defeat. "All right, all right, I'll try," he said, frowning tightly. "These people are absolute bastards, though."

"And right now, their mouths are watering for the easiest ten million they ever made. Your money, Eugene."

"But if I invoke the Act of God clause, they get nothing, right?" Eugene said, letting the words fall off his tongue. The frown began to melt. "Nothing, not a thing," he said, answering his own question, suddenly smiling. As hard as they had made him beg, work, and sweat to cobble this deal together — their nearly unending selfish demands, their noisy bickering over inane details, their lousy New

York manners — and now, holding ten million of *his* dollars as ransom; well, the thought of suddenly yanking the rug from under *their* feet was exhilarating. What fun.

"That's right," Alex said, reading his thoughts. "The only people who will walk away from this richer and happier are the lawyers and accountants who prepared this deal."

Eugene wasn't drunk but he had inhaled enough thick German swill that any ability to think with real clarity was hours behind him. Alex was right, though. Every word made sense.

After all they'd put him through these past months, if the sharks in New York refused to give him another thirty minutes he'd tell them all to piss off. Take a flying leap and kiss your own fanny before you hit the floor.

"Please, make the call," Alex implored him, looking suddenly apologetic. He glanced quickly over his left shoulder: Vladimir and Katya were eyeing him closely. Once they saw Eugene stabbing numbers into his cell phone, things could instantly turn ugly. Alex put a hand on Elena's arm and smiled pleasantly at Eugene. "Excuse me. In all the excitement today, I never had a chance to use the bathroom."

Without waiting for an answer he stood and left Elena with Eugene. Eugene's plump fingers were already stabbing his cell phone.

He couldn't wait. His only regret was that he couldn't watch their faces.

Alex approached the table where Katya and Vladimir sat. Both were glowering and trying to look utterly fierce. Why try? They could be wearing clown suits and sipping pink margaritas through striped straws; they would still smolder with menace. Alex stared directly at Vladimir and hooked a finger.

Katya was the smart one and he preferred to avoid her: Vladimir did his thinking with his fists and would be easier to fool. Not easy, but easier.

Vladimir had been watching the heavy American businessman at the table begin dialing numbers into his cell phone, and then — surprise — Alex standing up! Then walking in his direction! He turned to Katya. She shrugged noncommittally. Did the rich boy have a death wish? Where did he think he was going? Vladimir quickly pushed away from the table, stood, put a hand on the gun in his rear waistband, and trailed Alex.

The pair of hired guns by the exit were just lifting their pistols out of their laps when they saw Vladimir following behind Alex. They decided to sit and wait.

Alex offered a friendly nod as he walked past, then stopped beside a vacant pillar in the massive lobby and allowed Vladimir to catch up. The lobby, like the restaurant, was sparsely populated — it made it ridiculously easy for Alex to pick out Vladimir's people, a tough-looking couple lounging on comfort chairs right beside the entrance, smoking and glowering at anybody who passed by. And through the glass window, huddled directly beneath a fancy outdoor lantern, stood two more men in black jeans and black leather jackets. The moment Vladimir reached hearing distance, he hissed at Alex, "What in the hell are you doing?"

"What anybody in my position would do. The man at the table has to make a call to New York. It's not an option. I wouldn't want you to draw the wrong impression."

Vladimir opened his lips and was on the verge of speaking, but Alex cut him off. "His partners requested a thirty-minute extension. They want to add a few conditions. It's not uncommon. I probably should have warned you — antsy investors who come up with last-minute concerns, demands, and conditions. He's calling to nail down their issues."

Vladimir studied Alex. Nervous. Alex was fidgeting with his hands, his knees trembling so badly they were almost knocking together. Mr. Big Shot: all that money, all those businesses, one of the richest, most powerful men in Russia. Yet here he stood, nerves shot, ready to crumble. How utterly disappointing. Then again, Vladimir had worked damned hard to incite an earthquake of nervousness. In fact, he should be more worried if Alex seemed the least bit nonchalant. "If he's calling the police," Vladimir threatened, "he's arranging your death sentence."

"That's exactly why I'm talking to you right now. I knew you'd assume that."

"Is that right? Well, you're a bright guy, Konevitch, but don't think you can outsmart us. The local police will notify us the instant an alarm goes out about you," he warned. "There's no place you can go that we won't know. No place we won't catch you."

And it was true. During his long decades in the KGB, Sergei Golitsin had collected contacts and stoolies throughout Europe, all of whom now were struggling to create new lives in a new world, and wanted their dirty pasts as Moscow stooges and finks erased, buried, or forgotten. A fastidious bureaucrat with lethal instincts, over the decades Golitsin had kept every incriminating piece of paper he came in contact with. Within hours after he was "retired with prejudice" from the KGB, three large vans wheeled up in front of his old headquarters and were hurriedly loaded with forty years' worth of pilfered files. Box after box. Name after name, enough to fill several city-sized phone books. It was all squirreled away in a clandestine warehouse a few miles outside Moscow. Golitsin was sitting on enough dirt and compromising material to coerce and blackmail many thousands.

Among the names were the deputy minister

for internal security for Hungary, two captains and three senior inspectors in the Budapest police, all of whom were operating under harsh instructions to notify Golitsin the instant Alex Konevitch's disappearance, or death, became an item of police interest.

Vladimir thumped a threatening finger off Alex's forehead. "You're way out of your league, boy. The only way out of this is to get him to sign that money over to us."

"Believe me, I know that. I just want to survive this and get on with my life."

From his face and eyes it appeared he did know. Still, Vladimir thought it a good idea to rekindle his memory. With narrowed eyes he said, "Your pretty bitch will go first. Remember that. You'll have a moment to watch the blood draining from her head, to hear her last pitiful breaths. And you'll know it's all your fault. Then I'll kill you, too."

"I have to get back to the table," Alex told him, now looking paralyzed with terror.

"You've got twenty-five minutes to finish this. Not a second longer." He pointed at Alex's watch. "In twenty-five minutes and one second, I write off the money and start blasting. Now, take a few deep breaths," Vladimir said, "then get back in there and get us our money."

"It worked," Eugene announced with a triumphal slap on the table the moment Alex returned to the table. The lawyers in New York, a consortium of legal hit men who smelled an easy ten million for their clients, had yapped and howled a chorus of odious threats right up to the instant Eugene invoked the sacred Act of God clause. Like that, the curses and bullying died in their throats. Total silence. After that moment of stunned stillness, suddenly they couldn't shut up. They talked over themselves to extend Alex however much time was needed. And how was the poor man's health? the suddenly compassionate throng wanted to know. Damn shame about that awful accident, they collectively agreed — they couldn't have felt more sorry or sincere.

Eugene euphorically snapped his cell phone shut and laid it on the table. "They gave us thirty more minutes to hammer this thing out." He took a long congratulatory sip of beer and smacked his lips.

"Do you mind if we order a little food first?" Alex replied, sliding gently into his seat. "We haven't eaten all day. We're famished."

"No, no, of course," Eugene replied, feeling regretful once more for putting his friend through this. Then he thought again of his money, of ten million sailing away to his despised partners. Like that, he got over it.

Alex asked Elena, "What would you like, dear?"

She gave the menu a cursory glance and settled on a table salad and spicy German sausage dish. Alex ordered lukewarm chicken broth and a warm cola. He was famished, though his lips were so scabbed and swollen that solid foods were out of the question; at least three teeth were cracked or broken with exposed nerves a hot or cold drink would have brutalized; his jaw muscles were so achy, the thought of chewing was sickening.

Eugene loudly ordered another dark beer, a celebratory one this time, and mentioned to Alex, "Why don't you get started on reviewing the contracts?" In other words: I pushed fate once for you, pal, now get started.

Trying hard to look focused, Alex hoisted the thick sheaf of papers over and began leafing through, thoughtfully scanning the pages. His head throbbed. His body howled with pain. He forced himself to concentrate on one overriding thought: How to get out of this alive. How to elude the team of professional assassins seated only fifty feet away, fingering their guns, ready to blast away.

At least he had bought twenty-four minutes of relative calm to ponder his options — twenty-four minutes without anybody pummeling his body, or frying designs on his flesh, or uttering vile threats into his ear.

Eugene and Elena made small talk. How did she like Budapest? Lovely old city, didn't she think? Yes, very lovely indeed, she an-

swered with a strained smile and firm nod —
after what happened to Alex she would curse
this city to her dying breath. Did she enjoy
traveling with Alex? Oh, well, always quite an
adventure, she replied, tongue in cheek. And
how was life in Moscow these days? And so
on and so forth.

The last thing Elena felt like doing was
partaking in meaningless banter, but she had
to buy time for Alex to think, and she endured
it with phony grace. Eugene seemed like a
nice man, a few rough New York edges aside
— so why couldn't they sit there and just
enjoy each other's company in golden silence?
He could guzzle the beer he seemed to enjoy
so much, and she could dwell on their nightmare. Her heart was pounding. She was
forced to press her hands tightly together to
keep them from shaking.

Her back was to Vladimir and Katya, yet
she could sense — in fact, nearly feel — a
malevolent presence.

The food came. Between spoonfuls and
slow, careful sips, Alex maintained a pretense
of studying the documents, occasionally
scribbling on a page, a notation here, a notation there — meaningless chicken scratch as
he racked his brain for a way out of this.

Maybe he was overthinking this, he wondered. Maybe elaborate was the wrong approach; they should simply stand up and walk
out, thumb their noses at the gangsters, and

flee. Maybe this was all a big bluff. The more he thought about it, the more tempting that idea was. Would their kidnappers really open fire, here, in the grand dining room of one of the best-known luxury hotels in Hungary?

Back in Moscow, where such things were all too prevalent, maybe: okay, yes, without a moment of vacillation, they would blast everything in sight. But surely, in Budapest, the storied capital of a foreign nation, a peaceful, elegant old city renowned for its sophistication and exotic charms, different rules applied.

He glanced over his shoulder and caught sight of the two dull-eyed thugs by the exit, engulfed in the dense cloud of cigarette smoke swimming over their table. And then, for a fleeting instant, he and Vladimir locked eyes. Stupid question, he realized. Of course they would. They would blow away Elena, Alex, probably Eugene, the waiters and waitresses, other customers, and for good measure they'd nail the doorman and run away with smiles on their faces.

It would be a total massacre, a bloodbath. And it would be Alex's fault.

He had already signed over his companies and properties, coerced statements that, if he survived, would be completely worthless. The moment he set foot in Moscow, he would hire the best lawyers money can rent and rescind everything; he then would use his immense fortune to hunt down every last one of them.

They would know this, of course. And they would know there was only one way to be sure that never happened.

And if that required a massacre, a flamboyant atrocity in a pleasant, peaceful city, it would only persuade the next millionaire they targeted that these were serious people who meant business.

7

With only eight minutes left on Vladimir's deadline — and Eugene noisily draining what he claimed, with a suspicious slur, was only his third stein of beer — Alex finally settled on a plan he thought had a chance of success. He had conceived, chewed over, and discarded at least a dozen different ideas, from dangerously complex to ridiculously simple — from standing up and screaming "Fire!" to collapsing on the floor and pretending to suffer a massive heart attack.

Impressive intelligence was not his kidnappers' forte. But what seemed to be an advantage in his favor was also, ironically, a double-edged sword. Sociopaths like Vladimir could not be depended upon to make cool, rational judgments in moments of stress. Whatever Alex tried had better be trigger-happy-proof.

He looked up from the papers and matter-of-factly asked Eugene, "How did you get from the airport to the hotel?"

"Automobile. Why?"

"How? Taxi? Limousine service?"

"I drove, actually."

"Then you rented a car?"

"Yes, a rusty old orange Trabant," Eugene said, referring to the automobile mass-produced by the East Germans under the old system. Trabants were notorious for their atrocious workmanship, nonexistent reliability, and cramped lack of comfort. The automotive equivalent of throwaway razors, they were called, and that was a compliment; even junkyards didn't want them. He leaned back in his chair and chuckled, enjoying a private joke.

Elena asked, "What's funny? Surely there were nicer cars on the lot."

"You're right. Shiny Mercedes and speedy Beemers all over the place."

"Then —"

"Because Maria is a typical, spoiled American, without the slightest thought of how awful things were under communism. I thought she should experience firsthand the quality of socialist manufacturing." The drive had taken forty-five minutes and Maria moaned and complained every inch of it. Well accustomed to his money and all the perks it could buy, whatever memories she had of life on a secretary's paycheck were long behind her. She was horrified by this sudden dip back into the pool of poverty. Eugene relished every minute of it. His sole regret was that he

159

hadn't brought along a tape recorder so he could replay it again and again.

"That sounds like a novel concept," Elena noted, obviously wondering about Eugene's marital skills, or sanity.

"So is the car parked in the hotel lot?" Alex asked.

"The side lot. Why?"

"I'd like to borrow it," he said, rubbing the bandage over his eye and looking pained. "Elena and I have had enough taxi rides for the day. And as soon as we're done here we have to return to the hospital pharmacy for painkillers and fresh bandages."

"Of course."

"Also," Alex said, shifting from pained to apologetic, "I seem to have misplaced my wallet. The orderlies undressed me at the hospital to treat my injuries. It must have fallen out of my pocket. Do you happen to have some money I could borrow?"

"How much do you need?"

"I might have to cover the medical bills. How much do you have?"

"Two thousand in bills, another thousand in traveler's checks. American dollars, all of it. I exchanged two hundred into Hungarian forints, but Maria left with that."

"Dollars are fine. Two thousand should be enough."

Eugene dug into his pant pocket, withdrew the keys, then a fat wad of hundred-dollar bills, and slid them across the table. "About the car, only a strong hind wind will get you over thirty miles an hour, the shocks are non-existent, springs are popping through the seats, and the windshield wipers flop all over the place." He smiled for a moment. "Other than that, great car."

"Before the wall came down," Alex noted with an ironic shrug, "we all had to place our names on long lists, then wait years for the privilege to buy a Trabant. Some people were smart enough to sign up every year."

"Every year?" Eugene asked.

"Well cared for and driven minimally, that's about how long they lasted."

They lifted their glasses and silently toasted the marvelous new world.

Alex waved for the waitress, the same cute one Eugene had been nakedly admiring all afternoon. When she arrived he spoke in a low rasp that forced her to bend deeply over to hear him. He spoke for about thirty seconds, then slipped a hundred-dollar bill into her palm — two weeks' salary and tips for her. An enthusiastic nod and she rushed off, beaming.

Alex checked his watch — five more minutes and New York would be calling Eugene. In six, Vladimir and Katya would be blasting away. He fought the temptation to turn around and look at Vladimir and Katya, lifted up another few pages, and pretended to return to his work.

"What's he doing now?" Golitsin inquired into Vladimir's satellite phone. Copies of Alex's resignation letter and the appending contract relinquishing his properties had been faxed by the lawyer and now were stacked in a tidy pile on his desk. They sat there, less than two feet away. Close enough to where he could reach out and caress them. He had read and reread them six times. He could barely keep his hands off them.

A courier on a night flight from Budapest was en route with a chain around his wrist attaching him to a briefcase containing the legally vital originals. Just scrawl his name onto those originals, designate himself as the handpicked successor to Alex's empire, and voilà — he, Sergei Golitsin, controlled 350 million dollars. Possibly more.

Years of plotting and scheming and putting the pieces together were about to pay off. A few drops of ink and he would be one of the ten richest men in Russia; but throw in another three hundred million in New York moolah, and, well . . . he might be *the* richest. In the new Russia, cash was king. He was about to be seated on a mountainous throne of cash.

"He's still reading the contract," Vladimir eventually answered in a tone saturated with annoyance. He was so tired of being checked up on. "His wife and the American banker are talking."

"Talking about what?"

"Who knows? Who cares?"

"Can't you hear what they're saying?"

"No."

After a brief pause meant to expose the seriousness of his concern, Golitsin asked very quietly, "Why can't you?"

"Because," Vladimir replied testily, "we're seated in the middle of the room, at a vantage where we can keep them from escaping."

"Maybe Konevitch and the banker are planning their escape."

"Possibly they are. So what?"

"I'll tell you *so what*. Hundreds of millions of dollars disappear with them, you idiot."

"Two men are positioned by the exit to the restaurant. Two more by the exit to the hotel. That's three layers of security they would have to make it past. Also I have the Konevitches' passports, and their wallets, and he's nearly crippled. I'm telling you, he's not going anywhere."

Silence.

Vladimir rolled his eyes. "No matter what they try, he's dead."

Golitsin let more silence register his disapproval.

After a long moment, Vladimir said, "I gave him twenty-five minutes to produce the signed contracts or I start shooting. That was twenty-two minutes ago. I think I can keep him from escaping within the next three minutes."

"I still don't like it."

Vladimir could almost see the condescending scowl on Golitsin's face. So far he, Vladimir, had taken all the risks and done every bit of the dirty work. Plotting and overseeing the murder of Alex's executives, the kidnapping, the torture, obtaining the invaluable signatures — his handiwork, all accomplished without a glitch. He was quite proud of it. He had made Golitsin a very, very rich man. Was there even a halfhearted grumble of thanks? How about: Good job, Vladimir my boy, you really pulled this one off?

But more than anything, Vladimir despised being second-guessed and scolded by this deskbound lizard. The old boy hadn't been in smelling distance of real fieldwork in decades. And here he was, sticking his big nose into everything

Then again, Golitsin had promised him a bonus of one hundred thousand dollars, U.S., the instant this job was finished, three hundred if they bagged an additional 300 million of New York dough. A year of lurking in the shadows, of watching and killing — the money was so close he could smell it. No way would he give Golitsin an excuse to snatch it away. Yes, he was tired of being lectured and reprimanded, of having to endure the old man's biting insults, but in a few more hours, he reminded himself, it would be over. A few more hours and he would take his money, and then tell the old man exactly where to stuff it.

He fought the impulse to say, "Shut up and mind your own business," and instead meekly said, "Don't worry, boss. Less than three minutes. We're fifty feet away, watching his every move."

"You're an overconfident idiot. Don't mess this up."

With slightly more than two minutes left before the deadline expired, the lights suddenly went out in the restaurant. Like that, the room was pitched into darkness.

Nearly simultaneously, the kitchen door flew open and out marched a long line of waiters and waitresses, one after another, ten in all. The cute waitress with the impressive bosom headed the procession, proudly hauling a chocolate cake with ten lit birthday candles. The marching line was loudly slaughtering "Happy Birthday," in English polluted by thick Hungarian accents, and moving at a fast clip directly toward the table in the center of the room. Then they came to an abrupt stop, positioning themselves directly between Vladimir, Katya, and the table by the window where Alex and Elena were seated with Eugene.

The moment the throng was in place, stamping their feet and singing in a brash routine imported from an American restaurant chain, Alex leaped up from his chair, lifted the empty chair beside him, and hurled it with as much force as he could muster directly at the big picture window ten feet away. He had rehearsed this throw over and over in his mind. Over and over he told himself, ignore the pain from his dislocated shoulder, forget the severe burn on his chest. No matter how agonizing, put everything he had into this one chance. There wouldn't be another.

The moment the chair launched, he shut his eyes, held his breath, and prayed.

The chair flew through the air, and then, with a loud satisfying crash, the large plate-glass window shattered into a thousand shards and crumbled to the floor.

Vladimir was still holding the satellite phone, still smarting from the conversation.

Katya had been eavesdropping. Her elbows were planted on the table, her head craned sideways in a wonderfully successful attempt to catch every word.

She loathed Vladimir and found huge enjoyment in overhearing the old man browbeat and humble him. She had no love for

Golitsin either — a selfish, overbearing, snarling old tyrant she detested to her core. But she worked for him. She took his money and, without complaint, did whatever sordid work he asked of her. And why not? The money was damned good; actually it was merely adequate, but she wasn't about to complain. Two thousand a month in salary when thousands of KGB veterans were out on the street, wiping windshields of traffic-stalled cars and pleading for kopecks.

Plus he was cunning, corrupt, ambitious, and endlessly ruthless; in the bare-knuckle new Russia, with that résumé, she was betting the old coot would shoot quickly to the top. There were worse wagons to hitch her horses to, she reasoned. Besides, her other options were few and not overly hopeful. She had spent twelve years doing dirty work for the KGB before the wall tumbled down. Sadly, her skillset had prepared her for only one thing.

By twenty-six, she had thirty kills on five continents. All clean hits, all professionally flawless. Now thirty-one, her once lustrous hair had been peroxided, bleached, dyed and redyed so many times it hung in listless strands. Her skin resembled a snare drum in need of a rigorous tightening. Long years killing under the hot African and Afghan sun had prematurely aged her. She still had an attractive face, one that bordered on beauty, except for a detached iciness that chased men off. She cared less. Her tastes ran more toward women than men anyway.

Besides, sex didn't interest her generally, and emotions even less.

Unfortunately, that arctic demeanor was exactly what attracted Vladimir, who over the past year had come on to her more than a few times. Like many men with bulletproof egos, beating around the bush wasn't his preferred style of seduction. He barged right into the sweet talk, long, swaggering soliloquies of what he'd like to do to her. Much of it sounded physically impossible; all of it sounded vividly repulsive.

Katya encouraged him in the strongest terms to get lost or, barring that, try performing the acts on himself.

One dark night, while they were staking out a target from a parked van, he gave up on the subtle approach. Without ado, he rabbit-punched her twice on the side of the head, clamped his hands around her throat, and tried to rape her.

She wasn't entirely surprised by his foreplay. The brawl was brief. No quarter was given. His balls screamed with pain for weeks afterward.

She didn't nurse a grudge. Vladimir was an animal. Naturally, his urges lingered closer to the surface than most. She simply hated him a little more passionately than before.

And thus, at that moment, while Golitsin upbraided Vladimir on the phone, she smiled and hung on every word. Way to go, old boy. Oh please, don't forget my favorite part — call him an idiot again.

And thus, at the very moment the lights were extinguished, they both were pre-occupied with their own thoughts, off guard and flat-footed. One instant the restaurant was brightly lit and humming with small groups engaged in polite conversation; then, without warning, it went dark and the calami-tous mob of waiters and waitresses were clustered in front of their table, a gaggle of people in white uniforms stomping their feet and howling that stupid ditty at the top of their lungs.

A long hesitation. Then both drew their pistols and leaped to their feet. It was already too late.

They heard the glass crash and stretched their necks to look over the choir. They began hopping up and down, feeling like idiots. But between the darkness and the wall of kitchen staff, they were completely blinded.

Vladimir, who prided himself on being a man of action, for once was at a loss, frozen. Katya reacted first. She raised her pistol and fired three shots into the ceiling, rapid-fire — boom, boom, boom. It was absolutely effec-tive — and totally the wrong move. The first shot unleashed a wild fiasco; the next two wildly reinforced it.

Between the thunderous crash of the glass shattering and the upsetting flash and bang of the pistol shots in a dark chamber, the entire dining room collapsed into instant bedlam. Half the waiters and waitresses fell to the floor. The other half fled, screaming and hollering and clawing past one another in the general direction of the kitchen. Customers leaped to their feet, shoving over tables and chairs, banging against each other, racing for sanctuary wherever they could find it. Wails and shrieks and flailing bodies bounced around the room.

After an interminable thirty seconds, somebody flipped the lights back on. Vladimir and Katya stared wide-eyed at Alex's table. "They're gone," Katya screeched, and indeed, they were. Quite gone.

They were dumbfounded. They stood, mute, wide-eyed, gripping their pistols and gawking at the empty table. They took in the gaping hole that had replaced the picture window. They observed the heavy chair that hung on the window frame, dangling precariously. They didn't need to confer, didn't need to voice a single theory or weigh any half-baked suspicions. The facts were right before their eyes, unmistakable. They had underestimated Konevitch. A stupid amateur's mistake, and they had made it: plain and simple.

Konevitch had obviously confided to the

waitress that Vladimir and/or Katya were old pals celebrating a birthday, and obviously he persuaded, or more likely bribed, her to have the lights shut off and put on a little show to distract them. Just as obviously, he had faked the severity of his wounds. That harsh limp, that shambling gait, that lame shoulder: nobody that horribly mangled could've tossed that heavy chair, much less disappeared with such speed through the window frame. But he and his wife had successfully bypassed the layers of security. They had escaped, and were out there, on the streets of Budapest.

They were out there now, running for their lives.

Katya came to her senses and screamed at Vladimir, "Go out the window and find them. I'll get the others."

A response was a waste of time. He raced for the hole in the window and dove through, crashing hard on his knees on the concrete sidewalk outside. A loud curse exploded from his lips. The pain was sharp and intense. But his fury at being made into a fool hurt worse. He pushed himself to his feet, extended his pistol arm, spun on his heels, and scanned the surroundings.

Not a soul. Not out on the street. Not in the side parking lot. And not along the front of the hotel.

Alex and his party had vanished into the evening.

The hotel entrance was to his right and guarded by a pair of his men, making it unlikely, if not impossible, that Konevitch fled that way. He gripped his pistol hard and limped off in the other direction. There would be no warning this time. No second chance. He endured the pain from his bleeding knees and kicked it up to an all-out run.

Katya raced to the pair of thugs who were still seated by the restaurant exit, quietly congratulating themselves that they weren't in charge of this mess. When Golitsin learned about this screwup, heads were going to roll, literally.

She shrieked at them to follow her and went and collected the pair by the hotel entrance, then the two bored watchers outside. She ordered two of them to trail Vladimir before she set off, accompanied by the other four, in the opposite direction.

She signaled for the men to spread out, and issued one stern instruction. "Blow them to hell," she hissed.

8

A minute after Vladimir and Katya departed, the long white tablecloth was gently tugged back. Alex slowly raised his head and looked around. A waitress and two waiters loitered by the kitchen entrance, bantering about the bad people who had fired guns and chased all the customers away. The waitress was in tears, traumatized. One waiter looked ready to faint or flee. Otherwise, the palatial dining room was empty.

Alex stood and glanced over at the table where Vladimir and Katya had been seated. No corpses littered the floor. There were no dead waiters, and from what he could detect, no wounded patrons bleeding on the expensive carpet. He nearly fainted with relief. The three shots he heard were warnings or misses. Probably frantic or angered bullets fired out the broken window, he decided.

"Are they gone?" Elena asked from under the table, almost a whisper.

"Maybe. It looks that way," Alex replied in

a tone that conveyed half hope and half doubt. "Stay where you are another moment." He walked over to a waiter by the kitchen, a tall young man, considerably less fazed than the other two. He asked where the shooters had gone. Out of the building, he was informed — one dove out the window and disappeared and the other raced out of the restaurant, collected her evil pals, and dashed outside. Nothing more to worry about, Alex was assured. The bad people were gone. The concierge called the police. Any minute, the place would flood with cops.

Alex rushed back to the table, hefted the overnight bags over his good shoulder, and informed Elena and Eugene it was safe. Elena came out first and threw her arms around Alex, a hug she immediately lessened when he winced and groaned.

Then Eugene emerged, loud, upset, and furiously disoriented. He kept asking Alex why he had grabbed him, wrestled him under the table, pinned him down, and slapped a hand over his mouth. Alex tried leading him out of the room, but Eugene refused to budge until he had a reply, and it better be damned good.

"Long story. I don't have time to explain everything," Alex replied in a hasty effort to put him off, looking around and wondering what to do next. Open and shut, his plan had started and stopped at getting the killers out of the restaurant. Divert them, send them off on a wild-goose chase. Then he and Elena would make a speedy getaway in Eugene's Trabant.

But now, how was he to get to the Trabant in the parking lot without blundering into Vladimir and his people? And, he realized, if he left Eugene here, they might return and take their fury out on him. Eugene's yapping was growing louder. Alex waved a hand for him to calm down and attempted another explanation. "They kidnapped Elena and me, beat me silly, and forced me to sign over my companies. Now they're after your money, too. Let's go."

"My money?"

"Yes, Eugene, that's what I said."

"You know them?"

"We just met this afternoon. I don't want to get to know them better. Come on, we have to hurry." Alex glanced at the doorway to the dining room. He did not have time for these questions.

"Who are these people?"

"Eugene, please, shut up and help me. They're out there. Right now, they're combing the street, hunting for us. In a few moments, they'll figure out they've been hoodwinked and they'll be back. They're professional assassins. Are you listening?"

In the past two minutes, Eugene had passed from inebriated verging on tipsy to frightened out of his wits with Alex nearly smothering him under the table; he was finally settling on an emotion he could live with. Upset. Very, very upset. "Dammit, I'm not going anywhere. Why don't you just wait for the police?"

"Because they might be in on it. There's a very good chance they are. These people are unbelievably well-connected, better than you can even imagine, Eugene, and I can't . . . Listen to me, it's time to leave, now."

Eugene still looked angry and dubious — it *was* a lot to absorb — and Alex decided it was time to be blunt, and possibly a little deceitful. "It's not just Elena and me, they're hunting you, too. They want to kidnap and torture you, to force you to get your partners to wire the cash into my corporate accounts. They made me sign over the title to my companies, and now they want to steal your three hundred million, all of it. After that, they'll kill you."

Eugene suddenly felt nauseated. "They want to kill me?" he asked in a high-pitched voice. This was too much. He leaned back against a table and, drawing a few labored breaths, struggled to regain his balance; recapturing his composure was out of the question. He couldn't seem to think. He deeply regretted all those beers. How many was it? Eight? Nine? However many, the answer was: too many.

Alex placed a hand on his arm. "Yes," he said very quietly. "After they beat and torture you, after they steal all your money, yes, Eugene, yes, they intend to kill you."

Elena had been standing quietly, listening, and decided the time was right to throw her two cents in. Only shock would get this man moving, and she provided it. "Look what they did to Alex. Look at his battered face. Look, they nearly killed him, Eugene. They beat him for hours and burned him with an iron. That's what they'll do to you, too. Now, please stop wasting time. Do what Alex says."

With that, it finally sank in and Eugene offered the one response that felt appropriate at that moment. He vomited, a huge, boisterous gusher that splashed across the floor. He bent over, sucked in a few deep breaths, wiped the sleeve of his hand-tailored, thousand-dollar suit across his mouth and nose, then mumbled his first intelligent words of the night. "Get me the hell out of here."

Alex walked over to the same waiter he had spoken with earlier, politely explained what he needed, handed him the keys to the rented orange Trabant, and stuffed a hundred-dollar bill into his palm with the promise of another hundred the second the job was done.

Vladimir raced down the long alleyway and fought to suppress his exploding anxiety. He should have caught up with them by now, he realized. By his calculation, after they fled the hotel, this was the only route Konevitch and his wife and their plump friend could've taken.

Even if Konevitch *had* faked the severity of his injuries, Vladimir was damn sure he was at least partially lame. He had personally slammed that chair across his leg. Had smashed it down with such pulverizing force that it splintered into pieces against Konevitch's muscle, tissue, and bone. It was a miracle Konevitch could walk; running was out of the question, he was sure of it.

Also that short wife and flabby American banker were accompanying him. Vladimir was a fitness fanatic, a former Spetsnaz soldier who spent long hours in the gym buffing his superb condition. He had been sprinting, nearly full-speed, for four, possibly five minutes now.

He slowed to a hesitant trot, then an angry stomp for a few yards before he came to a dead halt in his tracks. He was breathing heavily. No, this definitely did not add up. He stole a quick glance at his watch: six minutes.

Six minutes.

A gimp, a fatty, and a small woman — a woman! — no way were they a match for his speed. It simply wasn't possible, he concluded with excruciating insight.

He quickly reviewed the possibilities. It was

a simple process of elimination; exactly the arithmetic he should've use six minutes before, he now knew. One, had they leaped out the window and run away in the other direction, the team posted outside the entrance would've seen them and blasted away. Two, had they instead exited through the lobby and out the hotel's front entrance, either of the two teams by the entrance would've bagged them. Open and shut.

There was, however, a third possibility. The least physically demanding possibility for a wounded man, as he thought about it — the most likely possibility, he realized with an ugly curse.

If only Katya hadn't barked at him to rush out the window. Stupid bitch. Like a snot-nosed rookie, she panicked. Rule number one: be sure what you *think* you see is what you're actually seeing. They should've yanked back all the curtains and peeked under all the tables.

Oh look, it's Alex and his friends playing peekaboo; ha, ha, ha — bang, bang, bang.

How simple that would've been. How deeply satisfying.

But no, they fell for Konevitch's cat-and-mouse game, and the mouse won. It was terribly stupid. But this blunder was definitely her fault, not his.

No, on second thought, the real blame fell on Golitsin's stooped shoulders. He approved the plan in the first place to drag Konevitch to the hotel. Okay, yes, Vladimir had claimed it would be easy. But of course there were risks. The greedy bastard knew that, but he wanted more money, money, money.

Konevitch baited the trap and the old geezer bit with every tooth in his mouth. He had nobody to blame but himself.

The satellite phone suddenly rattled at his waist. After a long hesitation, he pulled it off his belt and stared at it, consumed with dread, a new and surprisingly unwelcome emotion for Vladimir. Probably it was Golitsin. He would not answer it, not under any condition. He would just let it bleep and bleep until the old geezer got frustrated and gave up.

The thought of trying to explain this muddle, of trying to justify and excuse his stupidity, of confessing that he had allowed Konevitch to escape, was sickening.

On the other hand, maybe it was Katya. Maybe she was calling to say she had caught up with them; maybe Konevitch and his short wife and fat friend were already decomposing in a dark alley and out of their hair. Maybe their troubles were over. Oh, how he longed to hear those words.

So which was it? The devil or salvation? The bastard or the bitch?

He pushed the receive button and placed the phone firmly against his ear.

Golitsin said without a breath of emotion, "Your twenty-five minutes are long over. I'm assuming you lost him."

Vladimir felt a rush of fear bordering on panic. The voice was cold, so totally flat. For a moment he said nothing. He just stood there, tempted to throw the phone and flee as far and as fast as his feet could carry him. Find a new life in India or Zanzibar, for all he cared.

What could he say?

Golitsin snapped, "Your silence confirms it, you cretin. You were outsmarted by a complete dilettante."

"I still made you a fortune."

"So what?"

"Hundreds of millions. Doesn't that count for anything?"

"No." Just no.

"He hasn't escaped yet," Vladimir insisted, trying to sound convincing. The echo of his own bleating in the earphone, loud and whiny, shocked him.

"Oh, I think we both know he is long gone," Golitsin whispered, and he was right. "He and my three hundred million. All gone. Vanished. And it's your fault, you incompetent dimwit."

Vladimir stared into the dark, overcast skies. The alley was narrow and empty: no pedestrians; no lost tourists wandering in confusion; not even a smelly wino sleeping it off on a dark door-stoop. Just him, just a dead man sniveling into a clunky satphone. A scatter of small shops lined both sides of the street, all of which were locked and shuttered. Rain was pouring down in heavy sheets. A few lights burned in the apartments over the stores and the flickering glow from television sets refracted off several windows. The gloom contributed to his quickly deepening misery. "I'm sorry," he choked, mangling the words he had never before uttered in his life. He tried again, more clearly, more unctuously repentant, anything to mollify the menacing voice on the other end. "Truly, sir, I am very, very sorry."

"Are you?"

"Yes sir. Sorry, sorry, sorry."

"Well, sorry won't do, idiot. Sorry is for spilling coffee on my carpet. But losing three hundred million dollars? For letting Konevitch escape from under your nose? Just sorry?" Golitsin paused for a moment, then laid down the verdict. "When I am done with you, you'll learn the real meaning of sorry."

Vladimir reached into his waistband and withdrew his pistol. He took a deep swallow and said, "That's where you're wrong. You'll never get your hands on me, you ugly old bastard."

"Listen closely, moron. Wherever you run, I'll find you. You'll last days, long, terrible days, I promise that."

Vladimir laughed and the sound echoed down the alley and bounced off the walls, bitter and scornful. A few lights popped on. Concerned faces appeared in the windows over the empty shops.

"You think this is funny?" Golitsin hissed.

"Yes, I do. Absolutely. I'm laughing because I lost you all that money. Now screw yourself." Vladimir aimed the pistol at his left temple, held the phone right next to it, screamed, "Good-bye, asshole!" — and blew his brains down the dark alleyway.

9

The orange Trabant came to a screeching halt under the hotel's grand entryway, less than an inch from the steep curb. Alex, Elena, and Eugene scrambled through the rotating glass doors, looked both ways, then made a mad bolt for the car. Alex stuffed another hundred in the waiter's outstretched hand, mumbled quick words of thanks, and they squeezed and fought their way inside the car. The keys were in the ignition, the engine running. Elena climbed behind the wheel and punched the gas with gusto.

With an angry sputter the car lurched and coughed away from the curb, every bit as unsightly and underpowered as advertised. Only two years off the production line, it didn't look a day over a hundred. From bumper to bumper, nothing but peeling paint, dents, and vast patches of oxidation.

Alex couldn't have cared less. The car was perfect. Every rattle, every belch and spit from the perforated muffler was just perfect.

Nobody would expect a man of his means to be seen in such a creaky monstrosity.

For five minutes they drove without anybody saying a word. The rain battered the roof. Alex hunched down in his seat to disguise his height; Elena inched up in hers, straining to disguise her lack of it.

Thirty minutes of sitting under the watchful gaze of wicked people who intended to kill them left them moody and edgy. They peeked through the rear window incessantly. They thought they saw cars on their tail and breathed with relief when the cars turned off. Elena zigzagged through narrow streets, going nowhere in particular. Just away from the hotel. Just as far as they could get from Katya and Vladimir and the other killers. At a red light at a large intersection, she finally asked Alex, "Where to?"

Without hesitation, he said, "Out of Hungary."

"Not so fast," Eugene offered in a newly concerned tone from the backseat. "Alex, you need to see a doctor before we go anywhere." Now that they were out of danger, his good manners were kicking back in. "You should see how you look. A concussion, broken bones, internal bleeding, who knows how serious the damage is."

"Not a good idea, Eugene. I told you, these people are connected everywhere. They're former KGB, for godsakes. You're American, you don't understand what that means."

"So tell me what it means."

"They used to rule these countries. They can pull strings you can't imagine. The moment they recover their senses, they might even put out an alert to the Hungarian border police. Our names, our descriptions, and probably some trumped-up charges to warrant our arrests. Getting out will be impossible."

Eugene and Elena sat quietly and stewed on Alex's warning.

"In fact," Alex said after thinking about his own words, "it's safe to assume the alert's already out."

Another moment of silence, longer than the last one. A nationwide manhunt suddenly seemed like a possibility. Only a few years earlier this was a police state; they didn't have a prayer.

"Then the train station and airport are out of the question," Elena observed sensibly. "They'll alert those places first."

Alex nodded. "But I think they'll check hospitals and doctor's offices before they do anything else." He squeezed Elena's leg. "The nearest land border is our best chance." He twisted around in the seat and peered at Eugene. "You still have your cell phone?"

Eugene patted himself down. "It's gone. It was still sitting on the table when you pulled me down. I'll bet it's still there."

"Of course."

"Our passports, Alex, they have them," Elena remembered with a jolt. "Maybe it would be better just to stay here. Find a safe place and hide."

"I don't think so." Alex held up a clutch of small red booklets and waved them in front of her. "These were packed in a hidden compartment of my overnight bag."

Elena shook her head. Her husband's cleverness had long since ceased to surprise her, but to insist on bringing the overnight bags for the restaurant meeting with Eugene was an amazing stroke of clear thinking. She didn't need to ask about the fistful of little booklets.

But Eugene did. "Are those legal?"

Elena caught his eye in the rearview mirror. "Whenever Alex accompanied Yeltsin on overseas trips he submitted his passport for the required visa. Now that Russians are free to travel overseas, seventy years of curiosity about the outside world demands to be instantly vented. The visa office of the Foreign Ministry is choked with requests. Mountains of paper everywhere. And more often than not, requests with the accompanying passports get lost or misplaced in the logjam. These are former Soviet bureaucrats we're talking about. It's a miracle they find their way home at night."

Alex continued, "Two or three days out,

my office would call to complain, and liberally mention Yeltsin's name. Rather than hunt for a pin in a haystack, a clerk would just issue a new passport with the appropriate visa and send it by courier. That's the right expression, right? Pin in a haystack? Anyway, a month or two later, when the original turned up, it was returned by mail."

"Exactly how many do you have?" Eugene asked, enjoying his little peek into Russian inefficiency. A died-in-the-wool capitalist, he loved hearing about the sins of former commies.

"I honestly don't know."

"Guess."

"Ten. A dozen. Perhaps more."

Elena had twice gone along on Yeltsin's trips; she had three passports, one, of course, now inconveniently tucked in the back pocket of Vladimir's corpse. But Alex always shoved a few extras in his baggage, in the event the ones he or she were using got lost or stolen.

"There are two borders we can head for," Alex was saying, sharing the possibilities as he tried to think this through. "Austria to the south. Or due east, to Czechoslovakia."

"Okay, which?"

"I think Austria makes the most sense. It's closer. Also, I have part ownership of an advertising company in the capital. Illya Mechoukov is the president. A good man. I trust him. Better yet, the KGB had little influence there." He opened the window and took a deep breath. The night had turned cold. A frigid blast of air hit him in the face, but he felt dizzy. He briefly pondered the possibility that the exhaust was spewing carbon monoxide into the cabin. "Unfortunately, that border takes a visa. The Czechs and Slovaks, though, as former Bloc members, still have open borders for Russian passports."

"Where do you want to cross?" Elena asked, now that Austria was ruled out. She searched the rearview mirror. Nothing.

"Avoid the major arteries. Our best chance is a secondary or backcountry road. The guards at the smaller checkpoints will be the last ones alerted."

Eugene decided to join the discussion and leaned forward from the backseat. "Then what?"

"Then . . . directly to the nearest international airport. That would be Slovakia," Alex answered.

"Then Russia, right?"

"Maybe."

"I don't see that you have a choice, pal. You better get back there fast," Eugene advised.

"Do you think?"

"You better rescind those letters before anybody can act on them."

"I have other worries right now," Alex replied almost absently. He reached up and switched on the overhead light, which thankfully seemed to be the one thing in the car that functioned properly. He began flipping through passports and thumbing the pages.

"You know what?" Eugene announced, lurching forward in his seat.

"I think you're about to tell me what."

"Damn right I am. I think you got conked on the head harder than you realize. You're not thinking clearly. They could empty out your bank accounts in hours and, in a day or so, swipe all the investors' money in your banks."

"Don't you think that's a lot of cash to haul away?" Alex replied, curiously indifferent.

"You know damn well what I'm talking about. Come on, pal. They'll wire it all to a bank in the Azores or Switzerland. Then it'll shuttle around to a hundred banks and fall off the radar."

With no small amount of pleasure, Alex said, "I don't think so."

"Think harder."

"The people who forced me to sign those letters know nothing about banking. To move even a dollar they need my account numbers and the security codes."

"Oh."

"And those are all locked away in a safe in my office, guarded around the clock. They didn't know enough to ask about the numbers and I wasn't in the mood to educate them."

Elena reached over and patted her husband

on the leg. "You're a genius."

His nose was stuffed back inside the •
passports.

Sergei Golitsin sat behind Alex Konevitch's massive hand-carved desk and stared across it at the ten hungry faces around the long conference table. The irony of using Alex's own office as a command post to track him down and kill him was too delicious.

A phone was positioned directly in front of each man. A yellow notepad and a slew of satphones were poised within arm's reach. Empty coffee mugs littered the table. Ashtrays overflowed with snuffed-out butts. A large, 10,000-to-1 map of Hungary was taped to a wall, with dozens of little yellow and red pins stuck here and there. Another map, even larger, displaying the entire European continent and punctured with a similar mixture of multicolored pins, was fastened to the adjoining wall.

The men inside the room knew the address of Konevitch's unpretentious but nicely located Parisian apartment. They knew what hotels he preferred when he traveled, as well as the address of each and every office and subsidiary of Konevitch Associates outside the Russian border. A pin for each one, with a man or two now lurking at each destination. A mushroom of cigarette smoke rose from the table and swirled in cancerous eddies just below the ceiling.

Below them, the six floors of Konevitch Associates were nearly deserted. A handpicked crew of security guards ambled around the building; otherwise, the employees were home, cleaning up after dinner, mixing it up with their lovers, or snoring loudly in their beds. A few hyperambitious souls had tried to work late, but the guards had chased them out and shut down their phones and computers.

A sign was posted on the front door downstairs announcing a two-day holiday. A squad of burly guards would be placed there in the morning to make sure everybody got the message.

At that second, for the first time in two frantic hours, only one noise interrupted the sound of breathing — a buzzing that emanated from a specialist and his assistant employing a noisy instrument of some sort to crack a wall safe. The specialist had twice reassured everybody it was going "super splendidly." No hitches. No surprises, and Golitsin had good reason not to doubt him.

Six months before, when Alex Konevitch had ordered a personal safe to be installed in his office, the job naturally landed on the desk of his corporate security chief. Golitsin promptly handed it off to a black job specialist who once worked under him at the KGB, a master thief with an encyclopedic knowledge of safes and locks. Golitsin's instructions were precise and contradictory.

Nothing but the best brand on the market for the boss. Something sturdy, something imposing in appearance, something with a tidy reputation for quality, he'd emphasized; in other words, something that would duly impress its owner.

Just be damn sure the model was one he was sure he could crack; within two hours or less would do the trick nicely.

Golitsin's top deputy, Felix Glebov, eventually broke the awkward silence. "It's been three hours. Where is he?"

"Still running," Golitsin said, eyes blazing down the table with a look that could curdle bowels. "A scared rabbit, fleeing for his life." He paused briefly to scratch his chin. "Successfully, apparently, because he's up against a bunch of incompetent twits."

One of the twits, large, with a neck that moved like a tank turret, spoke up, a nervous attempt to deflect blame from his overgrown shoulders. "I have ten good people at the Budapest train station. Twenty more at the airport, a man at each ticket counter. All former KGB or Hungarian secret police. Another squad is hanging out at the arrival gate at Sheremetyevo Airport in the event they make it this far." Eager to impress everybody with his efficiency, he added, "They all have color pictures."

"Good for you," replied the next twit in line, a man with a skinny, pockmarked face and puffy eyes who lost no time launching his own accomplishments. "Only two minutes ago I got off the phone with the deputy minister of Hungarian Security. He has two children in private school and is cracking heads to collect the hundred thousand bounty I promised if he catches them. An hour ago, a red alert went out to all customs offices. They and the police have been notified a murderer and his accomplices are trying to flee."

He paused to be sure everybody heard the next point. "Katya and one of her people gave statements to the police. Said they witnessed Konevitch stick a knife in a man's back at the airport. Said they thought they recognized his face from photos in a Russian magazine, but couldn't remember if he was a movie star or what. Took them a while to figure it out, so now they're reporting it."

That last clever move was Katya's brainchild. Of course he felt no obligation to mention it now.

The next man, introduced by Golitsin to the others earlier that evening as Nicky — no last name, no formal introduction, just plain Nicky — sat for a moment, sucking deeply from a black cheroot, bored out of his mind, trying to entertain himself watching the safecrackers at work. Dressed head to toe in shiny black leather, down to his dapper biker boots, he was the only man present who did not get the executive-suite dress code. He was also the only non-employee of Konevitch Associates, the only one not hired by Golitsin over the past year for what they brought to this table.

Lacking a KGB background, he was also happily clueless about the reporting procedures.

Eventually the silence grabbed his attention and he noticed everybody staring at him. He crushed his cigarette on the tabletop, flashed an amused sneer, then held it long enough for everybody to get the message. Nicky came from a different world, one without silly protocols, a world with but one simple rule: rules are meant to be broken.

But even without the last name — despite never having seen him face-to-face — half the men around the table were sure they knew who he was. A photo of his face had hung in a place of honor on KGB walls long enough to grow mold. A much younger face, certainly. A little thinner, maybe, without the cute ponytail laced with gray that bounced when he strutted. One with considerably less scars, absent the gallery of tattoos on the neck, and certainly before the huge nose had been rearranged into a bent banana.

Nicky, aka Igor, aka Leon, or a half dozen other transient aliases he had used and thrown away in his illustrious career, was in fact one Nickolas Kozyrev, head of the largest crime syndicate in Russia.

How ironic that they were all now sharing the same table, smoking and sipping coffee like old pals. In their previous lives, they had spent countless hours chasing Nicky around the shadows. Typical gruntwork for the police ordinarily, except Nicky's kingdom had tentacles in every Russian city, webs that stretched across Europe and Asia, and bustling branch offices in Brighton Beach and Miami. Nicky was known and wanted by police forces from New York to Timbuktu. Three different American presidents and an army of other world leaders had bombarded two different general secretaries with strong requests to get Nicky off the street.

Among assorted other enterprises, Nicky wholesaled kidnapped girls to whorehouses, owned a string of porn studios, blackmarketed, smuggled arms, traded in stolen cars, gems, artwork, pushed heroin and an assortment of other illegal pharmaceuticals, and most recently, was making a loud splash in Russia's burgeoning executive kidnapping market. Wherever there was illicit profit to be made, Nicky pushed his sticky fingers in. Contract murder had long been a mainstay of his repertoire. The sheer breadth, expanse, and outright violence of his operation proved too considerable for the police to handle; not to mention wildly exaggerated suspicions that Nicky owned half the senior police officers in the country.

A quarter was more like it.

Thus the KBG was brought into the hunt and encouraged to use every filthy trick in its arsenal.

And despite every effort, despite years of exhausting work, they had never come close. Not even close.

"Tell me again," Nicky opened, his eyes dancing playfully around the table, "exactly how this guy got away."

He knew damn well how Konevitch escaped. They had already been over it, in detail. Twice. But he despised these former KGB boys. He would keep asking again and again, because it amused him to rub their faces in it.

Making no effort to disguise his irritation, Golitsin said, "Why does it matter? He got away. Now we'll find him."

"It matters because I say it does."

"Is that right?"

"Yeah, I'm just trying to figure out how all your morons got made asses of." His lips curled and he watched Golitsin. "Remind me, how old is this Konevitch guy? Who trained him to be such a Houdini? The KGB? The army?"

"Vladimir was the moron who let this happen. He was your man, last time I checked."

"Yeah, on loan to you for the past year, last time I checked. When I sent you Vladimir, he was a real killing machine. Your cretins polluted him, turned him stupid and clumsy."

Golitsin held his breath and counted to ten. An hour before, they had sniped back and forth like this for a full fifteen minutes. He gathered as much patience as he could muster and said, "Tell me what your people are doing."

Nicky had broken his spell of boredom and gotten his blood; he could wait until the next opportunity rolled around. He fought back a smile and said, "All right. Word's been passed to all my guys in East Europe. Since we got their passports, they'll need new ones, right? So what are they gonna do? Try and buy phonies, right? Every counterfeiter and half-assed fabricator in Hungary's been warned to pass word the second they make contact."

Golitsin nodded. Sounded good.

Nicky pulled out another black cheroot and lit up. "I got pickpocket teams working every train and plane station in Europe. They been told to keep a good eye out for a gimpy giant, a blonde runt, and a rich American fatty."

The twit who had just detailed his own efforts at corralling Alex at transportation terminals leaned forward and advised Nicky, "Consider giving them photographs instead. Our experience shows that visual representations always work better than verbal descriptions." He produced a crooked smile. "If you have fax machines, I'll provide copies."

He instantly regretted that he had opened his mouth. "Fax machines?" Nicky roared. He looked ready to bounce out of his seat and strangle the twit. "Oh, sure, moron. Hell, every pickpocket's got one. You know, stuffed in his back pocket." The other former agents at the table instantly hated the thick-necked dolt for his stupid remark. Little wonder they never caught Nicky.

Nicky planted his leather elbows on the table. "Listen up, asshole. They don't need no pictures. Pickpockets are . . . what? Observant, right? It's what they do. All day, staring at people, sizing 'em up. They can tell in a blink if a mark's got ten bucks in their pocket and who's got a thousand."

Another withering glare at the fool and Nicky clammed up. Why cast pearls before swine? He lit another cigarette and collapsed back into his chair.

The next man in line, in an earlier life the Ministry of Interior's liaison to Interpol, squirmed for a moment, stared down at the table, picked at a scab on his nose, then as quietly as he could, mumbled, "I called my former colleagues and alerted them that a warrant for Alex's arrest would be coming their way within hours."

Time for the next man in line to speak up. Nobody did, and the silence quickly turned deafening.

The man stole a quick sideways peek at Golitsin, who was staring back with a mean scowl. "And what are they doing about it?" Golitsin snapped, his scowl deepening.

This was not the question the man wanted to hear. "And they . . . they listened."

"Listened?"

"Well . . . umh, yes. Interpol won't do anything until a formal request is launched through appropriate legal channels. Can't really. The protocol is written in stone. It's a very bureaucratic and —"

"You're saying Interpol won't do anything?"

"No. I'm . . . I'm not saying that."

The other sharks around the table were edging forward in their seats, waiting for the fireworks to erupt. Oh yeah, pal, that's what you're saying, no question about it. "Then explain to me what you meant," Golitsin barked.

"We . . . that is, we, as executives of Konevitch Associates, we don't, well . . . we don't exactly have the legal authority to demand an arrest. Interpol wants to see a legitimate warrant before it will act."

The man reached under the table and with both hands gripped his knees together to keep them from shaking. His face was red. A jackhammer was going off in his chest. With pleading eyes he looked around the table for help, a meager sign of support, anything; a tepid nod of pity would be fine. Nine sets of eyes looked elsewhere. At the table, the ceiling, the white walls.

"Did you offer your contacts money?" Golitsin asked.

"Money, women, cars, drugs. Yes, anything their hearts desire."

Complete silence.

"And they swore at me and hung up."

"Then you didn't offer enough, idiot."

Nervous snickers around the table. They had all, every last man, heard the pistol shot reverberate through Golitsin's phone in that fatal final conversation with Vladimir. What a moment. Just the sound of Golitsin's throaty voice and that hardass Vladimir pumped a bullet into his own head. One for the record books, definitely.

More to the point, they had collectively witnessed the old man's response. He did not flinch or cringe or curse. Bang — not even a wrinkle of surprise. Actually, he smiled.

It looked, in fact, remarkably like the unpleasant little smirk he was offering Mr. Interpol at that moment. Wouldn't it be special if that smile ignited a heart attack?

Golitsin cracked a knuckle, then in a hectoring tone said, "Listen to me, idiot. All you idiots listen up. Konevitch doesn't have a game plan. He's improvising. If, somehow, they make it over the Hungarian border, they could jump on a late-night train or plane and end up anywhere in Europe. Only Interpol can issue orders broad enough to cover the entire continent. Only Interpol has instant access to charge card information. Only Interpol can forward warrants to police and border officials across Europe. Are you getting this?"

The man was scribbling notes furiously in a small notebook. Not a word had been said that he did not already know. If he shrank any deeper into his chair, he would disappear.

Golitsin stood up and walked in his direction. He bent over, got less than six inches from the man's ear, and muttered, "Get back on the phone and offer more money, moron."

Golitsin headed for the door, kicked it open, and slammed it loudly after he left. The room nearly collapsed in relief; everybody except Nicky. Watching these boys squirm and sweat was more fun than he could remember.

They all grabbed their phones and began making more calls, frantic now to find Alex Konevitch.

Golitsin took the stairs one at a time, down one flight, then bounced along a short hallway that ended in a small, well-lit conference room. A young lady, shapely and wonderfully attractive in red business attire, tight jacket, and a provocatively short skirt was seated patiently at the end of the long table.

A stout bodyguard stood in the corner and kept his mouth shut.

She looked up as Golitsin entered and acknowledged his presence with a cold smile. "How's it going, Sergei?"

Not many people dared call him Sergei. General Golitsin was fine; plain General better yet. His own wife and children called him General to his face and The General behind his back; he liked that most of all, the singularity of it. That had been his rank, after all — a lifetime title, one that reeked of power, prestige, and authority. He particularly enjoyed the look in their eyes when people learned it was not army, but KGB rank.

The informality of Sergei, though, was reserved for his equals; in his mind, there weren't many. Tatyana Lukin certainly wasn't his equal; she was the special assistant to Yeltsin's chief of staff, the youngest one, his right hand and chief counsel.

Nothing about that impressed Golitsin.

The Kremlin had more special assistants than mice, clawing around and trying to look and act more important than the replaceable coatholders they definitely were. But Tatyana came with another qualification, a priceless one. She happened also to be the chief of staff's mistress, the person who planted the first whisper in his ear in the morning, with final say at night. The chief was a lazy bureaucrat, a man who adored the many perks of his position and detested the maddening grind of daily work. His major qualification for his lofty title was that he was a more than willing drinking buddy for this sorry lush of a president. The whole Kremlin staff knew it. Anything of importance was therefore passed through Tatyana, who more than compensated for her boss's steady indifference.

She held a law degree from Moscow University, where she had graduated top of her class. A background check performed by his people revealed that those professors she couldn't awe with her mastery of law she conquered with her body. That got her to number two. Number one was a young genius who ignored sleep and consumed libraries, with an elephantine memory and a talent for oratory that would make a southern preacher blanch with envy. Two weeks before graduation, the KGB received a late-night tip — a female caller, the records revealed, who naturally insisted on anonymity — to ransack his room. The contraband was discovered under the bed, a stack of kiddie-porn magazines and nauseating videos, all with American trademarks, making them doubly illegal — all of which he naturally protested he'd never laid eyes on in his life. The next day, he was forced to goose-step across a stage to a chorus of boos and hisses from the entire student body, then hauled straight to jail.

His fourth day in prison, he was beaten to

death by a fellow prisoner with two young daughters and a hard-fisted aversion to perverts.

After that, three years as a state prosecutor. Tatyana never lost a case, not one. From the best his people could tell, she seduced at least two judges to acquire convictions of men who were flagrantly innocent. The rumors about her in Moscow's legal circles were rich and rife. She blackmailed and framed witnesses. She burned evidence contrary to her case, concocted false evidence, persuaded the police to force confessions, and so on. Golitsin believed every word of it. She was a scheming, conniving whore whose only scruple was to get ahead, whatever the cost. The old man admired her greatly.

Tatyana had the looks, the brains, the ambitions, and, more importantly, the chief of staff's balls in her hand. She could call him Sergei, or idiot, or toad for all he cared. He looked upon her as the daughter he wished he'd had, rather than the ugly cow he ended up with.

"Get lost," Golitsin barked at the guard, who shot out the door.

"Everything's on track," he informed Tatyana with a confident scowl. He moved around the room and collapsed into the chair at the other end of the table. "Just one unexpected glitch."

"Oh, do tell."

"Konevitch and his pretty little wife, they got away."

"Okay." Cool as ice, no shock, no histrionics. "Please explain that."

Golitsin launched into a brief recap. He left out a few embarrassing details, such as his own miserable role in dispatching Konevitch to the hotel. Nor did he feel it at all necessary to bring up the extra three hundred million that nearly fell in his lap, which he fully intended to keep for himself. When the doctored tale was done, he concluded, "We've initiated a manhunt. We're turning over all the usual rocks. I'm sure he'll turn up."

She had gorgeously thick black hair and was playing with a long strand next to her left ear. "And if he doesn't?" she asked, revealing no shock or surprise at this turn.

"Well, then he doesn't."

"But he signed the letters?"

"After a little persuasion, yes."

"And you now have the originals?"

"Signed, sealed, and delivered to my office an hour ago."

"And properly notarized by an attorney, I'm sure."

"Good assumption."

The lawyer in her seemed satisfied. "Does he know you're behind it yet?"

"Not yet, no. The name of his successor was left blank."

"Whose idea was that?"

"Who do you think?"

She raised an admiring eyebrow at that touch. As long as Konevitch didn't know who put this together, he wouldn't know who or what he was fighting. Time counted for everything. Hours were worth half a fortune. A full day was worth everything Konevitch owned.

It was brilliant, really. Keep him guessing and punching in the dark until they chose to expose themselves.

"Where do you think he'll go next?"

"If he's stupid, here. Moscow."

"But he's not stupid, is he?" she asked. A rhetorical question, really. The man was brilliant and full of surprises. Why else were they in this room, at this hour, rehashing his escape?

Golitsin grinned. "He was stupid enough to hire me."

"Good point." She laughed.

"Right now," Golitsin hypothesized in his usual way, as if it were a fact, "he's probably gone to ground. I think he's hiding someplace in Hungary. Trying to wait us out."

"Interesting. What makes you think that?"

"Deductive logic. We took their wallets, and we have his and his wife's passports. He can't get out. I limited the kidnap team to only ten people, and to the best of our knowledge, that's all he's seen. He has no idea how many more people are involved. But we won't underestimate him again. The torture was administered by one of Nicky's people, so Konevitch might reasonably guess the Mafiya is behind this. That alone will scare the crap out of him. He'll try to keep his head down, perhaps by driving around all night, or checking into a cheap fleabag long enough to lick his wounds. As long as he stays in Hungary, we're fine. In another ten hours it won't matter where he turns up."

She seemed to consider this. "Have you traveled overseas lately?"

"No."

"But Konevitch has, right?"

"You know he has. Between Yeltsin's trips and his own business, he's on the road more than he's here."

"Then it's safe to presume he has more passports."

"How do you know this?"

"Trust me. You know, I also usually accompany Yeltsin. I have seven passports with open visas myself."

A bored shrug. "So what? It really doesn't matter if he has a thousand. If he makes it to Austria or Czechoslovakia, we'll find him. Like I said, the key is keeping him away from here."

Tatyana stood up and moved around the table. She lit a cigarette as she walked, and a long trail of smoke curdled behind her. She came to a stop less than two feet from

Golitsin. A small hop and she was on the table, seated, legs swaying loosely from side to side. Long, lovely legs. She crossed one knee over the other and leaned in toward the old man.

He could smell her perfume, something wicked and musky — probably French, definitely expensive, a gift from one of her well-heeled lovers, he guessed. She had left the top three buttons of her jacket undone, he noticed, offering a quick peek at the chief of staff's playthings.

He spent a long moment taking it all in, the aroma, the pose, the alluring flare of her nostrils. She was just so perfect — a perfect blend of Asiatic and Caucasian, perfect teeth, perfect black, uninhibited eyes, perfect body. She leaned a little lower. "Who do you think he'll call first? What's your hunch?"

"I know who he'll call. Sonja."

"And who's she? The mistress?"

"No, the secretary. Been with him since the beginning. He relies on her for everything, an old lady he trusts completely. Treats her like the mother he barely knew." He pushed his chair back and stretched his short arms over his head. He was too old, too tired, and too callous to be seduced. He definitely admired the effort, though.

The message was received, and she produced an elegant little shrug; even the shrug was a turn-on. She took another pull off her cigarette. "So where's this Sonja? At home?"

"She was, yes, before we dragged her back here. She's seated at her desk at this moment, with a garrote dangling loosely around her neck. If he calls, she'll ask for his location or the new necklace will become unbearably uncomfortable."

"You don't miss much, do you?"

"No, I don't. But in the event we don't catch him tonight, tomorrow will be your turn."

She bounced off the table and with one hand began nimbly rebuttoning her jacket. "Relax, Sergei. Yeltsin's in China trying to mend a thousand years of bad relations. He'll be kissing Chinese ass for the next three days, bouncing around landmarks and ceremonies, drinking himself into a stupor at every opportunity. He'll be impossible to reach." She headed toward the door. "Everything on my end is taken care of."

Malcolm Street Associates was an opulent firm with an operations room fashioned to impress. Only the rare visitor was ever allowed inside, but to a man, they walked out whistling and shaking their head. Large flashing screens overloaded the walls, lights blinked, faxes whirred, computers hummed, phones always jangling with agents reporting in. Day or night, it was a beehive of dizzying activity.

The Vault, as it was called by its stressed-out inhabitants, occupied the entire top floor of the London headquarters, a five-story, stone-faced building located two blocks off Trafalgar Square. According to the brass plaque beside the front entry it had been established in 1830.

The tradition of maintaining eternally expanding profits fell on Lord Eldridge Pettlebone, an intimidating former police superintendent, number eight in the short line of managing partners, and at that moment a man who was annoyed almost to the point of bother. Twenty minutes before, a courier had fought his way past the doorman of his club and dragged him here.

A dead agent, and a missing client. One or the other, maybe. A twofer was unheard of, and the entire firm was reeling with distress. He paced around the long table where the firm's best and brightest were gathered, trying to catch up on a fiasco that had a long head start and took off at a gallop. He stifled a yawn, squared his shoulders, and tried to appear steady for the troops.

He had handled serious crises before, plenty of them. Nearly all came late at night. Each arrived with its own unique twists and turns. The first reports were always wrong, the second and third reports only more so.

"Who exactly confirmed Bernie Lutcher's death?" he asked, staring directly at one of the bloodshot-eyed assistants crowded around the table. This particular man, as a sad result of his previous time at a backwater desk in MI6, had the rare misfortune to be nearly fluent in Hungarian. That peculiar distinction earned him a turn on the hotseat, but he had worked himself into a lather and felt eager and ready for whatever Number Eight threw at him.

The young man straightened his tie, gathered his wits, and sat up. "The coroner of the Budapest police. The body was called in by airport security at one-fifteen, Budapest time. The police arrived a few minutes later. Bernie's corpse was transported to the city morgue, then placed in cold storage until six, when the night shift came on. The preliminary workup was done by a Dr. Laszlo" — he conferred with his notes — "Massouri."

Lord Pettlebone nodded, not at anything the man had said but a gesture to speed this up.

"We requested a full and immediate autopsy, of course. They begged off until tomorrow. That's our Hungarian friends for you. Even a ghastly murder in their capital airport doesn't put a hop in their step. But the preliminary cause of death," the man continued, browsing through his notes, "was a small knife puncture in the back."

He reached over and with a brash forefinger pointed like a dagger scraped an X slightly below the left shoulder blade of the man beside him. He plowed ahead. "A slight tearing around the incision suggests a twisting of the blade. The weapon was a stiletto, twelve or perhaps fifteen inches in length, only a few centimeters in width. Not a garden-variety weapon, I should say, more a specialist's tool, and it went directly for poor Bernie's heart." He waited a beat before he revealed this next revelation. "But his pupils were widely dilated, and his face also had a purplish discoloration, the visual by-products of oxygen deprivation. But no scarring or lesions from ligatures or bruises on his neck. As you know, this could be suggestive of poisoning."

"Assume both. He was poked with a coated blade," Pettlebone concluded swiftly, before the assistant could voice that rather evident opinion himself. "Let's further assume, hypothetically, the assassin was professional."

"Sorry, sir. Did I mention the dark bruise slightly below Bernie's breastbone?"

"Right you are. A pair of assassins." He examined the other faces. Knowing nods all around. "Witnesses?"

"Yes, and here's where it gets interesting," the man said with a relieved grin: this tidbit had fallen in his lap only ten minutes before. "The Budapest police were contacted about two hours ago by a Russian lady and man claiming to be her boyfriend. She swore she observed Konevitch stab his bodyguard in the back, then flee outside and jump into a cab."

"The client? The client stabbed his own security escort and fled?" Pettlebone sniffed and scowled. This firm did not hire out bodyguards, it provided security escorts.

"Quite right, sir. Alex Konevitch. Claimed she recognized him clear as a bell from the newsie magazines back in Russia. Seems he's quite the celebrity back home, being filthy rich and all."

Pettlebone removed his glasses and rubbed his eyes. "But it took her ten hours to recall who he was?"

"So she says."

"I don't suppose the lady has a name?"

Back to the notes. A few pages were flipped. "Ah, here — according to her passport, Alisa Petrova. It might be a phony, though. I had a nice chat with the detective who received her statement. Not much of a lady, in his words. A rough piece of work."

"So she saw Konevitch stab our man. Did she also see who punched him in the gut?"

"She didn't mention it, no. Though it might be prudent to consider the possibility that her angle of observation precluded it."

"Is that your considered opinion?"

"Well, if her view was from the rear, Konevitch is quite tall, and Bernie very wide. Fat, actually."

"But is that your opinion?"

It was as close as he was going to come to one. The man clammed up and stopped talking. He suddenly found the blinking lights on the far wall endlessly fascinating.

Pettlebone looked up and down the table again. "Can anybody here recall an instance where one of our clients murdered one of our employees? Anyone?"

A retired partner leaning on the far wall, an old man, who missed the excitement with apparently little better to do than hang around the headquarters, took the challenge. "Aye. Back in '59, if I recall properly, Clyde Witherspoon got offed by his man. Seemed Clyde was shagging the client's old lady. Got caught in flagrante and the client blew his pecker off." The old man shook his head and whistled in wonder. "Ten meters away, too. Quite a shot, that. Allowed poor Clyde a distressing moment or so to ponder the damage, then finished him with a shot between the eyes."

Pettlebone adjusted his glasses. "Yes . . . Well, thank you, Bertie."

After a quick survey of the young pups around the table Bertie smiled and replied, "My pleasure."

"Now, can anyone tell me why our client had only one bodyguard?"

"At his own insistence, I'm afraid," the head of scheduling replied with a disapproving frown. "We recommended four escorts in the strongest possible terms. The client wouldn't hear of it. Said it would be poor for business." He arched his thick eyebrows and looked up. "A record of that conversation is on tape, if you're interested."

Malpractice suits were rare in the trade, since potential claimants were usually dead, one of the few upsides in a business loaded with downsides. But they happened. The firm had been dragged through a highly publicized courtroom brawl eighteen years before. That experience still smarted: business did not recover for five years. Pettlebone was satisfied that the firm's backside was covered, and moved on. "And does anybody have a clue where our client disappeared to? Anybody?"

Apparently not. The best and brightest shuffled papers, sipped tea, and adjusted their striped ties.

"Right you are," Pettlebone said, placing his hands on the table and leaning forward. "Then let me hazard a guess."

The best and brightest collectively thought: Have at it, old boy. You always like your own theories better than ours anyway.

He lifted three long, bony fingers. "He's either running away from murder, kidnapped, or dead." They stared at the fingers and said not a word.

The collective response: Oh, spare me; a brain-dead copper two days out of the academy could summarize the obvious.

"But the former looks a little shaky, I should think we all agree." One finger flopped down.

The collective wisdom: You're getting warmer, old boy. That possibility was discarded by the rest of us well over two hours ago while you and your pathetic old chums were chugging sherry in your snooty, prehistoric club.

Another finger folded. "And the latter we can do little about but send a bucket of roses after the dust settles."

The collective rejoinder: In which case you'll fall back on your standard response — dodge for cover, shove the blame downward, and send three or four of us packing. The first report of Bernie's death was called into your office six hours ago; you fled for sanctuary in your club so fast there are burn marks on your office carpet. And how very convenient of you to forget your pager and cell phone, which we found conveniently stuffed in the bottom drawer of your desk, you sly old bastard.

"So why haven't we heard from his kidnappers yet?"

The collective response: twenty sets of eyes suddenly shifted upward, in the general direction of the ceiling. Why not, indeed?

Statistically, they all knew, kidnappers nearly always make their demands a few short hours after the fact. Like card players holding a blackjack, why let the pot get cold?

More shuffling of papers, more sipped tea, more tightening of ties. A recorder in the attic was silently capturing every word. The lads around the table had sat through Pettlebone's inquisitions before and to a man weren't taken in by his Socratic bullshit. The first fool who guessed wrong, on the record and imprinted forever on the device in the attic, would end up first on the chopping block when this crisis ended, one way or the other, and they shifted into the usual blamestorm.

Bertie, the retired partner, with nothing to lose, took a stab. "I don't suppose we'd hear anything if it's an inside job. These Russki millionaires are all surrounded by nasty chaps. Sleep with the wolves, one shouldn't wonder when one wakes up main course on a dinner plate. If it's insider work, the culprits aren't likely to bring in outside help, are they? What do you think?"

"Have we contacted his company?" Pettlebone asked, deliberately sidestepping Bertie's theory. The recorder in the attic was his own clever idea; he had no intention of leaving a magnetic trace that might not withstand scrutiny later.

Another of the bright lads in the middle of the table said, "I've spoken with his head of corporate security. Three or four times, in fact. Sergei Golitsin, a former KGB general.

Not a nice sort. The conversations weren't all that pleasant. Kept insisting that Alex's security outside Russia was our concern, not his."

"Had he heard anything from the kidnappers? A demand for ransom, a threat, that sort of thing?"

"Well . . . I did ask, sir."

"And?"

"He laughed, then cursed me and hung up."

"We're not going back to Russia," Alex announced with a very firm frown. After ten minutes of staring intently out the window, interrupted by occasional searches through the stack of passports on his lap, tossing ideas back and forth, he had finally made up his mind. "Too obvious," he announced.

"What's that mean?" Eugene asked.

"They're expecting it. In fact, they're hoping we'll try. We got lucky. I don't want to depend on luck again."

"Who's they?" Elena asked. Good question but one Alex didn't have the answer to.

"Certainly more than just Katya and Vladimir and the other goons we saw," Alex answered grimly.

"Did you see more of them?" Eugene asked. After all, his ass was on the line as well; naturally he wanted to know what he was up against.

"No, but they were too ignorant to put this together. They're working for somebody. And there may be . . . no, there definitely are more where they came from." But who knew how many more were in on this? They could be Mafiya, or they could be independents part-nered with the mob. For such a big score, there could be hundreds of them, possibly thousands.

And for sure, an employee, or a number of employees of Konevitch Associates, were in on it up to their larcenous necks. Somebody who knew Alex's travel plans. Somebody who knew the instant Eugene called his secretary to query about his whereabouts.

Alex knew exactly what this meant: some-body very high up in the corporate food chain was feeding the goons precious inside infor-mation and trying to put a noose around his neck.

He searched his mind, but quickly lost count of potential suspects. He now had several hundred former KGB people, more or less, on the payroll. Some were good people, smart, honest, and deeply relieved to be able to look themselves in a mirror with-out, for a change, wrinkling in self-disgust. Too many others were cutthroats in fancy suits. Nearly all were in security positions. Nearly all might have found a way to learn his travel plans. The security department was always notified in advance of his trips with a detailed agenda, a regrettable routine but one that was unequivocally necessary. Only a small handful, though, could've learned about Eugene's call to Sonja.

Where had it all gone wrong? Alex had once prided himself on personally hiring his chief lieutenants and a sizable number of his other employees as well. But the explosion of business happened so fast, Alex kept chasing more and more opportunities, and the need for more and more people became crushing. From one thousand to twenty thousand employees in less than two years. It was an old-fashioned gold rush: the lion's share went to the one who stampeded in with the most diggers and sifters. Supposedly qualified executives were being hired off their résumés, sans interviews, sans background checks, or even cursory calls to their former employers. Money beckoned. Each new opportunity begat others. Caution had long since been thrown out the window.

Greed. Money. He was printing it almost faster than they grew trees. They all wanted a piece of the action and too many were hustlers on the make. He swore to himself he would conduct a fierce purge when he got back and this was behind him. He could count on two hands the number of executives he fully trusted.

"Checkpoint's straight ahead," Elena announced, breaking into his deepening thoughts about who to sack.

Alex plucked two passports out of the stack, then carefully shoved the rest under his leg. Elena pumped the brakes and the car bounced and wrenched to a squealing halt. They held their breath and prayed.

The road was a two-lane, sparsely trafficked one surrounded by countryside and a light sprawl of quaint villages. The checkpoint itself was little more than a yellow crossbar, lightly manned, with a wood shack and a few flickering lampposts — nothing more than a hastily erected shelter placed there in the aftermath of the abrupt Soviet withdrawal and the helter-skelter opening of the borders.

A skinny young man in an ill-fitting green customs uniform approached from the passenger side. The sound of an angry generator, spitting and sputtering, came from behind the shack. No words were exchanged. He stuck out a hand and Alex, trying to match his air of lethargy, yawned and casually handed him two passports. Eugene shoved his out from the backseat as well.

The guard studied Eugene's first, then in awful English prodded, "You are American?"

"No, I'm from Brooklyn," Eugene replied with a stupid grin. The guard eyed him suspiciously, obviously unable to match a citizen from Brooklyn to the American passport. Just cool it with the wisecracks, Alex and Elena wanted to scream at him.

Eugene stuck his face out the window and smiled broadly. "Of course I am. Why, do you like Americans?"

"Oh yes. Americans good. Ronald Reagan is big hero for me. Every Slovakian loves this Reagan. He tells the Russians to go kiss his ass. You know him?"

The young guard was now smiling pleasantly. Not many Americans used this back-country crossing — in fact, none ever had, come to think of it. The heavy man in the backseat was the first American he'd ever encountered in person. He was obviously delighted and enthusiastic to try out his very limited English. Under improved lighting he looked barely old enough to be in high school, much less securing his nation's boundaries, with a lanky frame, pimply-faced, a pumpkin-sized head his features hadn't yet grown to fit. America was such a small land, of course everybody knew everybody.

"Oh . . . well, he's a dear old friend of mine. A dear, dear friend," Eugene rambled. "Ronnie and I . . . his pals call him Ronnie, by the way. Anyway, yeah, you could say we're big buddies."

"Ronnie. Yes, is better I think than Ronald. More friendly, yes?" The young guard was flipping through the back pages of Elena's passport, for no particular reason, since a Russian passport didn't require a visa. "He is really your friend?"

"I love him," Eugene declared loudly, anxious to like anything this kid liked. Stalin? — adore him. Liver? — my favorite meal. But it helped that it was true. He was a rich Wall Streeter and lifelong Republican without an ounce of guilt over the fortunes he'd made. He had no kind thoughts for those traitors from his tribe of millionaires who called themselves Democrats and did their best to get those tax-gobbling thieves back into the White House. Besides, it seemed like a great topic to keep this young guard's mind on other matters. Eugene told him truthfully, "I was one of his biggest contributors. Gave him lots of moolah. He had me down to the White House a few times. Nice place."

The guard was now measuring Alex's passport photo against his face. It was totally unnecessary. He was obviously dawdling to drag out the conversation. Why couldn't Eugene keep his mouth shut? Freedom was only ten yards ahead of them — if only Eugene would shut his yap.

The boy began thumbing through Alex's passport again, visibly more attentive to Eugene's ramblings about his hero than his work. He asked, not all that casually, "So you are big friend of Reagan's. Why then, you must tell me, you are traveling with these Russians?"

"Russians" spat out of his lips loaded with enough contempt to make it sound like he wanted to pull his pistol and blow Alex and Elena back to the gates of Moscow.

"They're old friends," Eugene replied, thinking fast.

A troubled look on the boy's face. He scratched his unwashed hair, shuffled his feet, and stared glumly at the passport. "This name, Konevitch, I think I have heard before."

"No surprise there," Eugene conceded in a quick rush of words. "Alex is . . . was . . . a dissident, a very famous one. He wrote brilliant essays about the rot of communism, they were smuggled out and published in the West." Eugene pushed his face closer and confided, "Guess how we met? Come on, guess."

Bunched shoulders. No idea.

"Ronnie introduced us. Get this — he told me personally that Alex's essays inspired him to tell the Russians to haul their asses out of East Europe."

The guard bent over and studied Alex's face more closely. His eyes narrowed and his lips scrunched with curiosity. Eugene's expansive lie suddenly did not appear all that clever. Alex tried to appear relaxed, humble, and proud, anything to look convincing. Would he become curious about Alex's injuries? Maybe he wasn't buying Eugene's bullshit. Or maybe he remembered exactly why the name Konevitch sounded familiar. Alex and Elena fought an overwhelming urge to hop out of the car and make a run for it. Just run as fast as their feet could go, flee into the nearest field, and hope the boy's marksmanship was as awful as his English. They squeezed each other's hands and prayed. The examination seemed to go on forever. "If he so famous," the guard eventually asked, fingering the passports, "why then you are traveling in this very awful car?"

Elena wagged a finger at that backseat. "In honor of our American friend." A knowing wink and she flashed her cutest smile. "We thought it would be fun for him to experience the full splendor of communist quality. He hasn't stopped complaining the entire trip."

The guard laughed, handed the passports to Alex, took a step back, and waved his arm. "Welcome to the *independent* Slovakian Republic. Drive carefully, if you please."

10

The drive through Slovakia to the airport proved mercifully uneventful. Slovakia, the former half of Czechoslovakia before the "velvet divorce" rendered it asunder, had at one time been its industrial breadbasket, a cauldron of sprawling factories that spewed out guns and bombs and other nasty devices for the Soviet army. That business had suddenly dried up: the country now resembled a ghost town; having survived sixty years of communism, it wasn't clear it would survive capitalism. The huge factories no longer belched smoke out of towering chimneys. Little traffic was on the roads.

They stopped at a roadside eatery and killed a few hours, engulfing coffee and battling to stay awake. Alex insisted on it. But even had Elena or Eugene considered it a terrible idea, they were not about to object. One look and they could see Alex was on his last legs. He slumped in the chair, could hardly lift his head, and rubbed his dislocated shoulder and kneaded his sore leg constantly. They could barely imagine how horribly his fried chest ached and throbbed.

The beating and torture had sapped his incredible energy. He spoke little, only when absolutely necessary. The words came out slurred in short sentences, almost a labored whisper.

Elena was worried about him. He should be in a hospital, for godsakes. Every bone in his body should be X-rayed, his wounds cleansed and rebandaged, his chest embalmed in a burn packet. Then he should be pumped full of miracle drugs until the grimness in his eyes melted, until laughing fairies were dancing inside his head. But a powerful sense of guilt was driving him, she knew. He blamed himself for this whole mess; for being rich enough that serious people would want to steal it; for not insisting that a hundred security men shadow him everywhere; especially, he was ravaged with regret for dragging her and Eugene into this.

And now he was shouldering full responsibility for getting them out of it.

The first round of coffee and pastries arrived. They dug in and ran through the situation. Alex summoned energy from some hidden reserve and summarized their situation. The easy passage across the border could be a sign that his fears were overblown, Alex told them; or it was just a fickle stroke of luck. So play it safe. Assume people were still out there, hunting, so they should drag it out awhile. With each passing hour, the searchers would become more tired. Tired meant sloppy. Better yet, it might mislead them into believing their prey had traveled much farther than they had. They would be forced to extend and widen their dragnet, increasing the chance of slipping through. When the time was right they would jump back into the car, drive straight to the airport, and have a quick look-see. If the airport was covered, this plan would go on the scrapheap, and they would devise another way to escape.

Elena wasn't sure Alex had enough left in him for this plan. A whole new one seemed out of the question.

So they sat and sipped coffee, the three of them, tense and keyed up. After the first cup, Alex excused himself and limped away from the table. By their fourth cup, Alex had returned. He collapsed into his seat and insisted they unwind and dwell on topics other than their troubles.

Eugene tried his best with lively tales about his slew of marriages, how they all belly-flopped into messy divorces. The stories were deliciously vulgar and quite funny. He had nicknames for each ex, wedded to a hysterical talent for mimicry. Number Two — Dallaszilla — apparently had an aggravating Texas twang, chewed loudly with her mouth open, and couldn't mutter a word without violently flapping her arms — a stuttering windmill stuck on overdrive. Eugene shucked his New York accent and produced an impersonation that was almost frightening.

This was the same ex who hired a PI to track her husband, then showed up at Eugene's suite at the Plaza, catching him red-handed with his newest mistress. The door burst open and Dallaszilla screamed and bellowed and howled with the unadulterated fury only a native Texan lady can manufacture. Her arms whipped around so hard, the mistress thought she was witnessing an epileptic fit and promptly dialed 911 for an ambulance. Eugene never spoke to the mistress again. He was furious with her. Forgiveness would never come. In court, he adhered to his lawyer's standard legal dictum — he denied, denied, denied — until three paramedics showed up to corroborate the affair. The judge happened to be a she, herself an aggrieved veteran of two nasty divorces with husbands who had philandered and then lied their way out of what she considered fair settlements.

His lawyer swore afterward that that gaffe cost him an additional five million dollars.

Elena found the stories hilarious. She laughed until it ached. For one brief, shining moment she almost forgot people were out there chasing, trying to murder them. Alex managed an occasional stiff smile, but had either heard the tales before or was pre-occupied, or exhausted.

They were back on the road at two o'clock. An hour later, after twice getting lost, they turned off a highway and entered the airport complex. Elena pumped the brakes and said, "You two get down. I'll cruise the terminal. See how it looks."

Alex reminded Elena, for the fourth time, "Be sure to check the cars in the lot," then both men tried their best to melt into the seats.

Crawling at fifteen kilometers per hour, Elena made a slow pass, quietly tapping the brakes and searching with quick shifts of her head. The airport turned out to be the aeronautic equivalent of a one-horse town, small, sleepy, with only one main building, and definitely shut down for the night. Few lights were on. A solitary janitor in loose gray coveralls was shoving a mop around the floor. That was it. She saw nobody else inside the terminal or loitering suspiciously in front of it.

Another twenty yards and a quick glance to her left. The parking lot contained only a few cars; all appeared dark and thankfully empty. Then, in one of them — yes! — in an other-wise dark car she could swear she saw the flicker of two burning cigarettes.

She slowed almost to a stop. She stared

hard at the car, then came to her senses, sped up, and retreated back the way they came, toward the capital. Alex and Eugene straightened up. "It's closed," she informed them, obviously surprised, obviously disappointed. "But in one of the cars in the parking lot, somebody was inside, smoking. I saw at least two cigarettes."

"You think it's them?" Eugene asked, bending forward with the help of Alex's seatback.

Elena replied. "I think they're just lovers too cheap to buy a hotel room. What do you think?"

"Yeah, I think it's them, too," Eugene answered.

Alex asked her, "What kind of car?"

"You know I'm not good with that kind of thing."

"All right, what color? This is important, honey."

"White."

"Not tan?"

"No, white. I'm positive."

"Big car, small car, medium, what?"

"A sedan. Fairly large. Four doors. I thought I saw an ornament of some sort on the end of a long hood. But it was dark, and by then I was scared, so I'm not sure. The car looked expensive, too, but how would I know? Are we through playing thirty questions?"

"Almost. Could it have been a Jaguar?"

"No, it was definitely a car."

Obviously they were through.

They drove for about five minutes in silence. A light rain began falling, and the wipers flopped wildly back and forth, never close to touching the windshield.

Apropos of nothing, Alex observed, "If you're interested, the doors to the terminal open at seven. A flight for New York leaves at eight every morning."

Eugene asked, "You knew the airport would be closed?"

"I thought it would, yes."

"And you knew about the New York flight?"

"Would it make a difference if I'd told you?"

"I don't guess it would, nope."

"But New York?" Elena asked.

"Yes, well, for one thing, the only open visas that match in both our passports are for America. Second, it's the one destination in the world where we'll be safe from these people. It's only temporary, anyway, until I get this cleared up."

Eugene remarked, "I'd offer you my place, but Maria will be there, and it's going to be a war zone."

Alex wasn't really in a listening mode and added, "We're not going together, anyway. It's time to split up."

"What's that mean?" Eugene asked, afraid he knew exactly what it meant.

"They're hunting three people, Eugene.

233

They believe we're amateurs and they believe we're afraid and insecure."

Believe? Well, they were certainly amateurs. And if insecure meant scared out of their wits, the bad people had it right on both counts.

Alex continued, "The point is, frightened amateurs stay in packs. They'll be looking for three of us, together, so it's time for us to divorce Eugene."

"You couldn't have picked a different word?" Eugene complained. Elena laughed, and Eugene joined her. Both were becoming giddy with exhaustion and the unrelenting tension.

Alex turned around and faced him, his face rigid with concern. "Eugene, you're a target because you're with us. They blew the chance to get your money. Nothing can bring it back, and they know that. Whoever they are, they're professionals. They don't care about you anymore."

"Hey, I'm having a ball being shot at, chased, and hunted by Mafiya goons," Eugene felt like saying. "This is the best idea I've heard all night, so fine, dump me off right here." But his conscience bothered him. Instead he said, "Look, what the hell, I'm in this up to my neck already. You're my friends and I'd like to make sure you're safe. Are you sure this is a good idea, Alex?"

"I'm not sure about anything at the moment."

"Except this, right?"

"Yes, and I won't change my mind. The very least I owe you is to get you out of this alive."

An unspoken thought lingered in that statement. Alex obviously wasn't optimistic about his own chances. Eugene looked at Alex and thought about arguing. It would be useless, though; Alex's mind was clearly made up. "What do I do?"

"Drop Elena and me off at the nearest big hotel in Bratislava. Find another hotel, check in for the day, catch up on sleep, find a nice restaurant with pretty waitresses, have a long leisurely meal, then drive back to Budapest and catch the first flight home. By that time, I assure you, the people hunting us will believe you're long gone." It was obvious he had thought this through.

"What about you?"

"We'll catch taxis from the hotel. Don't worry, I think I know what I'm doing."

Twenty minutes later, Alex and Elena stood beneath the overhang of a run-down hotel in downtown Bratislava. The streets were empty, the doorman was inside, napping. They watched Eugene putter off in the junkheap, spitting and spewing smoke out the noisy tailpipe.

Alex turned to Elena and said, "Now we

can discuss our plan."

"We couldn't discuss it in Eugene's presence?"

"He's better off not knowing. If the people chasing us get their hands on him, it's his best defense. Ours, too."

For the next few minutes, they stood under the awning and Alex told Elena what he hoped would happen.

11

The two taxis arrived at the terminal thirty minutes apart.

Alex was dropped off first, at 6:45.

Elena stepped out onto the curb at 7:14, a minute earlier than she'd been instructed, though it turned out not to be relevant.

Her instructions were clear and precise: Drive by the front of the terminal. If Alex wasn't standing and waving, alone, then howl at her driver to keep going and don't look back. Once they had Alex, they wouldn't care about her anymore. They wanted her only to get to him; if they had him, she was old baggage they could care less about. What was left of Eugene's 2,000 American dollars was wadded up and folded inside her bra. Use it, he told her, to find her own way to America, then contact her parents for help. Start a new life and don't look back.

But Alex was there, about twenty feet from the doors, waving, not directly at her, it seemed, but at some invisible person off in the distance. She tried hard not to stare at Alex as she walked right past him, then through the glass door and straight to the Continental Air counter. Yes, she had a reservation, she assured the smiling lady behind the counter. She held her breath and handed her passport across the counter. She was reaching into her bra for the money when the woman politely announced that the ticket was already reserved and prepaid, first class — and did she care for an aisle seat or window? Boarding started in fifteen minutes; she was welcome to use the VIP lounge until then. She had no idea how Alex arranged this, it wasn't part of the plan, but she smiled with relief and pleasure as the lady behind the counter ruffled papers and prepared her boarding pass.

First class? After all they'd been through, the idea of making a grand escape sipping champagne and munching on caviar seemed too good to be true. She felt like crying.

She sensed him before she saw him. A middle-aged man in a nice gray wool suit was staring at her. A quick glance in his direction, and he looked away. She took the ticket envelope from the smiling Continental representative and walked briskly in the direction of the VIP room. She kept her back turned to him for a few moments, then performed a pirouette that would earn a standing ovation. She looked him dead in the eye. The man almost jumped, before, suddenly, he discovered something on the magazine rack more interesting than her.

Her first thought was to scream. Just aim her arm at the man in the suit and scream full blast until her lungs hurt, until airport security rushed over to see what the fuss was about.

She kept walking instead. There was a knot in her throat and she tried hard to ignore it. She was an attractive woman, after all. Men stared at her: so what? She usually just ignored them. She was just on edge, she told herself. Paranoid people see big toothy monsters with lethal claws where others see squirrels. Maybe that's all it was, a sad, lonely little squirrel checking out the talent and dreaming of what would never be. She arrived at the door to the VIP room, looked back over her shoulder again, and there he was again, brazenly walking toward her! A little smarter, because his face was covered with a magazine. But the gray suit was a dead giveaway.

She was just raising her arm and preparing an earthshaking scream, when a firm hand grabbed her from behind. Panic enveloped her chest. She spun around, ready to kick and slap and howl like hell — it was Alex. "Don't worry about him, honey. Come on, step inside."

She stepped through the doorway and followed Alex to a table by the near wall, far away from the windows. Another man, this one in a blue wool suit, was seated, with his back against the wall, looping peanuts into his mouth. "Good morning, Mrs. Konevitch," he said, grinning between hard crunches. "I'm Eric. That fella outside's Jacob. I don't want to imagine what you've been through the past eighteen hours, but your worries are over." Another peanut in the mouth. "Jacob's watching the door and inside this VIP lounge is my territory. No bragging, but we can handle whatever comes up." A gentle slap on his forehead for effect. "Oh yeah, we're your Malcolm Street boys." The accent and demeanor were obscenely American — a thick twang ruthlessly tortured the vowels, broad, confident smile, black hair, tall and well built. Eric was leaning back on the chair, trying to appear relaxed and carefree. But Elena, the dancer, missed nothing about the human form. The body was coiled, ready to leap the length of the room and snap necks if the situation required. Ruthless blue eyes that never stopped wandering even as he spoke to her.

"Come on, Mrs. Konevitch, relax. You're safe. Take a load off your feet, please." He shoved a chair back with one hand, while the other hand plopped another peanut into the air; it sailed a full six feet before it fell and landed effortlessly in his mouth. His eyes never stopped darting around the room.

Elena nearly fell on her knees and kissed him. Eric in the nicely tailored blue suit could probably shoot with both hands simultaneously, hurl knives with his feet, and work an impossibly difficult crossword puzzle without missing a vowel. Let the bad guys try anything now. Eric would stack their bodies like cordwood.

The peanut fling was Eric's favorite trick, one that never failed to put the client at ease. That big lapdog smile again. "Fix yourself a cup of coffee. Don't skip them pastries, either," he suggested. Another peanut in the air — whoosh, it landed and was instantly compacted between two fierce incisors.

Alex took her arm. "Let's get a cup of coffee and talk."

They moved hand in hand to another wall where a wooden table sagged under the weight of coffee and tea urns, an enormous stack of pastries, and large containers loaded with eggs, bacon, flatcakes, and a few mushy concoctions unidentifiable to anybody but a Slovakian native. The smell of fresh-ground coffee was impossible to ignore. The only thing keeping her on her feet was the five cups she had swallowed at the café.

That half-life had expired an hour before.

Alex handed her a cup and saucer. "When I called the headquarters of Malcolm Street last night, they were in the midst of a meeting about our situation. A witness claimed I murdered my own security escort back at the Budapest Airport. It's —"

"What? That's ridiculous, Alex. Who claimed that?"

"A woman. A Russian woman. Her story was corroborated by her Russian boyfriend."

"Ridiculous. They murdered your bodyguard and now they're blaming it on you?"

"Yes, with a poisoned dagger, probably at the same moment as the kidnap. The security firm is dispatching a team to clear this up with the Hungarian authorities. There are big holes in the story. The woman's passport is a phony. The hit was professional and I'm an amateur. They're confident they can make this disappear."

Elena filled a cup with coffee. She snatched a Danish off the tray, stole a tentative nibble, and followed it with a deep sip. She couldn't remember anything tasting better in her life. "And they sent Eric and his friend to watch over us?"

"Eric and Jacob were covering a client in Prague; they were ordered to drop everything and rush here. That was them in the white Jaguar sedan last night."

The careful nibbling was over. She took a powerful bite from the Danish, neatly amputating half of it. "That was them? Smoking inside the car?"

"Not exactly."

"Then who?" she asked.

"You don't want to know."

"If you ever expect to sleep with me again, you'll tell me." The other half of the Danish disappeared into her mouth and she chewed it with vigor.

"Okay. Eric and his partner arrived about an hour before us. They drove by, just like we did. Two men were loitering outside the terminal. At nearly two o'clock, in front of a closed building, the killers couldn't have been more conspicuous or sloppy. Whoever's behind this apparently doesn't hold a high opinion of us. So Eric snuck back on foot, surprised the two men, and forced them at gunpoint into their car. The cigarettes belonged to the pair of thugs he captured. Eric was interrogating them."

"And what did they say?"

"They claimed they had no idea why. Just had orders from their boss to kill us."

"Who was this boss?"

"A name neither of us would recognize. It's irrelevant. They're part of a crime syndicate, gunmen at the bottom of a long chain doing what they were told."

"Where are they now?" At the bottom of a deep river, she hoped. After murdering one man, brutally torturing her husband, and trying their best to add three more kills to the tally, she hoped the weasels died slowly and horribly.

"I didn't ask," Alex replied. "I don't think either of us want to know."

"Don't be so civilized. I'd love to know."

"I doubt we would hear the truth, anyway."

Eric was suddenly standing at their side, as if he had materialized out of thin air. Tell me, did you kill them, she wanted to demand, and don't go light on the details. "Time to board," he said with that reassuring grin. "Jacob and I are on the flight, too. We don't get first-class freight, but we'll be tucked in the back in seats where we can observe you. So don't you worry. Kick back, drink all the champagne you can stand, eat till your stomachs are sore, then nap till that pilot says you're in New York."

The plane lifted off ten minutes after they boarded, at which point Alex and Elena were downing their second champagne, with plans to keep sipping until New York or they passed out, whichever came first.

Elena eased back into her seat and asked, "Will the bodyguards stay with us in New York?"

"No," Alex said, waving at the stewardess for a refill. "My company paid the bills. Somebody in the security division last night faxed a termination order to Malcolm Street, effective upon delivery. The people after us are thinking of everything."

Elena paused to think about that. "That's not a good sign, is it?"

"It's a terrible sign. Whoever's behind this obviously has control over my companies, for the moment anyway. But Eric and Jacob will stay with us until we're safely checked into a hotel. After that, we're on our own."

"And the crooks have all our money, right?"

Alex pushed back his seat, extending it fully to the reclined position; the champagne was working its medicinal magic and taking the edge off his physical pain. He closed his eyes. "Not without my account numbers and security codes, they don't. They're locked in my office safe. Until we get this cleared up, though, I can't access that money," he said. "Except for $2 million tucked in a Bermudan bank. A rainy-day fund I never imagined I would have to use. The account numbers for that fund are in my head, so no matter what, they can't touch it."

"Was that the best you could do?" she asked, laughing.

Alex was asleep already.

Three sets of steady fingers punched the keys in unison. The clack of computer keys was the loveliest sound Golitsin could remember, a rich symphony in synchronized harmony.

The operation lasted ten minutes. He stood, arms crossed over his stomach, watched over their shoulders, and enjoyed every minute of it. Clack, clack, clack — another five million sent here, another ten million there. Money was flying everywhere, massive electronic whirls of cash, shuttling from Konevitch's accounts to banks in Switzerland, Bermuda, the Caymans, and a few Pacific islands with tortuous names nobody could pronounce. Who cared to? The money would barely touch down, gather no dust, then clack, clack, clack — scatter off to the next bank. The wonderful process would proceed for hours.

Within ten minutes after opening time that morning, Alex Konevitch's immense personal hoard of cash was gone. Nearly two hundred million sprinkled around the world like fairy dust. The operation had been planned with exacting precision and rehearsed until the fingers of the pianists peering into the terminals ached and stiffened.

At noon, it would all be bundled back together in a dark Swiss vault where nobody could touch it but Golitsin.

In his pocket was the secret code for a new account at yet another Swiss bank only he had access to. He would sneak upstairs, punch the number into a computer he would dispose of afterward, and transfer all that money into a hole nobody could find but him.

A thirty-minute break for lunch. At one o'clock, the computer wizards would reassemble and the process would start again. This time on the hoards of savers' money in Alex's banks. Clack, clack, clack — not all of it, only fifty million, but enough that Alex Konevitch would be charged with looting his own bank and absconding into the sunset with that pretty little girl bride of his.

Two business reporters from *Kommersant,* the Russian equivalent of the *Wall Street Journal,* were at that moment cooling their heels downstairs. They had been promised the story of the year, how that wunderkind Konevitch had proved to be a rotten crook but was thoughtful enough to leave behind a letter transferring his businesses and properties to his trusted former chief of security.

"Yes," Golitsin would tell them with an appropriately grave nod, "for the sake of the twenty thousand employees, and for our valued customers everywhere," he, General Sergei Golitsin, "would restore the blemished reputation and keep the business up and running." Maybe you noticed the new sign over the headquarters entrance?

Golitsin Enterprises — it has a nice ring, don't you think?

By close of business the haul would be complete. Two hundred million of Alex's cash, plus fifty million more stolen from his banks — $250 million in liquid cash. Then, Alex's shares in his companies would be split with his co-conspirators, leaving Golitsin with probably another hundred million in stock. A moving van was already parked in front of

Alex's Moscow home, unloading the new owner's possessions.

■ ■ ■ ■

BOOK TWO:
THE EXILE

■ ■ ■ ■

12

September 1993

The promised call from Moscow had not been returned at ten; it was now eleven, so it was likely another broken promise, one in a long string of dashed hopes. Alex stood by the hotel window and stared down at the chaotic street seven stories below. Among the wash of humanity below, his eyes picked out the businesspeople — the lawyers, the money-men, the entrepreneurs, the two-bit hustlers — scurrying around this loud and important city in search of the next deal.

Alex's mind was locked firmly on the last deal.

From the bed, Elena kept a wary eye on him. She was deeply worried about him, but so far had not broached those thoughts. The bathrobe that hung loosely from his shoulders had not been removed in days. A man who put punctuation points on restless and driven, the past week had barely crawled out of bed. Ordinarily he required a mere three or four hours of sleep to recharge his juices; he was now edging toward twelve. The room-service meals were nothing short of delicious — at these prices, they better be. He shoved the food around on his plate. He squished everything into mush and rearranged it all into untidy puddles. The fork rarely left the plate; it even more rarely went near his lips. Elena calculated he had shed at least fifteen pounds.

He looked gaunt and haggard, thoroughly beaten. An insomniac in reverse; the excess sleep had left him listless and drained. The change since their arrival day in New York nearly three weeks before was more than alarming and there was no bottom in sight.

After they hopped off the plane at JFK Airport, they had dashed through customs and hijacked the first available taxi for a fast sprint into Manhattan, where they checked into this plush suite in the Plaza. After quick showers, they slept three hours. Then Alex dragged her out of bed and they flew out the door. They raced to and through a few local shops, pausing only long enough to stuff a few bags with new clothes, toothbrushes, razors, shaving cream — enough essentials, and no more, to squeeze through two fast and furious days, Alex insisted.

Moscow beckoned. Two days was pessimistic, he warned her; half a day was more like it. Yeltsin might even dispatch a military plane to haul them back. Should he request one? he openly wondered. No, he would demand it — along with an armed military escort to keep the bad guys at bay, an armored car for the ride home, and an army of investigators to round up the crooks. A quick dash around the corner and he darted into a crowded office supply store. Alex emerged a short while later loaded with furious determination, typing paper, a few notebooks, pens, a cell phone, a laptop, and somewhere in this frantic rush he found software to convert the computer fonts to Cyrillic.

That afternoon, fully armed, Alex began his all-out assault on Moscow. He set up camp in the nicely equipped business center on the ground floor of the hotel. With care, he selected a small desk in the far corner of the room where foot traffic was minimal. With his arsenal of pens and pencils, his supply depot of notepads and stacks of typing paper all neatly arranged, he plugged in his computer and launched in, daring anybody to poach on his turf.

For seven frenetic days, Alex lived there. He bombarded Moscow with phone calls and faxes. Between his new cell and the landline in the business center, he often had a phone loaded in each fist, sometimes speaking into both at once. His voice was enraged but controlled, precise, and quick. His ability to explain the story improved with each retelling, becoming shorter, honed to the gory essentials. Sometimes he juggled the listeners and bounced back and forth between conversations. The pace never withered except when Elena enforced a cease-fire long enough for hurried visits on doctors and dentists to repair the damage inflicted by Vladimir. If the ministrations took too long, Alex cursed and walked out. The leg was slow to heal. He lurched and hobbled from one lamppost to the next, in a crippled race back to the hotel. He couldn't wait to return to his battle station, to fire off another fusillade of phone calls to anybody who would listen, the next flurry of faxes to whoever promised to read them.

After seven long and exhausting days, the assault faltered almost as suddenly as it began. By day eight, it waned to a dull skirmish — a few aimless shots fired without energy or optimism. Nothing but lingering echoes of a battle that had been desperately waged and apparently conceded.

"Come back to bed," Elena told her husband, fluffing his pillow and giving it a loud, inviting smack.

"I'm not tired."

"Neither am I. We're in a glorious luxury suite in a great city. Make love to me, Alex."

"I'm not in the mood." A moment later, with his back still turned, "Sorry."

"Listen to me, Konevitch. I am so in the mood I caught myself winking at the toothless old homeless guy across the street. His name's Harry. He's heavy, and dirty, and has only one eye, but sort of a cute butt. Now get in this bed and do your damnedest to satisfy me before Harry shows up."

He never turned around — never even glanced at the skimpy black teddy she had secretly purchased the day before at Victoria's Secret and slipped into two minutes before in the bathroom. Two thimbles and a string would've been more modest. Nearly two hundred dollars for barely three ounces of fabric, but that was the whole point. She had painted her face, something she seldom did. Her golden locks were brushed to a high glean. She had saturated herself in so much perfume, a thick mist of vapors hovered around her skin. She was taking no chances. No corner had been unpampered or overlooked or spared. A bottle of ridiculously expensive champagne cooled its heels in a frosted bucket beside the side of the bed.

She had schemed and prepared this seduction. If she had to slam his head with a mallet, he would damn well get in the mood.

In a marriage that rarely passed three days without sex, Alex had not been Mr. Ready-and-Able since Budapest. He was in a black depression, trapped in a bottomless funk, and she would do her damnedest to bring him out of it.

She climbed out of bed and approached

him from behind. She grabbed his arm and spun him around. "Look what I bought for you. And I damn well better hear a gasp," she ordered. With that, she pranced and strutted and flaunted her sculpted dancer's body shamelessly, like a brassy stripper.

Three weeks before she wouldn't have made two steps before he tossed her on the bed and the ravaging began.

Ten steps. Twenty steps. Thirty.

He crossed his arms and weathered the distraction.

The hussy routine came to an abrupt halt. She squared her shoulders, took a deep breath, and looked him dead in the eye. "Get on the bed, now," she demanded, pointing a finger in that general direction.

"I warned you, I'm not in the mood."

"I can see that, Konevitch. But I bought this silly outfit, and primped and plucked my eyebrows and shaved my legs, and now I look like a whore, but I did this for you. You're not getting out of this if I have to kill you."

He took in the flared nostrils, the sparks in the blue eyes, the gripped fists, and he made the only sensible choice: a swift, meek retreat to the bed. He sat stiffly on a corner, enough to placate her — enough also to signal his stubborn indifference.

She sat on the opposite corner. She crossed her legs and for a moment did not say a word. Then, "Tell me what's happening. It's my life, too, and you're keeping everything to yourself."

"I'd rather not talk about it."

"I'd rather you do. No, I insist."

"Are we having a fight?"

"Not yet." She pulled a pillow over and rested it against her back. "But we're about to have a bloody world war if you don't tell me what's going on. I'm not bluffing."

"I don't want to depress you."

"Your depression is depressing me. Frankly I don't care if we lost everything. I'd actually be quite pleased if somebody else is now living in that musty old mansion."

"It's a good thing. I did, I lost everything. The money, our homes, our companies . . . everything."

"I thought the money was safe."

"Apparently they found the account numbers and security codes. They were better prepared than I anticipated."

"Well . . . it's only money, dear."

"A million or two is *only* money, Elena. But two hundred million in cash, and stock worth another hundred million, I think that deserves a slightly better modifier than '*only* money,' don't you?"

She had no idea it was that much. "Yeltsin won't allow it. He owes you everything, Alex."

A long sigh. "I can't get through to him. And believe me, I've tried. I've called his office countless times, and flooded it with faxes."

"Maybe he's busy. I'm sure that's it. This is urgently important to us, but I think he has a few other problems on his plate."

"No, I'm being stonewalled. I call and get foisted from one unimportant assistant to another. I know damn well what's going on."

"Okay, what is going on?"

"Somebody inside is pulling strings. Somebody clever and powerful enough to block me from Yeltsin. Each time it's a fresh new assistant, each time I have to start over from scratch. They're taking turns. They're trying to wear me down, and it's worked."

"You're smarter than they are, sweetheart. Shift your approach."

"Do you think I haven't attempted that? I tried every path into the Kremlin I could think of. Among many others, I've contacted the minister of security, the secretary of the Security Council, the minister of finance, the mayor of Moscow, even the chairman of the Central Bank."

"And what do they say?"

"They said it sounded terrible and promised to look into it." He turned away from her and stared again at the window. "That was last week's line. Now they won't take my calls."

She reached over and hauled the champagne bottle out of the bucket. Over the long days and nights they had stayed cooped up in the hotel she had managed to make only one friend, Amber Lincoln, a large, warm-hearted black woman who ran the phone bank in the basement. During Alex's week of furious activity, as Alex ignored her and as the switchboard people in the basement pulled hairs to keep up with his incessant requests for calls to various numbers in Russia, Elena had considered it the least she could do to reward their help by bringing food and an occasional bottle of wine.

This had been her only respite from Alex's bout of frenetic activity, and now his dark mood.

Champagne and sex were long overdue.

Her tiny fingers worked the aluminum cover before she handed off the bottle to Alex for the honors. "What do you think is going on?"

"Sergei Golitsin."

"The security chief? That ugly old toad?"

"He put this together, he and all the KGB crooks he brought into the company with him. He took over my company, and now has the nerve to rename it after himself. He stole everything I built, everything, Elena. He's now living fat and happy in our house."

He can have it, she thought, but said, "Everybody knows it's your company. He can't just steal it."

"Last week he fired every vice president.

Called them all into my office, and ordered them to depart the building immediately. Armed guards pushed and shoved them out onto the street. Remember Mishi? He said it was the most frightening moment of his life. Even before they were called in, Golitsin's thugs already had taken over their offices." Alex rubbed his eyes and stared off into space. "All those decent, hardworking people, now they're out on the street, unemployed. It's my fault."

"How was it your fault?"

"I was stupid. And worse, careless. I became desperate after the killings, so I brought Golitsin in to protect the company. I've thought about it for days, and the pieces have fallen into place. From the very beginning he was plotting to steal it. I'm a fool."

"No, you're brilliant. You're the most talented man I ever met, and the most decent. You just don't think like they do." He was gripping the bottle tightly, and she took it away from him. He was the least self-pitying man she'd ever met, but he was utterly miserable. Then again, everything he had built had been stolen, his life turned upside down. The frustration was boiling his soul. She went to work on the cork. She squinted and grunted and twisted with all her might.

Alex seized it back. A single hard wrench and — *POP* — gold liquid gushed over and dribbled onto the carpet. The bottle cost two

260

hundred bucks. Every drop was precious. She bounced off the bed and made a hasty scramble for the flutes.

Alex said, "The story spent five days on the front page of every paper in Moscow. I'm accused of stealing from my own banks and running off with the money. Can you believe it? They stole my money and they're blaming it on me. The prosecutor's office in Moscow is conducting an investigation. I'm being framed, and I'm not there to defend myself. I'm sure they'll issue an indictment."

She handed him a pair of tall crystal flutes she had borrowed from the dining room downstairs. He slowly filled them, one for her, one for him. She grabbed her flute and inched a little closer. Little of what he was now telling her was news. Over the past few days she had sneaked downstairs to the privacy of Amber's office and made her own calls back to Russia. She had her own sources, and if her husband kept her in the dark, she would use them.

Her family and a few close friends had fully apprised her about what had happened, the whole ugly story. For a few terrible days, Alex had been the talk of Moscow, with considerable interest throughout the rest of Russia. The story was irresistible and the press lunged into a predictable frenzy — on TV, in newspapers, and in magazines, Alex was loudly tried and all but convicted. The millionaire genius was on the lam. He had stolen the money and fled. Behind the glitz and glamour, behind that mysterious façade of quiet brilliance, he was nothing but a two-bit crook, a highway robber with a swollen IQ in a nice suit.

The day the news broke there was a frenzied stampede on Alex's bank: after two frightening days, though, it quickly stagnated to a mild panic. Only fifty million was supposedly stolen — a small drop from a massive bucket. And twenty percent interest, after all, was still the sweetest deal in town. The commercials with the lovely girl who adored men with interest and the treacly old couple fondly eyeing their shiny Mercedes flooded back onto the airwaves. Much of the money that had raced out limped back in.

As usual, the initial spate of news stories was brief and shallow and disgracefully inaccurate. Few details were known beyond the basic fact: Alex Konevitch was a lying, conniving thief who took off with a fortune. But somebody kept dropping more and more tips, inflaming interest in a bonfire that required no fuel. The stories turned longer, the lies more sensational and deceitfully toxic. Alex stole fifty million, a hundred million, a billion! He was holding out in a jungle palace in Brazil, guarded by snarling bandistas, flipping the bird and daring anybody to come after him. Using a false identity, he had checked into one of those California detox clinics, and now was doing cumbaya with the doped-out, besotted dregs of Hollywood. He was hiding here, in Moscow, in a plush safehouse protected by fierce syndicate killers in exchange for a cut of the loot.

The theories about Alex's wheres and whys changed daily. Alex had snapped under the pressure and flew out the door, laughing deliriously, hauling grocery bags leaking cash. Alex had plotted this theft from the start. Everything he built and accomplished was only to create the edifice for a massive heist; the only mystery was why he waited so long. Alex was bipolar and Jekyll finally smothered Hyde. A war was waged on the front pages as each paper tried to outdo the newest disclosures, the wildest suspicions. The same paper that dubbed him "The Kid with the Midas Touch" rechristened him "The Kid with the Sticky Touch."

Fortunately for Alex, Russians are bred to be jaded and skeptical. After seventy years of communist manipulation and distortions, any news fit enough to print was bound to be twisted enough to disbelieve. Besides, fabricating conspiracies is part of the Russian national character, and this story hit the street pregnant with lush possibilities. Golitsin's long career in the KGB did not work to his favor. This sounded like something the bad boys from the Lubyanka would cook up; and as everybody knows, old toads don't change their warts. Rumors and theories flew around Moscow, and ran heavily in Alex's favor.

Foul play was suspected, though nobody could put a finger on exactly how Golitsin pulled it off.

But the incredible idea that Alex would plunder his own bank and, before racing out the door, take the trouble to legally transfer everything he owned — not to his partners, not to his businesspeople, but to his chief of security, of all people — smelled rotten. What sense did that make? Besides, why would he care who snatched up the crumbs he left behind? And only fifty million from his bank customers? For a man rumored to have billions? Why squander his reputation and name for pocket change? And if he was willing to snatch fifty million, why leave behind billions more?

Even among those skeptics, however, very few pitied Alex. A rich man brought down, big deal. It was funny, actually. Live by the dollar, die by the dollar, seemed to be the general sentiment among a nation of former communists. Besides, nothing satisfies the average Ivan more than the spectacle of a high-and-mighty chopped down to his knees. Alex's downfall was weighed and deliberated around dinner tables with no small measure of delight.

"So what's next?" Elena took a long sip from the flute.

"I honestly don't know. I've tried everything I can think of."

She was now pressed firmly up against him, and between sips and explanations, he was stealing furtive glances at her threadbare teddy. She lowered her left shoulder and encouraged a strap to slip off. "What's the worst that can happen to us, Alex?"

"This is the worst."

"No it's not. Not by a long shot. We could be back in Budapest, dead."

"True enough. But if we return to Moscow, that could still happen."

"But they can't drag us back to Russia, can they? Without an extradition treaty, they can't touch us. They can add a library of charges but you're here. If they try, we'll just stay here."

"You wouldn't miss Russia?"

"A little, sure. But alive anywhere with you is better than dead there. But one thing's going to change."

He turned and looked at her.

"We're in this together. I wasn't involved in your business back in Moscow, I didn't need to be, and frankly I never cared to be. But our lives are different now. Our marriage changes with it."

"What does that mean?"

"From now on, no matter how depressing,

keep me informed of everything. I'm scared, but I'm not some breakable china doll, and I won't be treated like one."

"I'm sorry."

"Don't be sorry. I love you, and I want to help."

He put his arm around her. Elena slid back and dragged him down onto the bed. The champagne flutes tumbled to the floor. Three weeks of pent-up energy and the frustration of three hundred and fifty million in stolen dollars and stocks were compacted into the first long, smoldering kiss.

The expensive little teddy was quickly ripped off — it sailed through the air and landed on the lampshade. Alex paused only long enough to ask, "What time did you tell Homeless Harry to be here?"

13

The black limo idled in an otherwise empty parking lot that overlooked the ice-cold Moskva River. Mid-October. The sky was gray, overcast, and dreary; another winter that threatened to be long and harsh had produced its first cold snap. The driver had been ordered out of the car. He stood some twenty feet away in the bone-aching darkness, smoking, shivering, stamping his feet, and eyeing the heated car with considerable bitterness.

Three people sat in the rear.

They had agreed to meet like this, one or two days each week. They were bound together by the money and the single enduring emotion that thieves hold for one another: poisonous distrust. For obvious reasons, the three could not be seen together in public under any circumstances, so Golitsin took the initiative and arranged the inconspicuous rendezvous.

Tatyana Lukin sat in the middle, her splendid legs skillfully folded, impossible to miss or ignore. The men who were seated on each side of her — Golitsin to her left, Nicky her right — could barely stand the sight of each other. Golitsin hated to have his authority questioned. Nicky detested authority generally, and loathed Golitsin's prickly brand of it particularly.

Both men were arrogant, selfish, pushy, ill-tempered, and crooked to the core. They had so much in common it was scary. One was brains, one brawn, and for this to work they had to remain together. She was a woman; she could handle them. Without her to referee, they would have their hands around each other's throats in seconds flat. Tatyana liked to be needed.

She was saying, "I lost count of how many times he called. More than a hundred, probably. We're running an office pool. The operators in the basement are given a daily tag sheet of who to put the calls through to. Yeltsin still has no idea Konevitch is trying to reach him. He's seen the summaries of the news accounts, and heard —"

"And what was his response?" Golitsin interrupted.

"He called in my boss . . . the chief of staff," she added for Nicky's edification. "Said this did not sound like Alex. He wanted Konevitch tracked down so he could hear it straight from the horse's mouth. Asked my boss what he thought."

Golitsin smiled and rubbed his hands. "I'm sure you had already explained to him what he thought."

The answer was too obvious to merit a response. "He told Yeltsin he always considered Konevitch a conniving crook. Charming and likable, perhaps. But for sure, nobody earns that kind of money, they steal it. Warned him that he always believed Yeltsin allowed Konevitch to get too close. Whatever emotional or political bonds they shared, the only tangible connection was money. Konevitch didn't contribute all that cash out of the goodness of his heart. Plus, the Congress is filled with mutinous former communists who want to cut Yeltsin's balls off. He's walking a tightrope between trying to placate them and the frustrated reformers in his camp. They're always threatening to impeach him, and here's Konevitch, making a huge splash on the front pages. Exactly the kind of connection Yeltsin doesn't need."

Nicky yawned. Politics bored him to death. It made absolutely no difference to him whether commies or democrats or pansies in birthday suits were in charge. His business was bulletproof regardless of whichever idiots ruled the land.

"Did Yeltsin buy it?" asked Golitsin.

"He wasn't *not* buying it. He knows he's got enough problems already. There are dirty rumors regarding his daughter flying all over the city. She has almost literally hung out a sign saying, I'm daddy's little girl — leave your bags of cash here and I'll twist old poppa around my pinkie and bring home the goods."

Nicky perked up at this hint of corruption in high places. "Is it true?"

"Yes, and stay away from her," Tatyana warned with a knowing wink. "She doesn't know it, but she's already being investigated by the chief prosecutor. Bugs and undercover cops surround her everywhere she goes."

Nicky laughed and slapped his thighs with a loud thump. At least his brand of crook made no pretenses.

Golitsin merely grunted. He already knew about Yeltsin's daughter, of course. He could in fact educate Tatyana about how much little Miss Piggy had stashed in a Swiss bank, the account numbers, who gave her the money, and why. It was invaluable knowledge he had no intention of sharing.

"Tell you what, babe," Nicky announced. He leaned toward her and his left hand landed with a lecher's grip high on Tatyana's right thigh. "You still gotta get Konevitch. Put up all the roadblocks you want, eventually he's gonna find a way to get through. You thought about that?"

A twitch of irritation crossed Golitsin's face. "We'll take care of it," he sneered in Nicky's direction.

"Yeah? Like you took care of him in the first place?" Nicky snapped back.

"Stick to your own business." The two men glared at each other, Golitsin's face glowing with anger, Nicky sneering, as if to say, "You couldn't find a needle if it was sticking in your ass."

Tatyana waited until the men cooled off, then said to Golitsin, "Where's the money?"

"Tucked away in a safe place."

"I know that. Where?"

"None of your business."

"Okay. Will you take a little advice?"

"That depends."

"Don't be that way, Sergei. I'm looking out for all our best interests."

Golitsin sniffed and stared straight ahead. Bullshit. Given half a chance she'd rob him blind. She was smart and beautiful, and utterly without a conscience.

Tatyana plowed on. "You know why Konevitch was so popular with Yeltsin and his people? Money. He bankrolled Yeltsin's election. He bought them all their jobs. Literally. An election is coming in another few years, and believe me, they're scared. Yeltsin is being blamed for the mess we're in. His popularity's in the toilet and it'll take a load of cash to get him out of it. They'll miss Mr. Moneybags."

"You're assuming he'll still be alive in another year."

"I assume nothing. I'm just telling you there's an opportunity for whoever's clever enough and rich enough. Somebody is going to pump cash into the big hole Konevitch left. Why not us?"

Golitsin thought about it a moment. What was there not to like? Nothing, really. A million a year could buy a world's worth of influence; a few million, in the right hands, at the right moments, and who knew? It was a no-brainer, actually — he was only surprised he hadn't thought of it himself. He puffed a few times, stretched out the contemplative pause, then nodded. "Let's do it."

"Good decision," Tatyana said. "Funnel it through me. I'll make sure everybody knows where the money came from." And who inside the Kremlin arranged this infusion as well, though of course there was no need to point that out.

"How much are we talking?" Golitsin asked, suddenly concerned because it was his money.

"Not much. Relax, Sergei. A hundred or two hundred thousand a month, for starters. As the election draws closer, we'll increase it, have a real impact."

She had clearly thought this through and prattled a bit about the details — plans for secret bank accounts, blind contacts, how the money would be laundered, and so forth and so on, the typical architecture for large-scale graft and bribery. The irony that they were using Alex's money to replace Alex was lost on none of them. In fact, Golitsin had arrived at this meeting ready to pitch and hatch his own bright new idea about how to spend more of Alex's hoard of cash, and was waiting impatiently with his hands clasped to pop it. But Tatyana's suggestion fit right in, so he let her rattle on.

As soon as she finished, he said, "Do we all agree this has worked out beautifully?"

Nicky had been staring out the window. But he swallowed his usual nasty cynicism, looked over, and admitted, "Yeah, it's real sweet."

Tatyana merely nodded.

"Then why stop now?" Golitsin asked them, shifting in his seat and facing them. "There's lots of little Konevitches out there, building businesses and creating millions that are just waiting to be taken away."

Tatyana appeared thoughtful, though she had long held the same idea. The only surprise was that it took Golitsin so long to broach this rather obvious inspiration. In her mind, all along Alex Konevitch was just a guinea pig, a test case for them to see if they could pull this off and get away with it. Young millionaires were growing on trees these days, just waiting to be fleeced. But she played dumb and asked, "Do you really think that's a good idea?"

"It will even be easier next time, less risky.

None of the other rich kids have Konevitch's warm relationship with Yeltsin. We now know how it works, and we've got plenty of money to use for whatever we try. We'll get even better at it."

Nicky replied, predictably, "What's in it for me?"

Tatyana, speaking as the lawyer she was, answered, "Right now, Nicky, you get what our agreement called for, your share of company stock, and Konevitch's banks to launder your money. But you and the rest of your syndicate pals are making a very big impression. You've turned Moscow into a bloody war zone. The Russian people are screaming for law and order. Believe me, it's a sore topic in the Kremlin these days. The world is paying close attention to your fun and games, too. Yeltsin is tired of being lectured by Americans and Germans about getting your ilk under control."

"Talk, talk, talk."

"Not much longer, believe me," she replied, wagging a finger in his face.

"They have to catch us first."

"Adapt to the new rules. People now vote, Nicky. They make their displeasure known at the polls. Yeltsin knows he has to show tangible progress on the law-and-order front, and soon. A big crackdown is around the corner. Believe me, plenty will be caught."

"The dumb ones."

"That's right. The smart ones, like you, will get ahead of the curve."

"I like what I'm doing now."

"How much do you score in a year?" she asked him.

"Plenty."

"Don't play games, Nicky. How much?"

"Millions. I don't know. Thirty, maybe fifty." Twenty was more like it, but with Golitsin in the car he wasn't about to sound like a small fry. He squirmed in his seat and tried to look sincere.

"Not bad," Tatyana commented, arching her eyebrows. "How much did Konevitch make last year?"

"A lot, I guess," Nicky replied through gritted teeth. "I don't know."

"Around two hundred million. And there are others, like him, who will soon be hauling in billions. All of it considered legal, too."

"Billions?"

"Billions," she repeated, with cool enunciation, as if the word picked up velocity the more slowly it was pronounced. "It's time to take your game up a notch, Nicky, climb out of the gutter. Keep your whorehouses and drug business if they amuse you. But the real thievery, the big money, will be in big business. Billions, Nicky, billions."

Nicky adored that word, "billions." It rolled out of her lips so beautifully. She could repeat as often as she liked.

They chatted on a while, and — while the driver's toes turned black — settled on an equitable division of labor and responsibilities. Golitsin would scout the possibilities, determine the targets, and apply his devious talents to designing the takeovers. They had done it once, and the blueprint was perfectly adaptable for the next victim. Tatyana would build the political cover, grease the right palms, and buy their way into the hearts of Yeltsin's people. Nicky would continue to push whores and dope and gray-market cars, and bide his time until he was told who needed to be terrorized, or chased out of the country, or murdered.

The conversation ended right where it started, on the perplexing issue of Alex Konevitch. Nicky wanted him dead — as soon as it could be arranged, however it was arranged. Just dead. In a business with few troublesome principles, Nicky steadfastly adhered to one: the fewer witnesses the better.

Golitsin, too, wanted Konevitch dead. Very, very dead. For a man whose emotions generally veered between heartless dispassion and expressive fury, he had developed a fatal preoccupation with Alex Konevitch. It was unhealthy, he knew, he just couldn't help himself. He enjoyed thinking about how Alex would die.

Also, though nobody needed to mention it,

if Konevitch did eventually make contact with his old pal Yeltsin, this whole thing could come apart. The lush owed the boy wizard a huge debt. And no matter how hard Tatyana schemed and conspired, eventually Alex would break through — there were too many loose threads, too many suspicious connections, too many holes that could spring leaks. And as with all criminal conspiracies, they would inevitably be pitted against each other. The three of them knew beyond a shadow of a doubt that they would gladly hang the other two, if it came to that.

A legitimate investigation conducted by any halfway honest and competent official would be a catastrophe.

Tatyana confidently assured her partners she had a plan for their boy Alex, and ordered them to cool their heels until she told them otherwise.

The combination of champagne and sex worked like magic. The past three nights Alex had slumbered a more reasonable six hours. He was eating again, even exercising for two hard hours every morning in the nicely equipped hotel gym.

He was toweling off after a shower, preceded by a fierce early-morning workout. Elena lay on the bed nibbling toast and browsing through the morning paper. A delicious breakfast of eggs, bacon, toast, and fresh coffee had just been wheeled in for Alex when the phone erupted.

Elena was closest, and she lifted it up, expecting it to be room service. She listened for a moment, then in Russian said, "Yes, he's here," and handed the phone to Alex. "Some officer from the Ministry of Security."

Alex put the phone to his ear and identified himself.

"This is Colonel Leonid Volevodz, special assistant to the minister of security." The voice was deep, with the clipped, irritatingly authoritative bark of a career officer.

"What do you want?" Alex replied in kind, in Russian.

"I have your number because a week ago, the minister asked me to look into your complaint."

"Pass him my thanks." He squeezed his eyes shut, and for a brief moment found it hard to speak. "What have you found?"

"What have I found? Well, there are . . . shall we say, certain irregularities and incongruities in your story."

"You think I'm lying."

"Don't put words in my mouth, Mr. Konevitch. I think there also happen to be big holes in the reports about what happened."

"Then why don't we discuss those holes?"

"Fine. For starters, on the fifth, you flew on Flight 290 to Budapest. The —"

"Yes, I —"

"Don't interrupt me, Konevitch. I will talk and you listen until I ask you a question. Are we clear?"

The arrogance was so thick the man probably was exactly what he claimed to be, a high-ranking bureaucrat in an important ministry. Alex drew a long breath and said, "No more interruptions."

"One more and I'll hang up. Now, where was I? Ah yes . . . the flight manifest confirms this. Also, Hungarian customs show you arrived there at 1:05. Nothing shows that you reentered Russia, yet bank records indicate your personal accounts were emptied out the morning of the sixth. A few hours later, fifty million more was stolen from your customers. The terminals that ordered the transactions were traced back to your own headquarters." He paused a moment, then asked, "What am I to make of this?"

This was the first time Alex had heard the precise details of the thievery, and he spent a long painful moment taking it in. Oh, how he would love to have Golitsin seated in a chair in this room, to have his strong hands gripped around the old man's throat. He would squeeze and squeeze harder until every last detail poured out. How did you get into my safe? Where did you send my money? Who's in this with you, and where is it parked now? Alex said, "I was on a plane to New York during that time. If you read my fax, you'd know that. It's easily confirmed."

"I read your fax, Mr. Konevitch. But that's not the only possibility, is it? Maybe you had an accomplice who moved the money."

"But I didn't. Is that all?"

"Not quite. From the Central Bank, I obtained copies of the letters assigning your properties to Sergei Golitsin. One of our handwriting experts gave your signature a look."

"Go on."

"The writing is pinched, nonlinear, and extended. He believes it is your writing. But perhaps scrawled under conditions of discomfort or duress."

"After three hours of beating and torture, it wasn't my best work."

Elena handed Alex a piece of buttered toast and a cup of coffee. She raised her eyebrows. He answered with a wavering hand. He took a large bite and washed it down with coffee.

After a long pause, the colonel said, "About the fax you sent the minister, it raises many provocative questions. For instance, you implicate General Golitsin."

"I didn't implicate him, I said very clearly that he was behind this. He had people murdered, he had me kidnapped, he had me tortured, and he stole everything."

"We are talking here about a very distinguished man. A patriot who served this country nobly for many decades. These are serious charges. I need to question you directly."

"Fine. I'm in New York. Come and ask whatever you like."

"Not possible. My jurisdiction ends at the Russian border. My friends in foreign intelligence are understandably territorial. They become quite touchy if I forget my place."

"All right. We'll handle this by phone. Ask whatever you like."

"That is . . . unacceptable."

"Is it? Why?"

"For one thing, the case is very complicated and implicates some very important people. For a second thing, I like to see the face of the man I'm interrogating. And of course, everything will have to be checked out. Over the phone won't work."

"Neither will coming to Moscow, Colonel. They tried to kill me and they might want to finish the job. I explained that in the fax."

"I will personally provide for your security, Mr. Konevitch. Arrangements will be made. You have my word as an officer."

"I don't even know you."

"Look, the state prosecutor is preparing an indictment. Do you want your name cleared or not?"

"Don't ask stupid questions. I'm not setting foot in Russia until I read in the paper that Golitsin and his people are under arrest."

A long moment passed. It sounded to Alex like Colonel Volevodz had a hand over the mouthpiece while he conferred with somebody. Alex munched toast and drank his coffee.

Volevodz came back on and suggested, "Why don't we meet on neutral ground?"

"Who were you speaking with?"

"Are we having trust issues, Mr. Konevitch?"

"No, no issues. I don't trust you."

A long pause, then, "That was my secretary. Another call has come in that I need to take. Quickly, Mr. Konevitch, do you want to meet or not?"

"Make it a *very* neutral place, Colonel."

"Berlin. Is that neutral enough for you? You know Checkpoint Charlie?"

"Of course."

"Tomorrow, be there at three. Don't be late."

14

Colonel Volevodz had a crooked sense of humor; or, at the very least, a wicked conception of irony. Checkpoint Charlie, for four troubled decades, had been the fabled symbol of a divided world — socialism versus capitalism, the free world versus the chained one. This was where hooded prisoners had been exchanged between East and West, where tense, shadowy bargains had been fashioned that kept both sides from blowing each other into overradiated rubble.

Alex and Elena had caught an overnight, landed at stately old Tempelhof Airport, and took a fast taxi to a modest gasthaus near the city center, in a nontrendy neighborhood, an anonymous little place off the beaten track. They checked in under false names; they paid with cash.

The recently reunited Berlin was a boomtown. Towering cranes poked at the sky like a thick forest. Construction crews seemed to outnumber the city's population by two to one. Real estate prices in the eastern half of the city were racing to catch up with the inflated prices in the west. The West Germans were stumbling over themselves to gentrify their neglected, prodigal brothers to the east.

Alex stared glumly out the window during the taxi ride and fell ineluctably back into an old habit. Fortunes were being made all around him, new buildings being thrown up at a dizzying pace, a whole city being refashioned before his eyes. He conceived of ten ways he could edge himself into this market and produce millions. He felt like an Olympic sprinter whose legs had been amputated, seated in the bleachers, watching the rookies take their victory laps while he stared on in frustration, hobbled, unable to compete.

At three o'clock, Alex stood alone, at the west end of Checkpoint Charlie. The guardshacks, the lights, the swinging gates were still in place, unmanned though, and all too happily neglected. The long, narrow alley was now little more than a tourist trap, and a very popular one. People of all nationalities and complexions loitered around in herds, snapping pictures of the remains, wandering through the museum of a now dead era, pausing to ogle the graying old photographs of desperate people employing desperate, and often brilliant, means to escape the horrors of communism and make new lives in the West.

Volevodz kept Alex waiting twenty minutes. The message was unmistakable. You're an ex-mogul, a wanted felon, a sorry thief, a loser. I may be only a lowly colonel but I'm your only hope and you'll kiss my boots or else.

Colonel Volevodz finally marched around the corner of a short gray building, a middle-aged, tall, thin man in civilian clothes wrapped in a rumpled trench coat. Two young assistants dressed nearly identically accompanied him, both slightly behind, one to his left, one to his right. They strutted in step, like conquering military men, across Checkpoint Charlie from the east, no doubt attempting to concoct a cinematic entrance. The colonel stopped about two feet from Alex. They eyed each other suspiciously for a moment.

The colonel finally put out a hand. They shook without enthusiasm. Volevodz pointed at his two colleagues, who kept their hands in their pockets and edged a little closer. "Captains Kaputhcuv and Godunov. They're assisting me with this investigation."

"Thank you for coming," said Alex without a trace of warmth. He had dressed carefully for this meeting — the same tailored suit he had escaped in, cleaned and neatly pressed, with a stiffly starched, monogrammed shirt and silk tie completing the ensemble. He looked every bit the big-deal gazillionaire who could roil entire markets with a swipe of his pen.

"So, where is your wife?"

"Around."

"You are alone, then?"

"But you're not," Alex answered without really answering. "I'd like to see your identification."

"I don't believe you should be making demands, Mr. Konevitch. You're a wanted man in Russia."

"Welcome to the new Russia, Colonel. I'm a taxpayer with rights. You're my servant now. Identification, please."

"I can arrest you right now and drag you back to Russia. I'd be a big hero."

"Then welcome to Germany, too. You have no legal authority here."

The colonel's hands were in the pockets of his trench coat. Alex studied him carefully. He had a thin face, thin eyes, thin lips, and close-cropped hair molded to conceal a thinning spot on top. The face was neither mean nor nice, neither handsome nor ugly; the prototypically stonewashed face of a career Soviet functionary. He pushed one hand toward Alex — something round and hard poked forward against his trench coat. "Here's all the authority I need. My assistants are also armed. I can kill you right here." He paused to produce a hard grin. "Maybe I will."

Alex upped him with a tight smile. "A bad idea. For you and for me."

"To the contrary, it would be a great idea. It would solve a lot of problems."

"Look behind me at that big gray apartment building."

Volevodz's gaze left Alex's face.

"Keep going," Alex ordered, following the colonel's roving eyes. "Third window down on the right side. See the barrel pointed out the window?"

Volevodz's mouth nearly fell open when his eyes finally settled on something long, cylindrical, and dark poking out a window.

"Look long and hard, Colonel," Alex said. "That's one of three snipers I hired to protect me. If I lift my right arm, you're dead, all of you. If I die, you're dead. I had hoped not to do this, but . . ." He cranked his right arm halfway up, nearly to his waist.

Volevodz computed the new situation very quickly, then, in a fast rush of words, said, "Put it down! For godsakes, put your arm down."

"Hands out of your coats. Palms up. Shut up and do as I say. Show me your identification — then, maybe my arm will come down."

The hands popped out and so did the identifications. The hands were trembling. Alex glanced dismissively at the official-looking IDs in the fists of the two captains and snatched the colonel's for a closer inspection. It looked genuine enough, but what did he know? He threw it back.

Volevodz caught it and slipped it back inside his pocket. "You're not behaving like an innocent man, Mr. Konevitch."

"I wasn't treated like an innocent man."

"You've just threatened the lives of three officers of the Ministry of Security. This will be added to the already grave charges against you."

"You won't believe how much that worries me. Are you wired?"

"Why would I be wired?" Volevodz replied with a sneer.

"You wouldn't necessarily. I'd just like to be sure our frequencies don't interfere with each other."

"Oh . . . I see."

"You threatened to kill me. It's on tape. Who sent you?"

He stared at Alex a moment. Alex had chosen to stand in the middle of the check-point, well away from any walls or protective cover of any nature. Why was now clear. Volevodz and his assistants were trapped, out in the open, wildly vulnerable, and he briefly pondered the interesting question of how many bull's-eyes were painted on his forehead at that moment. He tried a smile and said, "I think we've gotten off on the wrong foot."

Alex crossed his arms and stopped smiling. "I'm here because you promised to help me.

You show up instead with guns and threaten to kill me. You have an interesting definition of a wrong foot."

"All right, all right. I made a mistake, a big one. I'm sorry. Let's start over." He tried to force the smile, and tried his damnedest to make it look friendly and sincere. "Can I call you Alex?"

"Sure. Why not?"

"Okay. Alex, as I said yesterday, I'd like you to return with me to Russia. If, as you claim, you're innocent, you can clear this up in court."

"Don't make me laugh. I won't be alive long enough to make it to court."

It was obviously a waste of time for Volevodz to contradict him; he'd just threatened to do the honors, here, now, in Germany, in a supposedly neutral corner. It was even more foolhardy to attempt to worm his way into Alex's confidence. A group of blond-haired, blue-eyed tourists wandered past, gibbering in some strange tongue. The eyes inside the skinny slits danced around a moment, then Volevodz observed, "There's a lady over there filming us with a camera."

"It's about time you started paying attention. Yes, you're being filmed, yes, your voice is being recorded, and yes, a bunch of guns in the hands of seriously nervous people are being pointed at you. At least four of these tourists wandering around are my people.

They're all armed to the teeth in the event you have friends lurking nearby. Don't try something stupid; I'm a very frightened, very desperate man. Any second I could maybe forget, and reach up, wipe the sweat from my forehead, and you'll all be dead. Now, why are we here?" Alex suddenly flapped his arms up and down, half slaps on his thighs like a penguin. "Quickly, Colonel."

"Settle down, Alex. I'm not here to kill you. I have a bargain for you."

"I'm listening."

"Stop that with the arms. It makes me nervous."

"Speak faster. My nose itches."

"All right, all right." He rubbed his eyes. Alex's preparations were not a total surprise. After being briefed on his unexpected escape from Hungary and the clever stunts he had pulled off, he had been warned to expect some sort of shenanigans. But Alex's eyes seemed to be boring into his soul, and he was having difficulty trying to maintain his nonchalance. "Certain friends are very impressed with your financial acumen. Frankly, it's a shame you've been chased out. You're a national asset for Russia. We admire what you accomplished."

"Who are your friends?"

"Powerful people."

"Give me some powerful names."

"Don't waste both our time. I don't know

all the names, anyway."

"All right, go on."

"They would like to enlist you to manage their finances. The money is parked offshore. You never have to come to Russia. It's work you certainly know how to do."

"And what do I get out of this?"

"Twenty percent of the profit. The fund contains hundreds of millions right now, but eventually will grow to billions. Your take, obviously, will depend on how well you invest it. It will be a reasonable compensation."

"Is the money clean or dirty?" Alex asked, ignoring the offer.

Volevodz shrugged. "What's clean money in Russia these days? Anyway, why should you care?"

"I don't. What about the case against me?"

"As I said, these are powerful people."

"How powerful?"

"Arrangements can be made." His forehead wrinkled and he pretended to think about it awhile. He reached up and massaged his sore neck. Alex towered a good six inches over him and had chosen to stand nose-to-nose. Volevodz was a tall man himself, used to being looked up to, and he hated having the role reversed. "A few witnesses might materialize and clear your name. The state prosecutor assigned to your case is a very reasonable sort. For a judgeship and a healthy contribution to his retirement account he might be persuaded to declare the case a dead end."

"Stop lying. My story was spread all over the front pages for weeks. I find it hard to believe it could be easily disposed of."

The colonel enacted a small shrug. "Sadly our police and courts are so overburdened, there is little pressure to close cases. Besides, in Moscow these days, a new scandal always eclipses the last. Such are the times you helped bring about, Alex Konevitch."

"What about my money?"

"Don't think of it that way." He attempted a feeble smile and placed a hand on Alex's arm.

Alex shrugged it off and backed away a step. "I was beaten and nearly killed. My wife was kidnapped and threatened. Three hundred and fifty million dollars were stolen from me. My businesses have been ruined and I've been publicly disgraced. How should I think of it?" Alex asked carefully, coolly, without a trace of rancor — a businessman dispassionately listing the credits and debits from a register.

"Water under a bridge, if you're smart. Or, if you like, a down payment on a new future. You're an exceptionally talented man, Alex. We're offering you the chance to make it all back."

"How kind of you."

"Get over it. In a few years, with a little elbow grease, you'll be right where you started. Maybe richer."

This offer was the last thing Alex had expected, and he needed a pause to consider what he was hearing and learning. It was almost laughable. Almost. Volevodz obviously was another cog in the rapidly growing conspiracy that robbed his life. Now they were offering Alex the chance to take the money they stole from him, to invest and nurture it, and produce fabulous profits that would make them even richer.

In return he would get a fraction of what was already his. It wasn't enough that the sharks took everything from him; they now were offering to make him a slave to their financial interests. And it was slavery. They would own him, a deal with the devil, and once he was in there was no way out.

They had his money, his companies, his homes — they now wanted to own him.

In fact, it was beautiful — for them, anyway. Alex would be the offshore front for their illegal activities, he would launder their money, keep it hidden and growing, and if anyone got wind of it, Alex would be there, the disposable frontman, holding the bag.

"You're a liar and the people who sent you are thieves," Alex said very simply, a fact he managed to express without sentiment. "So why should I trust you?"

"Do we have a deal?"

"Not yet. You're moving a little fast for me."

"I'm offering you a chance to live. Let's say you don't take this deal, okay? We'll hunt you down and kill you." ⁻

"I thought we were negotiating. Now you're making threats."

"All right. Negotiate."

"Twenty percent is too cheap," Alex told him. "A deal like this needs to be structured. If I increase the value of the fund ten percent or less, twenty percent is all I deserve. But if I beat that, my percentage needs to increase accordingly. Cap it at thirty percent if the value increases by fifty percent or more."

"What if you lose money?"

"I won't."

"You're quite the optimist, aren't you?"

"I gave you the pessimistic scenario. And any smart businessman builds in incentives to encourage better performance. I'm more than confident that I will easily produce returns surpassing a hundred percent a year. In that case, I'd like a five million bonus on top of the thirty percent."

Volevodz turned and traded surprised looks with his two assistants. "The man has balls."

"If you weren't a fool, you'd know I'm being generous. Find yourself another man with a track record like mine, the terms will be even stiffer. There are people on Wall Street who demand thirty percent even if they don't make you a dime. And if they know the money is tainted, or in any way questionable, they'll demand at least sixty percent. Don't take my word for it, ask around."

Volevodz became fidgety. "I will have to discuss this with my friends."

"Of course you will. You're an errand boy," Alex said, twisting the knife a little deeper. "You and I are through speaking. The next conversation will be with your boss or no one," he added. "If it's another rude flunky I'll hang up and never take another call."

Volevodz's eyes narrowed. Oh, how he was tempted to whip out his gun and blow this impertinent punk back to New York. He would, too, would smile and blast away, except he was at a severe disadvantage with all the guns pointed at him. "I'll bring it up," he mumbled, biting his lip.

"One other matter I'd like to bring to their attention."

"What?"

"Given my history with these people, I want some form of assurance I'll get what I earn."

"Like what?"

"I'm not sure yet. I'll think about it." He backed two steps away from Volevodz, then stopped and, treating it like a careless after-thought, warned, "Move two feet or make any effort to follow me — so much as tug a cell phone out of your pocket — and the nervous people with guns have orders to blast you to pieces."

Volevodz's mouth gaped open. A team of

five stalkers lurked around the corner, awaiting a call from their boss to jump on Konevitch's trail and track him to his lair, where they would add a little more pressure and help Alex make the right call.

He shifted his feet, suddenly remembered Alex's warning, and froze. He briefly pondered the amazing question of how he had been so thoroughly outwitted by a complete amateur. But before Alex could escape, he remembered to ask, "How do we reach you?"

"Same as before. Tell your boss to call my hotel in New York."

With that Alex turned his back and walked purposefully toward the west and freedom and Elena, who was pacing nervously behind the large gray apartment building, praying they had not overplayed their bluff. They held hands tightly and briskly walked two blocks, caught a taxi, got lost in the traffic, and eventually made their way back to the gasthaus.

Volevodz and his two aides stood in place, nervously wringing their hands. Their eyes never wavered from the window ledge six floors above. As long as the barrel never budged, neither would they. A flock of giggly Japanese tourists mistook them for tired old spies, perhaps sharing a reunion in a place of former glory, swapping lies and inflating old adventures. The tourists spent five minutes snapping pictures of the three scowling men in wrinkled trench coats. A bus arrived delivering a fresh batch of rambunctious tourists, who piled out and were instantly drawn to the attraction. Erupting with laughter, they yanked out the cameras and joined in the fracas. They were third-rate actors hired to lend a little authenticity to the site, one tour leader helpfully explained to his entourage, who laughed louder. "Absolutely third-rate!" one of the crowd yelled back. How badly the three men wanted to yank out the guns and start blowing holes through the crowd.

They felt like boneheads. Nobody spoke, nobody moved, they just gaped at the barrel pointed out the window.

After twenty excruciating minutes, they drew verbal straws. The taller of the two captains lost and gently inched forward, slow, limited scrapes across the cement, before he squeezed his eyes shut, uttered a loud curse, and hopped three rapid bounces. No shots were fired. No bodies bounced off the concrete. They threw caution to the wind and raced toward the base of the apartment house. They drew their guns and pounded heavily up the stairwell to the sixth floor. Puffing from exertion, they found Alex's hired sniper there, directly underneath a hallway window: a mop head rested on an overturned metal trash can, with its rusty metal pole poking out the window.

The three men stared at one another with

disbelief that quickly turned into red-faced humiliation. No debate was required or entertained; agreement was quick and unanimous — this petty detail would obviously only add unnecessary clutter in their report to Tatyana Lukin.

They were tired of hotel rooms. They wanted to get out and wander around this glorious city that reeked with such historical significance, to venture out and feel the soul of the German people. But they wouldn't. They agreed that it was too dangerous. It made no sense at this point to risk being picked up by Volevodz and his goons. Room service was contacted and they ate a quiet dinner in the room together.

Over dessert and a glass of wine Alex shared the details of the offer. Elena listened and withheld comment. The pros and cons were obvious. They were tired of living on the run, tired of looking over their shoulders, tired of going to bed each night and awakening each morning imagining the worst. And no matter how much Alex exercised, he was a man of restless energy and incredible intellect that needed an outlet. But the offer was humiliating, a disgrace, really. Still, the prospect of neutralizing the bad people trying to kill them had its pluses.

"What will you do if they meet your demands?" she finally asked.

"I may take it."

"Do you think Golitsin is behind the offer?"

"I seriously doubt it. I think he wants me dead."

"Then who?"

"That's the question. There are so many possibilities. I know of only one way to find out."

"So you intend to take the offer to discover who's involved," she suggested.

"That's the idea. If I say yes, I'll look for a way to smoke them out."

"Why you?" she asked, sipping from her wine. Good question.

"Partly because they're still afraid of me. That's why they want me inside and neutralized. Why else are they still working overtime to keep me away from Yeltsin? Bring me in, and they buy my silence."

"What's the other partly?"

"Golitsin has a partner. That's obvious. Somebody inside Yeltsin's inner circle, I'm nearly certain. But think about this, Elena. We know the syndicates are involved. We know Golitsin and his KGB friends are involved. And now this man Volevodz and his deputies show up."

"You think he really is with the ministry?"

"I'm sure of it. I made a call to a friend in Moscow and had him checked out. He's former KGB, but he's now exactly what he claims to be. And he is, in fact, conducting the investigation."

"So this conspiracy is quite big."

"Getting bigger by the day. It would help to know exactly who and what we're up against."

"And then?" Elena asked.

"I find another way to get to Yeltsin. I'll have names and evidence to shove in his face. If they can do this to me, Elena, they can do it to anybody. I'm sure they will. And if that happens, the damage will be immeasurable. Nobody will want to put money in Russia."

She was dressed in a long tight dress with a slit that stretched all the way to her waist; it clawed even more provocatively higher when she moved. The dress was not expensive and didn't need to be; she could justify drools in kitchen rags. She entered the restaurant and wound her way through the tables, where her date for the evening awaited impatiently in a long cushioned booth in the back.

Golitsin had arrived ten minutes earlier. He was deep into his third scotch, a fine, imported blend he had acquired a taste for during his years in the KGB.

The restaurant was the most exclusive and most breathtakingly expensive in Moscow. At that moment, anyway: city hot spots fluctuated monthly, and after three weeks of endless lines, of thousand-dollar bribes to the owner for a reserved table, this place was peering at oblivion. The tables were filled with other crooks and entrepreneurs who were choking down caviar by the bushel and gulping enough champagne to float the Russian fleet. Enough cigarette smoke filled the air for an artillery duel. Beautiful women seemed to be littered around every table, hanging lustily on the arms of seriously rich men, laughing at full volume over the slightest ping of humor, generally working hard to ingratiate themselves enough to let the party last another day, another week, another month, before they were replaced by a more eager bimbo with longer legs and a louder, faster quick-draw giggle.

Long live capitalism.

"Nice place. You have good taste," Tatyana said, smiling nicely, not meaning a word of it.

Golitsin did not get up or even acknowledge the phony compliment. She slid into the booth across from him and offered a nice flash of thigh. Her blue blouse was cut precariously low — if she tripped, or stooped even one inch forward, her breasts would flop out.

"How are things in the Kremlin?" Golitsin asked.

"Tense. Always tense. Disaster always lurking around the corner."

The waiter rushed over. She ordered British gin, straight up, no water, no ice. Golitsin tipped his nearly empty glass and signaled for a refill. A small band sat in the corner, dressed as Cossacks, playing old Russian folk songs to an audience playing a new Russian game.

Golitsin informed her, "Let me tell you why we're here. I'm hearing rumors."

"What kind of rumors?"

"Bad ones for the lush."

"How bad?"

"The reactionary forces are going to take him down."

"They've been promising that for years."

"They're beyond promising. They're hiring hooligans off the streets, arming them, and preparing a showdown."

An eyebrow shot up. "How reliable are these rumors?"

"Believe them. My old KGB friends say it will happen any day."

"What about Rutskoi? He involved?" she asked in a low whisper, meaning, of course, Aleksandr Rutskoi, Yeltsin's vice president, a war hero from the Afghanistan debacle Yeltsin had taken aboard in the hope that Rutskoi could calm down the right-wing wackos and former communists who loathed Yeltsin with a passion that bordered on madness. But the marriage was ill-conceived and soured from the start. It sped bitterly downhill from there. They were very different kind of men: one malleable and political down to his under-wear; the other the sort of military man who adored absolutes in everything but his own ethics. Aside from a few organs the only thing they shared in common was that they were both legendary blowhards with a bottomless lust for power. The two men now barely talked. Rutskoi schemed and plotted with his friends and allies in the Russian version of a Congress, undermining Yeltsin and his reforms at every turn. And Yeltsin worked hard to return the favor. Stealing a note from his American friends, he pushed his vice president into the shadows, and shoved him out the door every time there was a funeral anywhere in the world. "The Pallbearer," Yeltsin called him with considerable malice.

"In it up to his hips," Golitsin confirmed, finishing off his scotch.

Her gin arrived. She took a long, careful sip. "I know you hate him, but it would be bad luck for us and our plans if Yeltsin was toppled right now."

Barely paying attention, he now was looking over her shoulder at a man who had just swaggered through the entrance. Six leggy women of identical height and approximate weight and anorexic build were hanging off his arms, all with their hair died bright red, all dressed in identical red evening gowns. He thought at first he was seeing double, or triple, and it was time to cut back on the hooch. What a glorious time to be ridiculously rich and Russian.

"Maybe there's an opportunity in this for us," she suggested.

That got his attention. He shifted his rear and bent forward. "Like what?"

"Your old KGB friends now run the Ministry of Security and the security services. If there's bloodshed, they'll be Yeltsin's only hope."

"Yes, they will. What do we get in return?"

She was about to throw out an unconsidered answer when what had been a loud argument at the next table turned dangerously louder. Two millionaires were enjoying a heated argument over a business deal gone sour, both in full throttle about who had outcheated whom. One leaped from his chair and drew a gun. The two lovely blonde bimbos who were their evening entertainment screeched and hit the floor. The gunman was red-faced and howling curses, aiming the pistol in the face of the man across from him. It was such an everyday mess in Moscow business circles that the other patrons mostly ignored the fracas. They went about their meals, the girls laughed, the champagne flowed. Fortunately, like nearly every business in this raucous, crooked town, the restaurant had a protection contract with a crime syndicate. Two burly men hustled over, blackjacked the gun wielder into unconsciousness, kicked and pummeled him a few times out of habit, and dragged him out by the legs. Tatyana exploited the brief entertainment to ponder Golitsin's question more deeply.

The moment things settled down, she suggested, "How about this? In return we name the new attorney general."

It was a brilliant idea, of course. Golitsin saw the possibilities immediately. If they owned the attorney general, any potential Alex problems would go away. Nor, as they gobbled up other companies, would they have to look over their shoulders; they wouldn't worry about the legal authorities because they owned the head honcho. He bent farther forward and asked, "You think Yeltsin will bite?"

"If we time it just right, what choice will he have?"

He folded his hands behind his head and leaned back into his seat. "Wait till the blood is running, till the standoff reaches full pitch. Till he's absolutely desperate and has no choice. Great idea."

"Exactly. Can you deliver the Ministry of Security?"

He chuckled. Stupid question. "I'll appeal to their patriotism and I'll spread money around like there's no tomorrow. They may have demands of their own. I'll tell them to make a list."

The waiter arrived. It was nearly midnight, so they both went for the special, boar au gratin, which materialized almost instantly. Large slabs of it, buried under a ton of gooey white cheese and thick gravy. She drank measured sips of champagne with her meal, he stuck with scotch and drank without letup. She nibbled carefully and economically from the feast on her plate, he stuffed everything into his mouth and chewed with noisy vigor.

She stayed on small talk, but had another topic to discuss. A delicate one, and she wanted his stomach full and his incredible intelligence watered down with liquor before she made her move.

After desserts were delivered, she asked, "How do you like your new house?"

"It's wonderful." He tried to keep the nasty smile off his face, but couldn't help it. "I love sleeping in Konevitch's bed, knowing I took it from him. I hope he and his lovely brat are sleeping on a hard, bug-ridden bunk in a flophouse, surrounded by smelly winos and hacking dopers, and thinking about me."

"And how is business these days?" she asked, though she already knew the answer. She was sure he would lie.

As she guessed he would, he said, "Fine. Money's pouring through the doors."

She looked down and played with the silverware beside her plate. "I heard three of the subsidiaries are already bankrupt."

"Small setbacks," he replied smugly, waving for the waiter to haul over another glass of hooch. "We didn't want to be in hotels or restaurants, anyway. Lousy businesses. I'm getting rid of the bloat Konevitch left behind."

"Two more banks were just granted state licenses to exchange foreign currencies. You now have serious competition."

"They'll have to catch up to me. I won't make it easy."

"You kicked your price up to five percent for every ruble exchanged. They're offering two percent."

"Well, I give better service."

Better service, my ass, she wanted to say. Golitsin's posse of former KGB morons were ripping the guts out of Konevitch's business empire. The speed and efficiency was frightening. One of the twits had made the deplorable decision to shift the tourist company to a lower-fare airline. The first load of paying customers died horribly in a fiery plane crash. Worse, the passengers thought they were traveling to a sex vacation in Thailand; the plane was headed for a run-down health clinic in Poland.

The construction business was an unfolding disaster. Without Alex's name on the letterhead, no new contracts had come in. Nor, after the latest stumble, were they likely to. A huge high-rise under construction on the outer ring had collapsed in a spectacular heap. Ten workers crushed to death, twenty more in the hospital. The cause was an incredible decision by another of the twits to use less expensive wood beams in place of the thick metal ones clearly stipulated by the now enraged architects. Tatyana managed to pull a few strings and have the investigation squelched. The damage was done, though. Half the construction workforce quit on the spot; the other half were making ugly sounds about a strike.

Another twit, this one in charge of the bank, ignored the growing spread between government bonds and interest rates. A small, momentary blip on a computer screen and, like that, a hundred million, gone. Amazing.

The list of problems was endless, horrible, and growing. The car importing company shipped five hundred Mercedes sedans to the wrong cities, then hiked up the prices so high that the inventory was rusting on the lots. The hundred Mercedes convertibles that ended up in Yakutsk, a frigid penal colony near the Arctic Circle, were going to be a bitch to move at any price. The complicated computer program confused him, that twit whined afterward. And another idiot, this one in the arbitrage business, had purchased two thousand tons of the most expensive iron ore in history. He misread the code, thought it was silver at a great price, he insisted after he annihilated any possibility of the arbitrage business having a profitable year.

Another few months at this hideous pace and there'd be nothing left.

As per the original deal, Tatyana was a partner in Golitsin Enterprises — a hidden partner, of course — and she was quietly seething. From the beginning Golitsin had demanded Konevitch's cash for himself. His idea, his brilliant plan, his inspirational leadership; the instant gratification was rightfully his, every bit of it, he insisted. She had neither objected nor debated that point — she hadn't seen a reason to — and now she sorely regretted it. Looking back, it seemed so naïve. Stupid. But by any reasonable measure, at the time her take was around fifty million in stock in companies that were wildly flourishing and threatening to double or triple in a few brief years. At the time, that struck her as ample restitution for her part in the heist.

She doubted she could unload her shares now at any price. The smart money had already sprinted out of the banks; even the dumb money was pawing the exits. Lawsuits were piling up over shoddy workmanship, false promises, missed deliveries, slipped deadlines, and of course the furiously grieving families of the people slaughtered by that fly-by-night excuse for an airline booked by Golitsin's twits. Who knew what awful disaster would happen next? She had no legal friends, but plenty of attorney acquaintances, all of whom were eyeing Golitsin Enterprises with considerable intensity. They were salivating to get a piece of the action.

But Tatyana was a realist. Nothing she could say would change things. Golitsin, for all his brilliance and canniness, had no interest or talent for commerce. And his thugs had as much business running a company as three-year-olds playing with nuclear warheads. Tugging fingernails out of helpless prisoners was one thing; squeezing profit out of finicky customers quite another.

"I contacted Konevitch," she said, almost in a whisper.

"You *what?*"

She bent forward. "You heard me, Sergei. Konevitch. I dispatched an officer of the Security Ministry to make him an offer."

"You must have a death wish. You have no business free-lancing."

"Well . . . then forgive me. I'm looking out for both our interests." Even she couldn't make that sound authentic. Golitsin's face reddened, his eyes narrowed into angry slits.

"Answer me this, Sergei. How much interest are you getting from the bank where the money is stashed?"

"None of your business."

"It won't hurt to tell me. How much?"

"It's a big pile of money. A mountain, really. A little interest goes a long way."

"If it's a Swiss bank, about one percent, am

I right?"

"Around there," he snarled — not that one percent of 250 million was anything to be ashamed of. Besides, one didn't go to the Swiss for the interest.

"What if Konevitch could double it every few years? He's a genius. It will be easy to build in a few safeguards. He'll never actually touch the money. For a small share in the profits we'll be buying his golden touch."

"Not interested."

"Why aren't you? Because you're making a fortune from Golitsin Enterprises?" she asked with a constricted smile.

Since it was a privately owned company there was no financial reporting or formalized information flowing to the shareholders. He briefly wondered how much she knew. Too much, judging by the shrewd tone of her voice. He pulled a long sip of scotch, then admitted, "There have been a few small setbacks."

"Does Nicky know yet?" she asked, thrusting the knife a little deeper. "He's also a partner, last time I checked."

Golitsin flicked a hand through the air as if it didn't bother him in the least. He wasn't happy that she brought it up, though. Nicky definitely was not the sort of partner you wanted to disappoint with bad news. "What's your point?" he asked nastily.

"Two points. One, Konevitch is very good

at making money," she said, and the insinuation was clear and painful — Golitsin and his band of fools would alchemize gold into Silly Putty. "Two, if we employ him," she continued, "we own him. He won't run and tattle, because it won't be in his interest. And he'll be a co-conspirator."

"Where is he?"

"New York City."

"A big place. Where in New York?"

"I don't know exactly."

He knew she was lying. Her lips were moving, so of course she was lying. "If you don't know, how did you reach him?"

"Why does it matter? Are you in or out?"

"What do you get out of it?"

"A reasonable share of the profits. Nothing exorbitant, say thirty percent. It's my idea, after all."

Golitsin knew damn well what she was up to. She wanted to get her fingers on the money, the cash. His millions. She would set up this arrangement with Konevitch, then figure out a scheme to rob him blind.

Well, he knew damn well what he wanted, too. More than ever, more than anything, he wanted that boy dead. Just dead. That he was running Konevitch's companies into the ground — he was too painfully aware of the snickers and rumors roaring around the city — only made him detest the man all the more.

He sat back, drew a few heavy breaths, and struggled to clear his brain. Maybe killing him was the wrong approach. Maybe he was being impetuous and shortsighted. In fact, enlisting Konevitch in this scheme might be a great idea. It felt better by the moment — let the genius double or triple his money, get the boy's fingers nice and dirty, and if Konevitch made one wrong move, then find a way to blow the whistle and humiliate him once again. Why not?

He could always kill him.

He asked, innocently enough, but without commitment, "And how did he sound about the offer?"

"Interested. He made a few demands. Don't worry, I'll grind him down."

"All right," he growled, playing at phony reluctance. "Go ahead. Make the deal. See where it goes."

15

Early October 1993

Midnight, and Elena was lying awake, improving her English by watching an old American western. The tense gunfight was interrupted, midshot, by a tedious toothpaste commercial, so she casually flipped over to CNN for a quick peek at what was happening around the world, late-night. They were back in their suite in the Plaza, counting the days and waiting for whoever sent Volevodz to call.

She reached across the bed and shook her husband awake. "Alex, look what's happening," she said, almost yelling, aiming a finger at the flickering tube across the room.

Alex sat up and stretched, glanced briefly at the tube, and froze. At that instant, a line of tanks was pouring salvo after salvo at the Russian White House, Russia's rather less than elegant equivalent of a parliamentary building. The top floors burned brightly. Fresh shells were striking the sides of the building, sending showers of shattered glass and debris that bounced off the concrete apron.

An unseen male correspondent was providing commentary in a hurried, theatrical voice: "The Supreme Soviet, as the Russian Congress is still known, a week ago voted to impeach Boris Yeltsin and replace him with his hard-line vice president, Aleksandr Rutskoi. A few hours ago, in this very building, Rutskoi signed a decree announcing his own presidency. The fencing that has gone back and forth for months, the largely communist and right-wing deputies voting first to emasculate Yeltsin's reforms and power, and now to replace him, has finally erupted in violence. The past week there have been scattered skirmishes around the capital. Now there are two presidents of Russia. And now . . . the fate of democracy hangs in the balance."

Elena reached for the phone, called room service, and ordered two pots of coffee, with a fresh pot to be delivered every hour until she notified them otherwise. The drama, with overheated updates, unfolded throughout the night. Alex and Elena never budged. They sipped coffee, munched toast, spoke little, and watched in fascination. The troops surrounding the White House were part of the Ministry of Security. The trigger-happy tanks were courtesy of the army.

Inside the building, Vice President Rutskoi and a band of mutinous deputies, as well as a large clutch of armed thugs, were making their last stand. For the second time in two years, Russia's future hung over a bitter standoff at this same building. This time, though, the roles were reversed. Instead of Yeltsin flipping the bird at the old boys in the Kremlin, he was the one being flipped, the one who dispatched the tanks to flatten his opposition.

At seven the next morning the television showed Rutskoi and his humbled lieutenants waving a desultory white flag and scurrying from the still burning building. They were quickly slapped in handcuffs, forced into waiting vans, and driven off to prison.

The American president immediately issued a statement lauding a great victory of democracy, and a painful but desperately necessary move by his dear, dear friend Boris.

The screen quickly filled with talking heads who, as so often was the case, proceeded with silky conviction and utter certitude to get it all incredibly wrong. One graying authority in oversized horn-rimmed glasses made an analogy to Hitler's failed putsch in Munich. Another crowed that Yeltsin was the Lincoln of this era, a decisive, principled man who had locked horns with the devil and kicked his butt. Russia was saved, democracy triumphed, Yeltsin the hero of the hour, was the common refrain across network world.

Alex watched it all in sheer disgust. "They have no idea what they've just seen," he whispered to Elena, who was nibbling on a piece of cold toast.

"No, they're idiots," she agreed between bites.

"You saw who saved Yeltsin?"

"The Security people and the army."

"Yes, all former KGB people. You know what this means? Yeltsin cut a deal with them."

"How much trouble are we in?" Elena asked, though she knew the answer.

"A lot. This is the end of our Russian experiment in democracy. From here on, the old boys will take back what Yeltsin took from them, and there's nothing to stop them. The people who stole our money now have no fear. Even if I got through to Yeltsin, he's in their pocket."

"He won't lift a finger to help. He sold his soul," Elena said, finishing the thought.

The call came a full two days later. The voice was a woman's, Anna, throaty and sultry, no last name.

Alex cut off her attempt at pleasantries and opened the bidding. "You heard my requirements?"

"Volevodz explained everything."

"Good. What's your answer?"

"Thirty percent might be a reasonable compensation, but it will be structured differently. I'll draw up a contract that pegs your take a little more precisely." And along the way, I'll whack off as many points as I can get away with and add them to my own total, she thought, but didn't explain.

"I won't commit until I see the details," Alex told her very quickly.

"That's understandable. But forget the five million bonus. Out of the question."

"I considered it a reasonable request. Of course, I have no idea how big the base is. Volevodz mentioned several hundred million."

"So you were for shooting for the stars. I don't blame you. But let's say it's in the several hundred million range now. It will be more in the future, considerably more. Down the road, based on your performance, we can talk about a structured bonus. Not until we see how good you are."

"Who are you?" Alex asked.

Anna, actually Tatyana, laughed playfully. "Alex, you're smarter than that."

Yes, he was. Also a painfully good listener. She was playing it close to the vest, but she had already made one serious slip — "I'll draw up a contract." Alex took a moment and added it up. Female by sex, Anna obviously an imaginary name, a lawyer most certainly, from her voice late twenties, early thirties at the outside, and Alex guessed she probably worked in the Kremlin or held a senior government position of some sort. Also arrogant and pushy and sly — of course, that could fit almost any lawyer. From her tone of smug self-assurance, Alex suspected she was very pretty, possibly beautiful.

"Explain how this is supposed to work," Alex asked. "Obviously you have no intention of assigning me direct control over the money."

"Good guess. You'll work through a team of accountants and brokers who report to me. You tell them what you'd like to do, they inform me, not a penny gets moved until I approve it. You'll receive daily updates from them. Satisfactory?"

"It's not ideal, no."

"From your angle, I'm sure it's not. It looks perfect from mine."

"Listen to me. The best investments don't give warning. A difference between interest spreads, for instance, can last seconds. The same is true in the arbitrage game. It's a very narrow strike window — miss it, and you can forget about it. If you want spectacular returns, I can't be handicapped by time. How many people have to approve my decisions?"

"Nice try. Next question."

"Where's the money now?"

"Try again."

"How much is it earning?"

"You're starting to bore me."

"Am I? Look, I won't take this job if Golitsin is in the decision loop. I've read what he's done to my companies. What a disaster. He couldn't make two cents if it was raining dollars."

Another very serious mistake on her part. A long, revealing pause before she snapped, "Who and how the decisions are made is my business." Then, after another moment, "You'd better be done with your demands. Let me remind you, you're broke, on the run, and wanted for crimes here in Russia. But you can lose more, a lot more. I'm offering you a chance to make some of your money back."

"Your generosity chokes me up."

"I know. Do you want it or not, Alex?"

Alex glanced carefully at Elena, who was resting on the bed, biting her lip and trying her best to appear noncommittal and supportive of whatever choice he made — and failing miserably.

This was the moment; did he or didn't he? Yes or no?

"Not," he replied without hesitation.

"Don't be foolish. I'm offering you a great deal."

"A great deal for you. It stinks for me."

"Take a minute, Alex. Cool down and think like a businessman, be practical. You really have no clue of how powerful we are, do you?

How easily we can reach you."

"I'll take my chances."

"You'll regret it. Believe me, I'll —"

"I'd say nice talking with you, but it wasn't," Alex interrupted and pushed disconnect.

The instant it hit the cradle, Elena lifted up the phone and immediately placed a call to the hotel switch in the basement.

Her friend Amber, the head operator, had a live-in boyfriend who happened to work for the phone service that tied the hotel to the outside world. Amber promised to get right back with the phone number of their recent caller.

Two minutes later, Amber called with the number, which Elena hastily scribbled on the hotel stationery. Alex took it, studied it a moment — he did not recognize it — then stuffed it inside his pant pocket.

Elena sat on the bed, quietly pleased that her husband had refused the offer. An enormously talented genius at business he might be, but she was sure he was over his head with these people. He'd been surprisingly successful to date, and she prayed he didn't delude himself about why. Too much of that success rested on underestimation and beginner's luck. With each success the underestimation wore off. And luck could run out. Also, his plan had relied on Boris Yeltsin, an ambitious man she had never fully trusted.

Alex had seen him as an embattled figure struggling to end dictatorship and bring democracy to Russia. Elena was convinced that his own hopes had blinded him to the man's considerable faults. He was a politician, for all the good and bad that implied. Boris had grabbed a tiger by the tail, and the tiger was angry and hungry.

Boris would happily cram Alex into the tiger's jaws if that kept the resentful tiger from eating him.

"So what will we do?" she asked.

"Hire an investigator in Moscow. Mikhail Borosky always did great work for me. He's incredibly competent, and discreet. I trust him completely."

"I know Mikhail's good, but what's the point?"

"We won't know until he digs and finds out a little more. Maybe it'll help, maybe not. At least he'll have a few leads to go on."

"Do you want to get the companies back?"

He shook his head sadly. "You haven't been reading the business news online. What's left isn't worth owning. Golitsin is way over his head. Banking is a business built on confidence. In two short months, he's ruined everything."

"So what's the point of hiring Mikhail?"

"I want to learn more about these people."

"That will take time. Maybe a lot of time. What will we do in the meantime?"

"We're leaving. Right away."

"Are we in trouble again?"

"Big trouble. This sounded very much like a final offer. The lady became very threatening at the end of the call."

"Are you as frightened as I am?" Elena asked.

"Terrified," Alex admitted.

Alex went to the closet, lifted their suitcases and overnight bags, and hauled them over to the bed. Inside thirty seconds, they were cramming clothes and belongings into the bags.

"What's next?" Elena asked.

"Hire a lawyer and apply for political asylum here in America. I have a perfectly legitimate case. They'll kill me if I ever return to Russia."

"So we'll be Americans."

"Why not, it's a land of immigrants. We're young and we can adjust. What do you think?"

Elena was struggling to fold one of her new skirts, a red thing with a thousand pleats that defied her every effort. "It's different . . . but I think I'll like it," she said, a little tentatively, a little sad. Until this moment, she had never really believed that they had departed Russia for good. The thought of leaving their lives behind, permanently, was deeply unsettling.

"Is there someplace else you'd rather go?"

She shook her head. She would sorely miss

her parents and her friends. And okay, sure, it would be difficult to adjust to America's peculiar ways — people here were so flagrantly casual, so obtrusively personal, and their sense of humor was so weird. But she loved Alex, had from the moment she laid eyes on him — and her instincts told her this was the one place in the world where he would be happy, the one place he could be productive, the one place they would be safe.

"What will we do for a living?"

"Start over. Build a business of some sort."

"You know, Alex, if you could make a fortune in Russia, there's no reason you won't do the same thing here. I'll help you. In fact, it should be easier. America is a land of laws and respect for property. Rich people aren't despised here."

"We'll need a place to live," he said, and she readily agreed — just definitely not like the old one, she thought. A small, livable home, no servants, and definitely unpretentious enough that nobody made a point of spitting hawkers on their doorstep.

They began listing the requirements. A safe place, she said very firmly, with guards and doormen, where they could sleep without worrying about Golitsin's thugs. Great, but it would have to be in or very near a metropolis, he replied — a bustling, prosperous city where money grew on trees. Not too big a city, she countered, and that swiftly ruled out

New York and Chicago and Atlanta. California and Florida, in fact the entire South, and the Southwest, were too hot and miserably humid for their thick Russian blood. The Midwest was too plainly American, too parochial, and they doubted they would fit in. They were quickly running out of real estate.

An idea popped into her brain and, since time was short, and all other options were evaporating, Alex quickly agreed.

Washington. They would settle in that charming city, not too small, not too large, filled with impressive monuments, noisy politicians, and gobs of money. The more they considered it, the better it looked. They would find a nice home, stuff it with furniture, make a normal life, and quickly — and quietly — gather another fortune.

Plus, it was a city of lawyers, after all. It should be easy to locate a good one with loads of experience and contacts in immigration matters and get the paperwork started.

Alex warned, "We'll have to cover our tracks."

That sobering thought brought Elena back from her rosy dreams of the future-to-be to the here and now. "They'll keep hunting for us, won't they?"

"For a while, yes." He paused and looked at the window. "We have to mislead them on our way out. I'll need your help."

"Will this go on forever, Alex?"

"No. Not if we disappear and leave them alone. I think they'll forget about us, eventually. The idea is to be sure we aren't worth their time or effort."

By six, they had rented a car, stocked it with maps, and loaded the trunk with everything they owned. For a former mogul and his wife, it was almost pitiful — Alex's office supplies and what little clothing and toiletries they had gathered since their arrival. Alex checked out, with cash, then, accompanied by Elena, headed for the phone bank in the basement, where they discussed their plan with Elena's friend Amber. Ignoring her protests, Alex stuffed three thousand dollars into her palm with orders to keep a thousand or two for herself and spread the rest around liberally to select members of the hotel staff.

Amber pecked Elena on the cheek, hugged her tightly, and wished them both luck.

Fourteen hours after they departed, the team of killers arrived. They pushed through the door and began prowling the lobby, looking for their prey. There were six of them in all, five men and one lady, Katya, their old tormentor from Budapest, who had arrived only hours before, after being dispatched on a swift overnight from Russia. She was along to brief the new boys about Konevitch's elusiveness and ensure positive confirmation once the deed was done. At least that was the reason Golitsin had offered her and his partners, Tatyana and Nicky. A more truthful reply was that he did not trust Nicky. He wanted some of his own muscle involved.

The other killers were Americanized Russians, immensely talented at murder, citizens of Brighton Beach, connected through two or three shell companies to Nicky's expansive organization.

It had been easy enough to trace the phone number Tatyana handed Nicky after Konevitch told her to piss off; a swift look-see through the Manhattan Yellow Pages led them straight to the Plaza.

Alex was here, they were sure of it. His room number was the one mystery, but they would learn it quickly. Two men would remain downstairs in the lobby, one by each exit to block any attempt at escape. The rest would rush upstairs, employ a crowbar to burst through the doors, and toss the Konevitches through the window down onto the busy street below. If it turned out the room was on a lower level, knives and garrotes would do the trick.

The people at the reception counter refused to offer any information no matter how much Katya pleaded or offered in bribes. Customer confidentiality was an obligation taken quite seriously at the Plaza. Fine. The killers fanned out and began accosting maids and waiters, employees on the lower end of the pay scale, who might, for the right price, entertain a slight breach of hospitality ethics.

Katya, with considerably more experience in assassination matters, had a better idea. She took the elevator to the basement where the phone bank was located. The door was locked, so she knocked. A young woman opened it and Katya agilely stepped inside before she could be stopped. A large black woman who apparently was in charge pushed her rear out of her chair, stepped away from the switch console, and approached her.

"Sorry, you have to leave right now. This is a restricted area," she squawked with a posture that brooked no objections.

Katya spoke flawless English, but she hammed it up a bit, pretending she didn't fully understand. She slathered on the accent and said, "I am for my little sister looking. She is staying here, I am sure."

The black lady squared her heels and crossed her arms. "Then you need to go upstairs. Talk to reception. This is an employee-only room."

"Please, you must help me," Katya said with a long, uncomprehending frown. "She is named Elena. Elena Konevitch. She is here with husband."

Amber's big face retracted into a thousand suspicious wrinkles. "How come you don't know where your sister is?"

"She and her husband, Alex, they fled Russia. Alex does bad things there. Now is hiding."

"Bad things?"

"Yes, very, very bad. But our mother, she is most desperately sick. Dying, I think. I come because Elena must learn this." A long, pleading look. "Please, please, please, you must be of help to me."

Elena's big sister, my big ass. Who the hell did this Russian bitch think she was fooling, Amber thought. Her hands landed on her hips. "You missed 'em. Yep, yesterday they checked out in a hurry. Said they were headed for Chicago."

"Chicago?" Katya repeated, a little stunned.

"Uh-huh, Chicago. Said they were tired of New York and planned to settle there."

"Did they leave a forwarding address? A phone number, maybe?"

Amber's large hand popped out. Katya at first looked befuddled. The hand stayed put and she got the message. She yanked a twenty out of her pocket and slammed it onto the palm. The hand stayed put. Welcome to America, bitch. Not until four more twenties hit the pot did the hand retract.

"Nope," Amber said.

"They left no word? None?"

"That's right, none."

"Did they go by car, train, plane?" Katya was so disturbed at missing them, her concocted accent was melting.

"If I had to guess, he and your sister are gonna make themselves scarce. Be damned hard to find, know what I'm saying?"

Katya stared into her face for a long moment, spun on her heels, and departed. The door shut with a loud, angry bang.

At that moment, Maria Sanchez, an upstairs maid, was fingering the hundred in her pocket and recounting the same lie to two of the men on the hit team. Chicago, she told them with absolute certainty. She had overheard the Konevitches discussing the city as she cleaned their room two days before. Stacks of Chicago maps and travel guides sat on their bedside table; they sounded thrilled and eager to get on the road.

Amber figured she had at least bought the Konevitches a little time. A few weeks, maybe. With luck, a few months. But if the killers were serious, they would eventually track them down.

16

John Tromble was a man in a hurry. He had raced through a few years as a federal prosecutor, then sprinted through five more of a federal judgeship, and now was midway in his third year as director of the Federal Bureau of Investigation — the youngest ever, he reminded you quickly, in the event you failed to bring it up. He quickly stretched his long legs and speed-read a little more of the thick dossier produced by his staff in preparation for this trip.

He planned to spend another two years in this job, make a big splash, then pole-vault to the next level. A vice presidential candidacy wasn't out of the question; a senatorship should be easy pickings. Or barring that, open a private security firm and quickly haul in millions. With a mountain of cash, he could do whatever he wished. He read quickly, ate quickly, slept in a hurry, even had sex at astonishing speed. Everything he did, full speed ahead.

The plane was thirty minutes out from Sheremetyevo Airport, which apparently was on the outskirts of Moscow. If he were flying this damn thing he'd sure as hell find a way to make it in fifteen minutes.

Having slept since Washington, he had woken up thirty minutes before, showered, shaved, and slapped on a freshly pressed suit. He stole a quick glance in the mirror before he left the special cabin of this very special plane to make his final preparations for this very special trip. The rear of the plane was stuffed with as many American reporters as his aides and cronies could entice or cajole and cram aboard. The press would be shoved off five minutes before him. Oh yes, there they would be, a large, impatient mob at the bottom of the steps, snapping away as he made his majestic descent, capturing shot after shot of his photogenic face. The remains of a low-cal breakfast sat on the tray above his lap. He was sipping quickly and noisily from a bottled water, nose buried in the dossier, straining to avoid conversation.

Across from him sat Laura Tingleman, attorney general, and putatively his boss. She had worked through the entire flight since they lifted off from Andrews Air Force base twelve hours before. She was crumpled into her seat with her nose stuffed in her Black-Berry. She looked wrinkled, tired, and wrung out. She was a large, heavy, unimpressive-looking type, fifty years old, though she appeared a very poorly kept sixty, with a broad face that managed, somehow, always to convey panic.

This first year in her job had been unfortunate. For one thing, she was, quite publicly, the president's fourth choice. This happened only after it was revealed that choice one was doing the bedsheet tango with his underage nanny; Tromble had seen her, and to the man's credit, the nanny did not in fact look at all as if she was only fourteen; more like sixteen. This happened only after it was disclosed that choice two had taken numerous fat bribes from several very crooked oil companies. This happened only after it was discovered that choice three, a superior court judge in California, had spent his misguided youth dodging the draft, calling cops pigs, stuffing all nature of questionable substances up his snout, and barbecuing American flags. Perfect qualifications for a judgeship in California, but the rest of the country did not embrace his background.

After these train wrecks, Laura Tingleman had been found tucked away in a backcountry Montana circuit court, a low-key, competent judge who handled mostly divorces and small-time land disputes. Little to no political experience, no national exposure, zero controversial decisions, no overturned verdicts — all in all, Laura Tingleman was as apt to raise as much controversy as chicken soup. No bad habits, as best they could tell. Never married, thus never divorced; in fact, the lead FBI investigator who rummaged through her background even surmised that she might be a fifty-year-old virgin, if such a thing existed. Best of all, she was a woman! The first ever nominated for attorney general, and feminist leaders around the country growled that whoever opposed her would face a backlash of historic proportions.

It helped that she was a nice person, if deeply out of her depth, polite, respectful, and deeply religious, though not a zealot. Her nomination sailed through without a hitch.

Tromble detested her. There was room for only one legal superstar in this administration, one shining protector of America from the crooks, terrorists, and perverts who lurked in the dark shadows. And he, after all, was the whiz kid who came up the hard way through intellectual brilliance, sharp elbows, and unrelenting work. Yale undergrad, Harvard Law, and he had done his time in the legal trenches; she had been plucked out of Nowhere, Montana, for the plain and simple reason that she had no disputable accomplishments, or indeed any accomplishments at all.

And though it was true he had not been a popular prosecutor or judge, he had been greatly feared. The exception was cops, who adored him because he hammered defense attorneys and meted out terrifying sentences. His record of overturned verdicts was shocking.

In fact, the New York appellate court, tired of an exhausting docket overloaded with his weekly brutality, was about to serve notice of a review hearing when news broke that he was somehow, incredibly, on the president's short list for FBI director. The appellate judges were appalled. They gathered together in a private chamber and considered whether to blow the whistle on a judge they regarded as little short of a Nazi. No, no, one wise, notably liberal senior justice advised with a deep smile; don't shovel manure in a gift horse's mouth; at least John Tromble would be out of their hair. They could look forward again to being home by dinnertime and Friday golf.

In the expiring days of his outgoing presidency, the incumbent's predecessor, normally a moderate who had appointed two mild liberals to the Supreme Court, had spent his last political capital on the Hill to get Tromble this job. He took charge of ushering the appointment personally, called in every chit, used up every threat, and bent elbows until the sound of arms cracking thundered around the Senate. It was his finest hour. Had he poured that kind of energy and spirited determination into running the country, that southern governor who shellacked him at the polls would be back chasing skirts around some small southern town.

He was leaving his successor a poisoned chalice — a bundle of combustible, no-holds-barred, law-and-order ambition who would steamroll anything or anybody in his path, he confided to his chief of staff in a giggly private moment. He intended to sit back in his retirement and laugh at all the trouble John Tromble caused that southern boy. It was going to be horrendous.

And now, after two fairly low-key years in office, two years that were sadly unacclaimed, Judge Tromble had decided the time had come to kick it up a notch. Crime rates had dropped substantially under his watch, but the liberal press loathed him and credited a hundred other causes — from a diminishing appetite for crack, to all the hardened crooks already rotting in prison, to a religious revival in the Deep South and Midwest. He needed something — anything — they could not misinterpret or take away from him. He needed a signature issue, and he turned his fiercely impatient eyes on America's newest threat — international crime, foreign crooks on American soil, or maybe a little off it. First up, the Russian Mafiya.

Unfortunately for Alex and Elena Konevitch, their fates now rested in the hands of an attorney general in search of sea legs, and an

FBI director with omnivorous ambitions and a few fairly strange ideas about justice.

The long line of limos cruised to a stop on the cobblestone plaza. Tromble's aides and coatholders — the fanny-wiping brigade they were called by the jaded field agents — tumbled out in an unruly mass, took a moment to get organized, then were ushered quickly through the historic Kremlin doors, up two flights of stairs, and directly into the cavernous office of Anatoli Fyodorev, Russia's attorney general.

Introductions were handled briskly in a no-nonsense fashion. Several of Fyodorev's stone-faced assistants were gathered around the office walls, not introduced. Among them stood a very striking young lady in a breathtakingly short skirt who smiled nicely as the procession entered.

Fyodorev sat down on a tall chair behind a desk that looked bigger than Finland. Two chairs — little more than small stools, actually — were positioned before the desk. After a moment of confusion, Tingleman and Tromble edged precariously onto the chairs. Their knees were nearly in their faces, their elbows almost on the floor. They were forced to stare up at Fyodorev.

A representative from the American embassy took a standing position slightly behind them, notepad in one hand, pen poised in

337

the other. They had been assured that Fyo-dorev's English was exceptional — transla-tion was neither needed nor wanted. The embassy flunky's real job was to take detailed notes, and pay careful attention to anything the professional diplomats would have to clean up afterward. Shovel duty.

Fyodorev was the host and he opened with a long windy soliloquy about how, national differences aside, they were all in the same business. To wit, law enforcement. Spiritual brothers and sisters. Bonded by their com-mon enmity to criminals, and so on, and so forth — etcetera and double etcetera.

Fyodorev eventually wrapped up and Tromble summoned his important face and, before Tingleman could utter a word, quickly announced, "We're here to discuss bilateral cooperation in matters of crime."

"A nice term," Fyodorev noted dryly. "What does it mean?"

"Well . . . for starters, I'd like to offer you a few slots each year for your people to attend our FBI Academy."

"Why? Is it better than ours?"

The State Department flunky dashed off a few heavy notes on his legal pad. With limited success, he tried to keep the smirk off his face. Boy, this was going to be fun.

"I . . . well, yes, probably. It has a certain reputation. Also, we think you might want to place some of your people in our profiling center down at Quantico."

Fyodorev's elbows landed heavily on his desk. "Explain this term, 'profiling.' "

"It's, um, well, it refers to specialists who employ psychiatry to get inside criminal minds. We've found it quite effective. Serial killers, for example, tend to exhibit complementary patterns. If you can figure that out, you can stop them and find them."

A dismissive grin. "Russia has no serial killers."

"Works pretty good against serial rapists, also. Or serial arsonists, if you have any of those."

"We have neither. Those are American problems."

The State guy was now composing entire paragraphs.

Who is this guy kidding? Tromble thought. He was sure his leg was being pulled and he laughed. Fyodorev developed a very deep frown.

The hottie in the short skirt suddenly shoved herself off the wall and moved to a position beside Fyodorev's desk. She said to him, "Anatoli, we're being terrible hosts. It's been a long, tiring trip for our American guests. Maybe they would like coffee."

Whoever she was, she had an interesting relationship with Fyodorev, because his demeanor turned on a dime. The angered frown converted instantly into a gracious smile. "Yes . . . yes, you're right. Coffee, anybody?"

Tromble said yes, black, no sugar, no cream. Laura chose tea, doused with sugar and cream. One of the aides shoved off from the wall and scurried off to retrieve the refreshments.

The young lady with the glorious legs slid around the desk and, with a glowing smile and firm handshake, introduced herself. Tatyana something-or-other — she explained she worked not here, in the attorney general's office, but upstairs, for his boss. She was a lawyer who frequently advised Yeltsin on legal matters. This seemed to justify her presence.

"Why don't we all adjourn to the conference table?" she suggested, quite hospitably.

Why not? For sure, the current arrangement was a bust. They shifted from their stools and desks to comfortable chairs abutting a huge walnut block table by a large window. Tingleman and Tromble sat side by side, in an uncomfortable silence.

Miss Tatyana Whoever sat closely beside Fyodorev on the other side of the long, gleaming table. They made small talk about the flight and weather and a dozen other uninteresting topics. Once the coffees and teas were delivered and the room had cooled to a level of moderate tension, Tatyana said, "Let's not beat around the bush. What is it you'd really like to discuss?"

Tromble's briefing papers, prepared by a bunch of stuffy eggheads over at State, had stipulated that the Russians were consummate horse traders. Never arrive empty-handed: give a little, get a little. In that spirit, he had started — more accurately, he had tried to start — by offering them a few handsome concessions before he got down to his own request.

But if she could come right to the point, so could he. "Your Mafiya," he said very importantly.

"What about them?"

"Since the wall came down, they've become your biggest export. They're crawling all over our cities. They've turned Miami into a free-fire zone. Brighton Beach is a funeral parlor." Tromble worked up a nasty grimace. "They're a very nasty lot."

"Tell me about it," Fyodorev said, shaking his head with disgust. "Total vermin. The most ruthless, brutal criminals in the world."

"Yes, so we're learning," Tingleman replied, slightly irritated, not really clued in to what her FBI director had in mind for this visit. She had been told it was no more than a diplomatic meet-and-greet, part of the required protocol for her office, a chance to get away from the daily grind of Washington. "Our own Italian Mafiosi are civilized gentlemen compared to your guys. With your people, no finesse, no rules, no attractive

341

traditions. They kill over nothing."

"We're not proud of them," Fyodorev replied with an uneven shrug.

"I'm under great pressure from my president to do something about them," Tromble insisted, regaining the initiative.

A lie. His president could care less about anything that didn't register in national polls and outside Hollywood, where a fresh species of frightening brutes was always a welcome addition; the average Joe knew nothing about Russia's Mafiya and could care less.

Fyodorev looked sympathetic.

"I need a favor," Tromble continued with a friendly smile. "As you know, we have a small FBI field station at our embassy here in Moscow. Yeltsin personally signed the agreement. That was two years ago."

Tatyana noted, "And it expires in a few months."

"Exactly. Now I'd like an extension. Say, another five years. And I want to triple the size."

"How many of your people are here now?" Fyodorev asked.

"Four. Four overworked, exhausted agents," Tromble said sourly. "Two broken marriages, one newly minted alcoholic, one attempted suicide. Sad to say, it has become the most unpopular posting in the Bureau."

"Twelve would be a lot," Fyodorev countered, obviously cool to the idea. "This is, after all, Russian soil."

"I know, I know. But your Mafiya is huge, and growing fast. Ambitious, too. They're blasting their way into everything. Dope, whores, kidnapping, extortion. The bodies are piling up. Four agents barely make a dent. Besides, I hoped we would work this problem together."

"Together?"

"Well, yes. Presumably your people have a better handle on your own Mafiya than we do."

"I would hope that's the case."

"What if some of my agents worked full-time with your people?"

"Like liaisons?" Tatyana suggested, nudging Fyodorev with her knee under the table.

"That's the general idea. At our end, we're dealing with Mafiya foot soldiers. That's not working. Take one off the street, and in days he's replaced with two more. We presume that the heads of all these organizations are here, in Russia." Nobody contradicted that obvious point and he pushed ahead. "And you can put some of your people at my headquarters. We'll share intelligence, share everything we learn and tip each other off. Maybe perform a few big busts together."

Tatyana maintained a straight face, but her heart was racing. Oh, what an incredibly great idea: yes, we can share intelligence, the more the better. Wait until Nicky heard what had just landed in her lap. He would know everything the FBI was up to. He would learn the names of every plant, every snitch, every stoolie. Through her, he could set up his opposition and exploit the FBI boys to squash their American operations. It would be a windfall. Nicky's American branch would grow by leaps and bounds.

And it would all depend on little old Tatyana. She liked to be needed. Service like that doesn't come cheap.

A slight nod from Tatyana to Fyodorev, who glanced in her direction every few seconds.

"Of course we'll share the headlines?" Fyodorev asked, showing he and Tromble were kindred spirits.

"Wouldn't dream otherwise," Tromble lied.

"Why only twelve agents?" Tatyana asked. "And why only five years? Our Mafiya have been around for seven decades. They're such an institution, I hardly think we'll defeat them in only five years. Make it twenty agents. Thirty, if you wish. And a ten-year extension strikes me as much more reasonable."

Tromble reached both hands under the table and steadied his knees. This was everything he'd hoped for, times two or three. Ol' J. Edgar may have created the FBI and put it on the map, but he was determined to claw out his own storied place in Bureau legend. He was going to take America's only national police force and turn it into an international juggernaut. It would be twice as big before he was through: maybe more, maybe much more. He intended to have his agents in every damn embassy in every damn country in the world. A bigger operations center would be necessary, a real monster with dozens of lit-up screens constantly flashing the latest updates about Chink Triads, and Jap Yakuzas, French wharf rats, and Tibetan whatever-the-hell-they-weres. He would have a big seat in the middle of it all, a throne from which he could survey his crime-busting kingdom.

He bit his lip. "That all sounds reasonable to me."

"Good," said Tatyana with the great legs. She started to stand, then lightly tapped her forehead. She slid back into her seat, frowning, distracted. "There is, uh, one thing you can do for us, John. A favor. A very, very important one."

"Name it."

It was a gamble, but why not? How much was this worth to Tromble? She said, "There is a certain criminal who fled Russia. Alex Konevitch. He's hiding out in your country. He ran a large bank here that laundered billions of dollars. Mafiya money, in fact. When he learned we were on to him, he absconded with hundreds of millions, in dollars. A real crook."

"And he's in America?"

"That's right. We had a thread on him, but

345

he disappeared over a year ago. We had a lead that he was in Chicago. And maybe he is, but our best people have been unable to locate him."

"No problem. I'll put twenty agents on it tomorrow."

"You have your most wanted list" — she paused and looked him dead in the eye — "well, John, we have ours, too. He's number one on our list. The top dog, the most wanted bad guy in Russia. It's a great embarrassment that he has eluded us this long. He is unquestionably guilty. We want him back. Crooked bankers are a serious problem for us. We intend to make an example of him with a very big, very public trial."

"One week and he'll be in a Moscow slammer. I guarantee it."

The State Department representative coughed. "Uh, that might be a problem."

"Why's that?" Tromble asked, clearly irritated by the interruption.

"We don't share an extradition treaty with our Russian friends, I'm afraid."

"So what?"

That question, emerging from the lips of America's top law enforcement officer, a former federal judge no less, was unnerving. "It would be . . . well, you know, a big legal problem if Konevitch has diplomatic permission to remain in America. You can't just throw him on an airplane and ship him back here."

Tromble leaned over until their faces were inches apart. "I don't think this is any of your business."

Tatyana calmly watched this exchange. "He might be right," she said, twirling a strand of her gorgeous hair. "But let's be sure we're all clear on our deal. You can maintain your field station only if Alex Konevitch is returned to us. If not, there will be no cooperation. None."

The big black limo was parked in the small lot by the Moskva River. It was Tuesday. And they usually met on Tuesdays. The windows were cracked open. Cigar smoke billowed out. The car parked here once or twice a week. Week after week. Month after month.

The sheer sloppiness of it all amazed the man who sat and watched from a small non-descript car half a block away. He understood it, though. Hunters rarely looked back over their own shoulders. The people inside that car had every reason to be overconfident, and they were. He lit up an American Marlboro and cranked up his heater.

Tracking down Miss Tatyana Lukin had proven to be neither easy nor quick. Tracing the phone number Alex gave him to the Kremlin was simple enough — a small bribe to a phone technician was all it took. But the

Kremlin was an immense factory of bureaucrats of all manner and forms. They were not a talkative lot. It was such a snakepit of conspiracy and political fratricide that they spoke, even among themselves, in whispers. Outsiders were cold-shouldered as a matter of course.

Month after month of stubborn digging ensued. Six Annas were found and swiftly vetted. Unfortunately, none fit the broader profile and all were quickly rejected as dead ends. Mikhail had other jobs he had to balance with Alex's request, and a long, tiring period of frustration ensued. Dozens of trails opened, then grew cold. Leads looked hot then fizzled into disappointment. The staff at the Kremlin turned over constantly as Yeltsin chewed through prime ministers and assistants like a slaughterhouse. The number of potential suspects alternated almost daily. Was she one of those casualties? Maybe, like so many successful and well-connected political people, she had simply jumped into the private sector for the big bucks.

Mikhail Borosky had first encountered Alex Konevitch years before when Alex's firm had been hit hard by a few in-house embezzlers. A grizzled former cop, now a private investigator, Mikhail had been hired to find the crooks. No problem, they were greedy idiots. They drove up to work in their shiny new BMW 730s, which they stupidly parked in the office lot. Why not just hang out signs that announced: Hey, we're your thieves if you're wondering.

But Alex had been impressed. Only two brief days and Mikhail named the thieves. Steady work followed, nearly all of which involved in-house shenanigans of one sort or another. Mikhail handled it all with brutal efficiency.

Alex had been generous with the bonuses, always paid promptly in cash. The two became fast friends. There were occasional dinners that usually ran late. In his long years as a cop, Mikhail had specialized in combating the Mafiya, part of a handpicked cadre that was vetted and watched constantly for its incorruptibility and ruthlessness. Mikhail's strong suit was gathering intelligence, figuring out the corrupting webs of mob activity, bugging, trailing, and observing, collecting enough dirt on the hoods and thugs to ensure their convictions.

Alex enjoyed hearing tales that had nothing to do with business. But nobody in Konevitch Associates knew of their relationship. This secrecy Mikhail insisted on from the beginning. As long as he stayed hidden in the shadows, they would leave lots of breadcrumbs in their wake and the cat-and-mouse game would be child's play. Pay me personally, never call from the office phone, never mention my name. It made it so much easier for the bloodhound to find their trails.

After over half a year of hard effort, Tatyana had fallen into his lap by a stroke of luck, a complete fluke. He had befriended a pair of lowly assistants to the minister of finance, frequently accompanying them to a bar, a favorite Kremlin hangout where the coatholders schmoozed and networked. He plied them with booze and encouraged them to introduce him to everybody they knew.

One night, a gentleman at the next table was complaining bitterly and, after inhaling his fourth vodka, very loudly, about another Kremlin bureaucrat. Another staffer had knifed him in the back, had gotten him sacked. That sorry bitch, he kept calling her. Mikhail's ears perked up. Yes, but a tasty bitch, his companion noted with a garrulous laugh. The insults and bad jokes poured out and Mikhail's eavesdropping turned serious. No wonder the chief of staff always looked so exhausted, one said. Ha, ha. Yeah, but she's such a ballbuster, it's a miracle he still had his dingaling. More ha, ha.

Mikhail edged over to the table and began buying rounds for everybody. The fired staffer was drunk, and in no time became utterly drunker. The man had a bottomless bladder, but around midnight he ambled off to the men's room. Mikhail trailed two steps behind him. Over side-by-side urinals Mikhail offered him a cool thousand if the man could point out the backstabbing bitch the next morning as she made her way into the Kremlin.

One look, and he knew he had his girl. Everything fit, except the name. Then again, Tatyana to Anna had a certain ring to it. Alex had predicted she probably was attractive; she was that, and then some. Plus, she had a law degree. Over the next two weeks he tailed her everywhere, and it was fun, though not overly productive. Three to four nights a week she and her boss checked into a hotel. They drove into work together, holding hands and smooching like horny newlyweds. But she also took lots of extended lunch breaks in downtown hotels, not with her chubby middle-aged boss but a handsome, fit-looking young lad who apparently offered a little more in the sack. Click, click went Mikhail's camera. A little research and the young lad turned out to be Sasha Komenov, a star striker on the national soccer team. A little more digging revealed a little more dirt. Turned out pretty boy Sasha and lovely Tatyana were from the same town, had flirted and dated and wrestled together in backseats throughout high school. Her Moscow affairs came and went but Sasha was always there, lurking in her locker room after the game.

Late into the third week, he'd watched her disappear into the rear of a long black limo that took off at a gallop. Click, click. He hit the gas and followed. Next stop was a seedy, run-down nightclub on the city outskirts. More click, click, click. A short man with a large bent nose and graying ponytail dashed out of the club and clambered inside.

From his former days as a Mafiya crime-buster, Mikhail instantly put the name Nicky to the furtive figure wrapped in black leather. The limo's license plate told the rest of the story. It was registered as a company car by Golitsin Enterprises.

Usually the meetings by the Moskva lasted no longer than fifteen to twenty minutes. Today's meeting dragged on for over an hour. Big things were afoot, Mikhail guessed. At one point, Nicky climbed out, stumbled uncertainly for a few steps, then he whipped it out and peed in the open. More click, click with Mikhail's long, wide-angled lens. He chuckled to himself.

The most feared thug in Russia, Nicky Kozyrev, had a teenie weenie.

He made his weekly telephonic report to Alex that night. The pictures were bundled into a large envelope and sent off to the Watergate apartment.

17

Late 1994

The apartment bought by Alex and Elena
Konevitch was riverside, on the sixth floor of
the sprawling co-op building, gazing fitfully
over the brown muddy waters of the broad
Potomac and within yelling distance of the
majestic Kennedy Center. Even after a year,
Alex remained dismayed by how preposter-
ously small it was. A two-bedroom, one for
sleep, the other converted to a tiny, cluttered
office shared by the two of them. At an amazing cost of almost a million, it had to be the
most expensive eight hundred square feet in
the city.

But it was safe. Lots of important and
famous folks made their nests inside this
famous building — they demanded privacy
and good security, they paid out the nose for
it, and they got it.

Elena adored its simplicity. The small space
suited her fine — it was easy to clean. Alex
felt cramped, squeezed, slightly claustropho-

bic. He loved big, open spaces and frequently cursed Golitsin for stealing his home, for exiling him to an apartment that would be swallowed by his old bedroom.

The contract for the co-op, their phones, their cars, their insurance — everything was registered under Elena's maiden name. The name Konevitch disappeared from sight. On Mikhail's expert advice, to be on the safe side, every two months Alex flew in and out of Chicago, brief trips where he liberally sprinkled the Konevitch name around Russian nightclubs and neighborhoods. On the first visit he even signed up for local cell phone services with unlisted numbers. Maybe the bad people were still hunting them, maybe not.

Safe beats sorry every time, Mikhail advised him.

Alex and Elena were one year into their new life, and their new careers were flourishing. The requests for political asylum had come through ten months before. Their lawyer, Martie P. Jones, MP to friends, or to anybody, really, had been as good as advertised. Better, in fact. MP had started his career laboring in the trenches as a lawyer in the stodgy legal office at the Immigration Service. He knew exactly what buttons to push, with a Rolodex that would put the New York phone book to shame.

A few calls to the right people and Alex and

Elena's request was stamped "expedite." A few weeks later they were ushered into a sterile room before a small panel of serious people, sworn to honesty, and asked to present an abbreviated version of their sad case. The panel looked bored and impatient initially. That quickly changed. For starters, Alex opened his shirt and offered a long, nauseating gaze at the hammer-and-sickle emblem fried on his chest. A minute later, out popped the photos of Alex's overall physical condition, blowups of the photos taken by the doctor two days after they landed at Kennedy International. They were color and close up. MP accompanied the visuals with vividly horrifying descriptions — see, this is where the chair broke on his leg; the bruised lumps here, well, those are fractured ribs; and so forth. The wounds were brutal. Several members of the panel gasped and looked away. The verdict was returned promptly.

Approved, but only conditionally — welcome to America, land of the free and the brave — now go out there and make us proud you're an American.

Just one glitch: you must have a job — a place of permanent employment before permission to apply for full residency was granted.

Any job with a domestic corporation was also easily traceable, and therefore out of the question, so Alex immediately contacted his old friend Illya Mechoukov. They had met four years before, when Illya was first toying with the idea of jumping into mass-market advertising. No such thing existed in the Soviet Union, at least not in the same sense as in the West, where big companies spent billions each year shoving their names out into the marketplace. Illya was young, only twenty-five, and seized with the progressive idea that he would mimic the huge Western advertising firms. His business would explode quickly, he was sure, and the money would pour in.

A great idea that instantly hit a brick wall. Illya was odd-looking, with a hooked nose, unbalanced features, long woolly hair, and a thick black beard that looked revolutionary. But he was filled with brilliant concepts that poured out of his lips in quick, nervous bursts. He was inventive and wildly creative; unfortunately, he was also far ahead of his time. The former communists had no idea what he was talking about, or why it mattered. People went to stores. They grabbed the item off the shelf. The very idea of spirited competition sounded confusing, possibly immoral. The notion of trumpeting your own product struck them as haughty, self-indulgent, a blatant waste of money.

Three minutes into his initial pitch in Alex's office, Alex leaned across his desk. "Okay, I've heard enough. Here's the deal: I'm buying you. Not just your advertising, you. I'll fund your company, but you'll service my accounts before all others. I'll be the chairman of the board, you'll be the president, the chief of daily operations, and the brains. It's your show to run, and I expect great results."

Illya tugged on his beard and briefly considered this remarkable offer. "You're kidding."

"Yes, it's a joke. That's why I am about to write a check for five million dollars. Buy the best film and printing equipment on the market, hire good people, and call me if you need more."

The company was legally incorporated in Austria, close to Russia's border and surrounded by cutthroat Western competitors. Alex insisted on this. Rivalry was healthy. To survive, Illya and his people would be forced to absorb the best Western practices, sharpen their own wits, and bring that state-of-the-art knowledge to the Russian market.

Better yet, Orangutan Media, as Illya had named it, was not technically part of Konevitch Associates. To get through the doors of Alex's competitors the firm had to be notionally independent. The only legal documents that evidenced Alex's financial interests were filed with the Austrian authorities. Thus, Orangutan slipped under Golitsin's radar.

Alex now offered to represent the company in America, and the timing could not be better. The big American corporations were floundering in Russia. All those years of a wall separating the two worlds left the Americans clueless about the local culture, local wants, local psychology. What worked like magic in the good ol' USA, resoundingly belly-flopped in Russia. The Pepsi generation caused deep bouts of head-scratching; how could a generation be defined by some stupid soft drink? Doctors recommending this pill or that antidote were unconvincing. Russian medicine was dreadful; anything they recommended was promptly blacklisted from the family shopping cart. And as for all those sports stars hawking products, another bust; who cared what some muscle-bound freak gobbled or drank or rubbed on his body?

Alex would make the rounds of the big American companies and sell them on Orangutan Media — an all-Russian outfit with a native feel for how to pitch to a home audience.

Alex would work for commission only; he wouldn't hear otherwise. Illya was gaining traction with Russian companies, but the business remained an uphill struggle. Monthly payrolls were always uncertain. The costs of production in Austria were staggering. Russian companies remained skeptical about advertising, and proved hard-fisted and stingy. They undervalued it as a matter of habit.

Within six months Alex and Elena were

bagging millions in new accounts. They opened ambitiously with all-out attacks against certain large American candy companies and gargantuan consortiums that produced everyday household products, among other things. Most signed on — small, hesitant contracts at first, but once the clients gained confidence in this no-name Russian start-up, they couldn't throw enough money at Illya.

To cover more ground, Alex and Elena split up. Weekends were reserved for each other: rarely, though, was a weekday spent in the same town. She hit the big movie studios in Los Angeles, he bounced around the oil patch in Houston. The next week, Alex trolled New York City; he signed fat contracts to serve as subcontractors for three large Madison Avenue firms who recognized that their own efforts in Russia were failing abysmally. Two days later, Elena snagged a large Tennessee drug company with a slew of dietary products. A day after that, she hooked a New Jersey luxury cosmetics outfit that was salivating to decorate Russia's new class of uninhibited wealth. And so it went, week after week. Illya was elated. He tripled his staff and shifted the operation into an expansive new sixty-thousand-square-foot warehouse in Austria. It was expensive and risky, but what the hell. Spend money to make money, he figured. He struggled to keep up with demands that seemed to double by the week.

Their new life in America was coming together nicely. Over a million in commissions that first year. Not bad, but not good enough. The second year, they promised themselves, would be three million. With a little luck and more elbow grease, four million. Elena was happy. Alex was restless as always, but that was his nature, and part of his charm.

It was Saturday, and they had just finished a leisurely lunch at an excellent Georgetown restaurant followed by a brisk stroll along the lovely tree-lined canal to burn off the calories. Harold, the doorman, gave them a distressed look as they passed through the entrance on the ground floor. "Hey, Mr. K," he said in almost a whisper, "you got guests upstairs."

"I'm not expecting any."

"Yeah, well you got 'em. Guys in suits. They flashed badges and . . . hey, I tried, I swear I did. They wouldn't take no. They been up there about thirty minutes now."

Alex and Elena exchanged horrified looks. A race for the elevator and Alex punched six. They sprinted down the hallway. Alex gently pushed Elena aside before he stuffed his key into the door. No need, it swung open. He stepped through the entry, tense and ready to swing.

What a mess. The couches were overturned

and knifed open, their interiors gutted, drawers emptied on the floor, lamps broken, books torn apart. The place had been tossed with cruel deliberation. The new furniture and furnishings Elena had picked out with such loving care were ruined. Two men in gray suits loitered by the living room window, ignoring the glorious view of the river while they admired their own handiwork. They took quick looks at Alex and Elena but didn't budge.

"Who are you?" Alex demanded, making no effort to disguise his fury.

"FBI," came the prompt reply. Two sets of identification were quickly flashed, then quickly put away.

"Why are you here?"

"Welcome to America, pal," said one of them with a nasty sneer. "We had a tip you and the wife were harboring a fugitive."

"That's ridiculous."

"Yeah? Seemed real enough to us."

"Do you have a warrant?"

"What are you, a lawyer?"

"Show me your warrant or get out."

They rocked back on their heels and laughed. Take a strike at us, their body language screamed. Look what we did to your home, look at your wife's horrified face, and do what any real man would do. Go ahead, run across the room — throw your best punch. We'll slap your ass in cuffs, cart you off like trash, and, as an undesirable, have your ass on the next flight to Moscow.

Alex was mad enough to do it, but at that moment a third man strolled out of their bedroom. Alex glanced in his direction, and froze. The man was tall and thin, dressed in a rumpled trench coat, and wrapped in his arms was their home computer. He looked, in fact, remarkably like his old friend Colonel Volevodz — but it couldn't be. Not here, not now. This was America.

"Hello, Mr. and Mrs. Konevitch." Amazing — he even sounded like Volevodz, right down to the clipped arrogance.

Alex drew a few heavy breaths and struggled to get himself under control. He felt a large lump in his throat. He snapped at Volevodz, "I thought your friends in external security were territorial. What are you doing here?"

In Russian, Volevodz replied very coolly, "You're a wanted felon. I'm here to take you back."

"Then you're going to be disappointed," replied Alex in English.

"Am I?" Volevodz stayed with Russian so the Fibbies couldn't understand a word. He had arrived two weeks before, after a call from Tatyana to Tromble offering his services and expertise.

The Konevitches' year of dodging and ducking was over. No more hiding behind his wife's name. Nicky's boys had been chasing

362

ghosts in Chicago for a year, cowering in an embattled outpost in a forlorn corner of the city, and coming up empty. What they could not do, the FBI handled with speed and ease. A polite inquiry to the INS revealed the Konevitch address, working situation, and immigration status. Another call to the IRS revealed the full details of their financial status. All information the FBI gave Volevodz that he passed on to Nicky, via Tatyana. Hide-and-seek was over, a new game was about to begin.

One way or another, dead or alive, but on a plane to Russia, Konevitch was going to lose.

"I don't think I will," Volevodz countered, arrogance rising to full pitch. "You've tangled with the wrong people. There will be no second chance, Konevitch. You're a fool, you should have taken the deal."

"Think again. I have political asylum."

"I strongly advise you to come along willingly. This is inevitable, believe me. Make it easier on all of us."

"Get out of my apartment. Now."

A switch to English. "What will you do, Konevitch? Call the police? These are the police," he said, nodding his sharp chin in the general direction of the two agents by the window.

They smiled and waved. Real smartasses.

Elena bared her teeth and said to the two agents, "You should be ashamed of yourselves. Even in Russia, citizens aren't treated this way anymore."

"How much did you pay for this place?" one of the agents asked without a trace of curiosity. It was a statement of fact, an accusation, or, worse, a verdict.

"None of your business," Elena shot back.

"Nine hundred and seventy thousand," the agent replied, scowling. "Almost a million bucks. Lotta money. Cash, too. Where'd it come from?"

Alex placed a hand on Elena's arm — they were deliberately goading her. It would do no good to answer, so she stifled her reply.

"You stole it," the agent said, directing a long finger at Alex. "You robbed your own investors. You fled with hundreds of millions of dollars. You're crooks who lied to the immigration board to procure your status. You're nothing but lying thieves."

Elena had passed the point of rage. She was going to have her say, no matter what. "That's a lie. I don't know what this man told you, but he's a liar. You're stupid and he's a liar. Get out."

More smiles from the two agents. Large slack jaws, bunched shoulders, simple responses — actually they did look a little stupid.

Before things escalated, Alex decided to put an end to this. He stared coldly at the pair of agents. "Am I under arrest?"

No reply.

"Under investigation?"

The start of a nod, before it quickly turned into a crick of the neck that needed to be rubbed.

"It's time to call my lawyer," Alex announced, moving with feigned confidence toward the phone.

About two seconds passed. "There'll be time enough for that later," one of the agents said. It sounded like a threat.

Alex kept moving toward the phone. The agents appeared nonchalant, but the threat of a loudmouthed attorney showing up at this scene clearly unnerved them. No wonder. Without a warrant they had broken into a private residence, vandalized thousands of dollars' worth of property, then begun questioning a suspect without reading his rights. Worse, a foreign official without any legal status had been invited to the smashmouth party.

Any lawyer worth his salt would have their balls on a plate.

Alex lifted the phone and faced the two agents. "Give me your names. My lawyer will want them," he demanded.

They shuffled their feet and seemed to shrink. They exchanged matching looks of confusion.

"We'll be going now," one of them mumbled, one foot planted, ready to bolt.

"Not with my computer, you won't," Alex insisted.

"We're seizing it as evidence. Have your lawyer take it up with our lawyers," one said derisively. Having gotten the last word, and after firing off a final set of contemptuous looks, they walked quickly out of the apartment. Volevodz had that thin smile as he filed past Alex and Elena.

Alex slammed the door behind them, a loud shot that shook the walls.

Elena couldn't take her eyes off the mayhem in their apartment. Her only photograph of her parents had been torn out of the frame; it was on the floor, ripped into dozens of tiny pieces. The vindictiveness of it turned her stomach.

"Alex, I'm scared."

"So am I."

"What does this mean?"

"It means it's not over."

"Why would the FBI allow that man inside our home?"

"I don't know."

"We need to see MP, right away."

Alex lifted the phone.

Elena began picking up.

MP was at home, babysitting the kids while his wife shopped for groceries. He promised to drop everything and meet them at his office in two hours.

18

The office of MP Jones was on the second floor of a seven-story commercial building, almost dead center in the middle of M Street. MP was a graduate of Georgetown Law, a prestigious school, though not top five. He did it the hard way, four years of night school while he slaved at two menial jobs. Four years of pinching pennies. Four years of sprinting from class to McDonald's, where he pushed the torts and contracts to the back of his brain and shoved Big Macs and greasy fries across the counter. Four years of the cruel monotony of mac and cheese, of sleepless nights, of vying with full-time kids from wealthy families and wondering if this was the right choice. But he made it.

He graduated bottom third, but at least he had no onerous student debts. No interviews with big firms landed in his lap; sadly, no interviews at all. He had, however, passed the very difficult D.C. bar exam the first time around.

The Immigration Service was hiring and nobody else took his calls. Why not, he figured. Spend as few years as practical learning immigration law, then hang out a shingle and get rich quick.

Now it was him, two other lawyers, three stressed-out paralegals, and one very rude secretary who hated her job and couldn't wait till something better opened up. They called themselves partners. They referred to their setup as a firm. Nothing could be further from the truth. They were three struggling, scrambling attorneys dividing up the rent, a clutter of secondhand office furniture, and a few second-rate employees. No casework was shared, no fat profits divvied up at the end of a prosperous year. There were no prosperous years.

Married, with two kids and an attractive wife six months pregnant with the third, MP had cold sweats that it might turn out to be twins. They lived in a tiny, shabby ruin of a house he rented in a modest, run-down South Arlington neighborhood across the river.

Immigration cases, MP learned the hard way, paid squat. Nearly all his clients were poor, desperate people whose language skills were rudimentary, their earning power zilch. Too many were indigents assigned by the court. Hopeless causes seemed to be his specialty. They were booted out with regularity, which did not incline them to pay their legal bills. Immigration law, he had learned the hard way, was a poor man's game. Wealthy clients were scarce. The very few, mostly millionaires fleeing legal or tax troubles in their own lands, were bitterly scrapped over by every immigration attorney in the city; usually the large firms with dozens of lawyers to throw at their defense landed them with ease. MP had long since stopped hoping for a big score. His livelihood depended upon a backbreaking log of cases, and the oft-disappointed prayer that half of his clients might pay their bills.

But Alex and Elena Konevitch were different. An odd case, he thought as he stared at them holding hands across his desk. These were seriously frightened people. Probably had a right to be.

"So then the FBI just left? Walked out the door?" MP asked after listening closely to their story. A yellow legal pad was splayed open in front of him on his desk. Ten pages were filled with scrawls, questions, and other musings.

"With our computer," Alex clarified. "Can we get it back?"

"They entered without a search warrant?"

"Alex asked about it," Elena replied. "They didn't give him an answer."

"Okay, they didn't have one," MP concluded with the sad confidence earned through hard experience. Immigrants had few if any rights in this country. The police knew it and too often abused them in ways that would be unimaginable against a full-fledged citizen. Yes, Alex and Elena had been granted asylum. But what the government giveth, it can, and sometimes doth, taketh away. MP had seen it before. That the Feds would act with such callous abandon was not a good omen.

"You're sure you committed no crimes in Russia?" MP asked. He had repeated this same question a hundred times in preparation for their asylum hearings a year before. It wouldn't hurt to hear the answer again. He studied their faces, hard.

"None," Alex told him. "A traffic violation once. I parked illegally and paid the fine."

Blushing slightly, Elena said, "When I was sixteen, I was with a group who had been drinking and became a public nuisance. I was brought before a judge and released."

"You're sure you didn't steal anything from the bank?" This question, obviously, was directed at Alex.

"Not a penny. Fifty million was stolen, according to the Russian news. But by the people who took away my bank, not me," Alex answered quite resolutely.

MP seemed undecided for a moment. He ran his pen aimlessly across a page, trying to decide what to do next. "Could you step out for a moment while I make a call?"

They left and found seats in the small, cramped lobby. MP worked the phone for almost twenty minutes. It was Saturday, late afternoon. He was calling home numbers and getting the expected responses. The lawyers of INS were either out watching their spouses shop, clubbing divots into the back nine, or observing their kiddies tumble around soccer fields. He finally caught Tommy Kravitz, on a cell phone, apparently.

Kravitz was a lifer who did as little work as possible, an inveterate busybody who amused himself by knowing everybody else's business. The roar of a baseball game, live, loud, and raucous, made it difficult to hear.

"Who's winning?" MP yelled.

"Not the Orioles, damn it. Why do I root for these guys? I'm an idiot."

"You are an idiot, Tommy. Nineteen years in the INS trenches. You should've left ten years ago, gotten a life."

"Yeah? Hey, seriously, how's the money out there? Great, right?"

"Just okay. The kids love their new private schools, Terry considers our mansion in Great Falls to be too ostentatious, and I'm looking around to replace my six-month-old Jag with a Mercedes. The Jag picked up a small scratch on the bumper and it's just too embarrassing to be seen in. What do you think? Mercedes 500, or splurge and go all

371

out for a 600? It gets better mileage, that's what I hear."

Tommy laughed. "You're a lousy liar. Still got that same tiny shoebox in Arlington?"

"Yeah. The air-conditioning compressor went on the fritz last year, but we Joneses are tough. We'll sweat it out until Terry wins the lottery."

"Don't depend on her luck, pal. She got herself knocked up on your fourth date."

"Thanks for pointing that out."

"And that dented-up Chrysler minivan? That clunker still getting by the inspectors?"

"What do they know? We're driving it, anyway. Hey, you ever hear of a guy named Konevitch? Alex Konevitch."

A long moment of silence. Amid a loud roar, Tommy finally answered in a low whisper, "He your client?"

"Who scored?"

"Damn — that was a Yankee bat boy. The Orioles, remember? He your client or not, MP? Curious minds demand to know."

"Yeah, he is."

"Drop him. Just drop him, and run far, buddy."

"What's going on, Tommy? Tell me."

"I don't care if you were my brother. It's hush-hush, times ten. No can do. Mucho trouble's about to land on his head. Your guy's got problems he can't begin to imagine."

"Like that, huh?"

"Insist on cash, and make him pay you up front, MP. He has the dough, believe me. And count it real close — he's a rotten thief."

"Who's handling him?"

"Kim Parrish. That's not good news for you, either, pal."

The name was familiar: a vague memory, though. She had come aboard during his final year, when MP was more concerned with putting the INS in the rearview mirror than acquainting himself with the new associates he intended to leave in the dust. Like all new attorneys, she started out with the soft cases where she wouldn't embarrass the service — immigrants who snuck over a border or allowed their green cards to expire or committed some petty offense. Inside six months — record time — she was bumped up to the big leagues, the narcotraffickers, the big-time tax cheats, high-profile cases reserved for the best and brightest. She was old for a starting attorney, forty-five, maybe fifty. She was also smart and good, very good. Single, no children, intense, and very married to the law.

In a knowing tone, MP asked, "Who's pushing the case?"

"Are you deaf? I can't tell, MP. I swear I can't."

"Tommy, Tommy. That Gonzalez case, remember it? The one where you let the ball drop and the director wanted your —"

"Damn it, MP, I know I owe you. I'm not gonna say. Can't, just can't."

"I understand. I really do."

"Good. Believe me, if there was any way, I'd tell you everything."

After a brief pause. "So what aren't you gonna say?"

"You're a dogged bastard, you know that?"

"I can barely stand to eat with myself. Spill it, Tommy."

"All right, all right. For starters, I'm not gonna say the director was dragged over to Justice last week. I'm not gonna say the attorney general and FBI director reamed him purple 'cause he let this slimeball lie and cheat his way into asylum. I'm definitely not gonna say that this guy has the entire machinery of the Justice Department after his ass. I hope you're listening, MP. He's toast."

"Thanks for everything you didn't say, Tommy. I'll sleep better tonight knowing it's such an easy case."

"He's going home."

"He's got me as a lawyer."

"I'm telling ya, he's going home. Nothing you do will stop it."

"Watch me."

"You'll hurt yourself, pal. You're jumping in front of a steamroller. The heat on this guy's nuclear. Take the cash up front, then take a fast dive. Don't still be standing for the second round."

Tommy punched off, but MP still felt compelled to say, "I owe you one."

He called Alex and Elena and they filed back into his office. MP paced behind his desk, trying not to look overly concerned. The wrinkles on his forehead told a different story. They held hands as they fell back into their chairs.

"It's bad isn't it?" Alex asked.

"I'll be frank. Yes."

"How bad, MP?"

"The director of the FBI and the attorney general want you gone." He let this sink in, then continued, "I'm wondering why. Any ideas?"

"Yes, a few. My enemies in Moscow have powerful allies inside the Kremlin. They've obviously pulled strings with your government."

"But they can't ship us back, can they, MP?" Elena rocked forward in her chair, her hands tightly clenched beneath her knees. "They gave us political asylum. And there's no extradition treaty. If they send Alex back to Russia, they'll kill him."

"Those are the obstacles in their path. Ordinarily they're very powerful," he said, nodding thoughtfully, trying to balance optimism with his growing awareness of how serious this might be. He battled a temptation to jump out of his seat and scream, "Pack your bags and race for Canada. You haven't got a prayer."

"But . . . ?" Alex said.

"But they'll look for ways around them."

"What are these ways?"

"Every case is different, Alex. I can't predict. But I advise you to get your affairs in order. This can get ugly."

The first blow arrived Monday morning. Elena went to the bank to cash a check. They wanted to stay and fight, but they were realists. Flight might become their only option. To exercise that option they would need money, a hoard of cash, enough to get across the border and get settled. A withdrawal of ten thousand or more would trigger an immediate report to the IRS, and Alex was losing faith in all American authorities; so $9,999 it was. The teller, a plump young girl with a polite smile, punched the account number into her computer. The smile disappeared. She looked up with a puzzled expression. "Sorry, I can't cash this."

"You . . . What do you mean?"

"Your account's frozen." She was pointing at the screen Elena couldn't see.

"Frozen? How is it frozen?" Elena thought maybe her English was failing her, that maybe "frozen" was some enigmatic banking term like "overdrawn." A minor inconvenience that could easily be cleared up. "We have hundreds of thousands in that account," she insisted.

"Yes, I know. But the police or somebody has ordered the bank not to disburse any money from your account. I'm very sorry."

She felt like crying. Not here, though — not in front of all these strangers. She rushed outside and called Alex on her cell. She explained what had happened. He told her not to get upset, this had to be a misunderstanding. He would call MP, who would work a little legal magic and fix it.

They hung up and Alex immediately placed a call to his bank in Bermuda where the vast bulk of their money was parked. He was thanking God he had kept the account offshore, deeply relieved that he had not moved all that cash to an American bank where the interest rates were impressively higher. His business brain told him it was costing him thousands of dollars a year in lost income. A reckless waste. He had been sorely tempted a dozen times to just do it. Now he was pleased he had followed some darker instinct.

An assistant manager answered and quickly placed Alex on hold. A senior manager came on the line. "I'm sorry, Mr. Konevitch."

"What do you have to be sorry about?"

"There was nothing we could do."

"About what?"

"Well . . ." A lame cough. "Your account, sir, it's frozen."

The discussion lasted five minutes. Only an hour before, the governor of Bermuda had called in the head of the bank and read him the riot act. He himself had just gotten off the phone with a senior American Justice Department official who kicked him around like a third world tin can. Though Bermudan banking laws were notoriously loose, he was told that, in this case, the rules would tighten up. Ugly threats were traded back and forth, but in the end the outcome was preordained. Neither the governor nor the Bermudan banks wanted to be listed as havens for criminal money. It mattered not that they were — being accurately labeled was what they deathly feared. Tourism would dry up. Bermudan exports would sit on American docks, rotting. Bermuda, so dependent on rich Americans, would shrivel to a wasteland of empty beaches and foreclosed hotels, massive numbers of angry, unemployed people, etcetera. The governor remained steadfast for about three seconds before he crumbled under the onslaught of threats.

The FBI now had a death grip on both of Alex's accounts.

Not thirty minutes later, Illya called from Austria. "Alex, what's going on?" he yelled, clearly at the outer edge of reason.

"I have no idea what you're talking about."

"No idea? The roof's falling in here."

"Settle down, Illya. Take a deep breath and

tell me what's happening."

A long moment passed while his excitable protégé tried to order his harried thoughts. "This morning I was informed that our license to do business in Russia has been revoked. All day, we've been getting calls from clients canceling their contracts."

"On what basis?"

"The American clients were advised by the American FBI that we're a front for criminal operations."

"And the Russian clients?"

"No reason was given. They were just ordered by the Ministry of Security to terminate their relationships with us, or else."

Alex quietly cursed himself. The computer! He had password-coded his files, a false sense of security, he realized now, very unhappily, and a little after the fact. The FBI had talented specialists who probably could crack his password in seconds flat. He tried to recall what was in those files. Nothing. Everything. Too much. He had never imagined he would have to protect himself against this kind of police abuse. Not here. Not in America.

Everything he and Elena had done with Orangutan, the accounts they had brought in, the names of his contacts in Austria. What else? His bank records, of course — that accounted for how swiftly the FBI moved in and strangled their finances. A new thought struck him and his blood ran cold.

As coolly as he could, he said to Illya, "Pack your bags and get away, Illya."

"Why, Alex? I'm —"

"Don't ask questions I can't answer. Just get away, right now."

"Alex, I have three hundred employees. I can't. I have responsibilities and obligations here."

"Do you want to live?"

"Of course, but —"

"Use cash, Illya. Don't leave a trail. Don't call your family or friends. Find a place to hide where nobody will expect you."

Mysteriously, the line suddenly went dead.

The three men parked one block away in the white, unmarked van, turned down the volume, and sipped lukewarm coffee. They exchanged knowing winks and satisfied smiles. They were "press aides" assigned to the Russian embassy, a thin guise for intelligence operatives. Yes, run, Illya, run as fast as your legs can carry you. Dodge and hide, spend only cash, ignore your family and job, and disappear into the darkest hole in the universe. We'll still find you.

Volevodz had littered bugs in almost every square inch of the Konevitch apartment. The two Fibbies had observed him, had idly watched as he wandered around the Konevitch home hiding a listening device here, a bug there. They never said a word. After a while, Volevodz dropped any pretense of caution. They obviously didn't care. They had orders from on high to allow the Russian as much latitude as he wanted — as long as he didn't kill anybody. This was America, after all: a land of laws and inalienable rights. Beatings were questionable, they figured, in a gray area; guess it depended how bad the thumping got, the two agents decided.

The house phone was bugged as well. The men in the van could barely contain themselves when Elena had called that morning with the surprise news about the bank. Alex, we have no money. Oh Alex, how will we pay our lawyer? Alex, how will we buy food? The questions and pulled hair would come soon. Probably that night.

Another van, similarly equipped, and also filled with Russian "press aides," was parked half a block up from their lawyer's office. His phones, too, both at home and at work, were riddled with bugs. His house had been burgled the day before. While he, his wife, and two kids were doing the prayer thing at church, a team had entered through the broken back door. It was easy. A bad, decaying neighborhood. His neighbors generally stayed inside and very specifically ignored what happened outside their doors. His office, too, was wired like a sound studio.

So they knew the lawyer hadn't come in yet, was apparently still wandering the halls at INS, trying to fathom how bad his client's situation was.

Bad, pal. Real bad.

Neither the lawyer nor the Konevitches had the slightest idea how awful this was about to get.

19

The loud knock on the door came that night, slightly after midnight. Elena was sleeping with a pillow over her head, and never budged. Alex tried to ignore it, but the hammering grew more obnoxiously insistent, until he could stand it no longer. He slipped on his bathrobe and tiptoed quietly to the door.

He peered through the peephole. A middle-aged stranger in a cheap blue suit stood there, nervously looking around. Definitely FBI, Alex thought, though the demeanor was flagrantly different than the agents who tumbled their apartment on Saturday. This man appeared tentative, actually afraid. Alex opened the door.

The man inspected Alex's face, then asked in a low, raspy whisper, "You're Konevitch, right?"

"You know that or you wouldn't be here."

"Yeah, guess I do."

"Should I invite you in or would you rather just burst inside like your comrades? There's not much left to damage. A few chairs in the dining room. Two pictures we put back on the walls. I'll point them out for you. Take your pick."

"Lower your voice, all right? Step into the hall. Please."

"I'd rather make you come inside and drag me out."

The mysterious man leaned closer and lowered his voice to barely a whisper. "Trust me. We can't talk . . . not here, definitely not inside your apartment." His hand did something funny with his left ear, apparently trying to signal something.

Alex took a chance and stepped out. The agent reached over and gently eased the door shut behind him. He walked about ten steps and Alex followed. He turned around and they faced each other less than a foot apart. "Who are you?" Alex demanded.

"Hold your voice down. I'd rather not say. Did you do what they say you did?"

"Why ask? Your people already convicted me."

"Because I'm asking, okay?" The sour odor of a recently smoked cigar was on the man's breath. It mixed badly with the cheap after-shave.

"All right. No, I'm being framed. I swear it."

The agent almost smiled. Right, how pitiful. Why couldn't anybody come up with something original? "Tell you what. I really don't care if you did, or you didn't. I just don't like what's going down."

"Which is what?"

He played with the top button on his jacket and appeared indecisive for a moment. Then he apparently resigned himself to tell Alex everything. "A bunch of Russkis working in our headquarters. Tromble, the director, arranged it. I worked counterintelligence for ten years, right? I can smell it. These guys have former KGB written all over them."

"Colonel Volevodz?"

"Yeah . . . him and about three of his guys. Your apartment's bugged, you know."

"No . . . I . . . I had no idea."

"Probably your phones, too. Be careful."

"Why are you telling me this?"

"I'm a career guy, okay."

"So what? Volevodz is also a career guy."

"Yeah, but it's different." He wiped a hand across his forehead in frustration, apparently annoyed by being compared with some cold-eyed KGB thug. "Look, I'm taking a big risk coming here. But whatever you did back there don't justify what's happening here. I'm just warning you, be real careful."

"All right, I'm warned."

If anything, the agent suddenly became more agitated. He glanced down the long hallway, a long, searching look that indicated a high level of paranoia. He avoided Alex's eyes. After a moment he whispered, "One last thing."

"I'm listening."

"The Russian mob's got a contract on you. Don't ask how I know, I just know."

Alex should not have been surprised by this unwelcome news, but he was. Surprised and deeply unnerved. A long day of disasters was just capped by the Mount Vesuvius of bad news. He leaned against the wall and stared down at the red-and-black carpet.

"It's a serious contract," the agent continued, shuffling his feet and avoiding Alex's eyes. "Over a million bucks," he claimed, looking up. "These guys usually get people whacked for about five thousand. Apparently, you're quite valuable to them."

"Should I feel honored?"

"Scared shitless is how you should feel, Konevitch."

"All right, I do."

"Best we can tell, three teams flew in over the past week. That don't even account for the local players, of which there are too many to count."

"Your people know this for a fact?"

"Wouldn't be telling you otherwise."

"Where did this information come from? Do you have a source inside the syndicates?"

He shrugged his shoulders. "It's real, okay? Believe me or not, it's your ass."

"If your people know, why don't you protect us?"

"Because people high up don't believe you deserve it. They figure you did something to piss off the mob. It's your problem, not ours."

"Is that all?"

"That's all."

"Thank you."

A few seconds passed. The agent seemed to be arguing with himself before he blurted, "Look, forget about it. If things get tough, though, if you want advice or help, call me. Just not from your apartment. This is our little secret, okay?" He pressed a business card into Alex's palm. Special Agent Terrence Hanrahan, it read, with the usual array of office, cell, and fax numbers. "Remember, anytime you step outside, look both ways before you cross the street."

Alex nodded. The hand dropped and Special Agent Hanrahan walked quickly back down the hall, straight to the elevator. Alex returned to the apartment, stopped momentarily in his office, and rushed directly to the bedroom. Gently shaking her, he quietly awoke Elena. Placing a forefinger to his lip he handed her a notepad and pencil, keeping another of each for himself.

They spent the rest of the night writing each other notes.

Agent Terrence Hanrahan stepped off the

elevator on the ground floor. The Watergate doorman watched as he was quickly surrounded by five agents of the Bureau; they pinned his arms behind his back and roughly hustled him out through the door. No words were exchanged. A shiny black limo idled beside the curb.

A rear door opened and Hanrahan was shoved inside. A lean figure was slumped on the other side of the seat. The overhead reading lamp was on: the figure was paging through a stack of documents with blistering speed. Hanrahan found it hard to believe the man understood a tenth of what he was reading.

Tromble finally looked up. "Well?"

"Went down perfect. He's scared out of his wits."

"And he trusts you?"

"He's a smart guy, so I doubt it."

"But he at least believed you?"

"No question about that."

"And you think he'll call you?"

"Maybe. Depends, I guess, on how desperate he gets."

"You warned him about the contracts?"

"I did. Is it true?"

"Absolutely. My Russian friends say he not only embezzled from his own bank, he also stole millions more, from the mob. As if he didn't have enough enemies already. They want him as badly as the Russian government." He scratched his nose. "You remembered to mention the bugs?"

Hanrahan nodded. "His face turned white as a baby's ass. Why let him in on that, though?"

A slight smile. "We don't want Volevodz and his people to have an unfair advantage, do we?"

"Jesus, his own government, and now the Russian mob. I guess the only question is who'll get him first."

"Not really," Tromble said, glancing out the darkened window. "We'll beat them to him. Your job's to make that happen, Terrence. Don't let me down."

"He and that wife are going to be paranoid."

"Yes, I believe they will. That's the idea. You just make sure they realize America is more dangerous for them than Russia. I want them so hopeless they'll be more than ready for our offer, when it comes. We'll be their only help."

Hanrahan thought about it a moment. He had been an agent for eighteen years; Tromble was the fifth director he had served. By far, he was the toughest and most heavy-handed, but there was no question he got results. "And if they don't fold?"

"No problem. We'll turn up the heat. Pull out the stops and ship them back."

20

The three men sat in the white van, swapping American girlie magazines, sucking on cigarettes, sipping stale coffee, bored out of their wits. After that initial day of heart-thumping surprises and emotional terror, things had quickly retreated to a dull grind.

During the days, surprisingly little took place in the Konevitch apartment. Long bouts of silence, broken occasionally by tedious discussions about incredibly inane things — the laundry, the latest stupid game show on TV, Oprah, and so on. On Tuesday, the wife, Elena, read to her husband, out loud, a stream of interminable passages from *War and Peace.* Wednesday was *Anna Karenina*'s turn, which proved even worse. The men inside the van contemplated suicide, or rushing upstairs to drive a gag down her throat.

The Konevitches never left their building, or even their apartment, the best the men could tell. This had been a sore topic with Volevodz, who popped by occasionally to gather updates. As long as the couple stayed inside, the three listeners were trapped inside the van, crammed in with all the electronic equipment and debris from their meals. It seemed to shrink by the day; they were peeing in bottles, for God's sake. Theories and conjectures rumbled around the rear of the van. It was unnatural to stay penned up so long inside that cramped apartment. On the other hand, the Konevitches no longer had jobs. And money — actually the sudden lack of it — was undoubtedly a serious factor in their minds. Wasn't like they could afford to splurge on the theater or an expensive restaurant. Why not a movie, though? Better yet, a nice long stroll along the canal, like they used to? How much could that cost?

When it turned dark, things picked up and turned slightly more interesting. The Konevitches were like rabbits. Every night, for hours, groans and giggles, sheets rustling, and an occasional scream or "oh my God" to cap off the festivities. The first few times the volume had been kicked up full blast. The three men tried to imagine what was going on in that bed. Why hadn't Volevodz been thoughtful enough to plant a camera? It would have been so easy, they whispered among themselves. Eventually, the constant lovemaking only contributed to the enveloping air of misery.

It was almost as if the Konevitches knew all

about the three listeners, that they were taunting and rubbing it in.

The phone action had turned virtually non-existent. A few frustrated calls from their lawyer, who complained constantly about being stonewalled by his old friends in the INS.

An occasional call to order pizza and Chinese deliveries — that was it.

"What are they doing out there?" asked the note Elena passed over the dining room table to Alex.

A glance at his watch — 8:00 p.m. — and he scribbled a hasty response and flashed it to her. "Going nuts, I hope." After days of corresponding like this they had finally mastered the awkward art of balancing two conversations at once — inane verbal ramblings to mollify their listeners while they scrawled brief messages back and forth. It was tedious and slow, and absolutely necessary. They chatted in English and they wrote in Russian.

"Why didn't we buy a bigger place?!!!!" she scribbled back. "It's closing in on me, Alex. I can barely breathe."

Alex wrote, "At least the company's better in here than out there." Who knew how many Mafiya thugs were prowling nearby, trying their damnedest to collect the bounty? Volevodz knew their address — they had to assume he had somehow passed it along to the cabal in Moscow. So the thugs now had a firm fix on their location and Alex was sure they were huddled somewhere nearby, waiting. Going outside was out of the question. The first few days they had tried to suppress their terror, to find ways to cope with their anxiety and rearrange and repair their living conditions. Day three Elena had gone on a mad hunt for electronic bugs. She discovered six. They suspected there were more, plenty more, and they were right.

On day four, they agreed upon a strategy — they would work overtime to appear like they were going through the motions of a normal life, battling boredom, praying, and waiting for MP to whip a legal rabbit out of his hat and end this miserable nightmare.

They weren't fooling themselves, though. MP was a gnat battling giants. This was way over his head — over any lawyer's head, probably. At any moment, the people outside would become tired of this, and the next hammer would fall. And Alex, ever the clearheaded businessman, was sure things would become worse, whatever that meant.

With each succeeding day, the situation became more intolerable. Elena tried reading, watching TV, meditating — nothing worked. Nothing. Alex walked endlessly around the apartment, doing laps and searching for a solution. He thought best on his feet, and was wearing out shoe leather to find a way out of this.

They had no money. They were trapped inside this building. Unable to escape. Unable to communicate with anybody outside without the mice listening in. If there was a way out, it was up to them to find it. Alex patted Elena's knee and wrote, "Time for the bedroom."

They got up and together made the short trek down the hall. Alex loaded the tape they had produced the first night, carefully and quietly inserted it into the cassette player, then cranked the volume knob to maximum. He said to Elena, "Get your clothes off. I'm in the mood again." Neither of them had been in anything close to the mood since the visit from Agent Hanrahan with the terrifying news about all the bugs and the thugs waiting outside to kill them.

The idea that their every word was being overheard was sickening.

Elena kicked off her shoes, flung them hard against the wall, and made a point to sit heavily on the edge of the bed, with an accompanying groan from the springs. She opened the nightly banter. "You're always in the mood."

"And you're always beautiful."

"You're insatiable."

"And you're a doll." Then, "Take off your blouse."

"You first, with the shirt . . . that's it. Now

the pants."

They went back and forth, trying their best to make the listeners gag, then Alex sat heavily on the bed, right beside her.

They stared at each other a moment. Without another word, Alex pushed start and the tape kicked in. The sounds of the two of them sexually mauling each other shot full-blast into the listening devices.

They had nearly killed each other producing that tape.

Elena leaned close to Alex and whispered, "How many more days do you think we have?"

"One . . . twenty. Who knows?"

"What are they waiting for?"

"For us to break. Or run out of money and start starving."

"Why? What do they hope to gain?"

"They want us desperate. They have our money, and they've made us too terrified to step outside. It's a box, and the only way out is to accept their condition. A one-way trip to Russia."

"Maybe we should try to just make a run for it."

"How?"

"Disguise ourselves. Sneak out. Early in the morning when they're tired and their senses are dull. Create a diversion of some kind." She pecked him on the cheek, then pulled back. "You pulled it off in Budapest. We'll do it again."

"And go where, Elena? They have our passports."

"Montana, Idaho, Nevada. I'm past caring, Alex. A town in the middle of nowhere. Hot, cold, dry, wet, it no longer matters. Someplace small, neglected. America has millions of illegal immigrants. We'll live in the underground economy, find a way to blend in."

"I'll open a lawn service, and you'll be a maid. Is that the idea?"

"We'll be alive, Alex. And free."

He leaned over and touched her shoulder. "Listen to me. All of those millions of illegal immigrants don't have the FBI hunting them. The FBI doesn't know their names, doesn't have their physical descriptions, and could care less about them. We'd be looking over our shoulder every day. One day we'd wake up to a bunch of men in gray suits."

"But I'm tired of sitting here, waiting."

"Well, I have an idea."

"I'm willing to try anything."

"Unfortunately, it will take time."

"How much time?"

"Probably a lot. Probably too much. It's a complete gamble, anyway, an outside shot with a million things that can go wrong."

She stared up at the ceiling. "A million things can go wrong here. Tell me about it."

They whispered back and forth, while the men in the van, tired of the monotony of love and lust in the Konevitch place, squelched the volume and napped.

One block away, the lady and two men stayed hunched inside the car and, through a pair of powerful binoculars, kept a close eye on the front entrance of the Watergate. The year of hunting for Alex in Chicago had not agreed with Katya.

Nicky had a modest, not overly prosperous operation in Chicago run by a half-crazy, doped-out boss who put up the hunter-killer team, along with five of his own people, in a cramped, run-down rowhouse in one of the most crime-infested sections of the South Side. He called it a safehouse. It was barely a house, and anything but safe. Black and Hispanic gangs roamed the surrounding streets at will. They did not particularly cater to these Russians who were trying, rather unsuccessfully, to muscle into the local action.

The rowhouse quickly became a prison, a quite miserable one. The gangs were large, mean, and tough. A tiny bodega was positioned on a corner across the street. They hung there, blacks and spics in variously colored bandanas, mixing freely together, never less than fifteen of them. They sipped from canned beers, rapped back and forth, shared menthols, and glowered at the rowhouse across the street. They seemed to be honoring a local cease-fire among themselves, a temporary alliance against a common foe. For decades, they had battled and scrapped with one another for these streets — every inch of concrete, every crackhouse and whore's corner was a victory, paid in blood. No way were they going to let these Ivan-come-latelys have a piece of the action. At night they sometimes sprayed the rowhouse with bullets. They scattered when the cops arrived, only to reappear the instant the last blue suit departed. Once, a pair of Molotov cocktails sailed through the windows.

The Russians slept on the floors, and crawled on their bellies every time they passed a window. A stack of portable fire extinguishers was stored in the kitchen. First aid kits were in every room in the house.

Katya and her crew ventured outside as infrequently as possible. Two left on a grocery run one night and never returned. They may have fled. Nobody blamed them.

A few weeks later, a box with four ears was left on the doorstep. They studied the shriveled things and debated at length, but nobody could be entirely certain they belonged to Dmitri and Josef. Dmitri did in fact have two earrings. And okay, yes, Josef's ears were sort of large and floppy; but no one knew for sure.

It constipated the search for the Konevitches terribly. The first few months, Katya and her comrades snuck out only in the wee hours of the morning, trying to elude the gangs. Their car had been shot at more than they could count as they sped down the street. Nicky's locals had a firm fix on the Russian immigrant pockets of the city; naturally, this was where the bulk of effort was placed. At some point, inevitably, the Konevitches would turn up.

Occasionally, they got word that Alex Konevitch had been seen cruising a few local Russian clubs, flashing a wad of bills and bragging about the flourishing real estate empire he was establishing in the city. It sounded like Mr. Big Shot. And after flashing photos at various witnesses, they were sure it was him. Queries to the local phone companies had revealed a cell service account, though the number was unlisted and the phone service stubbornly refused to provide the billing address. That was it. No matter how hard they dug, no matter how many cops they paid for information, this was all they had.

Additional pictures of the couple were plastered everywhere. Hundreds more were pressed into the hands of Russian expats with vile threats about what would happen should they fail to snitch on first sight.

After those first few months, the hunters became dispirited — and worse, seriously frightened. The party outside the bodega seemed to grow bigger by the day. The Russians took to cowering in the rowhouse, contriving false reports back to Moscow, manufacturing hopeful leads that never existed. The lies would never be caught, they were confident of this. Nobody would dare run the gauntlet and pay them a visit.

Massive quantities of food and beer and vodka were stockpiled. They watched the same tired porn flicks, ate and drank heavily, and bickered among themselves. The men outnumbered Katya, and they cruelly exploited this advantage against her. They pressed her into service as their cook, their laundry lady, their maid.

Even the long year of killing in the Congo, her previous record for unadulterated wretchedness, paled in comparison.

Oh, how she hated the Konevitches. The last iota of icy detachment had melted months before. Her pouched eyes now burned with a scary intensity. It was all their fault, that awful couple. Why couldn't they just let themselves be killed? It would've been so much easier for everybody. How could they be so selfish?

When the call came from Moscow that the Konevitches had been found, living in Washington — and in a luxury co-op, of all places — she nearly cried. At four that morning, she and the rest of her team eased out of the bullet-pocked rowhouse, hauling their bags, and dodging a few farewell bullets.

The first day in Washington, she made six furtive passes around the Watergate and the busy streets surrounding the huge complex. To her trained eyes, the competition stood out like sore thumbs. The unmarked white van with too many antennas. The dark FBI cars splayed around like a drive-in movie theater, everybody watching, everybody waiting for the Konevitches to make a move.

They were all going to be sorely disappointed. They couldn't have them, not even a piece of them: the Konevitches were hers.

She sat, gazing hatefully through the binos, dreaming up unpleasant ways to kill them.

Mrs. Edna Clarke was ninety-two and still sprightly. She had lived in the Watergate from the day it was built. Her husband, Arthur, had been a managing partner of a large, prestigious law firm, before he passed, God bless him, at the youthful age of eighty-two. The past decade, she had stayed in her apartment, alone but for the kindred company of her three precious cats. She read and knitted and waited patiently for the good Lord to call her. Her children had pleaded with her to consider a nursing home. She wouldn't hear of it. This was her home, a place filled with wonderful memories of Arthur and the family they had bred and raised, through good times and bad, but mostly good. She would leave in a hearse, she vowed.

She just adored that lovely young Russian couple across the hall. The day they moved in, she had promptly rapped on their door, gripping a bottle of good red wine wrapped in a bright red bow. A housewarming gift. Not that young people practiced such things these days: they knew nothing about good manners. The Konevitches, though, were certainly different. They uncorked the bottle on the spot and insisted she come in and share a glass. And afterward, on weekends, they frequently invited her over for quiet dinners.

She and Arthur had led interesting lives. They had met in Europe during the war, where Arthur had been a legal star at the Nuremberg trials. They had dined with presidents and senators, as Arthur went on to work in civil rights and dozens of other things that were important and fascinating. At least fascinating at that time. Now they were just rotten old memories to most people. A pathetic old attic nobody cared to peek into. Not that Alex, though. He was so bright, so curious, such an accommodating listener. He sat on the edge of his chair and peppered her with questions until her brain grew tired and she creaked back across the hall to her bed.

On Edna's ninety-second birthday, they sprang for a ballet at the Kennedy Center — the Bolshoi on tour, no less! Edna had pushed and squeezed herself into a gown she hadn't worn since Arthur's death. Elena was friendly with a number of the dancers, and afterward she had escorted Edna backstage and introduced her around. What a lovely, lovely birthday. Her own children hadn't even sent gifts. Hadn't called, either.

So she did not think twice when Alex knocked and asked to borrow her cell phone. He promised to pay her back for any expenses incurred. Edna wouldn't hear of it, of course. Arthur had left her a bigger fortune than she could ever hope to spend. She had a perfectly good house phone, anyway. What did she need with that shrunken little excuse for a squawk box? She only bought it to see what all the fuss was about: a lot of hype and ado about nothing, she quickly decided. She could barely hear through it. Had to scream into it just to hear her own voice.

But Alex certainly seemed to be attached to that thing. She felt nosy, and guilty, but couldn't keep her eye away from that spyhole on her door. All day, day after day, it seemed, Alex was out there in the hallway, pacing back and forth, chattering like mad into that silly little device. Occasionally, he popped back into his apartment, only to reappear after a few minutes with that stupid thing nudged up against his ear again.

Odd behavior. A little suspicious, maybe; the way a man might behave were he, say, maybe having a secret affair. She drove that thought straight out of her mind. Such a nice, loving couple. He had to be talking business, she concluded; he was enough of a gentleman not to do it in front of his wife. Lord knew she hated when Arthur spent hours on the phone talking all that legal mumbojumbo with his partners and clients like she wasn't even there.

Shortly after midnight, the apartment door was opened with a skillful thrust of the pick, and gently pushed open.

Two men quietly entered, Mikhail Borosky first, then Igor Markashvili, a fellow PI whom Mikhail trusted devoutly, and occasionally employed for special jobs. Throughout the previous week, Mikhail and his client Alex had spoken over the phone every day, sometimes for hours. Things were getting ugly for the Konevitches back in America. Alex's patience with the people chasing him was exhausted. He had tried peaceful coexistence, forgive and forget, and they, apparently, wouldn't hear of it. Also they were targeting Alex's beloved Elena again. Mikhail could sense a deep change in his old friend. In place of Alex's cool, sober intelligence simmered a quiet rage. After a long dialogue, after many desperate ideas were thrown back and forth, they finally settled on a plan.

It would take time, though. Months, probably, if not longer. Mikhail encouraged his friend and client to just stay alive long enough to see it through.

The apartment was spacious, and also dark and empty. They tiptoed quietly in their sneakers, flipped on small flashlights, and fanned out. Nice place, high-ceilinged, wood-floored, furnished with expensive antiques, and kept neat as a pin by the lady of the house. The lady in question, Tatyana, was spending the night with her boss. Mikhail went to work on the phones, while Igor began littering listening devices at strategic locations around the apartment. Mikhail inserted a bug inside the phone in the living room, then another inside the phone on the bedside table. In less than fifteen minutes the job was done.

They slipped out as quietly as they entered.

The bugs were manufactured by a German electronics firm, highly sensitive, sound-activated little things that fed the noise to a small recording box hidden in the basement of the apartment building. There would be no need for Mikhail to conceal himself in a cubbyhole somewhere, battling sleep and boredom with an earphone pressed against his ear. He would stop in every few days, collect the old tape, reload a fresh one, then sit back in comfort over a cigar and scotch and listen for the dirt.

Only a few hours before, the two men had magnetically attached a small tracking device on the undercarriage of Golitsin's limo. Another, as well, was slapped on that cute little BMW convertible Golitsin had bought himself.

Breaking through the high-tech security system into Golitsin's mansion was close to impossible; also, frankly unnecessary. Who cared what the old man said, anyway?

At this stage of the operation, all that mattered was where he went.

Illya Mechoukov was soaking up the sun on a fold-out beach chair and gazing, without a serious thought in his head, through his shades at the Caribbean beach from the commanding perch of his balcony. In the four years since he founded Orangutan Media, he had not taken a single day of vacation. Not one. Just work, work, work. And even more work once Alex and Elena started roping in all those big U.S. firms.

He had no idea how exhausted he was, until this forced vacation landed in his lap. And this glorious little sun-drenched island filled with all manner of pleasantries was such a perfect place to unwind and forget all that pressure. The sun, the rum, the beaches, all those native girls and American tourist girls romping in the surf, competing to see who could show off the tinier bikini. At that moment, his eyes were feasting on two of the lovely little things down below, flaunting their bronzed bodies in little more than thin strings.

He never heard them enter his hotel room. Never knew of their presence until the garrote landed around his neck and was pulled back. The pain was vicious and unbearable. The garrote was held firmly in place for over a minute. His eyes bulged, his lips turned purple, as his hands clawed desperately at the rope.

Then darkness. He passed out, though he hadn't died. He was sure of this when they threw cold water on his body and revived him.

"What —" he tried to say before a big fist smashed against his lips.

He spit out two front teeth. He was on a bed, gagging and coughing up blood.

"We'll talk and you'll listen," a man told him in Russian. The man was a terrifying giant, nearly six and a half feet, with swollen muscles that stretched against his silly Bahamian shirt. Black curly hair covered his arms and half-exposed chest. In fact there were three men, Illya realized. The other two were dressed similarly in pink and yellow shorts, flowered shirts, dark socks, and leather sandals.

"Nice outfits," Illya mumbled, and was quickly rewarded with another fist.

"This is very easy. We have nothing against you," the one in pink shorts informed him.

"All you have to do is sign a simple statement and you're free."

"A statement? What kind of statement?"

"Do you want to live?"

"Of course."

"Then what do you care what the statement says?"

He really didn't. Not at all. A sheet of paper, official-looking and typed neatly in Russian, was shoved in front of Illya's face. A pen was propped in his hand.

He barely had time for a brief glance before the garrote around his neck suddenly tightened — something about a confession that Orangutan Media was a front for criminal activities. And something more, something about Alex Konevitch, before the world around Illya became a gathering blur. Somehow he scrawled his name at the bottom of the page before he subsided into darkness again.

When he awoke, the bad men were gone.

21

Tromble was seated behind his large desk, ruffling papers, pretending to read, a trivial excuse to keep Hanrahan and his team leaders waiting along the far wall, a spiteful way of showing his deep displeasure at their failure to bag Alex Konevitch.

After five minutes of this, Hanrahan thought seriously about rushing across the room and pistol-whipping him.

Eventually the director glanced up at Hanrahan. "It's been two weeks. Why hasn't Konevitch called us yet?" he asked in a tone suggesting this was all Hanrahan's fault.

"I don't know." It was five o'clock, Friday. The end of two long frustrating weeks, and Hanrahan was sure there was a happy hour somewhere with his name on it. He pushed himself off the wall and moved closer to the big desk. "They haven't left the building since our little chat. They're ordering in food, tiptoeing around their home, hunkering down. They're scared to death. They'd be

409

idiots not to be."

"Where are they getting the money? I thought we took care of that."

"My guess would be they had a little cash laying around. Not everybody lives off charge cards."

"How much money?"

Hanrahan said, "I have no idea. Probably not a lot. They're living off pizza and Chinese food. We've questioned a few of the delivery boys. They're using coupons, very spare with the tips. Indications are the kitty jar ain't all that full. They're trying to stretch it out."

"But you could be wrong?"

"Yes, I could be wrong."

"And this could drag out for months?"

"That's possible. Unlikely as hell, but I won't rule it out."

Tatyana from Yeltsin's office had been calling Tromble every other day. She was polite and courteous, but beneath that veneer, she was needling and nagging. She never missed a chance to remind him of his boast that Konevitch would be in Russia inside a week. He was tired of it. Twenty talented agents with hundreds of years of experience in battling organized crime had been identified and told to prepare for quick reassignments to Russia. Everything was ready to go, everything except this Konevitch guy.

"What are our Russian friends up to?" Tromble asked, leaning back and folding his hands behind his head.

"The white van's still here. Our guys snuck over and attached a very sensitive listening device on its side. The three boys inside are seriously unhappy campers. Starting to act a little strange. Get this. Yesterday they actually played a few rounds of Russian roulette." He shrugged. "I guess it's their national sport."

"What else?"

"The Mafiya's got a small presence. Last Tuesday, one of their people made a few fast laps around the area. She and two of their people are living inside a car about a block away. They sleep in it, eat in it, and wait."

The impatience on Tromble's face was palpable. Hanrahan, an old hand, was a veteran of countless stakeouts and several hostage situations. Patience is key. They take time. It's a psychological face-off, both sides playing mind games with the other. It's just a matter of who'll snap first. You can't rush it.

Almost predictably, Tromble said, "We need to do something different." After a pause that was meant to appear thoughtful, he pushed on. "Why don't you just arrest them?"

"On what grounds?" Hanrahan asked.

"I don't care. You tell me."

Hanrahan scratched his head. "Maybe some sort of immigration violation. Something simple. Overstaying their visas, maybe. From what the Russkis are saying, he lied to get his asylum. Maybe toss on a charge for fraud."

"Go with the overstayed visa."

"That's INS's territory," Hanrahan observed, quite rightfully.

"Good point. They have to get involved eventually. Why not now?"

Hanrahan slowly nodded. There was obviously more going on here than he was being told. The director was playing this close to the vest, but that wasn't unusual. In an effort to learn more, he asked dubiously, "So we pick him up on a simple immigration violation?"

"We'll throw on all the additional charges we want later. And we'll bring the press into this thing, maybe put out a statement that throws all kinds of dirt at Konevitch. I just want them in the judicial system for now."

"Them?" A brief pause and a look of disbelief. "Both of them?"

"Isn't that what I said?"

"What crime did she commit?"

"She married him."

Hanrahan cleared his throat and stood his ground. "So you want us to use her to pressure him? I wanna be sure I heard this right."

Tromble played with a paperweight on his desk. "Did I say that?"

Hanrahan didn't dare answer.

Tromble lifted up a document and pretended to read it.

Hanrahan wouldn't budge — they were skirting on the thin edge of the law already. Now Tromble was trying to shove him across it. He was two years from retirement. He had it all mapped out: a small home on a golf course in Florida, as little private consulting as he could get away with, divorce the hag he married, and find a new hottie who looked good in a skimpy bathing suit or wearing nothing at all. He wasn't about to put it all at risk. He wanted an unequivocal order in the presence of the two witnesses against the wall.

When it became clear they would stand against that wall all night, Tromble finally relented. Without looking up, he said, "He entered our borders under false pretenses. She accompanied him, and she participated in his falsified testimony for asylum. That makes her party to the conspiracy, and her role merits similar treatment."

"Got it. When is this supposed to happen?"

"Tonight. Late tonight. It's Friday and his lawyer won't be able to do anything until Monday."

The knock came at three in the morning. Alex threw on his bathrobe, again, and again tiptoed to the door. A quick peep through the spyhole — Marty Brennan, the co-op maintenance man, peered back with a worried expression.

Alex opened the door. "What is it, Ma—"

413

Marty was suddenly shoved aside by a crowd of eight people who barged inside, seven men and a stout woman dressed like a man. The agents fanned out and raced into every room in the apartment, which did not take long as it was so small.

From the bedroom, Elena screamed. Alex made a move in that direction before he was restrained by two men with thick shoulders and rough hands. They yanked his arms behind his back and with well-practiced efficiency fitted flex-cuffs around his wrists. "Who are you?" Alex yelled.

"Immigration Service," replied a voice from the small kitchen.

"We've done nothing wrong. We have political asylum."

"Past tense. You had asylum," the man corrected in a snarling tone, moving back into the room and positioning himself before Alex. "That's now suspended, pending review."

"Fine. We also have visas. The passports are in my briefcase," Alex told him, using his chin, awkwardly, to indicate the case resting precariously on the now three-legged living room table.

The man walked to the briefcase, deftly snapped it open, and withdrew two booklets. He flipped through until he came to the pages with the American visas — a millisecond of study before he looked up and frowned. "These are obvious forgeries."

"So is the American Constitution, apparently."

"Search the place," the man directed his people. Everybody but one man in the corner snapped to and began rummaging through drawers and overturning furniture, again.

Alex informed them, "The FBI tossed our place over two weeks ago. What do you expect to find?"

No answer. Alex turned away from the destruction and studied the one man who leaned against the wall, not participating. He wore a cheap gray suit like the others, though he was clearly more observer than participant. Alex directed his voice at him and said, "You must be FBI."

The man looked a little uncertain, then replied very amiably, "Good guess."

"I want to call my lawyer. He has all the papers regarding my asylum and legal status. I'm sure you want to see those papers, right?"

"Nope. Not tonight."

"What about my rights, sir?"

"Illegal immigrants don't enjoy rights."

"I want to be clear on this, sir. You're denying me the right to counsel?"

In one of many conversations with MP, the lawyer had advised him that something like this might happen. Ignore the indignities and offensive behavior, stay cool, don't get confrontational, no matter how bad the goading gets, MP had advised quite insistently. It

415

won't sound good at an immigration board hearing, or in a courtroom, that Alex, an immigrant, lacked respect for American authorities. Stay firm and polite. Gently remind them of your rights, and remember how many legal procedures they violate; later, we'll drag them through all that dirt in a courtroom.

But at that moment, Elena was tugged out of the bedroom and into the small living room by the female agent who looked like a drag queen in reverse. Elena wore only her nightie, a skimpy, nearly transparent garment that left little to the imagination. A few of the male agents were openly leering at her. Elena didn't care. She stared back with a ferocity that would make an armored tank wilt with shame.

The FBI agent also was sneaking quick lurid peeks at her, at least he was before Alex snapped, "Even the KGB didn't employ so many perverts."

The agent, who was named Wilson, shifted his eyes to his shoes and turned slightly pink.

"Are you married?" Alex asked him. No answer, so Alex again prodded, "Do you have a wife?"

"Yes." Still staring down at his laces like a shamed child.

"Would you enjoy seeing your wife treated this way?"

"How were we to know what she was wearing?"

"But you know it now, sir. And like sick perverts you're all leering at my wife. If you had any decency you'd allow her to go into the bathroom and get dressed."

Agent Wilson could not stop staring at his shoes, the tips, the laces, the stitching along the sides. His orders were clear and brutal. Humiliate Konevitch. Goad and provoke him into doing something stupid — any pitiful attempt at resistance, disrespectful behavior toward the agents, or, better yet, some mild act of violence. The charges against him were precariously flimsy, trumped-up bullshit that was dangerously toothless, if truth be told. His boss, Hanrahan, had demanded something a real judge could sink his teeth into.

But that "pervert" word really stung. Now looking at anything *but* the nearly naked, gorgeous blonde in the room, he said to the female agent, "Let her get some clothes and change in the bathroom."

Elena was led off, stomping angrily down the hall.

Alex leaned against a wall and resigned himself to watching the INS agents tear his apartment apart. The few pieces that weren't already broken — and those he and Elena had carefully and lovingly repaired — were now destroyed beyond repair. It was hard, grim work and, to their credit, nobody smiled or laughed this time.

After about five more minutes of frantic

homewrecking, the sounds of somebody pounding hard on a door at the rear of the apartment brought a sudden halt to the action. A deep woman's voice was frantically yelling, "What are you doing in there? Open up. I said, open this damned door! I mean it, I'm not fooling around."

The FBI agent, Wilson, suddenly lost his polished cool and dashed back to the rear bathroom. After a few moments of loud confusion accompanied by more ignored demands to open the door, Alex heard a loud crash. A moment later, Elena was dragged back into the living room, fully dressed now, in jeans, a loose sweatshirt, and a petulant expression.

"What were you doing in there?" the FBI agent demanded two inches from her face.

"I changed clothes."

"What else?"

Elena could not resist a big smirk. "Isn't that a rude question to ask a lady who was in the bathroom?"

Mr. FBI rolled his eyes and barked at the INS agents, "Search the bathroom."

Two minutes later, one of the agents reappeared, sheepishly gripping a wet cell phone in his hand. "This was hidden inside the toilet."

It was senseless to ask Elena if she had made a call. And equally a total waste to ask whom she had called. At that moment, their lawyer probably had his foot glued to the metal as he raced to the apartment.

"Slap her in cuffs," the FBI agent ordered. "Time to get out of here."

As they were led out the doors on the ground floor, somebody had obviously alerted the press. They were there in force, it was 3:15 in the morning, and they were swapping jokes about the infamous Watergate, sipping coffee, playing with the klieg lights, waiting for the fun to begin.

It had been a slow, dry week for the news cycle — the Hollywood brats were behaving surprisingly well; plenty of murders, but none gruesome or weird enough to break the threshold of public monotony with such things; and of course Washington hosted its usual political scandals involving graft and sex, but nobody cared about that anymore. The boys from the Bureau publicity machine had gone into overdrive and kicked up huge interest in this fast-breaking story. The Runaway Millionaire, they had called Konevitch. The number one most wanted man in Russia. A beautiful celebrity couple, and better yet, the news bureaus were promised all kinds of inside leaks and dirt to fan the public interest and give the story long legs.

A blonde woman lingered at the rear of the crowd, gripping a big pistol under her jacket, silently cursing that there were so many witnesses. The hell with them all, Katya swore to herself. Her orders from Golitsin were clear and unequivocal: make their deaths look like an accident, or a robbery gone wrong, or a joint suicide pact by the obviously distressed couple. But in her long, fruitful career of killing and assassinating, no target had ever pushed her buttons this way. The humiliation of the escape from Budapest was bad enough. But the full year of misery in Chicago, and to learn now that it was all because Mr. Smartass inside that big building had outsmarted her, again. Oh, she was long past caring what Moscow wanted. If she saw any chance for a clean shot, she would take it — just blast away with her forefinger glued to the trigger. Just keep firing until the Konevitches had more holes than a doughnut shop, then flee into the night and hop the fastest transport headed to Mexico. She rather enjoyed the idea that it would all be caught on camera.

She would somehow acquire a copy of that tape. She intended to spend the rest of her life watching herself blow them both to hell.

Suddenly, the doors flew open. Tightly surrounded by the clutch of agents, Alex and Elena were led outside, then halted for a brief cameo. Cameras flashed, film rolled, and dozens of unanswered questions were flung at the INS and FBI people. Katya tried pushing herself through the mob, but the reporters were veterans at this game; with the brutal skill of NFL linemen they shoved and pummeled her backward till she landed on her ass.

Alex and Elena were pushed through the crowd then shoved into the backseat of a large blue sedan. An FBI spokesman stepped forward and began issuing a statement as terse as it was obviously rehearsed: "Mr. Alex Konevitch is wanted for serious crimes back in Russia. He and his wife embezzled hundreds of millions from innocent investors and fled here. They've been living like jet-setters in America, hiding in one of the most luxurious buildings in the city, hiding from the Russian authorities and pretending —"

The door slammed shut and Alex could hear no more.

Next, a fast trip to the INS building, where the suddenly notorious couple were swiftly photographed, fingerprinted, and processed into the INS system for deportation.

Alex was handed a pair of orange coveralls and allowed to step into the men's room for a quick change. When he emerged, Elena was gone. He was led back outside and stuffed into a van, shackled to a floor bolt, then sped quickly to the Alexandria jail, where he was shoved into a holding cell filled with other miserable men, a mixture of Hispanics, Chinese, Albanians, and sundry other violators of the apparently whimsical immigration system.

22

The guard rattled his keys and called for Prisoner Konevitch to step forward. Alex pushed through the crowd of disconsolate men and appeared at the door. He had not showered in three days. He had barely slept, quick catnaps frequently interrupted by another prisoner stumbling over him, or a fresh internee being jammed into the overcrowded cell. He looked tired and unshaven, his hair greasy and limp. He smelled of stale sweat and urine.

He stepped through the door and two guards shackled his hands and feet before he was led in a series of awkward shuffles to the visitor area.

MP Jones was seated at a table, briefcase in lap, frowning and clutching his hands together. "Alex, I'm sorry this took so long."

"Elena called you Friday night, MP. Don't tell me you're sorry, tell me what happened."

"Games. I called every number I know at INS. Nobody would tell me where they took you. You should be in a D.C. cell. That's where you're domiciled and where you were arrested. Instead, they moved you here, to Alexandria, to throw me off the scent. Was it bad?"

"It hasn't been pleasant. I don't care about me. Get Elena out of this."

MP wouldn't look him in the eyes. "That's going to be difficult."

"Why? Arrange bail. Murderers get out on bail. Our apartment is paid for. Use it as collateral and get her out."

"Don't think I haven't already tried, Alex. Remember all those reporters outside the Watergate? The Feds are turning you into a showcase. You were big news over the weekend, all those crime and legal channels on cable had a field day. You got creamed in the papers and TV." He held up a picture cut from a newspaper. It showed Alex and Elena being led from the Watergate, cuffed and looking guilty as hell. "Apparently, they want the Russian government to know they're playing hardball."

"They want me, MP. Elena has done nothing wrong."

"The answer's no, Alex. They claim you're a flight risk."

"They can let her go. They'll still have me in jail."

"Alex, you're not listening. They want her in jail, too."

Understanding what MP was saying came slowly, but it finally struck with full force. He tried to swallow the huge knot in his throat. It wouldn't go away. The U.S. government was using Elena as a hostage, as leverage to force him back to Russia. He prayed her conditions were better than his. He hoped she was in a private cell. His cell was filthy and so thoroughly overcrowded that the men took turns sleeping on the hard floor. They fought with one another for a turn at the toilet, trading insults in an array of languages that only contributed to the frustration. The room was cold and noisy: between the sounds of a toilet constantly flushing and the constant drone of fearful men sharing loud complaints, sleep was nearly impossible. The food was awful, microwaved garbage mixed together on a tin tray.

MP pushed on. "By law, they can hold you four days before a release can be applied for. I've demanded a hearing tomorrow. They can't say no."

"What am I charged with?"

"An expired visa."

"But you can easily prove that's false?"

"Of course. As long as everybody sticks to the truth, it should be easy."

"Get Elena out, MP. I don't care about me, I don't care what it takes, get her out."

"I'll do my best."

■ ■ ■ ■

Yuri Khodorin's first hint of trouble was anything but subtle; five of his corporate executives ended up splayed out on tables in various morgues around the city. In less than three hours, five dead. An array of methods had been used, from shootings to stabbings to poisonings. The swath of killings spread from Moscow to St. Petersburg; it made it impossible to determine where the next strike might land, or, indeed, if there would be another.

On day two, this question was answered with an unmistakable bang. Six more dead. For sure, it was no longer an unlikely co-incidence, or a sated spike of revenge, or spent anger: the killings weren't incidental. They were deliberate, and they weren't about to stop.

At thirty-three, already Russia's second richest man, Yuri Khodorin was perched within one good, profitable year of landing at number one. Like Alex, he had started young and early, even before the crash of com-munism opened the door to huge money. He sprinted out of the starting block and cobbled together an aggressive empire as wildly diversified as it was vast, profitable, and hungry. Central Enterprises, it was named, an innocuous title for a holding company that had a grip on everything from oil fields to TV stations, including myriad smaller businesses, from fast food through hotels, and almost too many other things to count. It created or swallowed new companies monthly and spewed out an almost ridiculous array of products and services.

A pair of Moscow police lieutenants appeared unannounced at Yuri's Moscow office the morning after the second set of killings — an odd pair, one an oversized butterball, the other thin as a rail. They unloaded the bad news that the Mafiya was kicking sand in his face. And no, sorry about that, no way could the city cops protect him; they were stretched so thin they could barely protect their own stationhouses. But in an effort to be helpful they generously left behind the business card of somebody who surely could.

Day four opened with three of Yuri's corporate offices firebombed; suspiciously, the local firefighters were dispatched to the wrong addresses, and all three buildings burned to the ground. Insurance would cover the losses, but droves of his terrified employees were threatening to stop showing up for work. At the sad end of day four — having once more been refused municipal protection — Yuri bounced his problems up to the next rung. He placed a desperate call to the attorney general, Anatoli Fyodorev, and pleaded loudly and desperately for help. Fyodorev made lots of sympathetic noises, and promised an abundance of assistance of all sorts. He was just disturbingly vague about what that meant.

The best Yuri could tell, it meant nothing. Not when day five opened with a car bomb in his headquarters parking lot that slaughtered three more employees.

Late that evening, reeling from the brutally rolling shocks, Yuri sat in his office alone, brooding and speculating about the future. At this rate, there would be no future. He had been shuttling around to funerals all day, trying his best to console sobbing widows and their crying little children. His mood was ugly. He wanted to be left alone, to stew with self-pity.

His secretary interrupted this bout of dark depression and informed him that a man was waiting in the lobby. "Doesn't he have a name?" Yuri barked. He refused to give one, she replied. "Send him away," Yuri said. Think twice, she insisted; he claimed he might know a few things about the murders plaguing their firm.

"Nobody else seems to," Yuri muttered. "All right, show him in."

The man entered and fell into the seat across from Yuri's desk. There were no handshakes, no empty attempts at pleasantries.

Mikhail studied Yuri for a moment. Dark

cropped hair, rimless glasses, an efficient-looking type with a mass of excess energy he couldn't control. Constantly shifting in his seat, intermittently twisting the wedding band on a long, skinny finger.

This was Yuri's office, and he'd be damned if he was going to be outstared by anybody. He stared right back at Mikhail with a show of great intensity. The harder he stared, the less he learned — just a normal-sized, nameless male of about forty-eight years, with a hard, weathered face, dressed casually and nondescriptly.

After they stared at each other long enough, Mikhail broke the ice. "Alex Konevitch informed me that you and he were old buddies."

"We did a lot of business together, Alex and I. I miss him. Trying to keep up with him was a ball. He a friend of yours?"

"A good friend."

Yuri relaxed a little. "Where is Alex now?"

"America. Washington, D.C."

Yuri clapped his hands together in delight. "I knew it. All those theories about Brazil, or detox clinics, I always said they were bunk." Yuri's face turned grim. "Too bad he stole that money. Like I said, I miss him."

"That what you think happened, he ran with the money?" A year before this had been the most popular game in town — the Alex quiz. Where was the money? Where was Alex?

How much did he steal?

"Sure, of course." A furious nod. "That's what the news said happened."

"Great tale, isn't it? What's your theory about it?"

"I'm a big fan of the 'he snapped' camp."

"Just freaked out, grabbed as much as he could haul, and fled, huh?"

"Yeah, something like that. It probably makes more sense to me than it might to you. Tell the truth, I sometimes dream of doing the same thing."

"Having all that money isn't fun, huh?"

"Twenty-hour days, thousands of people who depend on you, constant crises where everything's on the verge of crashing down on your head. Oh sure, it's a blast." A brief pause, accompanied by a few more hard twists on the wedding band. "Now, who are you, and what do you want?"

"Mikhail Borosky. I did a lot of private investigation work for Alex. Still do."

"And what? Alex asked you to drop by?"

"Yes." Mikhail stretched his legs out and leaned back in the chair. "Alex asked me to keep my eye on the news. See who's next. Apparently, you're the guy."

A slight flinch. "Next? What does that mean?"

"It means you're at stage one of the same treatment Alex got. For some reason, you're getting it a bit rougher than he got. And they're a lot sloppier. I'm not sure why. Guess they're a little overconfident this time."

"I have no idea what you're talking about."

"Did you receive a visit from two of Moscow's finest?" From his tone, Mikhail already seemed to know the answer.

"Yes."

"A blimp and a beanpole, right?" It wasn't really a question. From a parking lot across the street, Mikhail had watched the pair enter the headquarters the day before yesterday.

A slow nod.

"They give you a business card recommending somebody who could put a stop to all this?"

Yuri tried to hide his surprise but found it impossible. This strange man knew so much. The card in question, in fact, sat on Yuri's blotter, in easy reach of his fingers. Only three minutes before, he had been within seconds of dialing the number and pleading for help.

Yuri shoved the card across the table. Mikhail bent forward and studied it a moment. The name on the card was unrecognizable and meant nothing. But the name didn't matter. If he bothered to check, which he had no intention of doing, the résumé would reveal a long career in the KGB and some kind of deep attachment or connection to Sergei Golitsin.

"You know the old story about the Trojan horse?" Mikhail asked, pushing the card back in Yuri's direction.

A careful nod. "Sure, who doesn't?"

Mikhail directed a finger at the business card. "There's your Trojan horse. Those two cops are crooked to the core. They were sent in to kick open the door. Once you call that number, the worm will find a way to let the barbarians inside your company."

"This is what they did to Alex?"

A knowing nod, and for the next twenty minutes Mikhail revealed everything that happened to Alex, how the scheme worked, the kidnap, the torture, being framed for the theft of everything he owned. The whole ugly tale. To verify his story, he passed Yuri morgue forms that confirmed the death of Alex's employees, as well as one of the statements prepared a year before by Alex that he had faxed to all the senior officials around Yeltsin.

Mikhail sat back and allowed Yuri time to read the evidence, to see the similarities, and to realize that he was indeed the newest target.

Long before he finished, Yuri looked sad, confused, and scared out of his wits. He gripped his hands together and studied his blotter for a long moment. "So what do I do now?"

"I think you got two options. One, take as much money as you can, and run."

After everything this man had just told him, option one sounded impossibly irresistible.

Screw option two. He had millions stored in a Swiss vault, a hoard of cash large enough to live happily ever after. A fraction of his current fortune of course, but he'd at least be alive to spend it. His private jet was tucked in a private hangar at the airport, fueled up and ready to go. He could have breakfast at his spacious London flat, or lunch at his favorite Azores resort. That indecision lasted seconds. The British have always been so very civil and accommodating to wealthy Russian exiles who drop by for breakfast, and asylum.

Mikhail allowed him a moment to bask in this hopeful reprieve before he warned, "Course, that option's not quite as clean as it sounds."

"Why's that?"

"They're still trying to murder Alex. They've got teams of killers hanging in his shadows. Also, they've somehow fooled the American FBI into shipping him back here. He's long past the point where he can do anything to them. They don't care. They still want him dead."

"What's option two?" Yuri asked very quickly, very solemnly.

"Fight them."

"Don't be silly. I'm a businessman. I don't know what I'm up against, or even who these people are."

Mikhail stood and began pacing in front of the desk. "That's why I'm here. I do know who they are. And every time they meet, wherever they go, I learn more. They're very powerful, very dangerous people. And they're very, very corrupt. It's a large conspiracy with lots of money that gets bigger by the month."

"Is this supposed to be encouraging?"

"If you're listening carefully, yes. That size now works against them. And, as I mentioned, after Alex, they've become overconfident and incredibly sloppy. Understand that this thing works only when they have complete surprise. They have to be in the shadows, totally anonymous."

"So what am I supposed to do?"

"For starters, forget the name on that card. I'll leave you the number of a former police captain. He's competent, tough as nails, a born street fighter. Call him first thing in the morning, pay him whatever he asks, and don't anticipate overnight results. Expect a few more killings and bombings. Over time he'll find a way to protect you and your people. If he needs money, write the check without questions. It's not just a matter of a few more guards and extra precautions. Alex tried that, and look where it got him. He's going to have to bribe people, and he'll probably need to buy you a little help from a competing syndicate. He's going to fight fire with fire."

"What are you going to do?"

"Stay in the shadows. Keep my eye on

them. Eventually, I might come to you for money. It might be expensive, but I promise it'll be the best money you ever spent."

"So you expect me to just stay tough."

"Way I see it, you can stay tough or get dead."

23

Tuesday, at 9:00 a.m., Alex was again called out of the cell and led to the booking area. Elena was already there — like him, she now was dressed in oversized orange coveralls. Chains ran around her leg irons, looped around her waist, and were connected to her handcuffs. This was so ridiculous, Alex thought; no, on second thought, not ridiculous, it was outrageous. She was being treated like a serial murderer when all she was accused of was an expired visa.

The guards set to work on him next. Within two minutes he and Elena stood side by side, in ugly orange suits and matching chains.

They were led outside and helped into the back of a long, windowless van. The chains were locked down to bolts on the floor before the guards left and shut the rear door.

It was their first chance to speak since Friday night. "I'm so sorry," Alex told her.

"Don't be silly. You've done nothing wrong."

He tried to rub his eyes but the chains wouldn't reach and forced him to bend over. Elena asked, "Are you all right?"

"I'm fine."

"Don't worry, Alex. They can't ship us home over this," Elena said trying to sound confident.

"I think they can do whatever they want." They wouldn't have long to speak, and Alex was avoiding her eyes, trying desperately to build up his nerve. He had spent the whole weekend considering this conversation. Rehearsing it. Playing with variations on the same theme.

There were no other alternatives, and he finally blurted it out. "Elena, I want a divorce."

She considered this a joke and laughed.

"I'm serious. We're getting a divorce."

"Forget it."

"I intend to ask MP to find a good lawyer to arrange it. Uncontested, it should sail through quickly. Don't fight me on this. My mind's made up."

"Alex, this is so stupid."

"I said don't fight me on this, Elena. They're using you to get to me. The moment we're divorced they'll forget about you."

"Did you meet somebody in lockup? Another man? I know how good you look in orange coveralls. I won't be thrown away for some weekend fling." She was laughing again.

"Damn it, I —"

"Shut up, Alex. Just shut up." She leaned back and closed her eyes. The van was moving. They bounced along in tense silence for a few interminable moments.

With her eyes still shut, Elena said, "We'll never have this conversation again. I mean it. I love you, and if you ever bring up the 'divorce' word again, I'll kill you. We're going to suffer through this together. I don't care what happens as long as we're together. Nod your head if you understand, or should I just kill you now?"

Alex bent forward and refused to look at her. The silence dragged on.

Alex eventually said, "You look good in orange, too."

"Check out my new jewelry." She rattled her chains, then bent over and they shared a kiss. Bad jokes, but neither was in the state to think up good ones.

After a moment, Alex said, "I think there's a chance you might get out on bail."

"Me? What about you?"

"MP's not hopeful. Neither am I. Jail might even be the best place for me right now. Did you recognize anybody in the crowd of reporters the other night?"

"From Budapest, that blonde she-bitch."

They probably had only a few minutes left. There was a lot Alex wanted to discuss and he began speaking quickly. "You'll have to go underground. And you'll have to sell our apartment," he told her. "I know you love it, and I'm sorry. But you'll need the money to survive."

"I hate that apartment. I'll be happy to unload it. After four days in a small, cramped cell, I suddenly love the idea of wide-open space."

"Set a low price and dump it quickly. Then find a cheap rental, one you can get out of quickly. You'll need all the money you can get your hands on. My legal costs are probably going to be enormous."

"What about Orangutan? No longer an option?"

"It's history. But I've got a new idea. Probably even better than Orangutan Media, something I've been toying with for a while."

The van was beginning to slow down. In a fast rush of words, Alex shared the rough details of his idea. Elena nodded. She would have to learn a lot quickly. The concept was great, though. It would mint money, if she could pull it off.

The van wheeled into an underground garage beneath the INS building. Alex and Elena were separated, taken upstairs in different elevators, then deposited in different cells and left alone to stew with worry.

Thirty minutes later, a guard arrived, unlocked the cell, and escorted Alex down

438

several long, well-lit corridors to a small courtroom. Elena was already there, seated at a table beside MP. Their lawyer had his back turned to Elena and was engaging in a conversation with an attractive, older, dark-featured female seated at what Alex presumed was the prosecution table. A considerably younger male colleague in a dark suit sat to her right, looking nervous and out of place.

Alex sat beside MP, who quickly bent around him and said to the prosecutor, "Kim Parrish, I'd like you to meet my client, Alex Konevitch."

Alex held out his hand and looked her dead in the eye. "It's nice to meet you."

The room was small. They were about three feet apart. She nodded but took a step back, said nothing, and studiously avoided his hand. Go ahead, MP was thinking from the sideline — take a nice long look at the man you're about to persecute. You'll be responsible when he lands in a coffin. He's young and handsome, and his wife is young and beautiful — they have so much to live for — but go ahead, ignore your conscience. Get them killed.

She understood exactly what MP was doing. A long awkward moment, then she suddenly buried her nose in the blank legal pad on her table.

A moment later, the judge entered through a side door. There was none of the procedural rigmarole Alex had observed on American TV. No announcement, no standing. No long perorations or lawyers being introduced. Apparently, immigration cases adhered to a less formal pattern.

Judge John Everston IV presided. He spent a brief moment surveying his court to be sure everything was the way he liked it.

Alex's and Elena's eyes were glued to the face of the man who held their lives in his hands. He was neither handsome, impressive-looking, nor even mildly judicial-looking, with a long, droopy face, thick, arched eyebrows that lent an impression of severe fierceness, scarecrow gray hair, and small eyes hidden behind bifocals that seemed impossibly thick and bleary.

John Everston had started out as an immigration attorney thirty years before, a fine, precise, hardworking lawyer whose service was eventually rewarded with a judgeship. His lawyer career had been spent in the prosecution trenches. He came from a long line of deeply rooted, well-heeled southern Virginia aristocrats. And though everybody assumed otherwise, banishing immigrants had been a job he utterly loathed, and nearly always was ashamed to perform. He carefully hid a soft spot for the miserable masses who flocked to America for a thousand different reasons and suddenly found themselves at risk of being booted out. Left alone, they generally turned into perfectly respectable citizens. The law had forced him to separate families, to dispatch honest, hardworking people back to a life of hopeless squalor, and occasionally to send them back to conditions that meant certain death. Thirty years of practicing law on both sides of the bench had converted him from a mild liberal to a fairly rabid one.

And like every liberal judge in the country — in his opinion, like any judge with half a brain — Judge Everston detested John Tromble and he loathed the attorney general for failing to reel him in.

His eyes took in the court recorder, the bailiff at his station along the wall, the attorneys at their appropriate tables, and the young husband and wife huddled miserably in their atrocious orange prison apparel. He finally settled on a small group tucked in the back of the small visitors' section — a pair of bespoke gentlemen in nice suits and a young lady dressed decidedly more flippantly in ragged jeans, a torn T-shirt, and plastic flip-flops.

The judge directed a long finger in their direction. "It's not often I get visitors in this courtroom. When I do, I always like to make your acquaintance. You look like a reporter," he suggested to the young lady; from the way she was attired, she could be nothing but. Jeans and a ripped T-shirt — he had threatened lawyers with contempt just for wearing distasteful ties.

Sally, the court recorder, and Harry, the bailiff, exchanged curious glances. The judge had never, ever before even acknowledged visitors on the few rare occasions any showed up. Now he was actually conversing with them.

"I am," the lady answered promptly and proudly.

"What paper do you represent?"

"New York Times."

He would've publicly laid into her about her indecorum, but the *Times* was so reliably and frantically liberal, she could wear a birthday suit for all he cared.

"Good for you," he pronounced. The judge's gaze slowly shifted to her left. "And you two gentlemen?" he asked, directing a bony finger at the men.

"FBI," the older one said, sort of shuffling his feet at the unexpected attention.

The judge's head reared back. He squinted through his thick glasses and peered down his long, skinny nose. "And to what do I owe the rare pleasure of a few of Mr. Tromble's boys in my court?"

"We're just . . . merely observing," he replied.

"Observing what?"

"It's . . ." The agent blinked a few times. He had a law degree, though admittedly, he had sailed straight into the Bureau after law school. Aside from a few occasions on a witness stand, he had never actually been forced to address a sitting judge. He took another stab, saying, "We, that is, the Bureau, has an interest in the status of this case, Your Honor."

"An interest. I see. And what interest would that be, Agent, uh . . . ?"

"Special Agent Wilson. It, uh, well —"

"Speak up, Agent Wilson. This is a small court, and I'd like very much to hear your replies. I'm actually dying to hear your reply. In ten years on this bench, I don't believe I've ever entertained visitors from your Bureau. This is a small, unimportant court, and the proceedings are normally quite tedious. I'm on the edge of my seat to learn what's so special about today."

It was becoming increasingly apparent that the judge was not overjoyed with their presence. Every eye in the small court was on Wilson. He desperately wanted to crawl under his seat.

"Your Honor, the accused is wanted for certain crimes in Russia, crimes that are under our scrutiny."

The long finger popped back up like a pistol. "In this court, he's not the accused, Agent Wilson. This is not a criminal trial and I don't want you to prejudice my judicial neutrality through any misleading impres-

443

sions. In here, he's simply a man who may or may not have overstayed his visa."

"Yes, I under—"

"Does he have a criminal record in this country?"

"Uh . . . no." A brief pause. "Not that we've yet discovered anyway," Wilson said, implying otherwise, and visibly proud that he was recovering nicely.

"I see. Well, it is not my jurisprudence or interest to try crimes that might or might not have been committed on foreign soil. Unless I misunderstand the law, I believe the well-known prurience of your Bureau also ends at the water's edge. Surely an agent of your distinguished agency might understand that," he announced, looking far down his nose.

"What I meant —"

"I really don't care what you meant. I care only about what you say. Precise legal terminology is important. Surely they taught you something about that in that FBI school all you boys go through."

Wilson was silently cursing Hanrahan for making him be here.

The judge waved a thick folder in the air. "I took the opportunity to review this case file. All your statements are in here, seven INS agents and yours, Agent Wilson. Eight of you, altogether. Eight! Eight of you involved in arresting this young, frightened couple. They look harmless enough. And, as I understand it, the charge for my consideration deals with nothing more serious than expired visas. Am I missing something here? Please tell me I am, Agent Wilson. Have they smuggled in one of those suitcase nuclear bombs? Committed mass murder or run one of those odious rape camps in Bosnia? Surely, they have. Please assure me I'm missing something here."

No, you're not missing a thing, Wilson thought, now visibly miserable. Not a damn thing, you mean old goat. His back was rigid. He could barely force himself to keep his eyes on this judge. He had faced down Mafia thugs, kidnappers, dope pushers, and never blinked. He was plainly terrified of this judge.

"I am only here because I was ordered to attend, Your Honor."

"And who gave you this order?"

"I'd rather not say."

"You'd rather not?"

"That's right, Your Honor."

His Honor rested his elbows on the bench and placed his sharp chin in his hands. "Is this some pressing matter of national security?"

"Yes."

"Yes?" His small eyes bored into Wilson like rockets.

"Uh, no."

"Precision, Agent Wilson. Which is it, yes or no?"

"It's not. Uh, no."

"I see." His Honor toyed with his pen a moment. Wilson was examining the door. His legs were tensed, ready to bolt. It was barely ten feet away. He was almost certain he could be outside, sprinting to his car, before the judge could fire off another question.

His Honor slipped off his glasses and leaned far forward. "Let me make this clear, Agent Wilson. Listen closely and pass this on to those whose names cannot be uttered in this court. The freedom and dignity of two human beings are at stake here. They are guests in our land, so the reputation of our great nation is at stake. If I find any hint of remotely unethical behavior, I'll make you wish you never heard of Mr. and Mrs. Konevitch. I watched the news reports over the weekend, and frankly, I am dismayed and alarmed. I seriously hope nobody in this court was attempting to humiliate or pressure these poor people. Are we clear on this?"

"Yes, Your Honor."

"I mean it." The public whipping was over. Wilson looked thoroughly whipped. His Honor redirected his eyes toward MP. "Mr. Jones, you may begin now."

The sound of Wilson's sigh of relief echoed throughout the room.

Without rising or missing a beat, MP said, "Thank you, Your Honor. I'm sorry we're wasting your time this morning over such a

446

trivial, ridiculous matter. The issue is whether or not my clients overstayed their visas." MP slapped his right hand with a theatrical thump on a pile of documents on the defense table. "I have here all the requisite forms proving they have valid visa status. Also documentation proving they applied for and were unanimously approved for permanent residency in the United States. I'd like to get this charge dismissed immediately so my clients can go on with their lives."

Kim Parrish suddenly bounced to her feet. "Your Honor, we've changed the charges."

His Honor stared at the ceiling a moment. Speaking in a generally upward direction, he said, "Miss Parrish, you heard what I just advised Agent Wilson?"

"Every word."

"You understand that this applies to you also?"

"It left little question in my mind."

"Then proceed. Carefully, Miss Parish."

"Thank you. In fact, we have now established that the Konevitches do possess entirely valid visas."

"I would have thought this rather simple fact could've been established before their arrests."

"As would I, sir." She frowned contemptuously at the younger colleague at her table, as if he was at fault for this stupid blunder. His role in this farce was apparently to take the blame, and he obediently shrank and cowered under the force of her fierce glare. She continued, "Regrettably, paperwork was misplaced. A simple administrative mistake. We were unable to confirm this fact until yesterday."

"And did you notify Mr. Jones, who is, after all, representing these people?"

MP decided this was a perfectly good moment to help her out with this difficult question. "No, this is the first I've heard of it. I'm caught between shock and surprise. As Miss Parrish is no doubt aware, I'm prepared only to contest the charges I've been made aware of." MP looked so sad and disgusted it was impossible not to feel an ocean of pity for him.

"What do you have to say to that, Miss Parrish?"

"I tried to reach Mr. Jones."

"Did you?"

"Yes."

"How?"

"Phone."

"Once? Twice? How often?"

"I made multiple good-faith efforts. I can't recall the precise number. Unfortunately, there was no answer at his office."

"Do you have an answering machine, Mr. Jones?"

"Yes."

"Is it left on after office hours?"

"Yes. Always."

"Miss Parrish?"

"Maybe I dialed the wrong number."

"I'm sure that explains it."

Now that it was firmly established that she was lying, she pressed on. "We're now charging the Konevitches with immigration fraud."

"Is this charge likely to change in the next few minutes?" MP asked, looking at the judge.

"It will not." She was getting creamed, and like a good lawyer, taking it in cool stride.

Alex was almost lost. English wasn't his native tongue, and the parries and thrusts shot around the small courtroom like lightning bolts. The questions and replies came without time to breathe or think. Not a word was wasted, no "uhs," no hesitations. Three first-rate legal minds were playing hardball with each other, with his life at stake.

The judge removed his glasses and rubbed his eyes. "As this is the first this court has heard of this new charge, can you honor us with a little more specificity?"

"Mr. Konevitch was heavily involved in criminal activity in Russia before he fled and came to America. He presented himself to the Immigration Service as a victim of political persecution. He deliberately constructed false facts to verify this status. Further, he claimed permanent employment with a company that has subsequently been discovered to be a fraud. It is, in fact, a front for criminal activities, including money laundering. Given those unlawful actions, we recommend that Mr. and Mrs. Konevitch be immediately deported back to Russia."

"Mr. Jones?"

"I'm not at all prepared to contest these absurd charges. They're obviously preposterous, and will be easily debunked."

"When will you be ready?"

"Two weeks, at a minimum."

"Then we'll reconvene in two weeks."

Like that, it was over. His Honor started to rise, before MP interrupted his progress. "I have another matter for your advisement, Your Honor."

His Honor sank back into his chair.

"My clients should be released on bond immediately. The charges that led to their arrest have already been disproved and disposed. They should not have to suffer a lack of freedom over what my colleague Miss Parrish has already confessed was gross negligence on the part of her department."

"Miss Parrish?"

"I did not state it was gross negligence. That's an outrageous distortion of what I said."

"Remind me. What did you say?"

"Simple bureaucratic oversight. Nearly two million immigrants a year enter our porous borders, legally or otherwise. As hard as our people work, well" — she stared down at her hapless associate again — "occasionally a few pieces of paper get misplaced in the shuffle."

The elbows landed on the bench again. "Miss Parrish, I admire your noble efforts to defend the reputation of your service. I surely do."

"Thank you, Your Honor."

"It is admirable and it definitely touches my heart. However, I spent fifteen long years in your shoes. So don't you ever utter such outlandish baloney in this court again. It was, unmistakably, gross negligence. The INS is overworked and severely understaffed, but that in no way excuses or ameliorates what happened here today. Now, what's your response to bond for these people?"

She never blinked. "We strongly advise that it be denied, Your Honor."

"Grounds?"

"According to the Russian attorney general, Mr. Konevitch embezzled many millions of dollars from the investors in his bank. He also fled with millions more that he stole from the Russian mob. He fled from there, and he will certainly flee from here. He is, by any stretch, a definite flight risk."

"Mr. Jones?"

MP paused and stared down at his legal pad for a long moment. Alex didn't have a prayer. MP knew this. Further, he knew better than to irritate the judge and risk losing his obvious sympathy by arguing otherwise. Alex seemed to understand this as well. He was vigorously nodding his head in Elena's direction.

"Mr. Jones?" the judge repeated, taking his tone up a notch.

"Those issues will be addressed in two weeks. Mrs. Konevitch, though, has been accused of nothing."

His Honor was tired of talking. He simply shifted his stare to Kim Parrish.

"The government," she replied, "would strongly prefer that she remain in custody as well."

"I do not react to preferences, Miss Parrish. You had better offer substantiation for denial."

"She's a flight risk as well."

"With her husband in jail?"

"Maybe."

"You need to do better than that, Miss Parrish."

"She was party to his falsehoods. She testified at his hearings, confirmed his lies, and served as his able co-conspirator."

His Honor bent far forward and peered down at his court reporter, who also happened to double as his appointments secretary. "Sally, what did I do last Sunday?"

"You played golf, Your Honor."

"I did?"

"Of course. You had your usual ten a.m. tee

time at Washington Golf and Country."

"And were you to ask Mrs. Everston where I was, what do you think she'd say, Sally?"

Sally produced a shy smile and blushed nicely. "She'd say you were at your county school board meeting."

"Am I on the school board, Sally?"

"No, Your Honor. Not for about five years now. It's the same tired old alibi you give her every other Sunday."

He redirected his gaze to Kim Parrish. "Mrs. Everston and I have been married thirty-two years now. You'd think she'd be on to me by now, wouldn't you?"

"I have no idea. I'm not married."

"Then allow me to offer a little wisdom from the trenches. The state of matrimony, Miss Parrish, does not confer infinite or absolute knowledge of spousal activities. Believe it or not, lots of married people cheat on each other, hide money from each other, and, in cases, even have additional wives and husbands. So as much as you might wish it, the laws of this land do not yet assign mutual guilt on married couples. I am not responsible for the horrible quilts my wife knits and afflicts on our poor children every Christmas. She is certainly not responsible for the three times Sunday that I regrettably shifted the lay of my golf ball and thereby cheated my partners into buying my lunch."

"Moving a golf ball and stealing millions

are wildly different offenses. I don't agree with your analogies, Your Honor."

"You don't?"

"Absolutely not."

"Bond will be set at $5,000."

"I protest, Your Honor."

"Of course you do."

Before Alex was led away, Elena squeezed his hand, but did not say, "I love you."

Instead she said, "Interactive Internet video?"

"Exactly. And call Mikhail for an update," he whispered before he was tugged away.

24

The destroyed remnants of a long working lunch were strewn around the table. The mess would be picked up by the secretaries shortly after the meeting ended. Laura Tingleman presided from the end of the long shiny table.

The chief lieutenants of the Justice Department were gathered on this Friday morning, as they were every Friday morning, for what had come to be known as the "Weekly Roundup," named in honor of her background as a Montanan. A city girl through and through, Laura Tingleman could barely tell the back end of a cow from the front.

The chief of the Civil Rights Division was just winding up a long, complicated report about the status of a suit brought by an Indian tribe nobody in the room had ever heard of. The tribe demanded the right to sue the shorts off anybody who used the name "Indian," or any variation thereof, or any reference thereto, or any image thereabout, in their product, team, school, or institution, or whatever.

The case had bounced around various lower courts for over a decade. A victory here. A successful appeal there and now it was on the verge of ascending to consideration by the Supreme Court. No fewer than ten civil rights lawyers had been involved full-time, dodging around the country every time the case changed jurisdiction. The tribe in question was quite small, comprising a husband and wife, a weird migratory couple who claimed they were pursuing the nomadic tradition of their forebears and could not be pinned down for any length of time. They claimed to be following buffalo herds, or locusts, or even slight changes in wind direction. Every move incited a new excuse. Coincidentally, their geographic shifts occurred every time they lost an appeal and needed to bounce the case to a different, more radically liberal venue; they staunchly insisted that their ancient native rights took precedence over the newly created White Man Rule, and some harebrained judge somewhere had ruled in their favor. They won legal permission for unlimited changes of venue along with infinite reasons for appeal.

The couple had once been named Antonelli, before they had it legally changed to Chief and Mrs. Stare at My Moon. They happened to be graduates of Yale Law.

The head of the Civil Rights Division and

the solicitor general squabbled back and forth. Civil Rights wanted to hand this hot potato to the solicitor general on the grounds that it was within spitting distance of the Supreme Court. The Court had yet to determine whether this case belonged on their docket, the solicitor general shot back, with his loquacious lips pursed. Yes, but the head of Civil Rights wanted his ten lawyers sprung. Also if the couple won, they would go on a legal rampage, suing for billions from schools and companies that apparently were brutally insensitive to the terrible slights they were inflicting on Indians. The costs would be huge, the backlash staggering.

Unfortunately, the White House was putting unbearable pressure on the department to roll over. The president felt the pain of what had happened to American Indians and he wanted to make amends for three hundred years of atrocities, for white men sharing their awful diseases, for stealing Indian land, for decimating the proud tribes. More succinctly, he wanted their votes.

It was a definite no-win situation.

As usual, Laura Tingleman deferred the decision for later — later being when it somehow resolved itself without her fingerprints. Time to bounce to the next issue, and Laura's chief of staff held up an article clipped, a few days earlier, from the *New York Times.* Said article concerned a Russian couple being prosecuted for immigration violations. Predictably for the *Times,* the article was slanted and not overly complimentary to the government's case. The word "railroad" was thrown around a few times by the defense attorney, who had been given suspiciously generous play by the *Times* reporter.

"Does anybody know what this is about?" Laura asked, searching the faces around the table.

Tromble bent forward. "I do, and so should you."

"I should?"

"Sure. From our Moscow trip, remember? This couple ripped off hundreds of millions and are hiding here. We specifically agreed we would return them to Russia for trial."

"I might have a vague recollection about it," Laura allowed. So much business passed through her office, she could barely keep it all straight.

"You were a little tired," Tromble allowed back. "You gave your word to the Russian attorney general. I'm just following through."

"How did it make the papers?" she asked.

Fortunately, Tromble had the answer. "The usual games, nothing to become concerned over. The defense attorney has no case. He knows it, too. He's trying to spin up the media and build sympathy. He and the *Times* reporter went to college together. She did him a big favor."

Nobody asked how he knew this. He wouldn't have told them if they had. If the Russians could tap and wire the lawyer's office, it was clearly a national security imperative for Tromble to have a few taps of his own. It was only fair to know what the Russians knew.

"Do we have a solid case?" Laura's chief of staff asked.

"It's in the hands of INS," he fibbed, smoothly and persuasively. "We're providing assistance from the side; only when they ask, though. Believe me, it's waterproof."

"How can you be so sure?" the aide countered. Every eye in the room swiveled to Tromble. How indeed?

Though the Justice Department was purportedly above the fray of politics, this was a liberal administration, and the White House had packed the senior appointed ranks with legions of die-hard, woolly-headed lefties. Tromble was the exception, the lone, fierce duck out of water. The others in the room detested him, and secretly, on a more ambivalent note, nearly all were convinced he was the right man for the right job — a tireless, efficient, ruthless hatchetman who ran his besuited stormtroopers hard. Behind his cover they could spout all the tree-hugging, abortion-loving, big government nonsense they wanted. In the first two years of his incumbency, national crime rates had plummeted a historic nine percent.

A Nazi he might be, but at least he was *their* Nazi.

"This guy Konevitch," Tromble explained with an air of authority, "was worth hundreds of millions before he fled. Nobody with clean hands makes that kind of money over there. Nobody. He's definitely a crook."

Heads nodding all around. Though few of them had ever set foot in Russia, the roomful of news junkies was well aware of Russia's sad descent into crooked madness. The rampant shootings in Moscow streets. The swift rise of the Mafiya. Vast fortunes being made by a handful of conniving thieves — a kleptocracy, Russia was now being called, and with good reason. Naturally this Konevitch man had to be crooked.

"He's the number one most wanted criminal in Russia. It's Russia, so that's saying something," he continued to the nodding heads. "There is no chance he is innocent. And from what we've learned from our Russian friends, he's already got a foothold here."

Laura was only too happy it was something so simple and straightforward for a change. She asked, "What help can I provide?"

One of her many legal advisors — a she, it happened — scraped forward in her chair, gazing suspiciously down the long table at Tromble. After carefully reading the article, she wasn't sure this was such a slam dunk. "We lack an extradition treaty with the Russians," she announced.

"So what's the best way to proceed?" her boss asked.

"Essentially, we have to prove the merits of Russia's case before an American judge," the aide answered.

"How hard is that?"

"It's been done before. Not with Russia inside this country, but we often use this strategy ourselves. In Colombia, for example, when we want a drug lord renditioned to our courts. We dispatch a legal team there, do a little show-and-tell before a Colombian judge, then they transfer custody to us."

"So we need a team of Russian prosecutors?"

"Pretty much. Assuming they have a good case, they display their evidence to our INS attorneys, and our people handle the heavy lifting in the courts. This takes time, though."

"How much time?"

"Sometimes years. Varies by case."

Tromble stared down the table at this busybody pushing her nose into his business. "The case will be heard again in one week. Konevitch doesn't have a leg to stand on."

"What if you're wrong?" his boss's legal aide asked, not backing down.

"No reasonable judge will decide against us."

"All right, consider an unreasonable one."

"Fine. If you insist, I'll call Russia and get a team over here right away," he conceded. The concession was of course entirely meaningless. He had not the slightest doubt that the Konevitches would land in Moscow long before a Russian team landed in D.C.

The meeting broke up with the solicitor general and head of Civil Rights in a corner, trading insults, and nearly fists, over Chief and Mrs. Stare at My Moon.

Tatyana was heavily preoccupied when her phone started ringing off the hook. She tried to ignore it, but eventually stopped what she was doing, rolled over, and put it to her ear. "What? Who is this," she snapped in Russian.

"Please hold for the director of the Federal Bureau of Investigation," a female voice stiffly instructed her in English.

The voice of John Tromble popped on a moment later. "Hello, Tatyana. Heard the news about your boy Konevitch? Made a big splash in the news on this side of the water."

"How did you get my home number?" she asked, unable to disguise her irritation.

"When I couldn't get you at the office, my boys in the embassy tracked it down."

"All right. Yes, I see that you've got him in jail. Why haven't you just shipped him here?"

"It's complicated. Not as easy as I thought. Listen, I need a big favor."

He explained what he needed, a team of Russian prosecutors, and Tatyana listened. Eventually, she replied, "Is this absolutely necessary?"

"Probably not. He goes back to court in a week. No way in hell he won't be deported. But the judge might act crazily. Call it a precaution, insurance."

"It will take time to get the case together."

"How much time?"

"A month or two, probably. Maybe a little longer."

"I thought you folks were already prepared to fry him in your courts. What's the problem?"

"John, please. The case is ready for Russian courts, not yours. Your rules of evidence are different, and we'll have to tailor it accordingly. There are also certain pieces of evidence we would find it embarrassing or troublesome to show foreigners. Dirty laundry we really don't want to showcase at a time when we're trying to attract foreign investment. Those problems will have to be cleaned up."

"Okay, yeah. I understand that."

"You can keep him in jail, can't you? A lot of powerful people here are opposed to letting you keep the FBI outpost in your embassy. I'm doing my best, but, John, it's a real uphill battle. Such a clear lack of mutual cooperation won't go over well."

Tromble started to say something, but she

cut him off. "President Yeltsin asked me about this case just yesterday," she lied. "He keeps asking if he needs to discuss it with your president."

"Hey, we'll find a way. I don't care if I have to bribe the judge or kill his wife. I'll find a way."

"Whatever it takes, John, whatever it takes. I'll put together a team of prosecutors and get them over there as soon as possible."

They rung off. Tatyana stretched, then rolled over, back into the muscular arms of Sasha Komenov, her boytoy soccer star. He drew away. "Who was it?" he asked in a petulant mood. He didn't speak English and understood not a word.

"Just some idiot law enforcement administrator from America."

"Oh, you're screwing him, too?" Sasha snapped. Lately, he was turning a little sulky about Tatyana and her extracurricular sleeping habits. It had never bothered him before, but after discovering a gray hair a few weeks before, he found himself suddenly torn with possessive urges.

"You're cute when you're mad. Come on and screw me now." She laughed.

Sasha crossed his arms and pouted. "Don't joke. I'm tired of sharing you."

"You're a fool. You've seen my boss. He's bald and fat and not the least bit interesting. He's so terrible in bed I have to pinch myself just to stay awake. He's so disgusting, I become nauseated afterward. I'm only doing this for us, Sasha."

"You've been saying that for years."

"And it's true. Listen, we're moving in on a huge fortune right now. Billions, Sasha, billions. My cut will be hundreds of millions, and as soon as I have it, I'll dump that old moron and quit my job. You and I will buy a big yacht and sail around the world. We'll never be able to spend it all. We'll die rich and happy."

The recorder in the basement whirred and caught every word.

The limo had been cruising around Moscow for an hour. It wandered aimlessly, in no particular direction, eating up pavement until the meeting in the back was finished. After picking up Sergei Golitsin at his big brick mansion, it had sped crosstown, straight to the comparatively smaller home of Anatoli Fyodorev, Russia's attorney general. He climbed inside and off it sped.

The tracking device on the undercarriage made it too easy to trail. After an hour it pulled back up to the curb in front of Fyodorev's home. Out stepped the attorney general, stretching and straightening his suit. And then Golitsin's big head peeked out. The old man said something, they both laughed. He handed Fyodorev a thick envelope. Right there, on the curb, the idiot actually opened it so he could count the cash.

Click, click, went Mikhail's trusty camera.

25

Court reconvened at ten o'clock in the morning on the second. Elena had driven herself and parked in the underground INS garage. She was dressed not in orange but in a modest dark blue frock that complemented her beauty, her blonde hair, her slim figure. She sat directly behind Alex, who was in his usual orange jumpsuit. They exchanged quiet whispers and handwritten notes while they waited for the festivities to begin. Alex had been permitted to shower and shave this time — though only after MP threatened his jailers with a noisy lawsuit for deprivation of dignity.

Kim Parrish sat at her table with the same youthful assistant perched anxiously to her right. Piles of paper along with several large boxes were stacked off to the side.

MP had offered her a warm, friendly greeting when they entered. She met it with stony indifference. She was openly furious with him over that nasty, rotten, one-sided *Times* article — earlier in the week, Agent Wilson had confided to her how MP had called in a favor from the *Times* reporter and arranged her public thrashing. She could barely stand to be in the same room with him.

As before, Judge John Everston entered punctually through a side door, hustling along, anxious to begin. He studied his court again. No reporters this time. None of Tromble's punks, either, he noted with satisfaction — nobody but a plump, middle-aged, long-haired fellow in the visitors' section who was sipping noisily through a straw stuck in a Diet Coke.

"Who are you, sir?" His Honor asked.

"An author," the man replied in an almost indifferent manner. "I'm halfway into a legal thriller that involves a few immigration matters. Saw this case mentioned in the *Times*. Thought I'd pop in and pick up a little authentic juice."

The man looked seedy, wildly disorganized, and poorly groomed. His threadbare blue blazer bore long streaks of mustard stain, and he was vigorously scratching his fanny. Sure looked like a writer.

When the judge did not throw him out, the man quickly settled his ample rear back into his seat. He dug a notebook out of a side pocket and loudly flicked his pen open. On the frames of his glasses were two miniature cameras. Tucked in his breast pocket, a highly sensitive microphone was capturing every word. In a small office two floors above, three federal agents were huddled before video screens, watching and listening to the proceedings with great amusement.

Agent Wilson laughed, slapped a thigh, and bellowed, "Hah, you old bastard, who's the smart one now?"

With his usual judicial efficiency, His Honor cut right to the chase. "Mr. Jones, we left off with your assessment that you needed two more weeks to prepare your defense. Are you ready?"

"I believe I am, Your Honor. But as there is no requirement for discovery in immigration code, I reserve the right to hear what the prosecution presents."

This reference was to the requirement in criminal trials for the prosecution and defense to share advance notice about evidence and witnesses they intend to present. There was no such obligation in immigration court. MP's retort was old hat. The judge nodded accordingly. He shifted his attention to the prosecutor. "Miss Parrish, make your case."

Without hesitation she said, "We'll open with the government claim that Mr. Konevitch lied to the immigration board about his place of employment."

She nodded at her young assistant. He apparently had another impressive purpose than being the meek target of blame for things gone wrong. He hefted up a number of documents and hauled them to the bench.

Miss Parrish said, "I'm providing annotated transcripts from the statement made by Mr. and Mrs. Konevitch to an immigration panel on April 15, to wit, they both were employed by a company supposedly established in Austria. The company so named is Orangutan Media."

Judge Everston licked his fingers and began noisily thumbing through the documents. "Go on."

"You'll also note three statements signed by Russia's attorney general, Anatoli Fyodorev. They detail several investigations by Russian federal investigators into the true activities of Orangutan Media. The —"

MP quickly interrupted. "Your Honor, we have not seen those statements."

"And you already established that, Mr. Jones."

"Yes, and surely it won't hurt to remind the court that my client came to America as a result of political persecution. The same government that provided those statements wishes him dead."

"Then you believe these statements to be false?"

"I haven't seen them."

"Well, they're in Russian. Can't read them myself. But let's assume, momentarily, that Miss Parrish is telling the truth. That's a reasonable assumption, is it not, Miss Parrish?"

"It is."

"Mr. Jones? Is Russia's attorney general lying?"

"Probably. I'll withhold judgment for now."

The prosecutor flipped a quick sideways smile at MP. She wasn't through, and he definitely wasn't going to like her next move. *Too bad your hack reporter friend's not here to see you gag and choke,* she wanted to tell him. Her errand boy hauled a few more papers up to the judge. "Your Honor, these are sworn statements from employees of Orangutan Media. They confirm the nature of the company's criminal activities. Please note the top statement."

"So noted. What is it?"

"A confession signed by Illya Mechoukov."

MP had never heard the name so he glanced over at his client. Alex's mouth hung open. He appeared to be in shock. He was massaging his forehead, openly pained.

MP bent over and scribbled a brief, questioning note to Alex.

"And who would he be?" the judge was asking.

"Mr. Mechoukov is the CEO of Orangutan Media. Again, it's in Russian, but he details not only the company's connections to money laundering for a notorious criminal syndicate but, more specifically, Mr. Konevitch's direct role in the nefarious activities."

Alex furiously scribbled a note back to MP. "Ask if the FBI was present," it said with a large exclamation point.

The judge was shuffling through several papers. "And the rest of these statements, who are they from?"

"More employees of said company. They all verify or expand upon the statement provided by Mechoukov."

"And how did you come upon these materials?" MP asked from the side.

She paused at this question, but only briefly. "They were given to me by the FBI."

"The FBI's a large organization. Who exactly, in the FBI?"

"I don't believe this is relevant, Your Honor."

"Should I give you my robes, Miss Parrish? Mr. Jones's question is quite relevant. This might only be immigration court, but the rules pertaining to chain of evidence remain in force. So long as you're making up my mind for me, you might as well look the part."

"Does your paycheck come with it?" She smiled briefly — a stupid mistake, one she immediately regretted.

His Honor did not smile back. "Miss Parrish, who in the FBI?"

"Agent Wilson."

"The same fellow who was present in this court two weeks ago?"

"I believe so."

"You believe so?"

"It is . . . was . . . whatever."

MP quickly interjected. "Did the FBI directly interview these people?"

"I . . . I believe so."

His Honor scratched his chin and asked, "Then where inside this arsenal of material are the statements by these agents?"

"If they were only observers, that wouldn't be necessary," she shot back.

"I asked if they took these statements, Your Honor," MP snapped.

"I heard what he asked," Parrish answered.

"I would like an unqualified response. Yes or no? They took the statements or they did not. They were present for the interrogations or were not," MP demanded, peering sideways at the judge. "Your Honor, if the FBI was present in any capacity, I request the names of the agents involved. Further, I'd like them to be deposed to confirm the authenticity of those statements."

In a room two floors above, Agent Wilson was loudly cursing. He drove a fist into a desk and instantly regretted it. It felt like he broke at least two knuckles. He hated lawyers. Such smartasses.

"It's not relevant," Parrish insisted, clearly rattled, and trying to squirm out of this line of inquiry. "The statements were taken by Russian law enforcement authorities. We should extend them the same trust and legal latitudes we afford our own police."

It was her first real mistake, and it was a whopper.

MP launched out of his chair; he was hell-bent to make her pay dearly for it. Directing a finger at her, he said, "Miss Parrish, are you telling this court that Russia's police are as credible as our own?"

She had said it, and it was too late to back away. "Yes."

"Have you ever heard of gulags, kangaroo courts, Solzhenitsyn, purges, Potemkin villages, Stalin, the Cold War, show trials —"

"Thank you, Mr. Jones," the judge burst in. "You made your point."

MP relaxed. "Thank you, Your Honor. I was starting to bore myself." He brushed a hand through his hair and shook his head.

It was a sly dig, skillfully delivered. Even His Honor cracked a hint of a smile.

A large scowl was on Parrish's face. She knew full well she had said something pathetically stupid. And she knew, equally well, that she had no choice but to breaststroke in quicksand. "I have no idea what Mr. Jones is saying. Nor does it sound at all relevant."

"Well, she might be the only person in the world confused about this," MP said with a nasty smile. "So let me clear it up. I'm saying the Russian police frequently use tactics that are abhorrent. They torture witnesses, employ blackmail and coercion, are notoriously dishonest, and sometimes even forge documents. If Mrs. Parrish is so naïve as to not be aware of this, I will gladly call in dozens of expert witnesses from the CIA and State Department to educate her. Or I can locate thousands of U.S. citizens who were granted political asylum — by her own department, I might add — after Russian police brutally tortured them and their families."

His Honor asked very nicely, "Miss Parrish, will that be necessary or will you simply concede this point?"

Parrish spent a moment grinding her fingernails into her palms. Was this a jury trial the damage would be enormous, possibly insurmountable. Fortunately it was an immigration case in an immigration court with an immigration judge. The rules were different.

She drew a few deep breaths, then tried gamely to repair the damage. "The prosecution is willing to concede that Russian legal authorities might occasionally employ a little excess vigor in the pursuit of justice."

Alex mentioned to MP, very loudly, "She means they rip fingernails out of innocent people and force them to sign untrue statements."

"I can interpret her words without your help," the judge said with a mildly aggravated expression. "Now sit down, Mr. Jones."

MP sat.

The judge removed his glasses and rubbed his eyes for a moment. Eventually he said to the prosecutor, "Can you produce any FBI agents who witnessed these interrogations?"

"No."

He turned to MP. "Can you produce witnesses or evidence that these statements are tainted or were forced?"

"I haven't been given the opportunity. They were sprung on us only five minutes ago. My client vehemently denies them. We would request the time to track down the signatories to interview them directly."

His Honor swiveled his neck back to the prosecutor. "I hope you have other evidence or substantiation."

This time her young lackey hauled two enormous cardboard boxes up to the bench. They overflowed with paper. Parrish allowed the judge a moment to peek over the lids and witness the massive volume of material. It would take at least a month to read it all.

"Your Honor, these are newspaper and magazine clippings collected and translated by our Foreign Service concerning Mr. Konevitch's considerable criminal activities in Russia."

Alex began scribbling more furious notes for MP. Parrish prattled on, describing the depth, complexity, and utter depravity of Alex's schemes and crimes. She referred to her notes frequently. She quoted freely from several of the more damning articles. About the abhorrent nature of Konevitch's crimes. Choice tidbits about the people this Russian mountebank harmed through his crookedness. The bankrupted investors who trusted him and were ruined. The thousands of employees laid off after he fled. The shock to the entire Russian business world and its incipient stock market. She requested that the accounts be entered into the record. MP scrawled a few questions. Alex dashed off hurried replies.

The moment she finished, MP observed, "I believe the prosecutor is aware of our contention that Mr. Konevitch was framed for these crimes."

"It's a common alibi from guilty criminals," Parrish replied dismissively.

"You doubt his word?" MP asked, slightly incredulous.

"Of course I do. Mr. Konevitch is listed number one on Russia's most wanted list. The Russian attorney general has issued a warrant for his arrest. The news stories in those boxes confirm everything he did, that he's now claiming he didn't do. I believe he is outnumbered."

MP turned to the judge. "I don't believe I've ever heard of a case where newspaper articles were introduced as evidence."

The judge was interested in where MP was going with this. "Nor I. On the other hand,

I'm inclined to accept her claim that the articles add a certain level of verification to the government claims."

MP smiled at His Honor and said, "Could I have a little latitude to explore this issue?"

"A very little, Mr. Jones."

He turned and faced Parrish. "Did you read the *New York Times* article published two weeks ago regarding this trial?"

"I may have."

"Would you like me to read it to you? I have a copy."

"No. I read it."

"All of it?"

"I just said I did. Every stupid word."

MP picked up the article from the table and waved it around for the judge to see. "Here's my favorite part," he said, smiling broadly. He read loudly and proudly, "Quote, 'This case is a travesty of injustice, a railroad, and the prosecutor is the chief engineer driving a train of lies and deceit,' remarked an anonymous source. 'If Konevitch is returned to Russia, he'll be murdered. His blood will be on the prosecutor's hands as surely as if she killed him herself.' End quote." MP smiled nicely at the court reporter. "Sally, please enter that into the record. Especially that literary part about driving the train of lies and deceit. I really like that line."

Parrish launched out of her chair. "I protest, Your Honor," she yelled, red-faced. "That obvious smear has no business being entered into the record."

His Honor briefly considered an intervention. There was no question about it; she was right, it definitely was a bald-faced smear. On the other hand, she was asking to have press clippings entered into evidence. Whether she liked it or not, she had given the defense attorney the opening to explore the issue: if he chose to crash through it in a Mack truck she had no complaint.

And frankly, such testy exchanges were rare for an immigration hearing. He pushed his chair back, folded his hands behind his head, and watched the interplay with huge enjoyment.

"Why not?" MP snapped back at her. "Didn't you agree with it?"

"I did not."

"Oh, come on, Miss Parrish. It was a great article. Well-reasoned, finely balanced."

"It was a shameful, slanted, slanderous piece of garbage, Mr. Jones. And you know it. It was too obvious the reporter was an old college friend of yours. She made no effort to get the government's side. Her behavior verges on professional misconduct."

For the briefest moment, MP paused. How did she know about their old college relationship? There was only one way she could, and MP pondered that ugly thought before he recovered his senses and pushed on.

"Then sue her," he snapped, struggling to keep his cool. How long had his phones been tapped? Who was listening in? How much had he divulged?

"I might sue you instead. You and I both know you provided that despicable quote."

"Fine. Sue me, then. I dare you." He waved the article like a matador with a red cape.

"I would love to. If it wasn't impossible to prove, I would take everything you own."

"Spare me the empty threats. Any lawyer worth their salt would end up owning the *New York Times* and shoving me into the poorhouse."

"Don't you dare patronize me. She'll hide behind the First Amendment. And you'll lie for all it's worth."

On a dime, MP was suddenly all warmth and compassion. He balled up the article and threw it on the floor. "You know what? I agree with you, Miss Parrish. What can be worse than being smeared and maligned by lies in the press? To have your reputation unfairly dragged through the mud? If a lawyer like you has no realistic recourse, what chance does a simple citizen have? He can sue, but what chance does he have? He can say it's all lies, but who'll believe him? Anonymous sources leak all the lying filth they want. The juicier the lie, the more quickly it spreads, picked up by one paper after another until it becomes an avalanche of lies. The more outrageous the lie, the more ink it captures, the more it's guaranteed to hit the front page, then another front page, then a magazine cover, and then . . . Well, it's all just so sad."

The constant use of "he" left no doubt he wasn't talking about her. Alex suddenly thrust a note into MP's hand. It read, "Ask if her bosses requested a team of Russian prosecutors to come here and prove the case." He read it, had no idea what Alex was talking about, or where this was coming from, but Alex *had* nailed it on the head about the FBI and Orangutan Media. He nodded.

Parrish decided she hated MP Jones. She had known exactly what he was doing from the beginning. It had just been impossible to ignore or deflect his assault in a casual manner. He had shoved her into a corner and forced her to battle her way out.

But at least he was finished, she thought with grim satisfaction. In fact, MP was just getting warmed up.

He said to the judge, "Your Honor, since Miss Parrish has asked to enter these news articles into evidence, I would like you to ask her, on the record, if she believes every word to be true and accurate. Is she confident these stories represent the truth?"

His Honor pondered this weighty request for a second. Was it fair and reasonable? Well, it was her idea to enter all this media rubbish

481

into evidence. "Miss Parrish, for the record, do you believe these articles to be true and accurate?"

For a moment she froze. In a thoughtful, halting voice, she eventually replied, "I won't attest for every word or every statement in every article. In general, though, yes, the articles convey . . . well, a fairly accurate portrayal of Konevitch's deplorable activities and actions." A perfect response. She was proud of her answer, so carefully measured, so finely hedged. She was glad MP gave her the opening. He had lobbed her the perfect softball to repair the damage she had already inflicted upon herself.

MP said, very carefully also, "Your Honor, could you please ask the prosecutor if it's true Russia's attorney general is dispatching a prosecutorial team here to share evidence of Mr. Konevitch's activities with her legal department?"

Parrish's mouth suddenly went dry. She had been informed of this news only two days before. A precautionary move, she was told, in the event this judge got stupid and produced an outrageous decision. It was confided to her in the strictest confidence. How did Jones learn about it? Who leaked it? How damaging was this? How much did he know? A hundred unanswered questions pinged around her brain.

"Miss Parrish?"

She had no choice but to answer truthfully. "Yes."

"Please ask her why the need for such a team?" MP asked, uncertain how Alex learned this little tidbit, but pushing the point for all it was worth.

"It wasn't my decision. I don't know," she replied, trying to get off the hook.

"Not your decision?" His Honor asked incredulously.

She replied lamely, "It was a departmental decision."

MP went for the kill. "Your Honor, please ask her the basis of this decision."

His Honor was already kneading his temples. "Good idea. Why, Miss Parrish?"

"I have no idea."

Once again, MP generously came to her aid. "If it pleases the court, I'd like to help my colleague clear up this mystery."

"It might not please her. It would damn well please me, though," the judge replied, shoving aside his decorum. He was sorely tempted to cite her for contempt. He had caught her lying several times. Her credibility was in shambles. Now he questioned her sanity.

Speaking with all the confidence he could muster, MP claimed, "It's obvious her own service has doubts about the outlandish claims made in the Russian press about my client. As for her faith in Russia's attorney general, it's obvious her superiors feel otherwise. They asked the Russians to come over here to prove their case."

"Is this true?" Judge Everston asked her with a look that nearly peeled the skin from her face.

She toyed with a thousand responses she could give him. Yes, it was true. And also deliberately taken out of context. No, she better not say that, she promptly decided; Jones would demand to know the right context. The right context was the FBI director and attorney general wanted this Russian couple expelled, no matter what.

She hated this case. It was rammed down her throat at the last minute, accompanied by dozens of vile threats if she flopped. But her job was to represent the interests of the United States government as best she could.

"I have no idea," she snapped spitefully, wondering what her superiors would say when they read the transcript.

"I am placing this case in abeyance," the judge snapped. He looked long and hard at Kim Parrish. If stares had weight, she'd be crushed under a hundred tons of barely controlled fury. "This might be the shoddiest case I've ever had the displeasure to observe. I am not happy, Miss Parrish. You've asked me to pull the trigger for immediate deportation when the gun's not even loaded."

She summoned the last tiny bit of her courage. "The government requests that Mr. Konevitch remain in custody until we ascertain the full validity of Russia's claim."

The judge reeled back and pretended to be shocked. "Miss Parrish, do you recall the warning I issued two weeks ago?"

"I do, Your Honor."

"And now you're asking me to approve indefinite imprisonment while you sort out whether Mr. Konevitch is guilty of crimes back in Russia?"

"I didn't say indefinite. We'll move this as fast as we can and notify the court the moment we're prepared."

"And when might that be?"

"A few months at worst. Possibly weeks." She didn't have a clue.

"Mr. Jones?"

Predictably, MP looked like a jackhammer was pulverizing his big toe. "It is grossly unfair for my client to remain in custody because the government arrested him on such spurious grounds. It's outrageous and —"

Parrish cut him off. "The alternative is that we release a possible criminal to escape his crimes, and possibly sin again. He has the resources, and he has fled before. As the huge volume of news accounts attest, Mr. Konevitch is an infamous fugitive in Russia. A celebrity thief. His case is being monitored closely by Russia's highest leaders and by his own people. Russia has made clear that the handling of this case will merit a strong reciprocal response. Thousands of American citizens are in Russia. They're at risk. We recognize and apologize for any inconvenience this causes Mr. Konevitch. But we emphasize the needs of the state over his personal comfort."

The slew of news stories in the boxes two feet from the judge's long nose suddenly weighed ten legal tons. The judge stared at the boxes that attested very clearly to Konevitch's infamy in Russia. For once, she had a good point.

His Honor removed his glasses and leaned forward. "With considerable reluctance, I'll approve this request, until this thing gets sorted out."

"Thank you, Your Honor."

"Oh, don't thank me, Miss Parrish. But do listen closely. I want Mr. Konevitch transferred to a federal facility. Get him out of that nasty holding cell."

"I understand."

"Find him a nice, comfortable place. I want him not overly taxed by our obvious inefficiency. Is this clear?"

"You have my word."

He bent far forward. "One of those country clubs with tennis courts, big-screen TVs hooked to satellites, and all the good food he can stand. A nice, white-collar environment without walls or barbed wire, where the worst lowlife in there is a tax cheat."

"I understand."

"The next time I see Mr. Konevitch I want him fat and tanned. He better be bored with gardening, and listening to all those fat-cat Wall Street lizards brag about their schemes."

"You have my word."

"I protest," MP said.

"Of course you do," His Honor said quickly, as he lunged out of his seat and fled from his own court.

26

The thrashing was horrible. Nothing less than deeply humiliating. It was the first time Kim Parrish had met the attorney general and FBI director. Oh, let it be the last, she prayed as they verbally tore into her. She gritted her teeth and mentally cursed, both of them. Neither was in her chain of command, but they were enormously powerful people, and it stung.

Her own director chose to stand off to the side, eyeing the line of fire and avoiding it at all costs.

She had turned fifty years old only two weeks before. Same age as the attorney general. Twelve years older than Tromble. Yet they lashed into her like a little schoolgirl who had failed to finish her homework.

"It's not all lost," Parrish protested weakly, almost vainly, avoiding their damning eyes. "He's still in custody. We'll have our day in court again."

"His ass should already be on a plane back

to Russia," Tromble yelled, slapping a hand on a table. "You blew it. A knockdown case, and you just blew it."

"It wasn't my decision to bring in the Russian prosecutors. I had them on the ropes until Jones used that ace."

"How did Jones learn about it?" the attorney general asked, plainly puzzled.

Kim Parrish shrugged. "You tell me."

Tromble stared down at his shoes. The profligate product of the wiretaps on Jones's office had been quietly reviewed that afternoon by a team of ten agents. No mention of it. Not in Jones's phone calls. Not even in private conversations inside his office. Not a hint, not a word.

He glowered at the INS director. "Your operation leaks like a sieve. Wasn't this Jones guy once one of your lawyers? Obviously one of your people tipped him."

"Maybe it was one of your people," Parrish's boss punched back, just as nasty now that the thrashing shifted toward him. "Myself and Miss Parrish were the only ones who knew. I sure as hell didn't let him know."

"When do these Russians arrive?" Laura Tingleman asked, cutting off the discourse. She hated confrontation.

"Could be months," Tromble replied, and with that, he suddenly had a new idea.

"Then another month or two for them to pass off their knowledge to one of your attorneys," Tingleman calculated to the director of the INS, choosing her language carefully, deliberately avoiding Parrish's eyes. That pointed "one of your attorneys" line was a clear shot — this girl either kicks it up a notch or find a replacement.

"Sounds about right," Parrish's boss replied, notably not going to Parrish's defense.

"So this might take six months?" Tingleman asked.

Tromble smiled and nodded. "Maybe longer. A year is a possibility. You'll have to call this judge," he advised her. "Tell him to be patient. Emphasize the importance of this thing."

She nodded.

Parrish's boss said, "I'll assign two more attorneys to Parrish's team. That'll speed things up."

Tromble looked at him like he was an idiot. "No you won't."

"I won't?"

"As long as Konevitch is in custody, what's the rush?"

"Hey, I've been your whipping boy every day to get this thing done. Why the sudden change of heart?"

The question did not faze him in the least. "Miss Parrish has been under unbearable pressure. Look at her, she's obviously exhausted. But the timing's no longer in the defense attorney's hands, is it? She needs to

490

take her time, get this thing done right."

The sudden shift to kindness was unnerving. Tromble walked across the room and slapped Kim Parrish on the back. "Good luck, Counselor. Knock a home run next time, or else."

The meeting was suddenly over, to everybody's surprise and Kim Parrish's complete delight. She nearly left a smoke trail she moved out so fast.

Then it was just Tromble and the attorney general. Alone. The two of them, together, all by themselves in the big office filled with overwhelming burdens and responsibilities.

Tromble turned to her and observed, "The judge released Konevitch to your custody. The second you give the word, he's going into a federal prison."

"Well, there's that very nice one in Pennsylvania. The one where all the Wall Street fat cats go. Out in the countryside. I hear it's lovely in a pastoral sort of way."

Tromble said, not very pleasantly, "You're not really going to let some pissant immigration hack boss you around, are you? Just roll over and bark for that guy?"

That stung. Tromble was right, though; he was a lowly immigration judge in a backwater court. And she was, after all, the attorney general. Her eyes were glued to his face. "What do you have in mind, John?"

"You understand how important this case is?"

"Remind me."

"The Russian mobs are climbing all over our coastal cities. They're the newest thing, and it's not pretty. They earn a ten on the viciousness scale. And now they're battling us, the Italian Mafia, and the black gangs, and the Colombians and Mexicans to get a foothold. The Russians are very good, and very, very violent. They learned how to thrive in the most totalitarian country on earth. Don't forget that. Imagine what they can accomplish in our wide-open liberal democracy. We're frighteningly vulnerable. Let them get traction, let them have an inch, they'll become another rooted criminal institution inside this country. Another cancer that's impossible to dislodge."

"And Konevitch is the key to this?" she asked, leaning on her plump elbows and watching him carefully.

"Yes, the Russians are quite clear on this. He's a very guilty man, Laura. The man stole hundreds of millions. They get Konevitch, and in turn we get twenty agents in Moscow, with full access to their intelligence about the Mafiya. They'll assign liaisons to us, and we'll trade information back and forth. It's a gold mine. We'll break the back of these Russian goons."

"I see."

"Understand this, too. This guy Konevitch is sticking his finger in our eye, Laura. It's a disgrace. The press is watching. A damned foreigner exploiting our own legal system to make you and me look like eunuchs. It's very dangerous for us."

She sank about two more inches into her seat. Her forehead added about ten wrinkles. Left unsaid was that Tromble himself had issued the boneheaded directive to cream the Konevitches on the front pages, and attracted all the public scrutiny. He regretted it now — it had been a terrible mistake — but the die was cast. If Konevitch wanted to make this a pissing contest, a waterfall was about to land on his head.

Tromble placed a hand on her shoulder. "You decide what damned prison he's going to. If he wants to play games with you, stick it to him."

"You're right," she said, feeling a sudden burst of something called determination.

"Pick the worst, festering pisshole in the federal system. Put him in with the worst scum in our society. Someplace hot as Hades, with crap for food, and unrelenting violence. Let him rot and suffer until he begs us to throw him out of this country."

"I suppose a little softening up might encourage him to see our side," she agreed.

Mikhail had managed at last to hide listening

493

devices inside the big black limo. For months he had looked for a chance. There just had been no openings. And it had to be unquestionably failsafe; getting caught would blow everything apart. But the driver had dodged into a coffee shop one cold afternoon, leaving the engine running and doors unlocked. Mikhail gently eased over, ducked down, and quietly opened a rear side door. He jammed one bug into the deep crevice between the rear cushions. For insurance, he attached another tightly to the undercarriage of the front seat.

The range was only half a mile, and that was on a clear day. It gave him two important edges, though. He could hear what they were saying and record every word. And he no longer had to keep the limo in sight during the weekly meetings on the Moskva. They were oblivious to his presence, so far. But Mikhail intended to die peacefully in his bed at a ripe old age.

The limo was parked there, right now, a few meters to the right of its regular spot overlooking the river. Mikhail was parked three blocks away, the receiver/recorder in his lap, volume turned up full blast. He was sipping carefully from a large thermos of coffee and listening intently. Golitsin, then Tatyana, then Nicky sat in the rear, in their usual order, performing their usual ritual, nursing drinks, arguing back and forth, plotting their next big heist.

Nicky, in his distinctively caustic tone: "I thought you said it was going to be easy. Kid's play."

Golitsin: "All right, I lied. So what?"

"So what? Nine of my guys dead. Two of my chophouses blown to pieces, that's what. Somebody's screwin' with my dope business, too. I had half a million stolen from a pusher last week. Every time I hit Khodorin's company, I get hit back, twice as hard."

Tatyana, in a soothing tone obviously intended to unruffle the feathers: "What makes you think Khodorin's behind it, Nicky? He's just a businessman."

" 'Cause we keep finding notes pinned on the corpses. 'Lay off Central Enterprises, or we'll kick your ass.' " A brief pause. "Hey, you know what? They *are* kicking my ass."

Golitsin, in an annoyed, slightly absent tone: "He never called."

Tatyana: "Who never called who, Sergei?"

"Yuri Khodorin. He never called my man to handle his company's security."

Nicky: "Yeah, well, sure as hell he called somebody. Somebody connected. I'll tell ya who he called. A real vicious prick."

Tatyana: "Well, we can't let him off the hook. Not now. The man is worth billions, Nicky."

"You know, you keep sayin' that. But I don't see your ass out on the street, takin' the lumps this guy's dishing out. I'm tellin' ya, this guy's smart."

Golitsin: "How smart?"

"Last week, a few of my guys went to lay a little dynamite in that warehouse. Same one we talked about last week. It was a massacre."

Mikhail laughed so hard he nearly choked on his coffee. He had overheard their plan the week before, and quietly passed it along to his old friend from police days who was now handling security for Khodorin — with brutal effectiveness, based upon what he was hearing.

Tatyana: "Is it possible another syndicate is going to war with you? That sometimes happens, doesn't it?"

"Oh, yeah, good point, I hadn't thought of that." A brief pause. "Stick with what you know. No syndicate leaves messages warning me to lay off this Khodorin guy."

Tatyana: "Come on, Nicky. We've invested months in this. Central Enterprises is perfect, just perfect. Five hundred million in cash reserves. Cash, Nicky, cash. We'd be idiots to walk away at this point."

Nicky: "It's his fault" — presumably pointing a finger at Golitsin — "wasn't he supposed to get one of his snoops inside? Whatever happened to that, huh?"

Yes, whatever did happen to that, Mikhail wanted to yell in their faces.

But for a few long moments there was

silence. Mikhail chuckled. He'd almost do this job for free. He couldn't wait to share this tape with Captain Yurshenko, the recently appointed head of security at Central Enterprises. They would crack a bottle of vodka, sit back, and bust a nut over the poisonous frustration on the other side.

Eventually, Golitsin, turning the tables: "All right, I'll find a way to get some people inside. Now what's the story with Konevitch?"

Nicky, speaking to Tatyana in an accusatory sneer: "Yeah, thought you said he was taken care of."

Tatyana: "It's under control. Tromble called this morning. Konevitch is in a federal penitentiary in Atlanta. Tromble swore he placed our friend in the nastiest hole in the universe."

Nicky, who presumably knew something about this subject: "I hear they got some places over there that are just unbelievable."

Tatyana: "We're cooking up the case to be presented to their courts right now."

Golitsin: "I have experts with decades of experience in this. Why don't I help you?"

Tatyana: "I don't think that's a good idea. The team that manufactures this evidence has to go over and present it to their lawyers. If you build your own lies, you should know your own lies, don't you think?"

Loud chuckles all around.

■ ■ ■ ■

Three days languishing at the federal transit center in Atlanta — while Justice hotly debated which of its many prisons was the most awful at that particular moment — proved to be a godsend. Despite frequent requests, nobody would tell Alex his eventual destination.

Two days after his appearance in court, he had been hustled out of the Alexandria jail by a pair of federal marshals whose only words to Alex were, "Say good-bye to the good life." A quick flight on a Bureau of Prisons 737 to a private hangar in Atlanta International was followed by a fast trip in a shiny black van to the sprawling prison facility in Atlanta. The moment he entered the transient center for what he was warned would be a brief stay, Alex knew he wasn't headed for the pleasurable resort the judge had ordered.

He was locked in a small cell with a repeat sex offender named Ernie, who favored small boys but settled for little girls, depending on his mood at the moment. Ernie was a leper, a small, oddly ebullient man despised and avoided by everybody. Even Alex could not bring himself to speak with the twisted pervert.

The transient prisoners moving through

this portal to hell were a mixture of hardened two- and three-timers, seasoned vets, and others like Alex, wide-eyed newbies about to be thrown into a frightening new world.

The old-timers adored the chance to show off their experience, and they acted like garrulous college kids returning from spring break. They hollered back and forth, spitting out stories, exchanging names of acquaintances in this prison or that. The only verboten topic was any mention of their newest crimes. Alex listened carefully to every word, every boast. He studied how they moved, their mannerisms, how they wore their prison garb. He took careful mental notes and absorbed every nuance. Head down, always, but stay alert. Avoid eye contact at all costs — a wrong glance in this milieu was an invitation to rape, or worse. Among enemies, among guards, among friends, it didn't matter — act indifferent, no matter what. Better yet, *be* indifferent, and trust no one. And the golden rule: never, ever, under any circumstances, snitch.

On day four, Alex's toe was jerked out of the water. He was led out of his transient cell by a pair of stone-faced guards, escorted through a number of cellblocks and hallways, across a large courtyard, and, after four hours of tedious processing — including another shower, another delousing, and another invasive body search — was shoved into his new home.

Ernie, his former cellmate, smiled and welcomed Alex to his new cell. The cold, unpleasant relations between Alex and Ernie had been duly noted by the authorities. Being trapped in a small cell with this pervert would surely kick up the misery level a few notches.

Ernie had arrived two hours earlier, enough time for a little interior decorating. The walls were already plastered with pictures of little boys and girls clipped from magazines.

Based on the most recent indices of prison violence and brutality — and only after the chief of Justice's Bureau of Prisons twice swore it was the pick of the litter — Atlanta's medium-security prison earned the booby prize.

The truth was that by almost every measure, Atlanta's high-security facility had an impressive edge over its adjoining medium-security counterpart — three more murders over the past year, eighty percent more vicious assaults, nearly thirty more days in lockdown, and an impressive seventy percent lead in reported AIDS cases.

That year, Atlanta's high-security prison was, without question, and by any conceivable measure, the worst canker sore in the entire federal system.

The medium-security facility, however, offered a big advantage, one that swung the argument in its favor. Because it was medium-security, Alex would be forced to mix freely and openly with the prison population. Two hours every day in the yard, socializing with killers, gangbangers, big-time dope dealers, rapists, child molesters, and assorted other criminals. Showers twice a week in a large open bay, with minimal supervision. Three meals every day in the huge mess, where violence was as pervasive as big southern cockroaches.

Alex Konevitch, they were sure, would be petrified. A rich boy from Russia who had pampered and spoiled himself silly with unimaginable luxuries. Nothing in his background had prepared him for this. They were sure he would panic and end up begging for a seat on the next plane to Russia. Or maybe he would run afoul of one of the inhabitants and be shipped home in a casket. Who cared? The Russians never stipulated dead or alive.

The tipping point, though, was the large concentration of Cuban criminals. The facility contained the usual toxic mix of Crips and Bloods, a large, swaggering White Power brotherhood, and an assortment of lesser bands that huddled together under a hodgepodge of quirky banners and social distinctions. But the Cubans ruled. They terrorized the other groups, ran roughshod over the guards, got a piece of all the prison drug traffic and black-market action, and generally did as they pleased.

The ringleaders were a long-term institution, a troupe of thirty cutthroats shipped over on a special boat by Castro at the tail end of the Mariel Boatlift. The Immigration Service had been tipped off about their impending arrival by a Cuban convict who hoped his little favor would be met by a bigger favor. This was Castro's biggest flip of the bird, he warned without the slightest exaggeration; a group of handpicked incorrigibles, men who had been killing and raping and stealing since they were in diapers. The dregs of the dregs — once loose on America's streets, the havoc would be unimaginable.

They were picked up the second they climbed off the boat onto a lovely beach just south of Miami, and sent straight to Atlanta's prison. It was unfortunate, but since they had been denied the opportunity to commit crimes on American soil, no legal justification existed to place them in a high-security lockup, where they clearly belonged.

On the second day of Alex's incarceration, a guard, acting on orders from the warden, tipped the Cubans that the new boy in cell D83 was worth a boatload of money. By Alex's third week in the new facility, the Choir Boys of Mariel, as they were known, decided it was time for the new arrival to make their acquaintance.

■ ■ ■ ■

Alex was one minute into his shower when three men surrounded him. "What can I do for you boys?" he asked, trying to pretend polite indifference, when every cell in his body screamed run. Just run. Don't look back, don't even breathe, just run.

The jefe of the trio, a small, wiry man with greasy black hair laced with gray, and long ridges of knife scars on his forehead and left cheek, stepped closer to Alex. "What you in for?" he asked with a strong Cuban brogue.

"Nothing."

"Nothing. Just visiting, huh?"

"All right, I was framed."

A light chuckle sounding like chalk scratched on a blackboard. "You and all the rest of us."

"It's true. I haven't even been to trial yet."

"You're Russian," the man observed, shooting past the normal prisoner baggage and getting to the point.

"I was. Now I'm American."

The man took another step toward Alex, ending up about a foot away. "I'm Cubano," he announced with a nasty smile and his chest puffed up. "I hate Russians. Biggest pricks in the world. You kept that bastard Castro in power."

The prisoners around Alex suddenly began

shutting down their showerheads and bolting for the towel room. A fire alarm at full blast could not have emptied the place faster. The three men surrounding Alex were fully clothed in prison coveralls, hands stuffed deep inside their pockets. They stank of old sweat and a thousand cigarettes. Apparently, they didn't visit the showers very often.

Alex swallowed his fear and kept rubbing soap in his armpits. "No, you mean the communists kept him in power," he said and glanced around. Act indifferent, he kept reminding himself. Don't look scared, don't crack a smile, control your breathing. Pretend that standing naked in front of these three goons is no more threatening than a lap around the prison track. The guard who had been loitering at the entrance had mysteriously disappeared, Alex suddenly noticed.

"And what? You weren't a commie?"

Alex shook his head. "Definitely not."

"Yeah, well, what's that?" He wagged a finger at the hammer and sickle on Alex's chest.

"A present from some angry former commies," Alex informed him, eyeing the other two men, who had fanned out a bit and now blocked his exit in any direction.

"For what?"

"Because I bankrolled Yeltsin's election to the presidency."

"You, by yourself?" A quick, derisive snicker

directed at his friends. "Just you, eh?"

"That's right, just me. I gave him the money to defeat Gorbachev."

This revelation was intended to defuse the confrontation, but instead produced a nasty sneer. "And you know who I am?"

Alex soaped his arms and decided not to answer.

"Napoleon Bonaparte. You ended communism in Russia, and me . . . well, I'm the short little prick what conquered Europe."

The man laughed at his own stupid joke — his friends joined him, loud guffaws that bounced off the walls. Alex forced himself to smile. "Actually, you're Manuel Gonzalez. But you go by Manny. Born in a small village, Maderia, you're forty-six years old, thirty-six of which you've lived inside prison. You've killed with guns, rope, and knives, but prefer your bare hands. You like two sugars with your coffee, no cream. Your favorite TV show is *Miami Vice,* though I suspect you always root for the bad guys." He paused and broadened his smile. "Have you heard enough things you already know about yourself?"

Manny's mouth hung open for a second before he reacquired his normal aplomb and its accompanying sneer. The sneer had a violent edge to it. "Smart guy, huh?"

"I've asked around a bit." With as much casualness as he could muster, Alex placed the soap on the metal tray on the wall. "I suggest you do your homework, too." He stuck out his hand. "Alex Konevitch. Have one of your boys look me up on the Internet."

"Already did that," he said, ignoring the hand. "You're rich, Konevitch, filthy rich. You ripped off hundreds of millions. I'm impressed. That's why we're having this little mano-a-mano. Question is, are you also generous?"

"We seem to have a tense problem, Manny."

"Maybe my English is not so good. What's that mean?"

"A bunch of former KGB goons stole my money and my businesses. The little that was left was seized by the FBI. I was rich, and now I'm broke."

Manny did not appear overly pleased with that response. He pushed his face within an inch of Alex's. "I'm not a man you want to lie to."

"Believe me, I know that."

Manny looked ready to whip out whatever was inside his pocket. "Yeah? Then you better —"

"Slow it down, Manny. Think about it. A man with hundreds of millions, would he be here, in this rotten excuse for a prison? This is America, land of the free and the brave, of all the justice you can afford. The rich boys are all eating steak and getting nice tans in the federal country clubs. I'm here, with you.

Put two and two together."

Rather than respond to that, Manny glanced at the man standing to Alex's left, a large, hairy monster named Miguel. Physical appearances aside, Manny was the muscle, Miguel the brain. They had been longtime compadres in Cuba, arrived on the same miserable little boat, and for almost two decades had shared a cramped, smelly cell on the second floor. Manny had the top bunk and stayed out front. He did the bullying, the enforcement, bought off the guards, and terrified the other gangs. Miguel slept on the bottom, and spent most of his time in the library thinking up schemes and scams. It was he who researched Alex's background after the guard tipped them off. And it was he who devised this coarse plot to shake Alex down.

After a moment, Miguel leaned forward and butted in. "Were you really the cashbox behind Yeltsin?" Not a word about that had been mentioned in any of the many articles about Konevitch Miguel had read on the Internet.

Sensing the sudden shift in power, Alex turned and faced Miguel. "Seemed like a good idea at the time."

"But maybe not, eh?"

"You're perceptive. After all, look where it got me," Alex replied, shrugging indifferently, as if he'd be as happy here, among these men, as lounging with a bunch of gorgeous ladies in skimpy bikinis at a Caribbean resort. He was nearly gagging on indifference. "The same former KGB thugs who stole my money put me here."

"Why they put you here, man?"

"They want me back in Russia, where they can get their hands on me, or dead."

"That right?" Miguel leaned his large bulk against the wall and thoughtfully twisted the small goatee at the end of his chin. With that admission this tall Russian had just made a fatal slip. A dozen questions suddenly popped into Miguel's mind. Would the Russians pay to have this guy whacked? Who did Miguel and his friends have to contact? How much was Konevitch worth dead? That was the big question.

Maybe the situation still held possibilities.

Alex was beginning to feel awkward. He was naked, vulnerable, and dripping wet. Who knew what they had hidden in those pockets? Any one of these three brutes would happily slit his throat and casually watch his blood spill down the drain. He reached over and shut off the spigot. "Mind if I get a towel and dry off?" he asked.

"Why not?" Miguel grunted and winked. "Who's stopping you?"

Alex began edging around him, carefully, in the direction of the towel room. "What do you want with money, anyway?" he asked over his shoulder. "You're in prison, what good does it do?"

The Cubans followed about a step behind. "Don't you know anything?" Miguel answered, wondering exactly how much this Russian, dead, might be worth. "Money's everything. Inside the joint, outside — makes no differences. Good lawyers, cigarettes, dope, smuggled-in girls, even guards."

Alex seemed to consider that a moment, then, rapidly changing the subject, asked, "Have you ever heard of AOL? America Online?"

Manny and the third, unnamed man exchanged puzzled looks. Totally clueless. Miguel thought he might've heard of it, a hazy recollection at best. But in an effort not to appear dumb, he produced a knowing nod. "Sure. What about it?" he asked, as if he could write a textbook on the subject.

"It's the new thing, an Internet company that's making money hand over foot. The stock could easily quadruple in the next few years, maybe more."

Miguel turned to his colleagues. "Advice from a hustler who ripped off millions back in Russia. Does this guy think we're stupid, or what?"

"You're forgetting something. I also made hundreds of millions."

This got a slight nod. He'd read that on the Internet.

"Point is," Alex plowed ahead, grabbing a towel and wrapping it around his waist, "you're losing out. The stock market's on a tear. You're trying to squeeze a few dollars from losers on the inside. The easy money's outside, the big money. It's perfectly legal and above board."

"Cons in the joint ain't allowed to buy stock," Manny chimed in angrily, as if that ended the discussion. From everything Miguel had told him about this Russian, he had been expecting the once-in-a-lifetime payday all convicts live for. Manny had lain awake on his bunk the night before, sweating in the intense heat, dreaming of the money and what he could do with it.

Like the rest of the Mariel Boys, Manny had an appeal for release grinding its way through the courts. They had collectively pooled their resources to hire a lawyer, a distant third cousin of one of the gang. The cousin offered an impressive discount, bragged about his many legal victories, and made lots of rowdy promises. He turned out to be a total loser. Between booze and gambling, Mr. Loser lost track of their paperwork with disturbing regularity; the only thing he turned out to be good at was consistently missing the deadlines for filings.

Mr. Loser had to go.

Miguel had asked around until he found the perfect mouthpiece. Mr. Perfect was a cutthroat from Miami who billed four hundred an hour and produced miracles. He was owned by the Colombians, a gaudy loudmouth who had earned quite the reputation for keeping their killers, mules, and pushers out of jail. Legal mastery was part of it; knowing which judges and prosecutors to help with their home mortgages and kids' college bills, the larger part. In his spare time, he was allowed to freelance as much as he wanted.

It was an outside shot, at best. Mr. Perfect was quite expensive. The billable hours would pile up. The case could drag on for years. And for such a large group, a band of thugs who definitely had not distinguished themselves as model prisoners, the bribes would be mountainous.

Mr. Perfect, though, was their only hope. The Cubans talked endlessly of walking out the gate and retiring in a small, lazy southern Florida town. Life would be so good. They would muscle their way into a few strip clubs and pawnshops, drink cerveza from dusk to dawn, cavort with the strippers, and put the ugly old days behind them.

Alex kept a close eye on Manny, who looked angry and frustrated that their mark turned out to have shallow pockets. He grabbed another towel and began briskly rubbing his hair. "You mean you can't invest under your own name," he corrected Manny in an even tone. "Have a lawyer handle your money. They represent you, they can't blow the whistle. It's in their oath."

Miguel shot Manny a look that said: This sounds interesting, so cool it, for now. "And how would this work?" he asked.

"It's simple. Surely you already have money and maybe you already have a lawyer in mind."

"Maybe we do," Miguel replied, exchanging looks with his pals.

"I have a friend on the outside who will set up a trading account. I'm assuming you have a way to communicate with the outside. It needs to be instantaneous. We'll be buying and selling every day. Throw in whatever cash you have. I can name ten stocks right now that are set to explode, and the spreads in commodities have never been better."

"How do we know you won't lose our money?"

"You know what a stop-loss order is?"

Miguel was through pretending he knew things he had never heard of. A slow shake of the head.

"With each purchase, you designate a trigger price that he programs into his computer. If the stock falls to that level, the broker is required to sell." Alex jabbed the air with a finger. "One push of a button and he dumps everything."

"That's all we have to do?"

"I told you it's easy, Miguel," Alex assured

him, leaving Miguel to ponder the interesting question of how Alex knew his name. They had not been introduced. Nobody had mentioned his name. How much did Konevitch know about the Mariel Boys? The suspicion struck him that the Russian had been expecting this shakedown, maybe even prepared for it.

No, nobody was that cunning.

Alex walked over to the clothing locker, picked up his underwear and dirty coveralls, and began dressing. "But don't worry," he continued. "The stocks I pick will never trigger a sell order. Tell your lawyer to watch the action for a month. If he likes what he sees, he can join the fun. Better yet, cut a deal. In return for handling his investments, he'll handle your case."

"And you," Manny asked. "What do you get?"

"Protection," Alex told him, tying his shoes. "Also use your influence to arrange a new cellmate. Ernie gets on my nerves. I'm tired of tearing down pictures of little children."

"Easy," Miguel answered for all of them. "One more question."

"Shoot."

A nice smile, followed by a quick shift of mood and demeanor. "You know what happens if you lose our money, Mr. Smart Guy?"

"I have a fair idea. Do I look worried?"

He really didn't. Not in the least.

The end of Elena's first month in the South Arlington rental apartment and she was beginning to feel at home.

The D.C. housing market was hot as a pistol and her real estate agent had pleaded with her not to drop a hundred thousand off the asking price. It was the Watergate, after all; why throw away money? Her neighbors would never forgive her; not to mention the Realtor's own bitter feelings about the seven grand shucked off her own fee. Elena dug in her heels and stood fast. Lured by the great discount, inside two days, ten couples lined up for a shot. A brief, vicious bidding war erupted. The escalation quickly shot through the roof. The dust settled $120K later, at least $20K more than average Watergate prices for a cramped two-bedroom.

The winners were a young Bolivian couple with no children but plenty of money and an open desire to tell everyone back home they were part of the la-di-da Watergate crowd. Elena drove a hard bargain. A hundred thousand down, in cash, she insisted, before the titles were checked and the closing moved along at its usual constipated pace. The young couple hesitated only briefly before Elena mentioned how much she liked the terms offered by the runner-up bidder. A hundred thousand in cash landed on the table.

Their business affairs had always been handled by Alex. She was proud she had done so well. She promptly put down twenty thousand on a top-of-the-line server built by Sun Microsystems, and arranged for furniture from a cheap rental warehouse. MP helped her locate an apartment, not far from his own shabby home in a run-down neighborhood. At seven hundred a month the price was right, and Elena signed the lease under the name Ellen Smith. A few of MP's clients with expertise in such matters swiftly produced a driver's license and social security card to match her new name. Charge cards could be traced, and therefore were too dangerous. She vowed to live on cash.

The landlord wasn't fooled and neither did he care. Half his tenants were illegal aliens. As long as they paid cash, in American bills, on time, they could claim to be Bill Gates for all he cared. The phone service, both cellular and home, and Internet service, were opened by and billed to MP's firm.

The only remaining trace of Elena Konevitch was her car insurance. She called the company, said she had moved, and gave MP's office as her new address.

The killers were out there. With Alex locked up, she was the only one they could reach, she thought. The killers were professionals with loads of experience. They knew countless ways to find her and would peek under every rock. She was on her own for the first time; every decision would be hers. She needed to be disciplined and careful.

In her college days, Elena had taken courses in computer language, and had been quite good at it. A fast trip to a local mall and her apartment quickly flooded with books about programming and all sorts of other computer esoterica.

She had one last thing left to do. Sipping from a cup of tea, she unfolded a note Alex had passed her in court. She dialed the number he had written out and waited patiently until the connection went through.

A male voice answered, "Mikhail Borosky, private investigations."

"Hello, Mikhail. It's Elena Konevitch. Alex asked me to call."

"Yeah, I just learned he's in prison," Mikhail replied. "He okay?"

"Fine. Probably safer inside than out here."

There was a pause for a moment before Elena said, "From now on, direct your calls and send all your materials to me, addressed to Ellen Smith." She quickly gave him her new apartment address, her e-mail account information, and then said, "The materials you've already sent are hidden in a safe-deposit box at a bank. I went through everything three days ago."

"It's incredible isn't it?"

"You're incredible, Mikhail."

"No, this is all Alex's idea. He's incredible."

Enough incredibles. "Things have changed," Elena told him, very businesslike. "I'm handling this now. Alex has kept me informed of your general activities, but it might be best if you filled me in on all the details."

"This could take a while."

"With Alex in prison, I find I have lots of time on my hands. Start from the beginning."

27

After an hour of wailing and gnashing, of fruitless attempts at denial accompanied by turbulent rantings and sulfurous threats directed at the messengers, the long procession of accountants finally packed up their books and spreadsheets and fled from his office. The door closed quietly, at last. Sergei Golitsin hunched down in his chair and stared at the blank white walls. He was angry and felt depressed. The number crunchers had been merciless. No punches pulled, no quarter given.

The export-import bank, the flagship of Golitsin Enterprises — and one of its last surviving companies — was careening off a financial cliff. The priceless monopoly on the exchanging of foreign currencies had long since expired. The competition had swooped in and undercut his rates with a vengeance. For a few months, the five percent fee he charged had pumped up the profits and hid the bad news: customers were fleeing in droves.

Then, almost overnight, as if a switch had been flipped, the customers melted away. One day small trickles were still coming through the door; then, without warning, severe business anorexia settled in. Golitsin had moved decisively and ordered an aggressive retreat on his inflated rates, four percent, then three, then two; as of a week ago, it was set at a paltry one percent. At that price it would take thousands of new customers pushing large fortunes through his vaults to keep the doors open. No respite. No flood of new clients, or even return business. The doors to his bank had grown cobwebs.

He now doubted he could lure any customers if he offered to pay *them* five percent.

Amazing, the damage caused by one unfortunate hiccup. One of his handpicked VPs, a magician in his former life in KGB counterintelligence, had gotten overconfident. Freewheeling with the bank's money, and reeling under unrelenting pressure from Golitsin to show a profit, he had made the bizarre decision to dabble in the speculation game. He made a brazen one billion bet on the unstable English pound. After a few short hours, it was nearly all swallowed in quicksand. A vindictive American currency speculator named Soros detected the move and whacked it with a thousand-pound sledgehammer.

Seven hundred million was lost, according to the squinty-eyed accountants who had just spent an hour cruelly detailing the urgent case for bankruptcy. Seven hundred million!

Golitsin could not squeeze even an ounce of solace from the fact that the idiot speculator would spend the remainder of his sorry life in a wheelchair, sucking fluid through a straw. Two kneecaps shattered into bony pulp. A face now unrecognizable to his own children. Big deal! It hardly compensated for the carnage — seven hundred million down the drain. What a mess.

After a year of horrible news, followed by worse news, Golitsin had at last reached a decision. A painful decision, and certainly humiliating. But it was also necessary, practical, and long overdue. Shove vanity aside. Managing businesses was not his forte. There was so little left to manage anyway. A few emaciated skeletons in a swarming sea of wreckage. The construction business had cratered into bankruptcy months ago. The arbitrage firm sank under the weight of ten thousand tons of North Korean "garbage" iron ore of a quality so poor nobody would touch it, at any price. The car import business had sputtered out of existence. The hotels and restaurants had been put on the block months before to pay off the ruinous debts accumulated by other struggling branches.

In fact, the feverish struggle to keep Konevitch's companies afloat had distracted and dislodged him from his God-given gift. What a waste! All those interminable hours exhausted in useless business meetings, listening to his sorry underlings concoct lies and excuses for their utter stupidity. The unending stream of crises brought about by the hapless dolts below him. From now on, he would focus his brilliance where it belonged: stealing other people's fortunes and businesses.

He left his office, walked downstairs, and climbed purposefully into the rear of his big black limousine. He barked at his driver to get it in gear and drive around until he was told otherwise. The motion would help him clear the cobwebs. A little medicinal relief wouldn't hurt, either. He yanked a bottle of imported scotch from the bar against the front seat and jerked the cap off. He positioned a tumbler carefully in front of him. A hearty tilt of the bottle and it was filled to the lip.

Feeling a new sense of purpose, he lifted the carphone, dialed a number in the Kremlin, drained the first long burning sip of scotch, and waited. Tatyana picked up on the third ring.

They wasted a few minutes on mock pleasantries and obligatory political gossip. The prime minister was about to be sacked. He was an idiotic little pencil pusher, bereft of ideas to bail out the crippled economy, and by general consensus a jerk. The old prime minister who had been fired before him — an even bigger jerk — had the inside track for a return engagement.

Golitsin drummed his fingers and waited. Tatyana obviously enjoyed recounting the tawdry gossip, and he let her ramble awhile before he got down to business. "Don't you find it curious how Yuri Khodorin has resisted our overtures?"

"He is a tough nut to crack," Tatyana agreed. "Nicky's taking a terrible beating."

"He's not the only one. I finally placed two of my agents inside his companies. Both discovered, somehow."

"How do you know this?"

"I was meant to. The message was quite clear. One found in his car with his throat slashed, the other disappeared. Went to work one day and hasn't been heard from in three weeks."

"They must've gotten sloppy," she said very coldly.

"They were handpicked. Veteran agents, both of them, and they went in with perfect covers. I don't think so."

"Then what do you think?"

After a brief pause, fueled by another noisy sip, Golitsin told her, "Khodorin has been tipped off. It's the only explanation."

"It's a good explanation. Not the only one, though. But assuming it's right, who would be behind it?"

"Alex Konevitch."

"Impossible."

"Is it really? They were friends before Konevitch fled. Business competitors, but they sometimes chummed around."

Tatyana considered this theory before launching into her usual nit-picking. "How could he get word out? He's rotting in prison, Sergei."

"So what? Solzhenitsyn smuggled out full-length novels, and that was from our most remote Siberian gulag."

"I do remember reading about that. He wrote them on toilet paper or something."

"Anything's possible."

"But how did Konevitch learn we were going after Khodorin?"

"Maybe Khodorin contacted our boy. Maybe Konevitch was watching. I don't know. It doesn't really matter."

"That's two maybes," Tatyana, ever the lawyer, observed, but without conviction.

"Then let's dispense with the doubts. We've tried the same tricks on Khodorin. The computer hacking, the murders, the bombings, the police visit, the in-house spies, all of which succeeded spectacularly with Konevitch. Khodorin's been ready for every single one. He's clobbering us at our own game.

It's not beginner's luck, and it's not coincidental."

Tatyana kicked off her shoes and planted her lovely feet on the desk. "So what do you suggest?"

"It's not a difficult problem."

"Then there must be an easy solution."

"There is. Konevitch, he has to die," Golitsin informed her. "And the sooner the better." His glass was empty and he refilled it with a flourish. It felt great to be back in the game, outthinking his opponents. He privately relished the vision of an OUT OF BUSINESS sign hanging on the bank in the morning. How nice it would be to wake up and have those worries behind him. He would hang the sign himself, he decided. Good riddance. "So where is our boy wonder now?" he asked, trying to suppress any hint of giddiness.

"A federal prison in Illinois. After seven months in Atlanta, it was felt he became too acclimated. Too comfortable."

"Too comfortable?"

"According to Tromble, Konevitch fit right into the life. Some band of Cuban heavyweights took him under their wing. He was living like a king. A security detail followed him everywhere. A Barcalounger in his cell. Special meals prepared in the prison mess hall. Can you believe it?"

Yes, he did. He was long past being surprised by Alex Konevitch. And, too, he was long past underestimating him. Probably, he decided, this explained how Konevitch blew the whistle on them to his old chum Khodorin — with help on the inside, there were a million ways Konevitch could communicate with the outside. "So you've failed to turn up the heat on him," Golitsin stated, but without his characteristic nastiness.

He had his own bad news to impart — bad news for her, anyway. No use getting her all worked up.

"Technically, Tromble failed. Not me," she insisted. "I've done everything I could. Our prosecution team arrived months ago. Konevitch should've been back in an American court a long time ago. The case is perfect."

"All right," he conceded very agreeably. "Then it's all Tromble's fault."

Suspicious from this burst of benevolence, Tatyana snapped, "What are you hiding, Sergei?"

Golitsin sank in his plush leather seat and cracked a small smile. She was so quick. He quickly recounted the sad tale about the rogue trader who shoved the export-import bank into insolvency. By nine the next morning, the bank would be shuttered. By ten, word would race around Moscow: Konevitch's once mighty empire had finally bled to death.

Tatyana's feet flew off the desk and landed

on the floor. "Oh, that's just great," she moaned. "Your idiots ruined me. My stock is now worthless."

"Mine, too."

"Oh, spare me. You have Konevitch's money, his mansion, his cars, his luxury apartment in Paris. What do I have?"

He was tempted to answer truthfully: A hundred thousand shares of nothing; you're broke and desperate, living on a mangy government paycheck. I'm your only hope — you need me more than ever.

Instead, he tapped his fingers on the car seat and sipped patiently from his scotch as she swore and vented for a few more minutes.

Eventually, he uncorked the cure to her troubles. "All the more reason to take care of this Khodorin business quickly. We'll divide the cash this time. I promise. Five hundred million, perfectly even, a three-way split. Same with his shares. And this time, we'll sell everything as fast as we can. We'll easily bag another billion or more."

He paused to allow her a moment to accept the inevitability of her situation. She was broke, for the moment; but not hopeless. With the right moves, in no time at all she could light her cigarettes with thousand-dollar bills. "The best way to get inside Khodorin's head is to kill Konevitch," he suggested.

"It will be quite difficult. He's out of reach,

behind bars."

"But not impossible. And if Khodorin wants to play games with us, he needs to be taught a lesson. There's no way for him to win."

"You're right," she mumbled. The brilliance of the suggestion finally dawned on her. "Meet our demands when the time comes, or we'll hunt you down. If the U.S. government can't protect Konevitch, there's no hope for you. Khodorin will collapse."

After a brief call on her cell phone to Nicky, and a long meeting with a few American specialists in the Foreign Ministry, Tatyana barked at the Kremlin switch to do whatever it took to connect her to the director of the American FBI. It took three operators thirty minutes to track him down. He happened to be in an FBI field office in northern Jersey, clustered with a team of agents who had just broken up a large counterfeiting ring. An inside informant had been turned a year before. Unlike so many other operations during Tromble's tenure, the investigation had been a model of law enforcement skill and restraint. Every nuance of legal limit had been adhered to, no shortcuts. The evidence was overwhelming and, in the view of the Justice Department's sharpest experts, virtually unchallengeable in court.

The three counterfeiters had been slapped

in cuffs an hour before. Tromble had arrived just in time for the press conference where he would make the announcement and bask in the glory. The podium was already set up, the large flock of reporters and cameras waiting with growing impatience.

An aide entered the room where Tromble was being fed enough information to fool the press into believing he had personally doted on every detail of the case, had personally overseen this masterstroke of crimefighting at its best. The aide cupped a hand to his ear and signaled his boss. Tromble cursed, then stepped out of the room and accepted the proffered cell phone.

Without preamble, Tatyana launched right in. "What's going on with Konevitch?"

"Sorry, no change," he told her, eyeing his watch, impatient to begin his briefing. All the big networks were there, all the big East Coast papers. "He's still up in Chicago. Believe me, it's a nasty place. One of our two worst."

"He's been there two months now, John."

"Almost three, actually."

"And it's been almost a year since you promised to deliver him to me."

"I know, and I'm sorry. He's tougher than expected."

"And how are the reports from Chicago?"

"Not promising. It's very curious. Somehow, he's wormed his way inside the Black

Power brotherhood."

"But he's white. Don't they discriminate?"

"Typically, yes. He's amazingly adaptable."

"All right, you've had your turn," she barked, suddenly turning aggressive. "Now I'd like to take my best shot."

"What are you talking about?"

"I consulted with a few of my experts about your prisons. I want someplace tougher. Much tougher, much more terrifying."

This greatly annoyed him and he made no effort to hide it. "I believe I know our prisons better than your so-called experts. Atlanta and Chicago are our worst."

"The worst *federal* prisons, you mean. Not your worst prisons, not by a long shot."

"That might be true, but the federal prisons are the ones I can influence."

She went on, unfazed. "It's my understanding that your Bureau of Prisons occasionally subcontracts with state prisons."

"Occasionally, yes. To alleviate overcrowding. Sometimes as a temporary measure until a prisoner can be moved. So what?"

"I further understand that the state prison in Yuma is unimaginably horrible. A nightmare of violence, killings, and rapes."

"Well . . . it's pretty bad. But Parchman down in Mississippi's probably a little worse."

"You don't seem to be listening, John. Like it or not, it's my turn to pick Konevitch's hellhole."

Tromble swallowed his anger. "So what do you want?"

"Switch him to Yuma. Do it immediately."

"He's barely been in Chicago three months."

"It's almost summertime, and the prison lacks air-conditioning. I want him sweltering in 120-degree heat, locked into a small cell he has to share with a complete sociopath. I want him mixed in with the general population, eating horrible food, and worried every minute of every day for his life. I want him more miserable than he's ever been."

"I think that can be arranged."

"If you want your agents in Moscow, you'll make damned sure it is. You've embarrassed me with my bosses, John. You owe me for a year of humiliation and lame excuses."

Before Tromble could say another word, Tatyana punched off. She leaned back into her chair and placed her feet back on her desk. The prison had been Nicky's choice. He knew of ten Russians inside Yuma, three of them hit men with impressive credentials. He swore that any one of them could do the job.

Courtesy of Golitsin's fat wallet, a bonus would be offered to sweeten the pot — $500K to whoever killed Konevitch. A way would be found to get this word inside. Quick results were expected.

The next idea was Tatyana's. To encourage

speedy action, the price would decrease by
$100K a month, until the job was done.

28

Warden Byron James leaned back in his seat and contemplated the glistening toes of his spitshined wingtips. He peered into the reflected face of Special Agent Terrence Hanrahan and informed him, "Won't take long."

"You're sure?"

"Damn sure. Ask around. This here prison's the rottenest sewer in America," he said very loudly, smacking his lips and looking quite proud about that boast.

"What have you done with him?"

A slow smile. "A week in solitary for starters. Moved him to D Wing today."

"What's that? High-security?"

The warden's feet hit the floor and he leaned forward. "Just say he's not in the best of company."

"Tell me more."

"D Wing's for the undesirables. Big-time dealers, gangbangers, Mafia hoods, Black Power brotherhood, and recalcitrants who can't seem to behave. Plus, he's got a special new cellmate, Bitchy Beatty."

"That supposed to mean something to me?"

"If you were an inmate . . . then yeah, damned sure it would."

Hanrahan was pretty certain it was best not to know. In the event he was subpoenaed later, total ignorance was his best defense. Curiosity got the better of him, though, and reluctantly he asked, "Tell me about Bitchy . . . ?"

"Beatty. Bitchy Beatty. Guess you might know him better as Benny Beatty."

"Oh . . . *that* Beatty?"

"Same guy. You know, before that awful assault thing happened." Hanrahan vaguely recalled the case, about three years back.

Beatty, formerly of one of those big Kansas college football factories, and in his second year as an All-Pro tackle for Arizona, had rushed into the New York Jets locker room with a baseball bat after getting creamed in a championship game. Like a whirling dervish, he spun and bounced around the room and brutally assaulted fifteen of the Jets' top stars. By the time he was wrestled down, the locker room was filled with busted teeth and broken bones, three shattered kneecaps, and more gallons of blood than anybody cared to measure.

Beatty got more than the max, ten to twenty: turned out the judge was a rabid Jets season ticketholder; turned out it would be five to ten before the Jets could rebuild and field a reasonable team. The furious judge threw away the sentencing guidelines and gave Beatty double what he gave the Jets. An appeal was pending. The grounds were solid, but it would be heard in a New York appellate court, of all places. His lawyers weren't optimistic.

Hanrahan asked, "How'd he get that nickname?"

"Short for 'bitchmaker.' Ol' Beatty misses all those groupie sluts something awful." A broad smile at the faces in the room. "Guess you'd say his cellmates are his surrogates."

Two special agents leaned against the wall and joined in the laughter, halfheartedly, little more than forced chuckles. They stopped as soon as it seemed polite.

This was the third prison inside a year. And the third cocksure warden who swore he would break Konevitch like a swaybacked pony. Konevitch had adapted to each new facility quickly, with surprising ease. Go figure.

As a prisoner in the federal system, though, he enjoyed one protected right they badly wished they could withhold: monthly visits from that pretty little wife, who appeared like clockwork. No matter where they moved him, no matter how closely the secret was kept, she somehow learned where he was. The Feds monitored his mail, an easy task, as there had been no mail — none coming in, none going out. That nosy lawyer of theirs peppered the system with requests for his location, but none had been answered. Somehow, though, she always knew where he was.

He attacked the library with curious regularity. The FBI accessed the records and followed his literary pursuits with their own deep interest. The law stacks were a common destination. Little surprise there. All prisoners fashioned themselves Clarence Darrows, able to outdo all those esquired incompetents who screwed up and got them in here. Every other day, it was books on computers, computer languages, FORTRAN and COBOL, and that new thing called the Internet all their kids were raving about. A few times a week, he hopped onto the library computer and typed away at blazing speed, nearly burning up the keyboard. Why, they had no idea.

Hanrahan turned away from the warden and, talking maybe at the wall, maybe at nobody, emphasized, "You know how important this is to us."

"Guess I do. I got a call from Fielder at headquarters. Said your guy, Tromble, wants this real bad."

Still looking away, like this wasn't a conversation. "Find a way to scale back his liberties. Turn up the heat as fast and hard as you like."

The warden, also now talking, not at Hanrahan but at some invisible spot on the ceiling, hypothesized, "Yeah, well, he could, I dunno, maybe misbehave or somethin'. I'd have to come down hard with a few necessary disciplinary measures."

"Yeah, but like what?"

"A few more weeks in solitary will get his attention."

"Don't. Believe me, don't. That was tried at both previous prisons. He folds himself into some kind of yoga posture and goes into a trance. Actually, he seems to enjoy the solitude."

"Two . . . ? Hey, I thought this guy was a cherry."

"Sorry, no, you're the third. The other two prisons he's shown a talent for building coalitions and finding people to protect him. He's clever. We have no idea how he does it."

The warden leaned back in his chair and threw his hands behind his head. "Well, your boy ain't met me yet," he boasted. "Ask around, fellas. The state always sends me the biggest hardasses. I got my ways of making 'em crack."

The two agents on the wall shared quiet smiles. It was the same speech, almost word for word, they had heard from both previous wardens. And in each prison, inside a few weeks, Konevitch was hanging out with the biggest badasses in the yard, getting extra food helpings in the mess hall, the recipient of all kinds of special largesse and favors, even from the guards.

As much as they hoped and plotted otherwise, somehow, some way, they feared Alex Konevitch would find a way to upstage this wingtipped, overconfident ass as well.

Bitchy missed football like crazy. All in all, though, prison wasn't all that bad, or even all that different. He more or less spent his time just as he did back in his cherished NFL days, eating voraciously, hoisting enormous weights out in the yard, and bashing heads whenever the impulse seized him. He had packed on another forty pounds of bad mood to the 350 he arrived with, all hard muscle.

Bitchy had scraped by with terrible grades in college, not because he was stupid, because he was smart. A full ride, with all the cute little cheerleaders he wanted, and bright little volunteers to stand in and take his tests. What dork would hide his nose inside books with all that fun to be had? Like many football hotshots, off the field Bitchy had always been spoiled rotten; it shouldn't surprise anybody that he now had a few serious impulse control issues. Anyway, the college was determined to graduate him phi beta pigskin, no matter what, even if he never went near class, which he seldom did.

The new boy was lying on the lower bunk with his nose stuffed inside a book, something about Web site construction. He was cute, real cute. A bit tall for Bitchy's usual taste maybe, but what the hell, variety was supposed to be spicy. So why not? He shifted his vast weight to the side of his bunk and peered down.

"Hey, I heard you're a transfer."

"Third prison this year."

"How come they moved you to this shithole?"

"Mutilation."

"What the hell's that?"

"I mutilated a man. I didn't kill him. Afterward, though, I suppose he wished I had." Alex absently flipped a page and continued reading.

Bitchy scratched his head. "That's a new one on me."

"In the statutes it sits between first- and second-degree assault. You see, in your American laws, it boils down to intent. I didn't want to kill him."

"What are you, a lawyer?" Bitchy hated lawyers. He'd been screwed royally by the five-hundred-buck-an-hour suit he'd hired to defend him, a pompous prick who barely protested when the judge doubled his sentence. He would dearly love to screw one back.

"Hardly."

Bitchy bounced off the top bunk. With incredible agility, both feet hit the floor at once, almost catlike. He was so damned big and blockish, his opponents habitually underestimated his speed, balance, and dexterity. But not after Bitchy got his huge paws on you — suddenly, everything about him came into terrifying focus.

He placed a hand on his zipper and was about to introduce his new cellmate to Mr. Johnson.

Alex calmly closed the book and looked at him. "I castrated a man," he informed Beatty simply, coldly. "He attempted to rape me in the shower. That night, after he fell asleep, I chopped it off. While he howled in pain, I cut it into small pieces. You know why, Benny?" He paused long enough to allow Benny time to consider this intriguing question. "It made it impossible to sew back on."

Bitchy's hand left his zipper and entered a deep pocket.

Alex said, "I hear you were a professional footballer."

A strange way to put it, but Bitchy answered, "Yeah. So what?"

"Did it pay well?"

This was getting weird. "Not well. It paid great."

"How great?"

"A five million signing bonus. Three million a year in salary. Why you askin'?"

"Where is all that money now?"

"None of your business."

Alex put the book down and leaned his back against the wall. "I suppose your legal costs consumed most of it."

Bitchy also leaned back against the wall. He was in the mood for a little man-love, but this guy seemed to want to chitchat a bit before they got down to action. At least he wasn't hollering and bouncing around the cell like his last cellmate. The Russian accent sure sounded cool.

"I got millions left. When it hits three mil, the lawyers can go screw themselves. The appeals stop."

"Smart. So how is it invested?"

"In the bank. Where else would it be?"

"Did nobody advise you that's stupid?"

Bitchy bounced off the wall. The hand came out of the pocket and suddenly balled into a beefy fist. "Watch your mouth. You're stupid if you call me stupid."

"Relax, Benny. I never said you were stupid. I said leaving the money in the bank is stupid."

"It'll still be there when I get out. How stupid is that?"

"A lot more of it could be there. Is that smart, my friend?"

"All right, Mr. I-know-so-much, what's smarter?"

"In the right stocks, it will multiply enormously. Real estate is a fairly good and safe investment also."

"That's not my thing."

"Have you ever heard of Qualcomm, Benny?"

Bitchy laughed. "Sure. I get it from the pharmacy whenever I get jock itch." He laughed harder.

"We'll look into jock-itch providers if you'd like. It's certainly a market you know well. That's more of a slow growth, long-term investment, though," Alex replied, very seriously. "It's a company that invented a brilliant new way to send sound and information down a wire, or even fiber-optic cable. The stock is set to quadruple. Do you understand time-division versus code-division encoding?"

Not a chance.

"Well, let me explain the deal. If you want me as a lover, I probably can't stop you. Of course you'll have to sleep with one eye open. When will that crazy Russian guy cut my dingee off?" Alex waved his hand up and down in the air. "He will, most definitely, he will . . . but when?"

It was said so matter-of-factly, Bitchy took no offense. Shifting to the third person helped; it took a little personal edge off the threat.

"Or," Alex pushed on, "I can be your investment advisor. I'll double or triple your money. That's a lowball estimate, incidentally. I know a great deal about the Russian market also. A little cash in the right ADRs would be very smart. Derivatives are doing quite well these days also."

Alex patted the mattress. Bitchy's broad rear landed on the bunk beside him and he said, "I have no idea what you're talking about."

"That's why you need me, Benny."

"Just for not raping you?"

"There are many attractive men in this prison. Do whatever you like, just not with me, okay?"

"Do I have to protect you?"

"That's not part of the deal, no."

"Make me that kind of dough and I'll slaughter whoever comes near you."

An indifferent shrug. "Probably a wise move on your part."

"So how's this work?"

"Easier than you might think. There are probably fifteen or twenty contraband cell phones in the block, am I right?"

Bitchy nodded. Fifty was more like it. The guards were always hunting for them, but as they grew smaller they became so much easier to conceal. Bitchy knew of at least four tucked away in the prison laundry, another six in the kitchen. Twist a few arms, and he'd have all he wanted. No was not a word Bitchy heard very often.

"Get me three of those phones, Benny. The batteries wear down quickly and can't be recharged inside our cell. You'll handle the expenses. Believe me, you'll be able to afford it. I use the phones to manage your money and whoever else I decide to call."

"And what if you mess up and lose my money?"

"I'll be on the bottom bunk. If I fail to keep my end of the bargain, you're not obligated to keep yours."

Bitchy crossed his arms and stared off at the far wall. Of the vast multitude of "investment advisors" at the pro draft who pounced hungrily on the newest batch of twenty-two-year-old, undereducated millionaires, not one of those greedy blabbermouths had offered a deal remotely resembling this. And if they lost it all through their own utter ineptitude, it was tough luck, pal, sayonara.

Really, how many investment advisors promised outright that if they failed in their promises, they'd bend over and take it, like they just gave it? "All right," Bitchy said, hands back in his pockets.

"Another thing. I'm going to teach you how to do this. If I make you all that money, I don't want you to turn around and lose it afterward."

"Will it hurt?"

"Only a little, Benny."

Benny laughed.

"One last thing," Alex said, returning to his book.

"Name it."

"Spread the word. The last two prisons, we pooled our money and increased our buying positions enormously. The more the better for you."

The day that marked the anniversary of eleven months since the Konevitch trial, Kim Parrish threw her long-overdue fit.

The team of state prosecutors had arrived from Russia six months before, four of them in all, all men, all wearing blockish suits made of a cheap, indescribable fabric. Only one spoke any semblance of English — just please, thank you, yes, but mostly no, and a dismaying variety of filthy curses.

The FBI paid for the works and put them up in the downtown Hilton. They immediately raised hell about the lousy accommodations. To shut them up, they were bounced a few blocks over to the Madison, a decidedly more upscale lodging. The complaints did not abate until the Madison succumbed and switched them each to thousand-dollar suites.

They ate breakfast, lunch, and dinner at the most expensive Georgetown restaurants, rented two Mercedes sedans, a snazzy black Corvette, and a shiny red Maserati. They spent their five-day weekends raising hell in California and Florida, before they fell deeply in love with Las Vegas and the legalized brothels nearby. They billed it all to the FBI — the first-class airfares, the whores, the gambling losses that quickly turned mountainous. Everything was billed directly to the Feds. They drank from dawn till dusk, got in fistfights in bars, picked up four DUIs, smashed up the Maserati, trashed one Mercedes sedan, and billed all that, too, to the FBI.

They arrived with two dozen large crates stuffed to the lids with documents. Everything in Russian. Everything, every word and comma, had to be meticulously and painfully translated into English.

Two more weeks were lost while Kim scoured the city for a competent translator. As the documents proved to be a thick maze of Russian legalese, not any translator would do. Kim interviewed a dozen candidates. Several American college graduates whose levels of fluency weren't nearly as impressive as their résumés. Five Russian émigrés who utterly failed the English test. A retired book editor who had translated two complete Tolstoy novels had seemed like her best bet. That one took a brief glance at the two dozen crates and bolted.

Eventually, Kim drove across to the river to the leafy, sprawling CIA headquarters at Langley. She had called ahead and was met by a man from the Russian analysis section. Downstairs, in the large marble lobby, she briefly described her problem. Mr. Spook smiled reassuringly and claimed he knew the perfect guy. On a sheet of paper he wrote the name and number of a Russian expat, a man named Petri Arbatov, a major in the KGB before he defected to the U.S. Petri had a law degree from Moscow University and in the fifteen years since his defection, he had also picked up an American JD from Catholic University. Petri demanded $600 an hour, a price that would've impressed the most expensive firm in New York. He insisted he wouldn't translate "da" to "yes" for a penny less. The price was outrageous, far beyond what she had intended to pay. She promptly agreed.

What the hell: Petri, too, could send his rather impressive bills to the FBI. If the Fibbies could blow through all that dough on a bunch of Russian cowboys whooping it up like rich Arab playboys, they better not even blink about all-too-legitimate legal expenses.

Kim rented a small, furnished fourth-floor apartment on Connecticut Avenue, they hauled up the boxes, rolled up their sleeves, and dug in. Petri proved to be a rare combination, an unemotional perfectionist — a short, thin, sad-faced man of few words who concentrated deeply and absolutely on his work. He consumed only one meal a day, always a thin broth he brought from home that he carefully spooned into his mouth. On such little nourishment, it was a miracle he stayed alive, much less endured the backbreaking load of work. He surrounded himself with both Russian and English dictionaries and waded through each document, word for word. He dictated. Kim typed. At six hundred an hour, he and Kim avoided expensive banter. They made it through three-quarters of the crates at a furious pace because they wasted nothing: neither time nor words. After four months and twenty days of eighteen hours each, she had no idea whether Petri was married, had cancer, children, was rich or poor, or even whether he lived on the street.

Thus she was hugely surprised when he slammed down one of the documents and turned to her. "You and I need to talk."

"About what?"

"Do you know what I did for the KGB, Kim? You've never asked."

"You were a lawyer?"

"More or less. I was the KGB's idea of a lawyer."

"Okay. What does that mean?"

"I worked in a legal section that specialized in what were termed special cases."

"So what? Specialization is the name of the game. I specialize in immigration law."

"Ask my specialty."

She decided to humor him. She smiled. "What was your specialty, Petri?"

"Framing. I framed people, Kim." He let that nauseating confession sit for a moment, then pushed on. "Only high-value targets. And I was the best, Kim, a remarkably talented lawyer. I could build a seamless case against anybody. A general secretary, a highly decorated marshal of the Soviet Union, a poet with a Nobel Prize, it didn't matter. Literally anybody, Kim. They gave me a name and I went to work. When I was done, any jury or judge would believe the accused was a capitalist pig with ten million in a Swiss account who had sex with his own children and lived only to destroy the motherland."

"Is this why you defected, Petri? Conscience."

He looked away. "Oh, I wish I could say yes." He seemed to sink in his chair. "I'm not so noble, I'm afraid."

"What happened?"

"One day, I went to visit another man in my section, a good friend of twenty years, who worked only three doors down from my office. He had slipped out to go to the latrine. He did something incredibly stupid, he left his door unlocked. This was totally against procedure, you must understand. Inexcusably sloppy. So I walked in. Documents were strewn everywhere. On his desk, his floor, everywhere. He was obviously well along."

"With what?"

"With me, Kim. He was building a case against me."

She moved closer, almost in his face. "Why?"

He refused to look at her. "An hour later, I was hugging a CIA man from your embassy and begging for help. I cried, Kim. I promised anything his bosses wanted — anything. I was about to get what I had done to so many others, and I was suffocating with fear. No level of betrayal was ruled out. They whisked me out the next morning." In a sad, resigned tone Petri added, "So I never asked my old friend, you see."

"You must have some idea."

"Competition, I suppose. You see, I *was* the best, Kim. I could turn a saint into a whore, a pope into a pimp, whatever I wanted them to be. The chief-of-section job was coming open. We were both vying for the job and all that came with it. A larger apartment, a chauffeured car, two weeks a year in a seedy KGB guesthouse in Ukraine. That's how KGB people operate."

"I see."

He rolled forward in his chair and planted his skinny elbows on his bony knees. "Don't look down your nose at my work. You have no idea the expertise or artistry it requires. Everything must be perfect, Kim. Documents forged with just the right dates, matching fonts, identical signatures, all the witnesses coached and carefully choreographed. It's police work and lawyer work and theater work rolled into one. You have to imagine the crime, Kim, dream it up out of thin air. Then dig a moat and build a castle nobody can assail. No detail can be overlooked, no knot untied. I must tell you, Kim, it's so much more difficult than constructing a real case with real facts."

"Well, I wouldn't know about that."

Petri lifted the document and began reading it again. He floated out of his past, back to the present. Nearly an hour passed before he looked up and asked casually, "How do you consider this case against Konevitch?"

"You know what?" She put aside the document she was reading and glanced over at him. "I'm impressed. I thought those four clowns were just drunken miscreants. Totally useless."

"But now?"

"Well, I was wrong. They're good. Very, very good. They've really delivered the goods."

"Will your judge be persuaded?"

Kim smiled. "The Konevitches will be back in Moscow faster than they can blink." After a moment, she asked, "What do you think?"

"Probably so."

"I just wish I had all this material at the first trial."

Petri nodded as if to say: Of course you do. "And what do you believe will happen to them at home?"

"Not my problem, Petri."

"My apologies. I offended you. Of course you can't worry about the people you kick out."

They returned to their work. They fell back into their normal pattern and quietly ignored each other for another hour. Petri thumbed through his beloved dictionaries and scrawled long, messy notes in the margins of a document. Kim pecked away on her keyboard, forcing yet another translated document into her hard drive — or trying to, at least. She began making mistake after mistake. She corrected, then corrected the correction, then repeated the first mistake again. Her brain and her fingers seemed to be coming unglued from each other.

With a loud curse, she finally pushed away from her desk. She wheeled her chair across the floor until she ended up less than a foot from Petri. "All right. What will happen to them?"

He quietly closed the thick dictionary. "Tell me what you think."

"All right. They'll be tried in court. Probably convicted. They didn't kill anybody, so probably they'll end up in prison."

Petri made no reply.

"Look," Kim said, more forcefully and with a show of considerable indignation, "all these crates of evidence from the Russians. Proof of intention, right? Why go to such enormous lengths and trouble if they don't intend to put them on trial?"

"As you say," Petri replied with a slight grin. The answer was now so obvious, it was staring her in the eye. She knew it. After all these months of sweat and hard work, and of unrelenting pressure from her bosses, it was only natural for her to suppress it. But pieces of it kept bubbling to the surface. Little fragments. Niggling doubts and caustic uncertainties.

The frustration was killing her. "Damn it, Petri, Konevitch stole the money. He's guilty. He plundered his own bank, he ripped off hundreds of millions."

"Is that so?"

She waved a hand at the crates stacked neatly in the corner. "Bank records. Statements from his own employees. Computer printouts of his transactions, police reports, three full investigations from three different government agencies. What more do you want?"

"You're absolutely right, Kim. Who could want more? It's all here."

"Damn right it is."

"A perfect little package, gift-wrapped, and handed to you on a silver platter." This skinny little lawyer who once made his living building perfect cases just wouldn't let go.

"Too perfect, isn't it?" she asked, bending forward and rubbing her forehead.

"Tell me how many cases you've tried."

"Hundreds. I don't know."

"Any cases where every detail matched up so well? Every date coincides, every witness saw exactly the same thing, every investigator came to identical conclusions? Everything so perfectly, so amazingly lined up? For a supposedly brilliant man, Konevitch left behind an astonishing ocean of evidence."

She was suddenly more deeply miserable than she had ever felt. It was inescapable now. She was fighting back a flood of tears. "No case is ever perfect."

She had reached the end of the journey. Petri sat back for a moment, allowing her to ponder the ugly magnitude of her discovery. Americans were so naïve about these things.

He then commented, "We never actually tried the cases in court, you know. Not our job, Kim. We built the perfect little cases and handed them off to others. Those trial lawyers, they all loved us. Such flawless gifts we gave them. They couldn't lose."

"I don't understand. Why hand them off? You said you were a great lawyer. Since you created it, you knew the material better than anybody."

"I often wondered that, you know. They never told us why. Perhaps they thought the man who designs the guillotine shouldn't actually be forced to pull the lever and have to stare at the head in the basket. Communists. They could be so incoherently humane in completely inhumane ways."

Kim wanted to jump out of her chair and bolt. Just run away from this case. Run as fast and as far as her feet could carry her.

He rolled forward in his chair and placed a hand on her knee. "They'll murder them, Kim. Oh, they might go through the motions of a trial . . . or they might not. They'll kill them, though, as sure as you and I are sitting here."

There was one question left for her to ask, one dark mystery to solve. "But Konevitch could be guilty, couldn't he, Petri?"

"You know the golden rule of my old KGB section?"

She forced herself to stare into his dark, sad eyes, to hear the wisdom of a soul soiled and ruined long before they ever met.

"Never frame a guilty man."

The first run at Alex Konevitch came shortly after sunrise. It came three weeks to the day after he stepped out of the dark prison van in Yuma. It came in a large sweltering room filled with sweaty men, less than a minute after Alex loaded his tray with his usual selection of soggy French toast and watery scrambled eggs, only seconds after he sat in his usual seat, at his usual table.

The offer had been smuggled in to the Russians a week before by a balding, nervous-looking guard named Tim. A double divorcé drowning under a serious gambling addiction, Tim owed his bookie, Marty, five thousand bucks after a sure-thing pony did the big choke on the backstretch. Before he placed the bet, Tim had vaguely wondered if his bookie had mob connections. Good guess. Turned out Anthony "the Crusher" Cardozzi was Marty's second cousin, a lifelong business associate, and quite serious about men honoring their debts. A month overdue on his vig, Tim now was seriously wondering if his state medical insurance would cover the destruction. Thus, when Marty relayed the offer — a favor for a friend, Marty intimated — Tim almost suffocated with relief.

Five thousand bucks forgiven, and two perfectly functional kneecaps — incredible generosity, just for delivering a simple message. Sure, no problem, Tim replied, vowing to give up gambling, and knowing he wouldn't.

The offer ignited a bitter quarrel among the Russians. Day to day a loose-knit group, they were bound by two common traits — they all spoke Russian, and all had ties of one sort or another to the Russian underworld. The big question — indeed, the only question — was, who would get first crack at Alex Konevitch?

After two days of passing increasingly malicious notes back and forth, the Russians gathered in a tight swarthy huddle in a remote corner of the yard to discuss the offer — a cool half million to whomever killed him within thirty days, declining in value with each passing month. They spoke in Russian, and they sparred loudly and heatedly, with no concern at all about being overheard.

The sooner the better — this point seemed elemental and was quickly agreed among the ten men. Why wait and waste a hundred grand? Point two was almost as easily settled — the first crack would be their best shot. Catch Konevitch before he knew of their intention to kill him. Catch him before he had his guard up. Catch him at his most vulnerable.

If that flopped, future efforts would become increasingly difficult.

The experienced hit men raucously laid claim to the honor. The killing game wasn't as easy as it seemed, one explained, and the other killers nodded with great gravity and solemn agreement. An amateur making his first plunge was likely to do something unfathomably stupid. Two of the veterans confessed how they had choked on their first jobs. Seemingly insignificant details that suddenly ballooned into big problems. A wrong glance here, a careless stutter there, that alerted the target. A case of last-minute jitters that turned paralytic. A lot could go wrong, and often did.

The thieves and pushers and kidnappers

weren't buying it. What was so hard? Bring something sharp, pick a vital organ, and poke it. No problem, as easy as cutting steak. The bickering intensified and verged on violence, before Igor, a clever accountant with a talent for money laundering, came to the rescue with a way to buy peace. One hundred grand from the bounty would be carved off and split among the nine Russians who didn't get to stab a hole in Alex.

Everybody wanted to argue about this for a while, but the compromise was irresistible, and inevitably accepted.

Now everybody benefited. And now everybody had a stake in doing it right.

Thus the lottery rapidly whittled down to four. Three had made a handsome living on the outside, killing people. Number four was a blowhard who loudly proclaimed two murders and launched into vulgar, descriptive bragging about his handiwork. They suspected he was lying, and they were right. Nobody could prove it, though; thus he had a tenuous, shaky seat at the table. But having settled on this logic, it was a short bounce to the next argument.

To nobody's surprise, this proposal came from the lips of Lev Titov, hands down the most productive killer in the group, if not the entire prison. It was plain common sense, Lev argued — the one with the most scalps on his belt should have the first shot. Having jumped off to an early start, at age fourteen, fulfilling every schoolboy's dream by strangling his math teacher, Lev went on to compile an impressive pedigree of homicides. He was legendary among certain circles, a remorseless assassin who killed without flair or even a telltale method. He had slain for himself, for the Russian army, for the Mafiya, and occasionally, when his short fuse got the better of him, for the hell of it. He was fussy and painstaking, and able to murder with a bewildering variety of weapons, from a deck of cards to sophisticated bombs. He once killed a man he suspected of cheating at chess by stuffing the checkmated king down his throat. Unpredictability and a certain amount of messiness were his only signatures.

A quick show of hands. Eight for. One puzzling abstention. Only the blowhard against.

Lev was the man.

One hundred grand would be split nine ways; the other four hundred would go into an account of Lev's choosing. A man who smiled rarely, Lev could not wipe the grin off his face. With seven years left on his sentence, he could at least look forward to a little gold at the end of the rainbow.

And so it was that at the moment Alex placed his tray on the table and casually fell onto the hard metal bench, Lev never even turned around. Why bother? After watching and studying his target for four days, he could write a book on Alex's culinary habits. He knew Alex would quietly sip his lukewarm coffee and wait for his big cellmate. Alex liked eggs, his cellmate adored French toast. It was a routine they shared, like an old married couple. The roommate would pour and scrape his runny eggs onto Alex's tray, and the French toast would land on the big guy's before they launched into their breakfasts.

The other nine Russians were strategically situated in a rough concentric pattern, precisely in accordance with the neat diagram Lev had meticulously sketched and handed out. Lev raised a clenched fist to signal the start. Immediately the other nine launched their trays in the air, then began indiscriminately pummeling every prisoner within reach. In a claustrophobic chamber filled with sweaty, grumpy men with a strong penchant toward violence, the spark was volcanic, the result horrific. It opened with an artillery duel of hundreds of hurled trays. Then four hundred men commenced an orgy of punching, kicking, tackling, biting, hollering, shoving, and general havoc.

Lev, seated almost directly to Alex's rear, watched with quiet amusement. He wouldn't budge until the riot approached full pitch. The sudden shift from order to madness overwhelmed the guards, who shuffled their feet and watched helplessly from the sidelines. From past riots, Lev knew he had three

559

minutes before reinforcements equipped with batons and riot gear arrived to break up the fun.

Lev slowly stood and stretched. He drew a deep breath and steeled his nerves. From his right pant pocket he withdrew a ten-inch shaft, a masterpiece of lethal perfection he had lovingly honed in the prison shop. The tip was pointy as a pin. Edges that could shave a baby's ass. The hilt was attractively bound in a coarse, fingerprint-resistant cotton fabric, a throwaway tool, a stab-and-leave-it special. And because of the commotion, a fast, quiet stabbing would be lost in the sea of violence. The odds of witnesses were about nil; the odds anyone would snitch on Lev even less.

Lev eased away from his table and through a series of short, stealthy steps quickly closed the seven feet to Alex. His target was standing now, back turned to Lev, thoroughly fixated on the raucous festivities, totally oblivious that this little party was all about him. Lev gripped the knife low. An upward thrust would be best, he promptly decided — up though the rib cage, then straight for the heart, or lungs.

But just as the blade was swinging up, something hard and powerful banged Lev's forearm. A nasty cracking sound, and the arm snapped. The shiv popped out of his fist and was instantly lost in the wild scuffle of feet.

The county coroner would later note that Lev's radius and ulna bones had both snapped and shattered. Simultaneous breaks with lots of splinters. A blow from a sledgehammer might account for it. A one-in-a-million kick from one of those big-time karate guys was another possibility.

One thing was sure — the force had been a ten on the Richter scale.

Lev yelped with pain and barely had to time to look to his left. A defense of any kind was out of the question anyway. A giant with frightening speed and gargantuan hands lifted him off the floor by his head. A quick jerk to the right, another snapping noise, Lev's neck this time, and he dropped to the floor like a discarded sack of disconnected bones.

His body was jerking involuntarily but Lev didn't feel a thing. No pain, no tingling, not even a mild sense of relief as his bowels and bladder emptied.

The big man was leaning over him, looking down into his eyes. "Hey, Alex," the man asked over his shoulder, "know this guy?"

"I've never seen him before."

"He knows you, for damn sure. He was about to shiv you."

In Russian, Lev managed to croak, "Call a doctor."

The big man looked bewildered. "What?"

Alex eased the big man aside and bent down until his face was two inches from

Lev's. "Who are you?" he asked, also in Russian.

"Call a doctor. Please. My body's not working."

"Give me your name."

"Can't breathe," he managed to gasp, and he was right. His spinal cord was severed; his face was turning bluer by the second as spinal shock settled in. "Hurry."

"Why me?" Alex asked.

"Money," Lev confessed.

"From who?" Alex asked, not budging, not making the slightest move to save him.

"I . . ." Lev tried to force a breath, but his lungs no longer functioned. "No idea."

The big man tugged at Alex's arm. "Let's go. Don't be standing here when the guards come."

"One last question," Alex promised the big man, then, staring into Lev's dying eyes, asked, "Are there more of you?"

Lev did not answer. The final act of his miserable life would not include snitching on his colleagues. He would not give Konevitch the satisfaction.

It was in his eyes, though.

Oh yes, there were definitely more killers out there.

They waited until they were back in the privacy of their small cell before either said a word. They sat on the lower bunk, kicked off their shoes, and pretended for a moment that it had never happened. Benny had not just killed a man. Nobody was trying to execute Alex. Life was every bit as good as it was yesterday, and tomorrow would be the same.

Eventually, Alex started it off. "Benny, I owe you my life."

"Just protecting my investment," Bitchy grunted as though it was nothing. His face betrayed him; he was obviously quite pleased.

"How did you know?"

"Oh, that. Well, the riot. There's usually one before a killing in here."

"I meant how did you know I was his target?"

"Didn't, necessarily. Protecting my quarterback in large mobs is how I make my living. You get an eye, or you don't get a contract. Who was that guy?"

"A Russian. I never met him."

"Why'd he want to shiv you?"

"Money, Benny — somebody put a bounty on me."

"A big one?"

"Quite large, probably."

"That's not good."

"Tell me about it."

"Any idea who's fronting the cash?"

"A very good idea, yes."

"Can you make them back off?"

"Sure, after I'm dead."

"Anyone else know?"

"I have that impression. The boys who started the riot, for sure."

They pondered the walls for a moment. Benny obviously was wondering what he had gotten himself into, hooked up with a Russian with a sumptuous bounty on his head. And Alex, just as obviously, was analyzing the same issue. How had the Russians found him? After a moment, that question answered itself. Somebody in the U.S. government had tipped them off; no other possibility made sense. But why now? And why here, in this miserable excuse for a prison? He was incarcerated, awaiting trial. In all likelihood, his next date with a judge would be followed by a quick trip to Russia. He posed absolutely no threat — or none they should know about, anyway.

Wait a few more months, and they could kill him at their leisure, in Moscow, in a small cell, in the prison of their choice. Kill him however they wanted, slow or fast, where nobody would ask questions later. So why now?

Benny broke the prolonged silence. "Will they try again?"

"What do you think?"

"I think I should find another cellmate."

"Good idea. I won't hold it against you."

Another moment of quiet passed. Alex studied his bare toes. Bitchy stood up, stretched, and produced a loud yawn.

"Thing is, Alex, you're trapped in here with these guys," Benny said, stretching his immense arms over his big head. "You can hide for 364 days, and on the 365th they catch you alone, in the shower, on the john, walking out of a meeting with your lawyer. That's it, game over." Then, as if Alex wasn't listening, "It's too easy."

"I'm already scared out of my wits, Benny. Thanks for making me hopeless."

"Just thought you should know."

"Now I know."

By 9:00 p.m. that same night, when Kim and Petri finally were allowed into the power chamber, the inquisitors were already settled comfortably in their chairs. After spending thirty minutes crashing in quiet huddles about how to manhandle an unruly INS attorney who was threatening mutiny, they had reached a decision.

Tromble sat at the middle of the table, tapping a pen, boiling with barely controlled fury. The head of INS, and the assistant district director, with the distinctly unhappy honor of being Kim's immediate boss, hunched down to his left. To his right sat the slightly inebriated chief of the Russian prosecutorial team, and a Colonel Volevodz, who had been frantically dispatched by Tatyana after a disturbing call from Tromble.

All were seated with unpleasant expressions

on one side of the conference table. The other side was barren.

Two empty chairs were arrayed in the middle of the floor across from them; the setting resembled a kangaroo court. In fact, it was. Kim and her translator were actually led in like prisoners by an FBI agent, one of Tromble's errand boys who in the hallway had coldly introduced himself as Terrence Hanrahan.

The arrangement was frightening. It was meant to make the hairs on the back of her neck stand up, and very briefly, it did.

Kim more or less stumbled timidly into one chair. Petri, with a sad, resigned expression, collapsed into the seat beside her. The INS director opened with a withering glare. "Miss Parrish, do you realize how much time, money, and effort's been put into this investigation?"

A cautious nod. "Of course I do. Nobody has worked harder on it than me."

"And now you say you want the case dropped?"

"That's exactly what I'm saying, sir."

"Because it's too perfect," he noted, dripping disbelief and skepticism all over the table.

"Because the whole thing is phony. The Konevitches are being framed by these people," she said, directing a finger at the two Russians at the table.

"What's the matter? Not enough evidence?"

"To the contrary, too much. It's too pat, too polished. It's obviously manufactured."

"Well, I heard of cases being dropped for lack of evidence. But for too much, and it's too good?" He shook his head from side to side, frowning tightly. "It's the stupidest thing I ever heard."

Petri and the two Russians glared across the table at each other. The lead Russian prosecutor suddenly lurched forward and snapped, "He is the one behind this." Other than an array of imaginative curses, in more than four months it was the most English Kim had heard pass his lips. And it was flawless, with barely a hint of an accent.

"Who's he?" Tromble asked, staring at the skinny, diminutive figure in the chair.

"That man," the Russian growled, directing a shaking finger at the small figure across from him. "The translator. The traitor. He defected fifteen years ago. His life's calling is to harm his motherland. If she's listening to him, she's crazy. He's obviously poisoning her brain."

Volevodz quickly jumped on the bandwagon and the two Russians spent about three minutes hurling insults and invective at the tiny Russian. Petri endured it with an unpleasant smile.

The river of castigations quickly became tedious, and Tromble eventually grew tired of it. He pushed forward and leaned across the table, redirecting the fire at the right source. "You're supposed to be a prosecutor, Miss Parrish, a lawyer. Remember your job. Leave the judgments to the men in robes."

The *men* in robes? She was already tired of all these boys ganging up on her. "I have an ethical responsibility to present an honest case. This is a travesty. You should all be ashamed to be taken in by these crooked Russians."

"The only people taken in were millions of poor Russians who trusted Konevitch. Of course the evidence is compelling. Guess why. He did it, he's guilty. He's a rotten slimy crook, who deserves whatever he gets. And when the Russians come along and prove it, you say they proved it too well. Do you have any idea how ridiculous that sounds?"

"Have you studied the evidence?" Kim asked, sounding frustrated, knowing full well how weak — no, how pathetically silly — her argument sounded. Toss this case away because it's watertight, too perfect, she seemed to be insisting.

"I have not, and I don't intend to." Tromble's elbows landed on the table, with his hands forming a steeple. "Why should I? I have you sitting right here telling me the evidence is rainproof, flawless in every way. No holes, no contradictions, no imperfections."

"I've made my position clear."

"Then I'll make mine clear. It's moving with or without you. Make your choice."

"Without me. Replace me. Find another lawyer."

The assistant director, Kim's immediate boss, was dismayed by how rapidly things were unraveling. Seven months of work about to spill down the drain. Another of his attorneys would have to replace her, then more months wasted while the new guy came up to speed. And frankly, Kim Parrish was the best he had. He produced a warm smile. "Kim, Kim, don't be hasty. You're a great lawyer. You have a fine record. A whole promising career ahead of you. Please, finish this case and put it behind you."

"I also have the prerogative to refuse participation in a case I believe to be fraudulent and shameful. Reassign me to another case."

Tromble was tired of this pussyfooting. He was unaccustomed to having his orders questioned, and he had an invitation to a big White House reception that evening his wife was dying to attend. He detested the president, a feeling that was deeply reciprocated, so this was the first invitation, and very likely the last. His wife had already spent two grand on a gown, dropped a cool five hundred on a faggy hairdresser, and threatened two years without sex if he was a minute late. It was long past time to put his big foot down. "Take this case, or you're fired."

"Then I quit."

"No you don't, you're fired."

"You can't fire me. I don't work for you."

The director of the INS had this one last chance to preserve the independence of his service, not to mention his own prerogative and prestige. Tromble had just violated the most sacrosanct Washington law — keep your fingers out of somebody's else's bureaucratic turf.

The director summoned forth every bit of his courage, looked Kim dead in the eye, and muttered, "Oh, you definitely are fired."

29

At 10:00 a.m., Elena arrived promptly for her monthly visit. She came in a rental car picked up at the local airport, a cramped bright purple economy model with a zippy little engine. She and Alex had done this routine fourteen times now. Different prisons, different states, different guards. But it was old hat. The routine rarely varied. Later, she would dump the car, hop a fast flight for Atlanta, wander through the huge terminal for a few hours trying to shake any followers, then at the very last minute hop another flight and bounce around the Midwest awhile. Everything paid for in cash. It would take her two days to return home but Alex emphasized that the time and money were worth it. This was not a game. People were out there, trying to kill her. No precaution was too great.

Her ID had been checked, she'd been patted down and searched, had her hand stamped, and was waiting quietly in a stiff plastic chair when Alex entered. The glass partition was perforated with dozens of small holes. An improvement, they thought, over the last prison, where they had been forced to whisper awkwardly over intercom phones. They were paranoid about bugs. It hampered their conversations terribly.

"You look beautiful," Alex told her. He did not mention the dark circles under her eyes. She looked exhausted and worn down by fourteen months of endless work, of living in the shadows, of leaping out of bed at the slightest creak of a floorboard. He was trying to hide how guilty it made him feel.

"I love you," she replied, her usual opening.

No need to ask how he was doing; how the new prison was working out; how he was being treated. Alex called almost every night from one of his three cell phones, and they chatted back and forth late into the night. She knew about Benny Beatty, and all about the "mutual fund" Alex was running for an ever-swelling pool of prisoners and guards. No different from the two previous prisons. Elena kept the records and managed the investments through a local Virginia broker she had picked for his efficiency and reliability. Checks arrived in the mail with great frequency from Alex's new clients in each prison, a trickle in the first month, before word spread and the floodgates opened. Elena promptly deposited the checks with the broker, and they were instantly invested. Every night Alex called with fresh instructions to be relayed to the broker the next morning. Execute this sell; buy five thousand shares of this; short this, long that. The stock market was roaring. The fund was beating it handsomely, and Alex's "clients" were elated. He couldn't walk ten steps in the yard without people pleading to join up.

The *Wall Street Journal* and *Investor's Business Daily* were delivered to his cell every morning by a guard who had emptied his entire 401(k) nest egg and handed it over to Alex's care.

Even Elena's broker was shadowing Alex's moves with his own money.

"How's Bitchy?" Elena asked.

"Fine. His appeal comes up next month."

"Does he have a chance?"

"I helped draft a letter for him to the court. It might help."

Over the past year, Alex had kept her well-informed about the characters he had met in prison. His ability to fit in with these rogues and villains and gangsters amazed her. The Choir Boys of Mariel with their relentless scheming to find a lawyer who could buy their way out. Mustafa, the glowering head of the Black Power brotherhood in Chicago, who kept ominously reminding "Brother Konebitchie" what would happen should the investments go south.

Bitchy Beatty was the most baffling one yet. Inexplicably, he and her husband had grown quite close. Odd bedfellows, though perhaps that was a phrase best avoided.

"What does the letter say?"

"He deeply regrets the pain and suffering he caused. He found God, God found him. When he gets out he intends to send hundred-thousand-dollar checks to each man he injured."

"That sounds nice. They should be impressed."

"I wrote the letter and forged his signature. Benny loathes the Jets for stealing his championship ring. He doesn't regret a thing."

Alex smiled and she laughed.

Alex leaned a little closer and lowered his voice. "The guard in the back. The tall one with blond hair. Name's George. He's your man."

Elena fell back into her chair, waited a moment, then glanced quickly over her shoulder. Three guards were back there but George was ridiculously easy to spot. Tall guy with white-blond hair leaning against the wall, pretending to be bored. He caught Elena's eye and winked effusively.

When they were finished, George would escort her out to the large anteroom to collect her coat and purse. They would brush against each other, a light bump that lasted seconds. Elena would hand George a bundle of computer disks. George would hand back a bundle of disks from Alex. George was the one with his whole 401(k) in the fund; in two short months, it had already doubled. Whatever Alex wanted, George would bend over backward to provide.

"Any new clients?" Alex asked, referring to their other new business venture.

"A few. General Motors signed up yesterday. I left right after they called. There wasn't time to update you."

"You do good work, Mrs. Konevitch."

"If she could write code half as fast as Mr. Konevitch, Mrs. Konevitch would have a thousand new clients."

For the time being, such talk was as romantic as they got. Their new business was roaring out the gate. The entire Internet world was going crazy with start-ups sprouting like poppies in a compliant Afghan field. None, though, had developed multimedia advertising technology as brilliant as Alex. The beauty of it was, Elena hit up pretty much the same clients they had enlisted for Orangutan Media. Same Rolodex. Same marketing contacts. Only the pitch differed. Alex leaned closer, until his lips were nearly pressed up against the glass. "What does MP say? Any updates?"

"No, the situation hasn't changed. He's furious. Says he's never seen anything like this. Keeps calling it a disgrace."

Alex appeared disappointed, though he tried his best to stifle it with a forced smile. "Tell him to relax, it's not his fault. We're up against the American and Russian governments, and I don't think any lawyer could prevail. I couldn't be happier with him."

"He's demoralized, Alex. He feels responsible. He wrote another long, bitter letter to the judge. Same theme as the last six. What happened to those high-sounding instructions to the prosecutor about putting you in a nicer place than this?"

"I'm fine, Elena."

"No, you're —"

"Relax, I'm fine. I actually had wine with a late dinner last night. Pot roast, fresh corn and potatoes, cooked by a guard's wife, served in the cell. Me and Benny over candlelight. He still thinks I'm cute, incidentally."

"You are cute. But you're not fine, Alex Konevitch. And don't tell me differently. You're surrounded by murderers and rapists and nasty gangs. You could get shooked in the showers by some crazy killer just because you stepped on his toe."

"Shanked," Alex corrected her.

"Oh, shut up." A few months before Elena had done something deeply regrettable; once done, though, it was impossible to erase. She had gone on an all-out binge of prison flicks, a response to her curiosity about what her husband was going through. She watched

576

them all, one after another, late into the night, night after night. For months afterward she was tormented by nightmares, waking up sweating and shivering. The images of brutal killings and chaotic beatings and jailhouse rapes came back to her constantly. Her precious husband was trapped inside a vicious building filled with barbaric monsters who snuffed lives for a pack of cigarettes.

Alex tried to shrug it off. Hollywood hooey, he called it. A bunch of cinematic nonsense, hyped-up tripe to shock and appall the ignorant public, he insisted.

He was lying. She knew better.

Thankfully, he had acquired no tattoos; none she could observe, anyway. But who knew what was lurking beneath that shirt, or under those baggy pants? And there was no doubt that Alex *looked* different. Harder, long greasy hair pulled back in a tight ponytail now, less expressive, a little slower to laugh, and his eyes darted around constantly, alert in a way that tore at her heart. Even his walk was different. No longer the old determined, upright clip straining to shave off a few extra seconds; it now resembled a slide more than a walk, slow, slumped, and slothful, with hands perpetually sunk to the bottom of his pockets. A survivor's walk. A way of saying he cared about nothing.

She understood but did not like it. Adapt, blend in with the natives, or you became bait to the strongest animals in the cage.

There was only one good thing about prison: sleep and exercise were plentiful. What else was there to do? Until this visit, anyway, Alex always looked remarkably refreshed and fit. He must've had a bad few nights, though, because this time he looked painfully exhausted. His eyes were bloodshot, with large bags underneath them. He hadn't slept well in days, possibly weeks.

"This is crazy, Alex," she uttered softly.

"It is what it is, Elena. Be patient."

"I've been patient for a year. I want you in my bed, where you belong. I'm tired of sleeping alone."

"I'm not all that crazy about sleeping with Benny, either. Have you ever heard an All-Pro lineman snore?"

"Stop it."

"And the smell. All that bulk. He comes back from his workouts in the yard, the paint falls off the walls."

Like Alex was an Irish rose himself. All the prisoners stank. They were oblivious to their own odors, but Elena was nearly flattened by the stench in the prison visitors' room. She wanted to bring Alex home and scrub a year of prison stink out of his skin. Then take him to bed and heal a year's worth of fear and misery and frustration and loneliness.

"Alex, are you sure you're okay?" she pressed, more emphatically this time. She was his wife. All this jokiness was an attempt to conceal something. He was far from okay.

Alex looked down and played with his fingers a moment — a slight twitch around his left eye, an almost imperceptible shift of tiny muscles, and she knew.

She bent forward until her face was pressed against the glass. "Stop lying. What's happening?"

"All right. Somebody tried to kill me yesterday."

"Yesterday . . . what happened?"

"In the yard, I was playing basketball when a man made a run at me. He was carrying a crude hatchet constructed in the prison shop. As attempts go it was stupid and clumsy. It had no chance."

Elena was perfectly motionless. This was the nightmare she had long dreaded. She watched him and waited.

"I was lucky," Alex informed her, trying to make it sound trifling, little more than a bad hand of cards. "Two of the cons on my team are investors in the fund. I threw the ball in his face, his nose shattered, he slowed down, they disarmed him. It wasn't all that dramatic." He left off the part about how his friends mauled the killer, stomping his hands and breaking both arms to be sure he wouldn't try again.

"Who was he? Why did he want to kill you?"

"A Russian. A former Mafiya gunman who

obviously wasn't as handy with an axe."

"I asked *why* he wanted to kill you."

A momentary pause. "Apparently, the people in Moscow are offering big money to whoever gets me." Then a more prolonged pause before he made the painful decision to tell Elena everything. "It was the second attempt."

"I see. And when was the first?"

"Two months ago."

"Two months? Why didn't you tell me before?"

"I've been quite careful since then. Benny follows me everywhere he can. I'm surrounded at every meal by a squad of our investors. A few of the guys watch over me when I shower, use the bathroom, use the library. They don't want their golden goose hauled out in a coffin. I'm only in danger when I leave my cell."

Elena reeled backward into her seat and struggled to fight her horror — she couldn't. "I'll call MP and have him insist on moving you to another prison. We'll raise hell. Hold a big obnoxious press conference. We'll —"

Before she could finish, Alex was already shaking his head. "I've already considered that. Don't. Don't even try."

"Why not?"

"I'm alive only because I've established a network here. At each new place, it takes three weeks to a month, at a minimum. I'd be completely naked."

"And if the investment fund for some reason has a bad month? A sudden market correction, for instance. That happens, Alex. How good will your protection be then?"

He forced a smile. "Believe me, I think about that every day. It certainly helps focus the mind."

She crossed her arms and did not acknowledge the smile. "And if you stay here, it's just a matter of time, isn't it? Say one of your new friends becomes distracted, or at the wrong moment bends over to tie a shoe. Maybe somebody slips a little poison in your food, or a little knife in your back."

"A lot could happen," Alex admitted, rubbing his temples. "They've been scared off a few times. A week ago, in the library, before some of my friends made a threatening move. Five days ago, in the shower, three men were approaching me when a guard showed up."

"I see."

"Look, I won't pretend I'm not worried. These are rough people, killers. They're watching me every day, looking for an opening. I know the odds."

"You have to get out of here, Alex."

"Believe me, that thought has crossed my mind. The past few weeks, I've lived in the law section of the library."

"There has to be something. You can't just let these people kill you."

581

About two cubicles down, a loud argument suddenly exploded between a prisoner and his wife. The woman was barely more than a child, maybe nineteen, dressed in a scant black leather skirt, black net stockings, a halter top that did more to reveal than conceal, false eyelashes that flopped like gigantic butterflies, and enough cosmetics to camouflage a battleship or capsize it. Only a moment before, she and the hubby had their faces pressed tightly against the glass panel, whispering sweet nothings back and forth, like they were ready to disrobe and grope each other through the divider. The husband suddenly recoiled backward, nearly tipping his chair to the floor.

"Oh yeah, you heard right. Your twin brother," the woman roared.

"My own brother. You're sleeping with my own brother," the husband wailed, slamming both fists like noisy gavels against the glass panel.

"Yeah, well . . . least I kept it in the family, since I know how much that word means to you. This time, anyways."

"You're a bitch. A whore. A backstabbin' whore."

She stood up and jammed her face up against the divider. "Hey, you noticed, finally. Guess what, idiot? I'm givin' it away to any fool who looks twice. They're thinkin' of naming a mattress after me. So what are you gonna do about it, huh?" she taunted.

Until this moment, the three guards in the room had looked on with an air of bemused boredom. Old hat, old story, happy days again in the visitors' room. A wife cheating on a locked-up hubby: what's new? A tired old scene the guards had observed a thousand times with few variations. Many marriages lasted a year, some more than two, very, very few beyond the third year of separation.

There was one inviolate rule, though, and this prisoner bashed it to pieces. He snapped, leaped to his feet, and, howling at the top of his voice, began trying to crawl and claw his way over the divider. Two guards lost their look of boredom and sprang into action. They yanked him off the glass, jerked his arms behind his back, and slapped cuffs on him. They began dragging him out as he hollered a bewildering array of curses at his wife.

His wife stood and loitered, arms crossed, watching it all with a smile that smacked of huge contentment.

Then, at the final moment before they yanked her husband through the door, she whipped down her halter, exposing two rather impressive breasts. With two hands, she cupped and then began juggling them. "Hey," she yelled at her husband, "remember these? Tonight your brother's gonna have a field day with 'em. And once I get bored with him, you know what? I'll bet I can get your father in the sack."

She tugged the halter back up, spun on her heels, and with a loud triumphant clack of high heels departed the room.

"Poor man," Elena remarked with a sympathetic frown after the tumult died down.

Alex bent forward and shook his head. "That's Eddie Carminza. He's up for bigamy. Five years in the joint, the max. She's one of four wives."

"My God, this place is crazy, Alex. You have to get out."

"Well, there is one thing we can try. Move the case out of immigration channels into a federal court. It's premature, though, and incredibly risky."

"You might prematurely die in here if we don't try something."

"I know. But there are two problems. Serious problems. One, federal court means different rules and procedures. MP isn't a criminal lawyer. Also he has no experience in the federal system. The rules of evidence and admissibility are stricter. It's too late to replace him, though."

"Can he handle it?"

"I'm not sure any lawyer can and MP is already holding a bad hand. And who knows how much ammunition our friends in Russia have provided the prosecutor over the past year."

"But Mikhail —"

"Mikhail hasn't found us the silver bullet. There's no legally acceptable proof that my money was stolen. No proof I'm being framed. Nothing to keep me from being shipped back to Russia."

"All right, what's two?"

"If we rush into federal court, and I lose, I'll be shipped right back here. We can try an appeal, and we will. But that takes time. I'll probably be dead long before."

"So it's a choice between very bad and awful?"

"More like between certain death and probable death."

"So what's this idea?"

"It's called a motion for habeas corpus. Technically, by shoving me into the federal prison system, they've created a loophole we should be able to exploit. It forces the government to show cause for my imprisonment. If a judge accepts it, the process happens very fast."

"How fast?"

"Three days after we launch it, we'll be in court."

"Oh . . . that fast." Elena stared at her shoes a moment. She began fidgeting with her hands. "Is it too fast?"

"Possibly," Alex told her. "We have a lot of enemies, here and in Russia. Everything has to happen at once. And everything has to succeed, or as my friend Benny puts it, it's game over. Also Mikhail will have to move up his time schedule. And we'll have to pray for a legal miracle."

"We're overdue for a miracle."

"I don't think it works that way. We'll have to produce our own."

"I'll call Mikhail the second I'm out of here."

"You have a busy weekend ahead of you. It's time to share everything with MP, then pray it's enough."

30

On September 18, 1996, one year and two months to the day since Alex's incarceration in federal prison, MP Jones bounced up the steps of the D.C. Federal Courthouse, one of the loveliest, most impressive buildings in a city littered to the gills with marble monuments. The day alternated between warmth and chill, the first hint that another long, humid summer in a city built in a swamp was coming to a close. Elena, along with a stout paralegal hauling a box of documents, accompanied him.

Two days before, Elena had called and frantically insisted on an emergency meeting. MP dropped everything and Elena arrived, pale, tired, angry, upset, and wildly determined. She told him Alex's idea and MP instantly launched a hundred objections.

It was too fast. Too risky. Federal court wasn't his thing. Besides, who knew what the Russian prosecutors and INS had cooked up, how much damning material they could throw at Alex? Elena insisted that she and Alex had entertained all the same reservations, told him about the four attempts on Alex's life, and that ended the discussion. MP called his clients with pressing cases over the next week and foisted their files off on other immigration specialists around town.

So they moved with deep nervousness through the wide, well-lit corridors, straight to the office of the federal clerk. MP signed in at the front desk, moved to the rear of the room, and waited patiently with Elena and his paralegal amid a clutter of other nervous lawyers until the clerk called his name.

He nearly sprinted to her desk. He proudly threw down a document and with a show of intense formality informed her, "I am introducing a motion for habeas corpus on behalf of my client Alex Konevitch. I ask the court for expeditious handling on behalf of said client, who has been incarcerated beyond any reasonable length and forced to endure immeasurable suffering."

The clerk, a large, feisty black woman, lifted up MP's motion and automatically plunked it into a deep wooden in-box, a vast reservoir filled to capacity with other such requests, motions, and lawyerly stuff. "First time here?" she asked without looking up.

"Uh . . . yes."

"This ain't no courtroom. Plain English works fine in here."

MP looked slightly deflated. "It's a habeas corpus motion." She chewed a stick of gum with great energy and stared intently into a computer screen. The sign on her desk suggested she was named Thelma Parker.

"I heard what you said," Thelma noted. "How long's your guy been in?"

"A year and two months."

"Uh-huh." Thelma did not appear overly impressed. "What facility he at?"

"At the moment, based on a federal contract, the state prison in Yuma. It's his third prison."

The reaction was delayed, but she slowly shifted her gaze from the screen and directed it at MP. "His third? Inside a year? That what you sayin'?"

"To be precise, inside fourteen months."

"What'd he do? Kill a warden?"

"An alleged visa violation."

"Come on, you bullshittin' me."

"On my momma's grave."

"That's an immigration matter. What's your guy doin' in a federal joint?"

"That's what we'd like the government to explain."

"He a U.S. resident?"

"That's one point of contention. The government said yes. Now it's saying no."

She poised her chin on a pencil. "That prison in Yuma, it's a badass place."

"So Alex tells me. He's locked up in D

589

Wing, mixed in with the most rotten apples."

She leaned forward, almost across the desk. In a low, conspiring, all-knowing whisper, she said, "Truth now. Who'd your boy piss off?"

MP played along. He bent over and whispered back, "John Tromble."

"Figures." She picked MP's motion out of the pile and smacked it down on her blotter. She paged through it, frowning and considering the request with some care for a moment. "Gotta cousin works over at the Bureau," she eventually remarked.

A sharp pain suddenly erupted in MP's chest. Idiot. Why hadn't he just kept his big mouth shut?

After a moment Thelma Parker added, "He hates that Tromble. Says he's the worst thing happened since J. Edgar pranced around in a skirt. Tell you what, you done this before?"

After manning this desk for fifteen years, she had seen thousands of lawyers pass in and out of her office. One sniff and she could smell a cherry a mile away.

MP allowed as, "My usual cases are in immigration court."

"Thought so. You never done this before?"

"Pretty much."

A large, plump elbow landed on her desk and her large chin ended up poised on a curled fist. "Now, don't you worry. Way this works is, your motion goes to a judge. Now, you could maybe get lucky and it might end

590

up in the box of, say, oh, Judge Elton Willis. He's a fair and judicious man. Then, assuming this thing gets stamped expeditious" — she winked at MP — "which might maybe happen about three seconds after you walk outta here . . . well, then the government gets three days to respond. Got all that?"

"Three days," MP said, winking back.

"Then it's show-and-tell time. This kinda motion moves fast. You got your stuff together?"

With all the humility he could muster, MP replied, "It's going to be an ass-kicking of historical proportions. They'll carry Tromble out on a stretcher."

"Uh-huh." A slow nod. "You got help? Sure hope you do."

"Pacevitch, Knowlton and Rivers. A classmate from law school's a partner over there. They're lending a hand, pro bono."

"Well, that's nice." Her eyes hung for a moment on the JCPenney polyester threads that hung loosely on MP's narrow frame. She smacked her lips and said, "No offense, but you gonna need a few thousand-dollar suits at your table."

In a career that alternated between roaring barn burners and droning recitations of intolerable boredom, Boris Yeltsin was producing the biggest thud yet. At least he was sober this time — what a rare and welcome change, his chief of staff was thinking, as he rocked back on his heels and briefly scanned the crowd. Nearly all of them were staring edgily at their watches. A few seemed to be asleep on their feet. He looked longer and harder, and for the life of him could not find one person who seemed to be listening to Yeltsin.

His boss liked him along for these things. Principally it gave him a reliable drinking partner for the long ride back to the Kremlin. Plus he could always rely on his trusted chief of staff to lie and say the speech was stirring and deeply inspiring. They were a pair of wicked old politicians. The lies flowed easily and landed comfortably.

A man in a black leather jacket bumped up against him. He took a quick step sideways, to get some room. The man edged closer.

The man suddenly turned and looked at him with a spark of vague recognition. "Hey, didn't I see you with Tatyana Lukin the other night?"

"Who?"

"Tatyana Lukin. You know, she works for you." The man studied his face more intently and continued, "I'm sure it was you. Walking into a hotel together on Tverskoy Boulevard. Same place you and she spend every Tuesday and Thursday together."

"You're mistaken," he replied in as much a hiss as a whisper. He tried unsuccessfully once more to edge away.

"No, there's no mistake. Here." The mysterious man pushed a plastic case into the hands of the chief of staff. All trace of phony uncertainty was gone. With a mocking smile, the mystery man whispered, "You'll want to listen to these alone. Believe me, you won't want company. You're mentioned a lot on these tapes."

Before he could reply, Mikhail jogged away in the direction of the road, where he jumped into an automobile with the engine running and sped off.

The chief thought about just tossing the case away. Fling it as far and as hard as he could; forget about it and walk away. Instead he opened the lid and peeked inside — just two unmarked cassette tapes and a few photographs. He tucked it into his inside coat pocket and decided he'd get rid of it after he got home. Who knew what was on those tapes? Why risk having some stranger find them? Who knows how bad it might be?

He arrived home at nine that night, fixed a tall glass of vodka, and removed his jacket. He felt the weight of the plastic packet; he had nearly forgotten it. He withdrew it from the inside pocket and walked directly to the trash can. He promptly dropped it inside, then stared down at the case for a moment. He should listen to it, he decided: maybe the man that afternoon was a blackmailer. Who knew?

The photos fell on the floor when he pulled the tapes out, and he let them lie there until he knew what this was about. He selected the first tape and inserted it into the cassette player on his desk, sat back into his desk chair, and sipped quickly from his vodka.

It whirred quietly for a moment before a petulant male voice he didn't recognize said, "Who was it?"

"Just some idiot law enforcement administrator from America." This would be Tatyana: no doubt about it. He reached over and turned up the volume.

"Oh, you're screwing him, too?"

"You're cute when you're mad. Come on and screw me now." A loud laugh. Definitely Tatyana's throaty laugh.

"Don't joke. I'm tired of sharing you."

"You're a fool. You've seen my boss. He's bald and fat and not the least bit interesting. He's so terrible in bed I have to pinch myself just to stay awake. He's so disgusting, I become nauseated afterward. I'm only doing this for us, Sasha."

"You've been saying that for years."

"And it's true. Listen, we're moving in on a huge fortune right now. Billions, Sasha, billions. My cut will be hundreds of millions, and as soon as I have it, I'll dump that old moron and quit my job. You and I will buy a big yacht and sail around the world. We'll never be able to spend it all. We'll die rich and happy."

By then the chief of staff was choking and coughing violently. The vodka popped out his nostrils, dribbled out his mouth, and spilled down his double chin. He clutched his chest and thought he was having a heart attack.

He lurched from his chair and rushed to the cassette player. He punched stop, rewind, then listened again, and then repeated the sequence three more times.

He put the machine on pause and sat back and rubbed his temples. He felt the onset of a crushing brain-splitter. "Nauseated." "Terrible in bed." "Bald and fat, and not the least bit interesting." The torrent of nasty words kept tumbling in his mind. The headache quickly progressed from a five to a ten on the Richter scale.

That bitch. That lying, deceitful, two-timing, impertinent bitch.

Settle down, he told himself. He actually voiced it, out loud in the big, empty room — relax, take a few deep breaths. Get a grip, for God's sake. He walked over and refilled his glass with vodka, then sloppily filled a second and third glass; it never hurt to be on the safe side. He carried them back to his desk, positioned them carefully and in order, freshest to least freshest, pushed start on the cassette player, then settled back to hear everything. It was going to be horrible, he knew. And he swore he would endure every last word.

Halfway through, he rushed to the trash can and picked up the photos from the floor. The first showed a smiling, handsome young man dressed in the uniform of the national soccer team. He had no idea who he was, just a strong suspicion that it was his whiny voice on the first tape. The second showed the justice minister accepting a fistful of dollars from a man whose face he thought he recognized.

An hour later, after listening to the second tape, after repeating it once, as he had with the first tape, he knew more than he had ever cared to about Tatyana Lukin. The sheer stereotypicality of it was hard enough to swallow; he was just one more old, middle-aged, cuckolded fool, stewing with anger, self-pity, and regret. Worse, she had used him from the very start. There she was bragging to her boyfriend, Sasha, about how she was running the entire machinery of the Kremlin while her fat, drunken bore buddied up to his big pal Boris. There simply were too many barbs to remember; but also too many to forget.

"Well, guess what, bitch," he grumbled, lumbering drunkenly up the stairs for bed. "Tomorrow, the fun will begin."

The girl was tall and blonde with skinny legs

that stretched from the ground to the sky, pretty blue eyes, and she was at least forty years younger than him. She was even younger than his two granddaughters. If it didn't matter to her, sure as hell it made no difference to him. She gripped his arm and squished her ample breasts against its soft plumpness.

"You are so funny, General, I just can't get enough of you."

"I'll bet," Golitsin slurred as they staggered and swayed, holding each other up, in the direction of his shiny little Beemer in the rear parking lot. The Lido was behind them, the newest city hot spot where the big-deal millionaires gathered in their relentless quest for the best orgy in town. Somewhere between his fifth and eighth scotch — such a blur that he lost count — the girl had become attached to his arm. Between his tenth or twelfth scotch, at some now indeterminate point, he decided they were deeply in love.

"What did you say your name was again?" he asked her.

"Nadya. Please remember it, General. I've told you ten times already. I really don't want you to ever forget me."

Golitsin was again admiring the streamlined legs that seemed to stretch up to her armpits, when three men stepped out of a dark alley. Two lunged straight for him. One banged his arms behind his back, the other shoved a filthy rag in his mouth and then, very quickly, a coarse dark hood over his head. The girl started to step back and scream before the third man clamped a hand over her mouth. "Shut your trap, tramp," he growled, and flashed a knife to show her the request was serious.

A black sedan pulled up, seemingly from nowhere, and squealed to a jarring stop three feet away. Golitsin was bundled roughly into the rear seat before two of the men spilled in beside him. The other man released Nadya. She stepped back and winked at him. He winked back, before she disappeared into the night. He climbed into the front passenger seat and they sped away.

Twenty minutes and ten miles later, Golitsin was shoved through a large doorway, dragged about forty steps, then shoved down hard onto a stiff wooden chair. His hands were tied, quickly and roughly, behind his back, and his chubby legs were roped to the legs of the chair.

The hood was removed and tossed onto the floor. With a loud spit, the filthy gag flew out of his lips, though it took a moment for his eyes to adjust. Another moment before he realized there were five of them in all. They were gathered in the middle of a large, empty warehouse with a high, corrugated ceiling and an oil-stained concrete floor. They wore dark jeans and black leather jackets. Rough faces all around. There were more tattoos and earrings and facial scars than he cared to count. A few misshapen noses.

Syndicate thugs, that's all, nothing to be overly alarmed about, Golitsin told himself.

And they had made a mistake, a big one. They were nothing more than common, everyday kidnappers who threw out a random net and stupidly dragged in the meanest shark in town. Oh yes, this was a real boner, one they would deeply regret, and he decided to inform them of this right away. He worked up his most scary sneer. "Do you punks know who you're messing with?"

"Punks," one of them answered. Whack! — Golitsin's head bounced to the side. A spray of blood shot out his nose.

"Don't you dare strike me again. You —"

Whack, whack, whack.

"All right, all right. Enough," Golitsin insisted.

Whack, whack.

"Please . . . I . . . I said that's enough."

One of them pulled over another wooden chair, reversed it, then eased into it. Their faces were three feet apart. He looked about fifty, older than the others, and carried himself like he was in charge. A hard, weathered face. Dark, piercing eyes. "Listen up, Sergei. This can be hard or it can be easy. Understand?"

The punk had called him Sergei. He knew

his name! It wasn't a random kidnapping after all. Golitsin even, very briefly, entertained the notion of reminding this scum of his proper title: General. But maybe flexing his muscles at this instant wasn't such a good idea. Maybe it was a terrible idea, in fact. That last whack had left him with a splitting headache.

"Can we talk?" Golitsin asked, trying his best to sound reasonable and unctuous.

"Sure, Sergei." He leaned closer. "But it works like this. I'll talk and you'll listen."

The other four men slapped their thighs and roared with laughter. This was funny? This wasn't the least bit humorous. These punks were just begging for it. "Can I at least have your name?"

The man in the chair, said, "For tonight, Vladimir. Let's not worry about what to call me tomorrow. First, you have to give us a reason to let you live that long, Sergei."

"There's no need for these threats. What do you want?"

"Let's start with the easy one. Where's the money?"

"What money?"

A long sigh. "Do we really have to go through this, Sergei?"

"I'm a simple retired officer with a family. I am struggling to survive off my pension. It's not much. Perhaps we can work something out."

From somewhere behind his head, whack, whack, whack.

"Enough! That's enough!" he wailed.

"The money, Sergei. Where's the money?"

"What money?"

"Two hundred and fifty million. The money you stole, where is it?"

How did he know the exact amount? Golitsin briefly wondered. Only a handful knew: Tatyana, Nicky, and of course, the victim knew, not that it mattered. He was rotting in prison, after all, counting the days until his return to Russia.

"Maybe," Golitsin suggested — he squeezed his neck down, hunching his shoulders, trying to avoid another whack — "maybe if you told me who you're working for we can work something out."

Whack — the ducked head and bunched shoulders were a wasted defense. It felt like six hands were slapping the back of his head. He heard his own voice whining and pleading for them to stop.

And eventually the slaps did subside. But Vladimir allowed him no time to recover his wits. "Pay attention, Sergei. This is invaluable advice. You've never been on this side of the torture rack, always the other side, watching and enjoying the show. Fifty years of screaming victims begging for quick deaths. Are you listening, Sergei? Do you understand?"

The voice was so very cold, so flat, so casually captivating; amazing how mesmerizing a voice becomes when it controls the pain.

How many times had Sergei heard that same droll pattern over the years as he watched one victim after another suffer and scream their guts out, until they eventually snapped, until they signed whatever was put before them, signed anything to make the pain stop — accusing their own mothers, sentencing their own children, confessing sins they never came within ten miles of committing. Oh yes, he definitely understood.

He slowly nodded.

"You know how bad this can get, don't you?"

Another nod — yes, yes, of course he remembered. Tears were now rolling down his fat cheeks.

"The pain is going to become intense, Sergei. I don't want you surprised by it. You're going to wish you were dead. You'll beg us to end it. We won't kill you, though. You can't feel the pain unless you're alive. Sorry, but we need you to feel everything."

"Wait!" Something was bothering him. All this talk about torture, and the name of this cruel man. There was a connection there, he was sure of it.

"Why wait? Do you want to tell me where the money is?"

"Vladimir? Yes, Vladimir. Like the Vladimir who worked for me, right?"

A quick shift of the eyes to the floor. "I have no idea who or what you're talking about."

Golitsin stretched as far forward as he could. "He a friend of yours? Is that what this is about? I am so sorry for what happened to poor Vladimir. He killed himself, you know. Suicide. How tragic."

The interrogator jumped out of his chair. Turning to the other four men, he directed a finger at one and said, "Get the BP cuff and monitor his blood pressure. He's old and fat. We don't want him slipping away on us."

The man dashed off.

"Get the tools," he barked at another, who also disappeared into the darkness. To the other two, he said, "You look bored. Work on him while we wait."

They moved up and the slapping began again. No punches, everything open-handed, a relentless fusillade of girly slaps obviously meant to add shame to his pain. Golitsin wailed and screamed, all to no avail.

Vladimir walked to a corner of the large warehouse, yanked a cell phone out of a pocket, punched a number, then cradled it to his ear.

Golitsin was being slapped silly. His cheeks, the back of his head, occasionally his ears, which really stung. He howled and moaned, begging them to stop. Eventually, his chin sank to his chest. His head began lolling wildly with each smack.

He bit down hard on his tongue, choked back his screams, and played opossum for all he was worth. Just stop those infernal slaps, he prayed with all his might. And after a moment, the prayers were answered. They did stop. One yelled out, "Vladimir, he's out cold."

"Don't worry about it," Vladimir replied, sounding distracted, then returned to his phone conversation.

Golitsin fought to control his breathing and prayed they didn't catch on. He could overhear Vladimir speaking louder now, unconcerned about his ability to eavesdrop.

"No, don't worry. We've only gotten started." A long pause. "Look, I've done this before. I —" Another pause. "Nicky, you have my guarantee, he'll tell us everything. Everybody does. We start ripping off the body parts, and they all —" Pause, then a nasty laugh. "I know, I know, Nicky. Look, by the time he's got no fingers or toes, his kneecaps are pulp, he'll spill . . . Yeah, okay, you, too."

Vladimir flipped the phone shut and returned to the scene of torture. A scream was going off inside Golitsin's head. Nicky! That rotten son of a bitch. That lying, thieving, betraying bastard. These were his people, he realized, and he fought the urge not to scream and threaten these people, to unleash all the rage he could muster.

One of the boys returned a moment later

with the BP monitor. He quickly slapped it around Golitsin's right arm and tightened it up. Then the other fellow reappeared lugging a large dark suitcase, which he set down on the floor.

"Open it. Get the tools ready," Vladimir told him.

Golitsin heard the locks snap open and the noise of the lid hitting the cement. He didn't want to look — he had no desire at all to see what terrible ghoulish instruments were inside that damned case — he tried to fight it, just squeeze his eyes shut, he told himself; ignore them and ignore it. But it couldn't be helped. The curiosity was just too irresistible; he had to know, had to see what they had in store for him. Slowly, ever so slowly, he cracked open his right eyelid, just a hair. A tiny, tiny sliver, and he peeked.

Vladimir and two of his boys were bent over the now open case, rummaging through the contents, apparently deciding which tool should lead off.

Oh, Christ. Oh, no. The bastards had bought out the entire torture store. Three or four razor-sharp saws of various sizes and types, wicked things, so sharp and shiny. A small blowtorch. An iron, just like the one Vladimir used to scorch the hammer and sickle on Konevitch. A slew of gleaming surgical instruments employable for everything from eyeball gouging to nut-crunching.

Golitsin could put a name and use to every instrument: a vivid picture of their exact use.

How many nights had he spent watching with sick fascination as the boys in the basement at Dzerzhinsky Square found all sorts of inspired uses for these things? Every instrument in that case, he knew them all like a mechanic knows his shop tools.

He squeezed his eyes shut and bit his lip, but it just slipped out. A moan of fear just clawed its way up his throat, into his mouth, and it popped right through his lips.

Five sets of eyes instantly snapped in his direction.

Vladimir smiled. "Ah, Sergei, you're back." With a befuddled expression, he asked, sounding mildly frustrated, "Listen, I can't seem to make up my mind. How would you like us to start?"

"You keep those damned things away from me."

"Well, you see, we're a little past that point. Come on, Sergei, I'm trying to be generous here." He laughed and the others joined him. "So, what will it be?"

"I swear I don't have any more of the money."

"None?"

"It's gone."

"All of it? Two hundred and fifty million?" Vladimir asked, dripping skepticism.

"Yes, it's spent, every penny. I swear it."

Golitsin wasn't about to hand over his fortune to Nicky, no matter what. They could cut and slice and dice him however they wanted — not a red cent.

Vladimir bent over, studied the contents inside the case for a moment, then made up his mind and picked up a saw. "Well, that's too bad," he muttered, shaking his head.

"Please, you have to believe me. I was stupid and greedy. I wasted it all on idiotic things. It's all gone."

Vladimir was now ten feet away. With a finger, he was testing the sharpness of the blade as he moved closer. Two of the boys were now hovering directly behind Golitsin. They pinned his arms and squeezed his neck. He squealed but their grips only tightened.

"Where to start, where to start, that's the big issue now," Vladimir said. The piercing, hard, dark eyes began searching Golitsin's body. "Why not toes?" he asked very reasonably. "Start at the bottom, start with the little things, and slowly work our way up."

He bent down and pulled off Golitsin's shoes, then yanked off his socks. The plump white toes were wiggling, trying to curl under his feet. Vladimir carefully selected the big toe on the right foot. Using two strong fingers, he clamped the toe, poised the saw, then looked up. "I should warn you that I get a little carried away. Once I take one, I generally get all ten. You can answer everything, and I just can't stop," he warned, looking slightly remorseful. "It's, oh, I don't know, something wrong inside my head."

"Okay, okay, I have the money. Don't . . . oh, please, don't touch that toe."

Vladimir gave the toe a little pinch. Golitsin nearly bucked out of the chair. "Switzerland. A Swiss bank," he muttered in a fast rush.

"You wouldn't be lying, would you? I hate liars."

"No, no, I swear. Switzerland."

"What bank?"

A momentary hesitation and Vladimir suddenly had the saw pressed firmly on the flesh, right at the base of the big toe. "Lucerne National. All of it. Every penny."

"How much?"

"Two hundred."

The saw bit ever so lightly into his flesh.

"All right, all right . . . 220."

"You blew thirty million already?" Vladimir looked like he was ready to just whack the toe off. Nothing to do with disbelief, just anger.

"I'm . . . I'm sorry."

"I'm sure you are, Sergei. Now the hard questions."

Golitsin couldn't take his eyes off the saw.

"Are you ready, or should I just cut now?"

"No, please no. Ask anything."

"The account and security code numbers. Concentrate. What are they?"

"I . . . I don't have them in my head. My office. We have to go to my office."

Whack, whack, whack.

"Oh, God, all right." And like that, a fast rush of numbers spilled out of his lips.

As he spoke, another man, this one hiding in a back room, punched the numbers into a laptop computer, and they shot like lightning bolts through the Internet, straight to a large mainframe in Zurich. It took two minutes before the money — 225 million and change, it turned out — was shunted into a new account, in a different Swiss bank, coincidentally only two blocks down from Lucerne National.

The man with the computer stuck his large ponytailed head out of the doorway. He gave Vladimir a thumbs-up.

"What will you do with me?" Golitsin asked.

"Why would I do anything with you?"

"You mean you're not going to kill me?"

"You know what? My instructions aren't real clear on that point." Vladimir stroked his chin and played at indecision for a moment. "You're broke now. A fat has-been loser with nothing to fall back on but a tiny pension and the tragic memory that once you were rich. Should I worry about you?"

"No, absolutely not. Definitely, no. You're right, you've ruined my life. I'm nothing, a sorry loser. I don't even know who you are," he lied.

"Well, I'm not so sure." The man dug a hand deep into his coat pocket. He appeared to be fishing around for something. Perhaps a gun or a knife. "Maybe, just to be on the safe side, maybe I should —"

"No, please," Golitsin pleaded, and words kept spilling out his lips. "I'll leave Russia. I promise, I'll be on the next train. I'll disappear and you'll never hear from me again. Please let me live."

The man stared at him with an impenetrable expression for a moment, then finally he shrugged his thick shoulders. "I guess it saves the trouble of what to do with your big, fat corpse."

Golitsin nearly groaned with relief. "Yes, exactly. I don't want to be a burden to you."

"Around nine in the morning the workers in the factory across the street come to work. Scream loud and hard, Sergei. Who knows, maybe they'll come and save you."

The tools were packed back inside the case, and within five minutes Vladimir and his boys had turned off the lights and scattered into the night.

After half an hour, Golitsin tried his hardest to close his eyes and float away into sleep. He so badly wanted to sleep. The fear and terror left him drained and exhausted, but he couldn't shut his eyes. The anger and resentment kept bubbling up. By 9:30 the next morning, he would make Nicky pay dearly for every humiliating moment, and for every dollar the bastard stole. He wasn't sure just how yet. It would be slow and horrible, though. And very, very painful; he promised himself this.

He leaned back on the chair and dreamed of Nicky's death.

The rumor started early that evening. Moscow's underworld loved rumors almost as much as gossip, the juicier the better, and this one took off like a rabbit with its ass on fire. By midnight it was bouncing through brothels, thug hangouts, drug dens, was being murmured by pickpockets on the street, and becoming a consuming point of interest in the bars frequented by the city's syndicate chiefs, who at that hour were just starting their day.

Somebody wanted Nicky Kozyrev dead. Somebody deeply serious; serious in the way that counted most in this town, serious enough to back up this gripping desire with big money. This was the salient point. This kept the rumor roaring all night. Five million dollars — five million to make Nicky's heart stop. Unconditionally, up to the assassin's discretion, nothing off-limits, no bounds — by bullet, by car accident, by poison, who cared? A stake through his black heart had a nice ring but dead in any form was fine. Five million excellent reasons for Nicky Kozyrev to die.

Three syndicate chiefs had been contacted by a Chechen mob that had been hired as underwriters by the source of this generous venture. For good and obvious cause, the benefactor preferred to remain anonymous. A select group of witnesses were invited to a small apartment in the city center, five suitcases of cash were hauled out of a closet and opened for display, though it was far too much to count. But for sure it looked like more than enough. This is it, they were told — this is what five million dollars looks like, up close and personal. Not an empty promise, no bluff, the real deal. Now get out and spread the word.

In a city where five thousand bucks will buy you all the corpses you wish, five million was going to kick-start a gold rush of assassins.

A few bookies put their heads together and gave thought to creating a betting pool. Nope, why bother? There were no competing odds. Open and shut. At five million bucks, Nicky was dead.

At three that morning, Nicky's chief bodyguard — his most trusted lieutenant, a lifelong friend from the same impoverished back alley of Novgorod — gently eased open Nicky's bedroom door and peeked inside. They had raped and killed and pushed dope together for three long, enjoyable decades. They had dodged the cops and KGB, swindled, murdered, and beaten too many to remember. Oh, the warm memories they shared. He snuck quietly inside. He hugged the wall, crept ever so slowly, never setting foot off the carpet. Nicky liked dark rooms. Nicky wouldn't sleep anywhere with windows, and this one was like a coffin. Nicky's loud snores bounced off the walls. The whore sprawled across his legs was shot so full of heroin she wouldn't have heard a T-80 tank pass three inches from her ear.

A pistol was in the bodyguard's right hand with a round chambered and the silencer screwed on tight. A pencil flashlight was in his left hand, with a finger poised to turn it on at the last second. He was ten feet away. Then five and the pistol came up. At two feet away, he suddenly felt something kick him in the chest. He flew backward, smashed against the wall, and crumpled in a bleeding heap on the floor. It was funny, he thought; he never heard the blast until a millisecond after his left lung blew out his back.

A moment later, Nicky was over him, peering down through the darkness into his eyes.

"It hurt?"

"Yeah, like a bitch."

"Why?" Nicky asked.

"Five million," his best friend managed to grunt.

"From who?"

"Who knows? Who cares?"

"For real?"

"Oh, it's real, Nicky."

"Why you?"

"Stupid question."

"Five mil. Yeah, you're right."

"Yeah, and you're dead."

Nicky pumped two more bullets into his best friend's mouth, straightened up, then tossed the semicomatose whore out of his room.

He locked the door behind her and moved a large dresser in front of it. He stopped and thought for a moment. Who put the price on his head? Five million was a very big level of enthusiasm. Who hated him that much? Who had the motive? Who had that much money?

After a split second, a name popped into his brain. Golitsin. It made perfect sense; in fact, no other name made any sense. He lifted his cell phone and dialed a number from memory. A voice answered, and Nicky said, "Georgi, it's me."

"Hey, I heard you got a big friggin' problem." Georgi laughed.

"Word's gotten around, I guess."

"It's five million, Nicky. You're the talk of the town."

"Good point. Here's the deal, Georgi. You owe me two million for that dope deal, right?"

"Hey, I got it right here. Deal was you don't

get it till tomorrow night."

"Scratch that."

"Seriously?"

"As a heart attack. Put out the word, one and a half million to anybody who whacks Sergei Golitsin. Rest is yours to keep."

"Maybe I'll whack Golitsin and keep all of it."

"Your option, Georgi. But Golitsin better be dead, or you're next." They rang off.

He returned to his bed, sat down, and cradled the pistol on his lap. Five million!

His best friend was right. Nicky was dead. It might take an hour, a day, maybe a week, but he was, without debate or uncertainty, a dead man walking.

By eight in the morning, Tromble had assembled the full team in his office. The usual cast of characters: his pair of compliant hey-boys, Agents Hanrahan and Wilson, Colonel Volevodz, and the head Russian prosecutor, and a fresh pool of INS legal jockeys, now backed up by a pair of eager youthful hot-shots from Justice. They sat, pens gripped, notepads poised, and awaited guidance from the great man himself.

"Really, it was to be expected," said one of the Justice boys, named Bill. Bill's area of expertise happened to be anything that happened five minutes before.

"Well, I didn't anticipate it," remarked Jason Caldwell, wiping a remnant of his morning shave from behind his left ear. After the harsh dismissal of Kim Parrish, Caldwell had been handpicked personally by the INS director, a hotshot gunslinger flown in from the San Diego office, where he was legendary for booting Mexican ass back across the border. Caldwell was a loudmouthed blowhard pretty boy without an ounce of pity for anybody accused of anything. He did deliver, though. He took the toughest, most ambiguous, most troubling cases and never once thought twice about the truth or consequences.

He made his ambitions well-known among his peers, among whom he was not now, nor had he ever been, overly popular. The INS job was a stepping stone, a temporary government job from which he intended to run for Congress, and he intended to eventually head the immigration panel, and they would all have to line up to kiss his ass. He was, by every stretch of the imagination, perfect for this job.

He had spent one month reviewing the vast hoard of evidence compiled, translated, and organized so strenuously by Kim and Petri. The hard work had been done for him, a perfect slam dunk; all he had to do was show up in court and smile brilliantly for the cameras. The past month he had mainly strutted in front of full-length mirrors, rehearsing and polishing his lines, admiring his courtly prose, and gearing up to kick a little Russian ass.

The motion for habeas corpus and switch to a federal court came like a bolt out of the dark. No warning. No threats, no hints preceded it. But MP's sneak attack bothered him not in the least. He looked forward to it, actually. Glad Alex and his hired gun did it. The chance to escape from the largely ignored immigration courts into the federal big leagues, and with such a high-visibility case, appealed to him immensely. He had no doubts he would do great. He was Jason Caldwell — if Konevitch had any clue he was up against the scourge of Mexico he'd book his own flight to Russia.

Tromble brought the meeting to order briskly. A few comments about the importance of the case. A blistering reminder about the need for victory at all costs. A hard stare around the table as he dwelled on the somber imperative of sending Konevitch home to pay for his many sins.

The Russians listened without comment. Volevodz detested America — he wanted desperately to get back to Russia, where he expected to pin on a general's star in recognition for bringing home the bacon. The head Russian prosecutor hoped Caldwell would blow it. Just choke and fumble and get his ass kicked. He prayed the case would drag on forever. He and his three comrades all had lady friends out in Vegas, a bunch of big-breasted showgirls who partied without stop and weren't overly picky about their men. And after losing nearly a hundred grand in FBI dough at the tables, he and his pals were finally starting to win a little back.

"You. Who's the judge?" Tromble asked, squinting at the two Justice boys whose names he couldn't remember because frankly he didn't care to.

"Elton Willis," replied Bill, only too proud to be here in the office of the FBI director.

Tromble looked like a lemon had been stuffed in his throat. "Oh, not Willis."

"He has a fairly good reputation," Bill argued, obviously not getting it.

During his brief tenure as a judge, Tromble and Willis had attended a few legal conferences together and, on one sour occasion, had even shared a podium for a spirited debate on civil liberties, one of many legal topics about which they held diametrically different views. The audience were other judges and the results were predictable. Willis was intelligent, methodical, measured, with a former Jesuit's grasp and approach to law. To put it mildly, the scholars and justices in the audience didn't seem to grasp the subtlety of Tromble's theories. It wasn't the first or last time he'd been pelted with boos, but it was probably the loudest.

"He's a lefty wimp," Tromble growled, daring anybody to contest this conclusion. He leaned back in his chair and cracked his knuckles. "You ready for the show?" he asked Caldwell.

"It's a knockdown case. In and out inside one or two days."

Tromble traded glances with Hanrahan. "What's the one thing we've overlooked?"

No clue.

"Publicity. Press. We need to bang Konevitch on every front page," he said, almost predictably.

Caldwell loved this brainchild. "Great idea," he announced quite loudly. "If we don't, the defense will. Better to preempt them."

"Our Russian friends need to see we're serious. All this time, but we haven't forgotten them."

"I could hold a few press conferences," Caldwell agreeably offered.

Tromble cleared his throat. "Well, we'll see if we need you." He paused briefly. "Hanrahan, tell the boys downstairs to kick it in gear. See if *Nightline* or *Good Morning America* has an opening for me. And call that blonde lawyer over at Fox News, you know the one. She always has an opening for me."

"Pretty short notice. We've only got two more days, boss."

"Tell them it's the biggest trial of the year."

Hanrahan looked away and pondered the tabletop. "Maybe that will work, maybe not." Truth was the newspaper and TV people were tired of his boss and his unrelenting attempts to steal ink and camera time. He was a preening spotlight hog, a master at shoving himself before every camera in sight. The boys downstairs in the public affairs office were working eighty-hour weeks, but had flat run out of angles, lies, and lures to get him press time.

"All right," Tromble said, thinking up a fresh angle quickly. "Tell them I intend to be a witness at this trial. A historic occasion. First time an FBI director has ever been on the stand."

"Good idea," Hanrahan said.

Caldwell offered no objections. Go ahead, give it your best shot, he was tempted to shout. Bill this as the biggest trial of the century, if not forever. You'll be a witness, but I'm the prosecutor, it's my show, and I'll damn sure find a way to make you second fiddle.

The meeting broke among frothy promises to make sure Konevitch would at last have his long-overdue appointment with justice.

31

The front steps of the Federal Courthouse looked like a convention for something. A few dozen TV crews were gathered, klieg lights in place, cameras loaded and ready to roll. Another dozen print reporters milled around aimlessly, drawn and stoked by the buzz fed by the FBI's impressive publicity machine.

Inside the court another dozen journalists were already seated at the rear benches, pool reporters who would rush out and share the dirt and drama with their less privileged brethren.

At one table sat a clutch of five lawyers, led by Jason Caldwell, looking rather resplendent in his fine new five-hundred-buck Brooks Brothers suit, bought in honor of his break-out debut. It matched his blue eyes. It would look great on camera. A pair of INS colleagues sat to his left, and on the floor beside them rested a large stack of evidence. The two boys from Justice were banished to a shallow space on the far side, though their exact purpose in the trial was an open question, especially between themselves.

At the defense table, MP huddled importantly with a pair of well-dressed guns from Pacevitch, Knowlton and Rivers, one of many monster firms in a city where lawyers outnumbered ordinary citizens three to one. Directly to his right sat Matt Rivers, a law school classmate who had served as best man in the hastily arranged wedding between MP and his by then noticeably pregnant bride.

Top of his class, in his third year, Matt had been wined and dined by big firms from New York and Chicago. But he chose PKR, as it was commonly known. He was drawn by its no-holds-barred reputation, a feared powerhouse, a collection of divisions that did many things from corporate through criminal, with branch offices in six American cities, and ten more spread around the globe. Notice that PKR was involved in a case often had the terrifying effect of getting even the most recalcitrant opponents to promptly initiate settlement talks. PKR's unwritten motto was "pile it on," in honor of the firm's willingness to throw a hundred lawyers at a troubled case. However many lawyers were committed against it, PKR doubled it and wrenched up the hours, drowning the competition in useless motions and watching it sink in exhaustion. To put it mildly, PKR did not like to lose. Matt's competitive streak — aka his killer instinct — had been identified early and carefully nurtured and cultivated. The cultivation included partnership within five years: three hundred thousand a year, plus bonus, plus car.

Though their lives and fortunes diverged, Matt and MP still lunched together every few months and shared tales from the opposite ends of the legal profession. There was one condition that was strictly followed; Matt picked the eating hole and paid the check. This law was laid down in the early years after MP took Matt to Taco Bell; no longer accustomed to such fare, Matt's stomach rebelled with horrible violence.

At Alex's behest, MP had approached his old pal a few months before for a favor. MP was seriously outgunned, and Alex pressured him to find some reinforcements, but since funds were short, to find somebody willing to do the work for the promise of the publicity it might generate. Tromble seemed to be doing a masterful job at stoking that publicity, and Matt took MP's appeal to the firm's management committee. It was a simple and quite common request; assign one or two lawyers on a pro bono basis. The bulk of the work would be handled by MP: all he really wanted was the firm there, in the background, throwing its weight around, striking fear in the opposition. A simple immigration matter failed to fuel the committee's enthusiasm until Matt launched into Alex Konevitch's fascinating background and the strange nature of his supposed crimes. Interest swelled, then the partners on the committee became curiously fired up about the whole idea.

Two years before, PKR had joined the pell-mell rush of Western firms pouring into the new market of democratic Russia and opened a small, struggling branch in Moscow. The PKR boys in Russia were immediately hired by a free-market oil company battling to fend off a vicious takeover by a shady consortium with heavy government contacts. One day before the first hearing, PKR was notified by the Ministry of Justice that its lawyers had just been disbarred, and its branch office was no longer welcome. The PKR lawyers were all booted out. The oil company was swallowed up two days later.

What a great way for PKR to shoot a big middle finger back at the Russian government, the senior partners agreed. Among its many fine attributes, PKR never forgot a slight.

Thus, seated to Matt's right was Marvin Knowlton, the K in PKR, a distinguished-looking eighty-year-old gentleman, a legendary scrapper talked out of retirement for this one brief return engagement. He cut a striking figure, with the deep tan of a permanent

Florida golfer that contrasted nicely with his long silver mane. The old lion's presence in this court was a warning to whoever cared to pay attention. In his trial lawyer days, Marvin specialized in suits for defamation, rights violations, and libel. He sued at the drop of a hat. He rarely lost.

The strategy was simple. By introducing the motion for habeas corpus — thus forcing the government to show the constitutional basis for Alex's prolonged detention — Alex and MP were moving it out of immigration and into federal court, a system with more rights protections for the accused. Also, there were appeals in this system, a chance for a second, or even a third hearing. MP would take first crack at defending the Konevitches. If he lost, the cutthroats from PKR would take over, commit a dozen more lawyers, and go for blood.

For the time being, though, Matt and Marvin were expected only to look threatening, listen to MP's arguments, and be prepared to step in only after things went wrong, which, after reviewing the evidence, in their collective view, was the likely outcome.

To MP's rear sat Elena in a simple blue pantsuit and white pumps, clutching her hands, praying fervently. Occasionally she stopped talking to the Lord long enough to throw a hateful glare at the defense table, the people who had so cruelly persecuted her husband.

At the last moment, Alex was led through a side door by two big marshals straight to the defense table. He had been offered the chance to shower and change into something more presentable, like a suit and tie. He politely but insistently refused. He sported the same dirty white trousers, soiled white shirt, and grungy flip-flops he wore in prison. His face had accumulated at least four days of thick, dark stubble. His hair was still pulled back in a tight, greasy ponytail.

Even MP had argued otherwise, but Alex adamantly insisted — let the judge and all the reporters see what had been done to him. The sight of him in such a sorry state would displace any thought of a fat-cat millionaire. Whatever he had been before, now he was just another simple guy cruelly oppressed and abused by the state.

Alex shambled in fits and starts to his chair, shoulders slumped, head and eyes down. He feigned a pained expression and very gently began to ease himself into the chair. A lady in the third row leaned over to somebody a few seats down and muttered loudly and indignantly, "You see that? The poor guy's been gang-raped by those animals."

The cue was perfect. MP and Matt immediately jumped up and made a dramatic show of helping poor Alex get more comfortable. And as though she hadn't seen her husband in months, Elena clutched her throat and emitted a strangled wail that bounced around the courtroom walls.

At just that moment, the rear door flew open and in marched John Tromble, fresh from a fast flurry of interviews on the courthouse steps. His eyes roved around the courtroom, settling finally on the prisoner at the defense table. It was his first look at Alex Konevitch, up close and personal, his first glance at this irritating man who had occupied so much of his time and attention over the past fourteen months. He took in the prison garb, the shaggy beard, the unkempt ponytail, the exhausted eyes, and he responded instinctively — he smiled.

This response was fully observed by the dozen pool reporters in the back rows, who launched into noisy whispers among themselves.

Tromble moved with important purpose to the front row where an aide held an empty seat for him. He had not been in a courtroom since his days as a judge, but he felt his presence would send a strong message to the court.

A moment later, a side door quietly opened. Judge Elton Willis walked out, black robes rustling, and moved straight to the bench. The bailiff announced him, everybody stood, the judge sat, and the court fell back into its seats.

Elton Willis was fifty-nine, surprisingly short, with jet black skin and dainty facial features. A former Jesuit priest, he awoke one morning and decided God's will wouldn't be settled in a church, but out on the streets where the battle between good and evil was waged with terrible force. He turned in his vestments and spent five years dishing slop in soup kitchens and mentoring young black children in Washington's brutal slums, before becoming deeply discouraged. Any illusion that he would save the world was crushed by crack, guns, and the unrelenting violence of the streets. So many of the kids ended up dead or in the legal system, with poor representation, and were shunted off to prisons they would bounce in and out of for the rest of their lives. It was time to take the battle up another level. He finished law school at the University of Virginia, where the novelty of a former Jesuit studying a lower law greatly amused the faculty, then returned to Washington, where he established himself as a defense attorney to be reckoned with. Rich clients were banned. If a prospective client passed through his door dressed in a suit, he was promptly sent right back out the door.

As a federal judge, he now waged the battle between good and bad from a high bench. Jesuits tend to be hard men of great intelligence. Elton Willis happened to be harder and smarter than most.

His eyes wandered around the court for a moment. In a quiet voice, he quickly summarized the matter for consideration, and in a louder voice established a few ground rules. This was not a jury trial. In fact it wasn't a trial, it was a habeas corpus hearing mediated by a judge. He did not cater to theatrics, asked the attorneys to object only when absolutely necessary, and emphasized that brevity was next to godliness. He offered threatening scowls to both lawyers, underscoring these points.

Opening statements were made by both attorneys. Jason Caldwell led off and couldn't help himself. After months of primping and prepping, he was like a Hollywood starlet at her first premiere. He paced and pranced around the floor. Half his remarks were addressed to the judge, the other half to the yawning journalists in the back row. Unfortunately, he was also an effective attorney with a sharp tongue and a strong case, and, long before he was done, Alex Konevitch sounded like the personification of evil. He deserved to be in prison, and possibly executed. At the very least he should be dispatched to his own shores for a long-overdue appointment with justice.

With a final flash of his freshly bleached teeth at the reporters in the back, he returned to his seat.

MP pushed himself only halfway out of his

chair and said very simply, "My client has endured fourteen miserable months in prison, convicted of nothing. I request an immediate release."

He sat. That was it, nothing more — a tiny drop in a vast ocean that screamed for a long and indignant rant.

Caldwell felt like standing up and applauding. He was going to pound MP Jones into dust. This was going to be so easy. He stood and called his first witness, Colonel Leonid Volevodz, to the stand.

The colonel marched to the witness box, was sworn in, and sat.

Caldwell sidled up to the witness stand, Perry Mason absent the wheelchair. "What's your position, sir?"

"I am the special assistant to Russia's minister of internal security."

"And this would be equivalent to our FBI?"

"You might describe it that way." He leaned back and coolly crossed his legs.

"What is your relationship to the investigations concerning Mr. Konevitch?"

"The lead investigator for my department. The crimes were so severe and crossed so many areas, eventually I was ordered to oversee the efforts of all three government investigations."

Caldwell turned around and nodded at one of the INS lawyers at the crowded table. The lawyer seized a bundle of papers and rushed to Caldwell's side. He selected then held up one clump of papers. Caldwell asked, "Can you please identify this?"

Volevodz bent forward. "That is an English translation of the Ministry of Justice investigation."

"And this?"

"The Ministry of Finance investigation."

"And this?"

"My own investigation."

"And do these three investigations draw similar conclusions?"

"Identical conclusions."

"Could you briefly describe those conclusions?"

"Briefly? Konevitch stole 250 million dollars. He gutted and bankrupted his company. He almost single-handedly ruined the credibility of the Russian banking model. It is impossible to summarize in a short statement."

Caldwell turned his back to the colonel and smiled at the peanut gallery. "Yes, I imagine it is. Do any of these investigations differ in any serious regard?"

"No. The facts were easily established. The evidence was overwhelming. Perhaps a hundred different investigators reached the exact same conclusion."

"That Konevitch is a crook?"

"A thief. A liar. A confidence man."

"Was Konevitch ever asked to return to

Russia?"

"Yes, by me. I pleaded with him. Twice, on two separate occasions. I assured him of a fair trial. I offered my personal protection. If he was innocent, he could clear his name."

"Twice?"

"That's what I said."

"And how did he respond?"

"He laughed. He pointed out there was no extradition treaty between our countries. He stuck his finger in my chest and said he would hide behind your flag."

Caldwell couldn't resist that opening. "He would hide behind our flag? The Stars and Stripes?"

"His exact words."

Another document was held up and splayed open. Caldwell asked, "Can you identify this for the court?"

The thin eyes squinted again. "It's the indictment issued against Alex Konevitch for his crimes." He leaned forward, as if he needed a closer look. "It's signed by Anatoli Fyodorev, Russia's equivalent to your attorney general."

Caldwell looked at the judge. "Your Honor, we submit these investigations and indictments as evidence that Alex Konevitch committed serious crimes in Russia, and later he lied and covered up these crimes when he fled here."

The stack was handed off to the clerk, who

quickly assigned a number to each one before she arranged them in an orderly stack on her desk. Alex was seated in his chair. He showed no surprise or even concern over the seriousness of the testimony.

His Honor looked at MP. "Would you care to cross-examine?"

"I would not, Your Honor," he answered without looking up.

Volevodz was released. The next witness was the chief Russian prosecutor, who was identified and properly sworn in.

He sat and Caldwell approached. "Could you please describe your role in this investigation?"

"I was ordered by the state attorney general to prepare the indictment and legal case against Alex Konevitch."

"He's a wanted man in Russia, I take it?"

"Number one on our most wanted list."

"Do you believe he's guilty?"

"That would be a matter for our courts to decide."

"But Mr. Konevitch claims your courts are unfair."

"Ridiculous. Under the old communist system, maybe. We are a democracy now. Our courts are every bit as judicious and fair as yours."

"So he would be allowed to hire a lawyer?"

"As many as he can afford. If he can't afford any, the state will appoint one."

"He would be allowed to present evidence on his own behalf?"

"Just like here, Mr. Caldwell. Konevitch will enjoy the full benefit of innocence until proven guilty."

"Are you aware that some Americans have a poor impression of your legal system?"

"Are you aware that some Russians have a poor impression of yours?"

"Touché." Caldwell decided to step out on a limb, directed his gaze at Alex, then asked, "Why would Mr. Konevitch feel he can't get an honest shake in Russia?"

The Russian also directed his gaze at Alex, who nodded politely but otherwise appeared indifferent.

"Maybe an honest shake, as you call it, is the last thing he wants."

Caldwell paused and waited for the loud but inevitable objection from MP Jones. He had led this witness. He had openly encouraged an act of naked conjecture — how could the chief prosecutor possibly know what Alex was thinking?

Silence. MP sat in his seat, doodling on a legal pad. He looked bored out of his mind. Beside him, Alex appeared to be studying MP's doodles, as transfixed as he would be by a da Vinci or a Picasso.

"Thank you," Caldwell said to his witness, then studied the ceiling a moment as though he needed a little help from the Lord to remember his next point. He snapped his fingers. "Oh, another question. The money Mr. Konevitch stole? Did you ever find it?"

The chief prosecutor looked at Alex. "Some of it, yes. We tracked a few million to a bank in Bermuda."

Another of Caldwell's aides hustled over and shoved a sheet of paper at the witness.

Caldwell asked with construed curiosity, "Would this be the account information?" What else could it be?

After a careful examination, "Yes, this is it."

"How much is currently in the account?"

"Two and half million dollars."

"That's it?"

"Yes, that's all."

"I thought he stole 250 million dollars. Where's the remainder of Konevitch's money?"

"It's not Konevitch's money, sir."

"No?" A look of surprise. "Well, whose money is it?"

"It's money he robbed from poor people in Russia. They trusted him and are now bankrupt. We won't know where he stashed it all until we get him home and he confesses. Only then can those poor people be repaid."

Caldwell let that fester a moment — all those miserable victims back home starving and freezing while they waited for Alex to give them back their money — then said, "Are you familiar with a company named

Orangutan Media?"

"I most certainly am."

"How are you familiar with this company?"

"It became the subject of police interest a few years ago."

"How did this come about?"

"The result of a tip from a source inside one of our crime syndicates. A Chechen mob, a nasty group involved in a number of criminal activities, from kidnapping to drugs to murder."

"Sounds like our Mafia."

"You should be so lucky. Compared to these people, your Mafia's a Boy Scout group. After the tip, a wiretap was installed and the police heard Konevitch arranging payments and transfers of cash. He was using Orangutan as a front to launder syndicate money."

"What was the nature of Orangutan Media?"

"Reputedly it was an advertising company. And it was established in Austria to evade our scrutiny. The syndicate money came into the company under the guise of client contracts. Orangutan turned around and gave the same money right back to the syndicate as subcontractors. It was all very neat."

"It sounds quite elaborate."

"Not really. It's a very common shell game. Child's play for a sophisticated financial mastermind like Konevitch."

"And you have Mr. Konevitch on tape discussing these arrangements with a syndicate?"

"Right there on your table," he said, pointing at the defense table. "The taped discussions are in Russian, of course, so I left them back in Russia. They would be incomprehensible to you, anyway. I therefore turned over paper transcripts to your people."

"Yes, you did." The aide took the cue and hauled a bunch of papers to the bench. "We introduce these translated transcripts," Caldwell said very slowly, with another flash of teeth. "As well, I submit statements collected by state prosecutors from a number of Orangutan Media employees confessing to the schemes inside the company."

He held his breath and waited in anticipation for Jones to jerk out of his chair. Without the tapes there was no way to verify that the written transcripts were accurate, or indeed whether any tapes even existed. There had to be an objection this time — a noisy protest infused with enraged anger would follow, he was sure.

In fact, Jones looked ready to jump out of his seat before Alex reached over and grabbed his arm. Alex briefly whispered something into his ear. MP relented, relaxed back into his seat, and went back to doodling on a yellow legal pad.

Caldwell silently congratulated himself. A

brilliant move, and he couldn't believe he got away with it. Having the chief prosecutor in the witness chair obviously nullified the discrediting strategy Jones had pulled off in immigration court. Welcome to the big leagues, pal.

Caldwell triumphantly announced, "I'm through with this witness," and returned to his seat.

Judge Willis peered down from his perch at MP. Jones was still focused intensely on his yellow legal pad, which now was cluttered with aimless squiggles and shapes. "Mr. Jones, do you wish to cross-examine?"

MP looked up. "What? . . . Uh, no, thank you, Your Honor."

"You're sure?"

"Yes, quite sure."

Willis rubbed his eyes for a moment. "You heard what the witness presented?"

"I did."

"And you're sure you don't want to ask him a few questions?"

"Very sure."

"Is this your first time in federal court, Mr. Jones?"

"Yes sir. Very first. It's much nicer than immigration court. Quite lovely."

"I'm glad it appeals to your tastes. Do you understand how our procedures work?"

"I believe I do, Your Honor."

"Once I release this witness, he cannot be

recalled."

"Then please do it quickly. I don't know about you, but he was becoming tiresome, Your Honor."

This caused a twitter of laughter among the reporters.

His Honor did not appear to get the joke. "I advise you, Mr. Jones, to think harder about questioning the witnesses than trying to entertain us with humor."

"Can I be blunt, Your Honor?"

"You can try, Mr. Jones."

"I don't wish to waste your time."

"To the contrary, Mr. Jones, I'm here to listen to both sides. It's an adversarial system, by design. I encourage you to participate."

"Well, I don't want to encourage him to tell more lies."

"I see. The witness is released."

Caldwell rose to call his next witness, but the judge put up a hand. "Hold on a moment." His eyes turned to Alex. "Can you please rise?"

Alex stood.

Judge Willis leaned far forward on his elbows. "Are you aware your attorney has no experience in federal jurisdictions?"

"In fact, he emphasized the same thing last week."

"I'm sure you're in a great hurry to get out of prison, Mr. Konevitch. I'm just wondering if this hearing might be premature."

"On the contrary, my arrest and imprisonment were premature, Your Honor."

"Do you have adequate knowledge of our legal system?"

Alex directed a look at Tromble, who was seated, legs crossed. "I've been imprisoned the past fourteen months, without trial. You could say I am quite familiar with this legal procedure. Soviet law operated the same way."

Willis pinched his nose and forced himself not to scowl. "Are you content with your representation? The question is on the record, Mr. Konevitch. Because if you try to appeal my decision based upon incompetent representation, it will now be clear that you knowingly settled on Mr. Jones."

MP blinked a few times at what was obviously intended as a very public putdown. It was humiliating to be treated as a featherweight but that wasn't the most painful part. Worse, part of their strategy cooked up by him and the PKR boys relied on Alex having valid claim to poor representation. So far, MP had availed himself of every opportunity to portray utter incompetence. Let the prosecutor get away with as much as was legally advisable, do your best to sit and look stupid.

A great idea, in concept, that was suddenly falling apart.

After a moment, Alex stated very clearly, "I'm happy with my counsel," then collapsed into his chair.

And so it went for the remainder of the morning. An hour break for lunch before Caldwell resumed calling more witnesses who confirmed and reconfirmed and elaborated powerfully on the inescapable fact that Alex Konevitch was a crook, a flight risk, a criminal who had to be incarcerated or he would flee and never be heard from again. Three FBI agents were paraded to the stand, followed by two Foreign Service officers with recent experience in Russia, each of whom had observed firsthand the public furor caused when Konevitch disappeared with the money.

MP politely and firmly declined to cross-examine each one. The clock read 4:30 when the last prosecution witness was excused from the stand.

Judge Willis checked his watch, then said, "Sidebar with the opposing attorneys."

MP and Caldwell joined His Honor in a small, tight cluster beside the bench.

The judge glared at MP. "Did you not in fact submit this motion for habeas corpus?" he whispered.

"I certainly did, Your Honor," MP whispered back.

"Why, Mr. Jones?"

"Why? Because my client has been incarcerated in federal prison for fourteen months. He's been bounced through three different prisons, each progressively more hazardous and miserable than the last. He's been submitted to several bouts of solitary confinement, and deliberately assigned cellmates categorized as Level Five inmates. I'm sure you're aware that prisoners reach this distinctive category only after they prove they are a grave danger to other inmates and to the guards. In short, somebody in our federal government wants my client dead or willing to submit to instantaneous deportation."

"Those are grave charges."

"I believe that's an understatement."

"Now, may I be blunt with you?"

MP nodded.

Still in whispers, His Honor unleashed a day's worth of quiet anger. "Since you requested this hearing, you are supposed to do something other than sit and doodle on a yellow pad, Mr. Jones. The American legal system is designed to allow a spirited defense. You are obligated to occasionally object to statements that are challengeable, and cross-examine witnesses and poke holes in points you believe are contestable or unsubstantiated. I am dismayed by your behavior. I find it egregiously outrageous and, frankly, incompetent."

"I apologize. I promise I'll try to appear more engaged."

"I'm sure your client will appreciate that."

He turned to Caldwell, who was biting back a smile. He could barely contain himself. His bosses had warned him that Jones was wily and tough and full of surprises. This was the guy, after all, who booted Kim Parrish's ass out of the ballpark. "Hey, who's the tough guy now?" the scourge of Mexico wanted to ask. He was tempted to move two inches from Jones's face and just break out into laughter.

"Mr. Caldwell, do you have more witnesses?"

In fact, three more he planned to question that afternoon. But, hey, what the hell — he could dispense with all of them. After the catastrophic damage he had administered — none of it challenged, all cleanly admitted — why pile more humiliation on top of ten thousand tons of misery? They were nothing more than confirmation witnesses, here to build on already well-substantiated facts. The judge was ready to rule in his favor right now.

"One more. It can wait till morning."

"Then unless you gentlemen disagree I intend to adjourn until nine a.m. tomorrow."

Neither attorney objected in the least.

His Honor looked at MP again. The look was anything but kindly and compassionate. "You had better do some soul-searching tonight. You requested this hearing. If I don't see a spirited attempt on your client's behalf in the morning, I'll cite you for contempt."

The instant the judge dismissed the court

and the side door closed behind him, the mad scramble was on. Like the shot that starts a race, Caldwell scuttled for the door. He raced through the wide hallways, shoved open the huge outer doors, and nearly lost his balance as he went careening down the big steps.

Three dozen cameras and reporters converged on him at once. He pushed back his hair and produced his most handsome smile for the friendly cameras. "Ladies and gentlemen, I'm Jason Caldwell, and I'm prosecuting this case. I'm sure you have lots of questions. One at a time, and don't interrupt my replies."

Tromble crashed out the doors just as Caldwell finished his windup. Without even glancing back, Caldwell very smoothly said, "Surely you all recognize our beloved FBI director. He has been providing assistance to me on this case. Limited assistance, though it has been somewhat helpful. I just want to express my appreciation. If you haven't heard, in fact, he will be my first witness tomorrow morning."

Tromble wanted to punch him. Grab his throat and begin throttling. Instead he forced a smile, produced a firm, dutiful salute for the cameras, and sprinted off to his limousine, yelling over his shoulder, "Sorry, I don't have time for questions."

Caldwell remained on the steps for two hours. No question was too trivial to answer.

No reporter too insignificant for an endearing smile and a long, thoughtful reply. He bravely withstood the fury of interest until the reporters remembered their deadlines and wandered off into the Washington evening.

32

It was called the Tsar's Suite. At an enormous five thousand square feet, it was furnished with rare and wondrous antiques, loaded with marble and teak, and crammed to the rafters with a staggering array of personal luxuries. Two separate baths, either one big enough to swallow and wash a squadron of sweaty horses. An entire wall of picture windows overlooking the glorious Moskva River and Moscow's twinkling lights.

The sumptuous dinner had been prepared by a four-star chef and delivered by three waiters who hung over the table, willing to cut the meat and spoon-feed the thoroughly spoiled customers. Whatever they wished for, a dollop landed on their plate, delivered by a gold ladle. A sip of wine and the crystal goblet was instantly topped off.

By ten, the chief of staff and his mistress were stuffed and sated, slightly lightheaded from the wine and champagne, ready to retire to the sumptuous pillow bed in the gargantuan bedroom. The chief dispatched the waiters with huge tips.

Tatyana was cradling a snifter of sherry and staring wistfully out the window at the sky full of stars. "This was a wonderful idea," she said.

"Isn't it?"

"The most romantic thing we've ever done."

"What can I say? I love you."

"I love you, too."

"Do you?"

"Of course. I love you, love you, love you."

He stared across the table at her. "Will you marry me?"

"I would love to."

"You're sure?"

"Yes. Just . . . obviously not right now."

"Why not now?"

"Yeltsin needs you. The country needs you. I won't be a distraction from your important work."

"I can handle it. After all, we see each other at work."

They had been through this same argument a hundred times, a conversation they had rehearsed so often it was stale. A brief loving glance at her paramour. "But I'm not sure I can. We've been through this. In case you haven't noticed, darling, I stay pretty busy, too."

His elbows landed on the table. "You're

sure there's nobody else?"

"Absolutely," she snapped. She fell back on her usual defense, a deep pout. "Now you're acting like a jealous idiot."

He reached into a pocket, withdrew a photograph, and casually tossed it across the table. "Recognize this guy?"

She glanced down and didn't flinch or so much as squint. "No."

"Look again. You're sure you don't know him?"

She picked up the picture. "Who is he? He looks sort of cute."

"Nobody. Just thought you might. Until yesterday, he was a star striker on our national soccer team."

"Was?"

The chief began playing with a small fork. "That's right, was. Seems he experienced a terrible accident. Collided with another player and broke his leg. Also destroyed ligaments in his knee . . . actually both knees, I'm told. Then somebody ran over him with cleats and broke his nose and kicked off an ear. Poor fellow. Such a rough sport. His soccer career is definitely over."

Tatyana gripped the photograph a little harder.

Her boss said very amiably, "Just thought you might know or at least remember him."

"I'm not a soccer fan. Why should I?"

"It seems he went to the same elementary

and gymnasium as you. Same small village. Same age, too."

"What's his name?"

"Sasha Komenov."

"I have a vague memory of the name." A well-feigned expression of dawning recognition. "Oh, yes, I think I do remember. A chubby little boy covered with pimples. Obviously, he looks different now. We were all so young back then."

Her boss swallowed a deep sip of sherry, then bit down hard on his lip. "How about a little music before we retire, dear?"

"Something romantic would be nice." She sipped carefully from her sherry, trying not to vomit. Poor, poor Sasha. She stared out at the city lights and tried hard not to imagine how her boytoy looked with a blown-up nose and only one ear. She failed miserably. The image just wouldn't disappear.

Her boss moved to the entertainment console, gritted his teeth, punched play on the tape machine, and waited for the sound of romance to start.

A moment later came the sounds of Tatyana and her freshly disfigured Sasha thrashing in the sheets and prattling away about what a disgusting, nauseating dork her boss was.

Tatyana spun around. She and her boss looked at each other for a moment, he with his eyes narrowed into betrayed slits, she unable to close her mouth. The damning tape droned on.

Tatyana screamed, "What in the hell is that?" She knew damn well what it was. Disaster. Her apartment was bugged. Some nosy-body had been listening and, worse, recording. But for how long? Who? How sloppy had she been, how much dirt was on those dreadful tapes?

She quickly ended up with the one question all lawyers ask at a moment like this: how screwed am I?

"That?" he answered, jerking down the volume. "Oh, just the sound of you being fired."

"What? You can't."

He smiled. "Yes, I definitely can. Listen, it's fun. I'll do it again — you're fired." He pushed stop, and they stared at each other. Then, once more, because he loved the sound of it, "You're fired."

The snifter of sherry tumbled out of her hand, landed on the marble floor, and crashed into a thousand tiny shards. An apt metaphor to what was happening to her life. She bounced out of her chair, stamped a foot, and said, "Don't be a fool. Without me, you won't last two minutes. I've been carrying you for three years."

"I won't deny it."

"While you and your pal Yeltsin have been keeping the vodka industry afloat, who do

650

you think's been keeping the office running?"

"Won't deny that, either. You worked like a dog."

She tried a smile. "Look, darling, we can get past this."

"I already have. I hired your replacement this afternoon. A real clever young fellow with endless energy and an incredible knack for organization. He'll be happily seated behind your desk in the morning."

"You bastard."

"You bitch."

She grabbed her coat and began stomping for the door. She threw it open with a loud crash and immediately three men in blue uniforms lunged at her. They spun Tatyana around and slapped cuffs on her wrists. She tried screaming and thrashing, but it had no effect, and she soon stopped.

Her boss watched with fierce satisfaction, then mentioned to his former lover, "Ooops, did I fail to mention there's a second tape?"

A second tape? She was suddenly sure she was going to become sick.

"I turned it over to our new attorney general. It's you talking with your crooked friends about all your illegal schemes." He mocked her with a loud laugh. "Hey, you know what else? Maybe I failed to mention that your stooge Fyodorev was also fired and arrested this afternoon."

"You lousy bastard."

"A postcard from prison would be nice. Be sure to let me know where you land."

So many of them were gathered in such a tight two-block circumference, it resembled a convention of killers. There were strutting pros with big-league experience, an all-star team of deadly assassins. A clutch of third-rate mobsters ambling for their first kill. And a sprinkling of ambitious young amateurs hoping to get lucky. It was every man to himself, or herself — a few women's suffrage types were lurking in the shadows as well.

They hung out in parked cars and vans, smoking and sipping coffee, eyeing Nicky's hideout, waiting for a break. Going inside was ill-fated stupidity. This had been tried rather unsuccessfully by one bold idiot before he was driven off by a furious hail of bullets. About twenty of Nicky's bodyguards were in there, armed to the teeth, guarding their turf. Poachers weren't welcome. A few snipers were perched on rooftops, fighting off the cold. The apartment building across the street from Nicky's holdout, a real dump, had suddenly experienced an unaccustomed flood of subleases. Responding to loud knocks on the doors, the inhabitants found themselves confronted by tough-looking men shoving thousands into their fists for what was promised would be a brief dislocation. The far side of the hall, the one that did not face Nicky's safehouse, couldn't draw any interest at any price.

The street had only one coffee shop, a cramped, neglected little place run by a chubby old babushka with a million wrinkles and a toothless smile. She was suddenly rolling in customers, nasty-looking sorts who demanded coffee day and night. She struck a deal with a sandwich and soup joint six blocks down. She imported their goods, tripled the price, and made a killing. To date, she was the only one making a killing, literally or figuratively. She quietly rooted for Nicky to last another few weeks.

Late on Tuesday evening, a new car joined the party, a big, shiny black Mercedes that slid to a curb and idled for hours. Instantly, a dozen hungry sharks took note of this latest entrant in the Nicky sweepstakes.

Throughout the night, the car never budged from the curb. At four in the morning, four men stepped out. They stretched and looked around. All were dressed in nice suits, wildly out of character for this game.

A moment later, a fifth man embarked from the car and stepped out onto the curb. Short and fat, he wore a double-breasted blazer with a hundred gold buttons that sparkled in the moonlit night. He stretched his cramped legs, looked around very briefly, then waddled off in the direction of the coffee shop. The four men followed at a discreet distance, an obvious deference to their boss that marked him like a whale swimming among minnows.

Golitsin ran in the wrong circles. He had no clue that photos of him with a million and a half bucks painted on his backside were circulating throughout the city's heavily populated underworld. Later, the city coroner would find it impossible to discern exactly which of nearly a hundred bullets fired in the willy-nilly hailstorm was the precise cause of death. The five through the heart were certainly candidates, though the ten in the brain had the odds in their favor.

Six of those ten, however, were fired from different guns, different ranges, and different angles. Unfortunately the shattered brain gave up no clues as to which bullet struck first, or indeed, which produced the most lethal damage. Frankly there was too little brain left to consider. So much of it was scattered on the concrete, bits and pieces too small to scrape up.

The logjam was settled after an intense three-day bombardment of whispered threats and intense pleadings, when one of the shooters secretly offered to split the reward fifty-fifty — of the many other offers that poured in, nothing was over a third.

Three-quarters of a million dollars!

The coroner's last troubling doubt instantly vanished in a cloud of certainty.

■ ■ ■ ■

The third day in his self-imposed bunker was the one that got to Nicky. Three days and two nights of sitting in the same pitch-dark room, cradling his gun in his lap, counting down the hours and wondering when it would end. Three days of waiting for the inevitable. His own bodyguards made an occasional foray. Day and night, Nicky could hear them out there, exhorting one another, loading up on booze and dope, trying to stoke up the nerve.

Early on the second day there had been a chaotic rush at the door — a stupid, clumsy attempt with bodies bashing against the reinforced wood. Nicky emptied his pistol and smiled blissfully at all the satisfying howls and screams.

Later that same night, a second attempt. Smarter this time. Well, slightly more sneaky, anyway. One of the idiots crawled up to the door, planted a hand grenade against the wood, pulled the pin, then scuttled away for his life. Nicky became dismayed and depressed by the stupidity of his own handpicked bodyguards. It was a miracle he had survived this long. Anticipating them was child's play. Everything in the room — the furniture, the mattress — everything was piled up against the door. The pile of junk absorbed the blast and shrapnel nicely. When the boys showed up, Nicky emptied his pistol again. Another lovely chorus of screams and howls, and Nicky laughed long after they had retreated back to their refuge.

They were through being careless and stupid. No more suicidal rushes, no more dragging bullet-riddled corpses down the hall and trying to figure out how to dispose of them. Now they were trying to wait him out: if he snoozed, he was dead. They took shifts and listened for his snores. There was no food in his room. The bathroom was across the hall so water was a problem, too. But there was heroin and cocaine in abundance. Nicky pulled a fresh snort every hour. Every fourth hour, the needle slid back into a vein. He sat on the floor, pumped up on dope, erupting with delirious chuckles that echoed down the hall.

His best friend's corpse was three feet away, bloated like an overinflated balloon. The smell was intolerable, but Nicky's nostrils were so crusted and blocked up with white powder he had no idea.

Late on the third day the idea took root in his exhausted, drug-addled brain. He thought about it more, and liked it more. No, he loved it. In a lifetime of great ideas, it would be such a grand finishing touch. Long after he was gone, they would still be admiring his final masterstroke. His last finger at all of them.

He reached over to his friend's dead hand and pried the flashlight out of the rigor-mortised fist. He found a piece of paper and pencil and scribbled a brief, perfunctory note.

Holding the note in one hand, he put the pistol in his mouth and without a moment of hesitation blew out the back of his head.

His bodyguards waited an hour before they drew straws. They dispatched the losers first, frightened scouts who scuttled past the door and prayed Nicky didn't blast them to pieces. Everybody had heard that last shot an hour before. The debates and quarrels were noisy and fierce, but they just weren't sure.

Nicky was so clever, so diabolical. It wouldn't be beneath him to fake his own suicide just to lure a few more of them into his sights.

Finally, they tiptoed down the hall, broke the door down, and crashed inside. Somebody flipped on the lights. Between the rotting corpse and the fact that Nicky had used the floor as a toilet, the stench was like a dropkick in the nostrils. They pinched their noses and eased over to Nicky's body against the wall.

The note was gripped tightly in his dead hand: "I, Nicky Kozyrev, claim the five million dollars for my own death. You pricks figure out which of my many bastard kids are first in line. Send it to him. Or her. I don't care."

33

The trial opened on time. By 9:15, John Tromble was seated in the witness chair, duly sworn to honesty, waiting impatiently for this snotty, pretty-boy, headline-robbing prosecutor to kick it in gear.

The moment was historic, unprecedented, actually. No FBI director had ever sat in a witness chair — or, more accurately, none not accused of crimes themselves. One more groundbreaking achievement to tack on to the growing legend.

The evening news the night before had been an Alex fest. Every morning paper on the East Coast led off with the story about the Russian runaway millionaire who had been dragged out of the Watergate — a national landmark of sorts, after all — and was fighting deportation and a long-overdue appointment with justice in his own land. Legal experts held sway on the evening and late-night talk shows, and were still there, sipping coffee and yammering away, for the morning shows as well. Maybe they slept at the networks.

The general consensus was that Alex's legal team was getting its tail kicked and the result appeared inevitable. The only objection came from a big-time radical, highly esteemed member of the Harvard Law faculty, who posed the perverse theory that if Alex Konevitch was a foreign citizen, American courts had no purview over him. After getting laughed off two shows he disappeared back to his classroom.

Alex himself was back at the defense table, looking, if anything, more tragically decrepit and miserably ill-kempt than the day before. His beard was thicker, darker, more pronounced. Heavy circles under his eyes betrayed another long, sleepless night.

From the stand, Tromble stole a quick look at him, then quietly suppressed another smile. A few of the morning articles had mentioned his instinctive reaction as he entered the court the day before and first saw Alex; the mentions weren't overly flattering.

The pretty boy ambled up to the witness stand. "Could you please tell the court your name and title?"

It was a stupid, fatuous question, but Tromble played along. "Judge John Tromble, director of the FBI."

"And that would make you the nation's top law enforcement officer?"

"Technically, that honor belongs to the attorney general," he said with a condescending smile as if everybody should know this.

"Do you believe Alex Konevitch committed crimes in Russia that merit deportation?"

"I wouldn't know about the crimes. Russia's courts will decide that."

"But you reviewed the evidence against him?"

"My people reviewed it. I've seen summaries." Another fatuous question — Tromble obviously had more important things on his hands than sifting through piles of evidence.

"Is this evidence compelling?"

"Overwhelming."

"What would happen if Mr. Konevitch were to escape?" A slight frown. "I mean, escape again."

Tromble appeared thoughtful, as though he had never considered this possibility. "Well, it would be a flat-out disaster."

"Why?"

"Because a great deal of modern crime is international these days. Just as our corporations and businesses have expanded across borders, so have criminal syndicates. International police forces have to rely on each other."

"And you believe Mr. Konevitch's escape would hinder this cooperation?"

"He is what we would call a high-profile

criminal back home. If we let him slip away, we would hear about it from the Russians in a million unfortunate ways. It would probably cripple our efforts against the new wave of Russian criminals."

"This is called reciprocity, is it not?"

"That's one word for it. If we want them to hand over our crooks, we have to hand over theirs. If we want their help to combat crime in our streets, we need to help them."

"That seems like common sense," Caldwell remarked, as if anybody would argue otherwise. "Now, why was Mr. Konevitch placed in federal detention?" Avoiding the "prison" word was a nice touch. Detention sounded so much more pleasant: little more than a mild inconvenience for Alex while things were sorted out.

"My understanding is that the immigration judge ordered this step. You should ask him why."

"Would you care to guess?"

Another thoughtful pause. "All right. The escape rate from federal facilities is demonstrably lower than county facilities. Our Russian friends tell us that Konevitch has hundreds of millions stashed away. Sad to say, he could probably buy his way out of almost any county jail in the country. And if he disappears again, he won't make the same mistake of living out in the open next time. I expect he would flee the country, change his name, maybe get a face-job, and find haven in a more criminal-friendly country, say Brazil, or a Pacific island. He's got plenty of money to spread around and buy favors and protection. It might be impossible to find and bring him to justice."

"Should he remain in prison? As a former federal judge, you're certainly qualified to answer."

Judge Willis's head snapped up and jerked hard to his left. The question was rude and an impertinent breach of protocol. True, this was Caldwell's first performance in a federal court. But he should still know better. And Tromble definitely knew better. If he answered, either way, it was an unforgivable violation of legal courtesy. This was, after all, what Willis was here to decide. Judges, even former ones, do not prejudge or inhibit or attempt to preempt other judges. Certainly never in public. And above all, not in their own courtrooms.

Tromble pretended he didn't see Willis or understand the slight, though he betrayed himself with a slight smile. "It would be an unimaginable blunder to let him out before his immigration status is decided. Only a fool would even consider it."

Willis's eyes shifted from Tromble to MP Jones. He exerted every pound of silent pressure he could muster to encourage the attorney to rise from that chair and unleash a loud, heated objection. Come on, boy, for godsakes, let him have it. The question and answer begged for an objection. Willis *needed* that objection. He so badly wanted a chance to slap down Tromble right here, in the presence of the entire court, that he nearly screamed objection himself.

Jones just sat, wide-eyed, listening attentively with a flat expression. At least for a change he wasn't idiotically scrawling doodles on that stupid legal pad. But not a word. Not so much as a raised eyebrow or parted lips.

"Your witness," Caldwell said, and nearly strutted back to his table.

Judge Willis continued to stare at MP. In a clenched tone that managed to convey both disapproval and regret, he commented, "I imagine Mr. Jones, in the interest of saving our time, has no desire to cross-examine."

Very slowly, MP pushed himself out of his seat. "Maybe a few questions, Your Honor."

"Well" — for a moment the judge was almost too stunned to reply — "proceed then."

MP didn't budge from his table. He glanced down at Alex, who seemed to shrug as if to say: Okay, why not?

"Mr. Tromble," he began, openly ignoring the official title, "your presence today suggests this is a very important case to you."

"More important than some, less than others," Tromble said, grinning and choosing a nice middle ground.

"As FBI director, at how many other trials have you appeared as a witness?"

Tromble wasted a moment rubbing a forefinger across his lower lip, as though this question required considerable thought. "I guess none."

"You guess?"

"All right, none."

"How'd this case come to your attention?"

"I don't exactly recall."

"You don't? Being the director of the FBI and all, I thought you were a smart guy. You recall nothing?"

"It might surprise you, but the FBI handles tons of cases a year. Nobody expects me to remember every detail."

"Do you recall any conversations with any Russian government officials about Alex Konevitch?"

He scratched his head. "Not exactly."

"Inexactly would be fine."

"I don't recall any."

"Then may we assume you did have such conversations, but just can't recall them?"

"No, you may not."

"Again, Mr. Tromble, did you or did you not discuss the Konevitch issue with the Russian government? Yes or no."

"No. If I did, it was only a passing reference."

MP lifted up a piece of paper from the desk

and pretended to read from it. Then, in an annoying tone suggesting he knew everything, he asked, "That Russian colonel and head prosecutor, how'd they get over here?"

It was an old lawyer trick meant to rattle the witness. Tromble, an observant judge in his day, had seen it a thousand times. He handled it coolly, leaning back into his seat and replying, "The Russians have a compelling interest in this case. They were sent to help us prepare his extradition."

"Extradition? Do we have such a treaty with the Russians?"

"No. I . . . I misspoke."

"You mean you spoke your mind."

Caldwell showed none of MP's inclination against objections. "Objection," he yelled, launching from his chair.

"Sustained."

MP turned back to the witness stand and shook his head. "All right, Mr. Tromble, describe your role in deciding which prisons Mr. Konevitch would be incarcerated in."

"That was decided by the attorney general."

"You had no input? None?"

"Believe it or not, I stay fairly busy running the FBI. Federal prisons aren't my bailiwick."

With a condescending roll of his eyes, MP said, "Oops. That was another of those troublesome yes-or-no questions, Mr. Tromble."

"All right, no." Strictly speaking, the truth,

666

although he looked uncomfortable.

MP bounced back to the issue of Colonel Volevodz and the team of Russian prosecutors. "Who paid for their trip? Who handled their expenses?"

"How would I know?"

"That was going to be my next question," MP answered skeptically.

Tromble lived by the motto "better to give than receive," and the derisive tone from this pip-squeak immigration lawyer was starting to grate on him. He gripped the sides of his chair and snapped at MP, "Was that a question?"

"If it makes you uncomfortable, we'll come back to it later."

MP went on for another two hours, bouncing quickly from subject to subject, tossing in as many insinuations as he could get away with. Occasionally he returned to an old topic, forcing Tromble to plow and replow old ground. Same questions, repeated with minor variations, and saturated with a rising tone of disbelief.

Caldwell objected as often as he dared, most often simple harassment objections intended to disrupt the flow, but eventually the judge warned him to cool it.

After two hours, Tromble was tired of sitting in the same hard wooden chair. He was tired of this disrespectful lawyer, tired of this Russian crook fighting an overdue trip back to Russia, and tired of the rude questions. He was tired of the judge, tired of the entire routine. He regretted he had subjected himself to this. He squirmed in his chair but couldn't seem to find a comfortable position.

MP suddenly left his position behind the defense table and moved to a place about two feet from Tromble. He paused very briefly, then leaned in. "Mr. Tromble, I'm a forgetful type. Did I hear you take an oath to tell the truth on this stand?" MP paused for effect. "The whole truth, absent equivocations, quibbles, or bald deceptions."

That was it. Tromble shifted his bulk forward and nearly spit in Jones's face. "Don't you dare lecture me on integrity, you two-bit mouthpiece. I'm a respected public servant. I will not be addressed this way by you. If you have another question you will call me Judge or Mr. Director. Those are my titles."

MP smiled. "You may go, Mr. Tromble."

Tromble leaned back into the chair. He planted his feet and didn't budge, not about to let this third-rate legal loser boss him around.

After a moment, Judge Willis leaned over and said very loudly and very firmly, "Mr. Tromble, if you're not out of my witness chair in three seconds, I'll cite you for contempt."

Lunch was a welcome reprieve. Alex and

Elena were led into a small conference room and allowed to share a quiet meal in privacy. Outside, two deputies manned the door. Ham sandwiches, a fat deli pickle, chips, and ice-cold sodas, all bought and delivered by the court, were waiting in paper bags on the long conference table.

MP and his PKR pals lunched in a separate conference room three doors down. After fourteen months apart, Alex and Elena deserved a little time together, they figured. Left unsaid was that it might be the last time, and they should be allowed this last chance to be alone.

Besides, MP had a few testy legal issues about rules of evidence he wanted to bang out with the guns from the big firm. He had picked up a few lazy habits in immigration court that could get the book thrown at him in a federal venue. The afternoon would be the decisive battle — it would be very touch and go — and the boys from PKR wanted to iron out any kinks.

Caldwell, they knew, was eating with a *Post* reporter in a fancy restaurant a few blocks over, conducting a premature tutorial about his brilliant and inevitable victory. A PI employed by PKR followed him every time he left the court, and via cell phone kept his bosses apprised. Easy work, since the INS prosecutor, shipped in from out west and acclimated to the relative geniality of immigration courts, was too naïve to understand how things were played in the big leagues. At that moment, the nosy PI was seated one table over, enjoying a cheeseburger and Coke; Caldwell was a loud braggart and PKR's gumshoe was whispering into a cell phone and relaying every word of importance to a junior PKR associate in the hallway, who raced in and informed his bosses inside the conference room. PKR played for keeps.

Caldwell was oblivious to what was coming. He should be in a tense, sweaty huddle with the best and brightest at Justice, preparing for the assault Alex had gone to over a year's worth of difficult trouble to prepare. While Caldwell munched away on a cucumber salad, sipped a large diet Pepsi, and prattled on about his courtroom mastery, a surprise attack was being prepared.

A last-ditch effort was the only way to describe it, a desperate throw of the dice they would never contemplate against a more seasoned and tested brawler. It was a wild-haired idea of the sort that could come only from a legal novice — Alex himself.

After five days of painful consideration, the pros from PKR warned that it should be attempted only as a last resort.

Its only chance was to catch the government flat-footed.

The moment the conference room door

closed behind them, Alex and Elena kissed and hugged. Then Elena stepped back and said, "Mikhail called this morning. The news from Moscow is good."

"Describe good."

"Golitsin and Nicky Kozyrev were shot dead last night."

"How?" No smile, no satisfied grin — just "How?"

"Mikhail did everything you asked. He talked Yuri Khodorin into putting up five million for Nicky's death. An easy sell. You said it would be, and it was. Yuri was fed up with his people being butchered, and tired of Nicky Kozyrev trying to destroy his business."

"Who killed him?"

"He killed himself, Alex."

"How poetic. And Golitsin?"

"This is just a guess on Mikhail's part, okay?"

Alex nodded.

"Nicky learned about the bounty on his head. I mean, he was meant to learn about it, wasn't he? He apparently assumed Golitsin was behind it."

"No trust among thieves. Let me guess, Kozyrev repaid the favor?"

She nodded.

After a moment, Alex asked, "And Tatyana Lukin? What about her?"

"Fired and arrested. The tapes and photos

Mikhail gave her former boyfriend worked like magic. He also sacked the attorney general."

Alex finally allowed himself a smile. He had caused two deaths and destroyed two lives. Of course, they had tried to kill him, numerous times, and made his life as miserable as they could. The smile was distant and cold, though — the grim smile of a very different man from a few years before. "So that's it," Alex said. "No more enemies in Moscow."

"We're safe from them forever, Alex. We only have to worry about here."

Alex stared down at his flip-flops a moment. He asked Elena, "How much time do we have left?"

She checked her watch. "Forty-five minutes, more or less."

He walked to the table and picked up a chair. He carried it to the door and jammed it quietly but firmly in place underneath the large brass knob.

He turned around and looked at Elena. "Are you hungry?"

"Not in the least. You?"

The food was shoved out of the way. Elena's pantsuit flew off in two seconds; the prison suit took even less time. They landed on the tabletop and put their heart and soul into using forty minutes to make up for fourteen months apart.

Left unsaid, but certainly understood by

both of them, was that this might be their last time.

MP called his first witness.

The rear door of the courtroom opened and Kim Parrish walked quickly down the aisle. Caldwell's head spun around so fast he nearly snapped his neck. He traded a look with Tromble, now seated directly to his rear.

Neither man was the least bit happy to see her.

She was duly identified and sworn in, then sat perfectly still in the witness chair while MP warmed up.

"You're an attorney?"

"Yes."

"And you worked at the INS legal office?"

"Same place you used to work. The district office that includes the District of Columbia."

"And you once handled the case of Alex and Elena Konevitch?"

"At one time I was the lead attorney for their persecution — I mean, prosecution," Kim replied, deliberately mixing up her nouns. She looked at Alex. He smiled and offered a thankful nod.

"But no longer?"

"No."

"Why not? Isn't it unusual to be removed from a case you initiated and took to immigration court?"

"Nearly unheard of. I asked to be reassigned from the case."

MP raised an eyebrow. "You asked? From such a big, important case? Why? I imagine any INS lawyer would die for a case like this. All this attention, all those hungry reporters out on the steps. Mr. Caldwell, over there, is so giddy he can barely contain himself."

"Objection," Caldwell howled, scowling at MP.

"Sustained."

MP ignored Caldwell and acted like the objection was meaningless. "Why did you ask to be removed, Miss Parrish?"

"Because . . . because, over time, I became convinced Mr. Konevitch was being —"

"Objection!" Caldwell yelled again, nearly bouncing up and down in his chair.

"Grounds?"

"Miss Parrish is in violation of attorney-client privilege."

"Sidebar," the judge snapped. The huddle formed beside the bench.

MP brought Matt. Because he didn't want to be outnumbered, Caldwell brought Bill, one of the useless Justice boys who did his best to appear fierce and disguise his general sentiment, which was thoroughly confused. He had no idea who this lady was, what was at issue, and even less idea of his role in this case.

The judge examined the four faces, then

whispered to Caldwell, "Make your argument."

"Her knowledge of this case was gained through her employment by her client, the state."

"Mr. Jones?"

"Her employment was terminated. She's free to testify as she likes."

"She remains bound by her oath as an attorney," Caldwell insisted.

"You should have thought about that before you people sacked her," MP shot back.

"I'm inclined to agree with Mr. Caldwell," the judge intervened, strongly wanting to do the opposite, but he couldn't will the law against Caldwell's side.

"I'll restrict my questions," MP said, trying to mask his disappointment. Matt nodded at him. Good move.

"She should be dismissed," Caldwell complained.

"She's a private citizen now. She can testify," His Honor said. "But within limits. Be careful, Mr. Jones."

"I'll be watching," Caldwell sneered at MP.

"Watch hard," MP sneered back. "I enjoy an attentive audience."

They returned to their respective seats. MP spent a moment rearranging his thoughts, then asked, "Miss Parrish, do you recall a team of Russians sent over to help with this case?"

"I do, yes. Five of them in all. An investigator and four prosecutors."

"And do you recall who paid for this?"

"The FBI."

"All of it?"

"Yes, their full expenses. They've been here about a year."

"Where are they staying? Such a long way from home, what are they doing? Don't they get bored?"

Kim's eyes narrowed. She sent her answer like a rocket straight at Tromble. "At the Madison Hotel. Four of them, in separate thousand-dollar-a-night suites. For almost a year now, and they've racked up incredible bills. They eat at our most expensive restaurants, fly away first-class to Vegas every weekend, whoring, gambling, and drinking unimaginable amounts of liquor. Every bit of it is billed to the FBI."

"A rough estimate. How much would you guess the FBI has wasted on these crooked clowns?"

"Objection, Your Honor."

"Sustained. Watch your language, Mr. Jones. How much, Miss Parrish?"

"Millions. Many millions of taxpayer money. As I said, they've been here a year, living like spoiled kings."

MP returned to his seat.

Frankly there was no reason on earth for Caldwell to cross-examine Kim Parrish. His earlier, well-timed objection had slipped a noose around MP and put her in a box. No real damage had been done. Who cared about the Russians? Let them impregnate half the showgirls in Vegas. Bet the whole national treasury and lose it in a bad roll of the dice. Big deal. It had nothing to do with whether Konevitch should remain in prison.

But he was angered that Kim Parrish chose to turn on her own department. It was betrayal and he damn well knew how to make her pay for it. Time for a little discreditation.

He stood and asked, "How did you become a defense witness?"

"I don't understand the question."

"It's very simple. Did Mr. Jones contact you, or vice versa?"

"I contacted him. After I was —"

Before she could finish that thought, Caldwell cut her off. "Are you still employed at the INS, Miss Parrish?"

"No, I quit."

"You mean you were fired. You went to Mr. Jones because you were angry and wanted revenge."

"I mean I quit. Then Mr. Tromble fired me."

"No, you were fired by the director of the INS."

"I don't recall you being in the room. I was fired by Mr. Tromble because he refused to allow me to resign from what I considered a shoddy case."

Caldwell immediately turned red. He looked at the judge. "Strike that response from the record."

"You asked the question," the judge replied, "and you challenged her to elaborate. I'll allow it."

A stupid mistake. But so what? The damage was minimal. An ambiguous little defeat in the midst of a big, clear-cut victory. At least his well-timed objection had smothered her from exposing the really damaging stuff.

Kim was dismissed and MP called his next witness. Parrish walked back up the aisle and was passed by a poorly dressed, diminutive man slowly shambling in the opposite direction.

Petri Arbatov was sworn and seated.

MP spent a moment walking him through his background — for the edification of the judge and audience, he dwelled on it at some length. KGB for twenty years before his sudden defection. A law degree from Moscow University, but no mention of the law degree from Catholic University.

MP didn't ask, and Petri didn't offer.

The crowd in the court hung on every word. With few exceptions, none had ever seen a real live KGB agent, up close and personal. Petri was their first peek at a living, breathing KGB agent — and he looked so small, so crushed, so sad. Who could believe this was the fierce demon portrayed in all those Cold War cinema thrillers and spy novels? Why hadn't we won the Cold War thirty years earlier? Having spent no time in courtrooms, Petri looked nervous and his opening responses were halting.

Next, a few warm-up questions to put the witness at greater ease. How Petri came in contact with this case, his interview with Kim Parrish, and so forth.

MP said, "So you were hired to translate the documents given to the INS, via the FBI?"

"It is how I make my living these days. I translate for American firms doing business in Russia."

"Are you still a practicing attorney?"

"No. I quit the profession sixteen years ago."

"Why?"

"The work I did for the KGB, I suppose. It left a certain taste."

"What kind of work would that be?"

Petri looked around the court for a moment and let the suspense build. "My job, Mr. Jones, was to frame people," he answered slowly, drawing out the words.

Petri spoke quietly, and the reporters bent forward as they spent a few minutes delving into that legal specialty. Fascinating stuff. People were on the edge of their seats, and never budged. How to frame a perfectly innocent man, ten easy steps to a surefire trip to a gulag, or worse.

Then, from MP, "And what did you conclude after you reviewed the material about Konevitch from Russia?"

"Objection," Caldwell barked.

"Grounds?" Willis asked, leaning his chin on his fist.

"Uh . . . attorney-client privilege again."

His Honor peeked down at Petri. "Remind me, please. Are you still a practicing attorney, sir?"

"Not for many, many years. These days I'm a simple translator."

MP confidently asked, "Did you sign a contract that precluded you from sharing what you learned?"

"No. I merely stated my price and Miss Parrish hired me."

The judge said, "Then overruled. Please answer the first question."

Petri looked at Alex seated at the table. "After looking at everything, I concluded that Mr. Konevitch was being framed."

"Why?"

"There is a certain stench to such things, Mr. Jones."

"An odor? An actual smell? Explain that."

Petri directed a finger at Colonel Volevodz seated at the rear, now in his capacity as an official observer. "Take that man, Mr. Jones. He might tell you he works at the Ministry of

Security, but he was definitely career KGB before this. He might claim he's merely enforcing the law, but his hands are covered with blood. It's a stink no shower will erase."

Every neck in the court craned to examine Volevodz. A more charming man might have smiled or chuckled disarmingly — at a minimum shaken his head in pretended disbelief. Volevodz tried to bore holes through Petri with his skinny, mean little eyes.

Oh yeah, no doubt about it. There's the guy from the Hollywood thrillers — KGB down to his undershorts.

"But the documents?" MP asked. "Did they actually smell?"

"Well, you see, the key is to produce a perfect case. These four prosecutors your FBI is caring for, they are experts at this. That's exactly what they did."

MP led him through this for a while, the craftsmanship of how to string a noose with lies, forgeries, and planted evidence. Then he shifted on a dime and asked, "Incidentally, were you present when Miss Parrish was fired?"

"I was there, yes. Seated right beside her. But she wasn't fired."

"The prosecutor claimed she was."

"He's wrong, or he's lying. She quit."

"Why did she quit?"

"She reported to her boss that this case was phony. Cooked up. A sham."

MP paused to allow this to sink in, then asked, "What happened?"

"She is an honorable person, Mr. Jones. She did something I never had the courage to do."

"Which was what, Mr. Arbatov?"

"She tried to get the case dropped."

MP affected a look of huge surprise. "The attorney in charge wanted it dropped?"

"Yes."

"Well . . . why wasn't it dropped?"

"She was brought into a room with that man" — he pointed out Tromble, who was trying desperately to ignore him — "and her INS bosses. She begged them to drop the case. They refused quite rudely. She then asked to be reassigned, as is the prerogative, indeed, the responsibility of any attorney who believes a case is improper. They yelled at her. She resigned, then that man" — another damning finger aimed at Tromble — "screamed at her that she was fired."

MP thanked him and walked away. Petri sat quietly and looked at Alex. Alex looked back, nodding his head, a silent acknowledgment to an old countryman who had refound his conscience.

When offered the chance to cross-examine, Caldwell passed. He knew next to nothing about Petri Arbatov. What he did know was that the man was a legal minefield, and further questioning would only reinforce the damage.

Besides, the damage wasn't really that bad. Tromble looked like a mean horse's ass; like that was news to anybody. And maybe he lied a little on the stand. But that was Tromble's problem, not Caldwell's.

Frankly, the more he thought about it, Caldwell was quite pleased. There was room for only one ego on this side of the case — one shining exemplar of truth and justice — and this skinny, tired little Russian just blew Tromble right out of the saddle.

When time came for the summary, Caldwell would strongly note how the Russian "expert" had offered an opinion — not a fact, but a baseless opinion pulled out of thin air after concluding the case was, in his own words, too perfect. And he was heavily outnumbered. The word of a self-confessed framer of innocent men against that of the entire Russian government; a reformed, democratic government, he would stipulate quite loudly, not the corrupt old dictatorship this Petri Arbatov had sent people to the gallows for.

The little Russian was released and he nearly bounced out of his chair. He and Volevodz exchanged hateful looks as Petri passed up the aisle. MP announced that he had no more witnesses.

MP remained standing, though. He looked at the judge and asked, "Could we have a moment, Your Honor?"

"Take all the time you need," Willis replied, strongly intimating that time was not on his side.

Alex stood, too, then Matt, and for a moment they gathered in a tight triangle and conferred in tense whispers.

"What do you think?" Alex asked MP.

"We're in trouble. Big trouble," MP told him bluntly. "Kim was our star witness. But Caldwell blocked us from unloading her most damaging testimony."

"You don't think Petri repaired that?" Alex asked, searching their faces.

Matt, the pro with years of big-time criminal experience answered for both lawyers. "Caldwell will cream him in his closing. I certainly would. The opinion of a man who admitted framing people against the word of an entire government. The issue is credence, Alex."

MP nodded at this candid observation. "That's exactly what he'll do. If I try to counter it in my closing, it'll only sound defensive."

"Then let's go with it," Alex stated very firmly.

MP and Matt exchanged looks. Both had badly hoped to avoid Alex's proposal. Legally speaking, it was fraught with difficulties. After a moment, Matt mentioned to MP, "He hides it well, but I think the judge is sympathetic."

MP nodded. Not enthusiastically, but nonetheless it was a nod.

Alex said to both of them, "It's all or nothing. Bluff, and do your best."

"I hope you're the lucky type," Matt replied, clearly believing this was crazy.

"He wouldn't be here if he was lucky," MP replied dryly.

Alex and Matt fell into their seats. MP remained standing. Finally, he announced somewhat hesitantly, "I'd like to submit a little evidence."

Matt handed him a tape player, a compact Bose system with small but thunderously powerful speakers. Alex arranged the system on his table, carefully directing the speakers toward the prosecutor's table, while the bailiff strung an extension cord and plugged it in. Next Matt handed Alex a tray loaded with about twenty cassettes. Alex noodled through the tapes and finally settled on one that he carefully withdrew. MP took it and inserted it neatly into the recorder. Alex's finger hovered over the start button as MP said, "This is a phone call to Miss Tatyana Lukin, special assistant to the Kremlin chief of staff. She's a lawyer who also serves as legal advisor to Boris Yeltsin." Alex stabbed play.

First, the sound of a ringing telephone.

"What? Who is this?" A woman's voice in Russian, and the annoyed tone came across loud and clear.

"Please hold for the director of the Federal Bureau of Investigation." A female voice, bored, in English.

"Hello, Tatyana. Heard the news about your boy Konevitch? Made a big splash in the news on this side of the water."

"How did you get my home number?"

"When I couldn't get you at the office, my boys in the embassy tracked it down."

"All right. Yes, I see that you've got him in jail. Why haven't you just shipped him here?"

"It's complicated. Not as easy as I thought. Listen, I need a big favor."

"John, you promised me Konevitch."

"Well, just listen. Some of these judges here are pigheaded. I need you to cook up a case for me."

"Why?"

"Because I can't just throw his ass on a plane. Look, Tatyana, I really don't care about the details. Understand? Come on, your guys are supposed to be real good at this sort of thing."

"What sort of thing is that, John?"

A long silence. "Look, give me whatever you like, just be damned sure it sounds convincing."

"Is this absolutely necessary?"

"Probably not. He goes back to court in a week. No way in hell he won't be deported. But the judge might act crazily. Call it a precaution, insurance."

Caldwell finally came to his senses and, doing something he should've done a minute before, yelled, "Objection, objection."

Alex reached over and cranked the volume up full blast until it drowned out Caldwell's voice. The voices on the tape howled out of the speakers and filled the courtroom.

"You can keep him in jail, can't you? A lot of powerful people here are opposed to letting you keep the FBI outpost in your embassy. I'm doing my best, but, John, it's a real uphill battle. Such a clear lack of mutual cooperation won't go over well."

An unintelligible mumble from Tromble before she cut him off. "President Yeltsin asked me about this case just yesterday. He keeps asking if he needs to discuss it with your president."

"Hey, we'll find a way. I don't care if I have to bribe the judge or kill his wife. I'll find a way."

Caldwell was now on his feet, screaming "Objection!" at the top of his voice.

Alex pushed stop. The tape finally went quiet, though it seemed to echo for a long moment. He glanced around and studied the faces in the court.

Tromble was melting into his chair. Every eye in the court was on him.

Directly to his front, Caldwell spent a long moment in terrified confusion. Eventually he repeated, an octave higher but more quietly this time, "Objection, Your Honor."

"Sidebar," the judge replied and scrambled off his bench. Again Matt accompanied MP, and this time he added Alex to his entourage. Again one of the Justice boys accompanied Caldwell, who arrived red-faced and furious.

"Lawyer's meeting," Caldwell snapped, directing a finger at Alex. "He has no business here."

"His presence is necessary to establish the provenance of the tapes," MP answered very nicely. "This is a hearing, not a trial. What do you say, Your Honor?"

"That might be a good idea," Willis answered, still a little shocked by what he had heard.

"That's clearly an illegal, inadmissible tape," Caldwell snapped, at the judge, at MP, at anybody in earshot.

"To the contrary," MP argued in a voice dripping with phony confidence, "it's legal and quite admissible."

"Was it taped with the consent of the conversants?" Caldwell demanded.

"That's American law," MP replied with a smug smile, trying to bluff his way through.

Alex quickly interjected. "This tape was made in Russia. Russians are allowed to tape and wiretap to their heart's content. No law bans it. In fact, it's our national pastime."

Caldwell had no idea whether that was true or not. "Your Honor, please," he pleaded, "it's blatantly inadmissible. Obviously the product of a wiretap."

His Honor looked at MP. "Well?"

"Yesterday, the prosecution introduced into evidence a wiretap provided by the Russian chief prosecutor. It concerned the supposed activities of Orangutan Media. I didn't challenge him on whether the tape was the product of a legal warrant, and am now dismayed that he's even making this argument. He established the precedent. I should be accorded equal latitude."

"Do you have more tapes, Mr. Konevitch?"

"About twenty here. Another fifty or so in a safe-deposit box."

"Are you requesting to play all of them?"

"Not at all," Alex replied. "My wife and I picked out the most damning ones."

"These are all conversations between Tromble and this lady?"

"No, just one more of those," MP insisted, borrowing a bit of Alex's confidence. "I'd love to play it. It's the one where Tromble brags to this lady about all the terrible prisons he's sending Alex to. He promises her that he will keep my client suffering until he snaps, until he begs to be returned to Russia."

"And what material's on the rest of the tapes?"

"Tatyana Lukin had two . . . well, I guess you'd call them business partners."

"Go on."

"Nicky Kozyrev, a notorious syndicate chief. This is a guy with Interpol and Russian police records long enough to stock a library. And General Sergei Golitsin, a former KGB deputy director hired by Alex as his corporate chief of security."

"These are phone conversations?"

"Some," Alex replied. "Most were captured as the three of them sat in back of a fancy limousine."

"And their role in this affair?"

It was time for the lawyers to take over, and MP answered, "Glad you asked. They stole Alex's money and his companies. Then they framed him. Then they orchestrated his persecution here."

"And these tapes prove those accusations?"

"I'll leave that for you to decide."

"And how did you come by these tapes?"

"My client."

"And how did you acquire them?" he asked, peering now at Alex.

"I hired a private detective. He did the taping and sent them to me."

After a moment of quiet consideration, the judge suggested, "Let me tell you what worries me, Mr. Jones. For all I know, your client had those tapes produced by actors."

It was Matt Rivers's turn at bat and he opened with a mighty swing. "My firm had the tapes analyzed over the weekend by a reputable laboratory. A clip of Tromble doing

690

a TV interview was compared against the tape you just heard. Perfect match. Identical voice print. That analysis is included in our submission."

"I see."

"Also, they compared Miss Lukin's voice from the tape you just heard against the remaining tapes. It's her speaking to Tromble, and it's her speaking with her co-conspirators."

"And these tapes are in Russian?"

Matt's turn again. "We hired three actors to role-play in English. We're submitting the originals as well. You can check the accuracy of the translations if you wish. No expense was spared. They're quite good."

Matt couldn't wait for the judge to plow through them. The actors were professionals, used by New York publishers to make audio-books. Over a very busy weekend, they rehearsed together for hours. Not only did they reproduce the conversations with passion, conviction, and fluidity, but they captured the small but important details that add a certain verisimilitude. The sounds of Nicky's furious snorts. The menace in Golitsin's voice. The woman who did Tatyana was nothing short of spectacular, a purr so spot-on you could almost picture her seductiveness.

Caldwell looked like a whipped dog. It was obvious which way the judge was leaning.

His case was falling apart before his eyes. He could do nothing to prevent it. The sad truth was, he was dying to hear the tapes himself.

The judge said, "I want to hear them in my chambers before I decide. I expect both of you want to be present," he said, looking at the lawyers, then at Alex. "Not you. This is a matter for lawyers to hash out."

Three minutes later, court was adjourned until further notice. The solemn-faced judge issued one last ominous instruction: Tromble would be present when the court reconvened. It was an unchristian sentiment, and he felt mildly guilty about it, but Tromble had done him no favors, and he fully intended to repay it.

The judge and lawyers disappeared to his chambers. The reporters straggled out to join their colleagues on the front steps where they would share the incredible events of the morning and file as much as they could before court reconvened. Within minutes, the legal talking heads were back in the studios, on the air, sharing updates, squawking away, and shoving opinions and predictions at whoever cared to listen. The opinions were divided and, hotly debated.

Half thought the judge might make a rare exception since this was, after all, only a habeas corpus hearing, where the benefit of the doubt normally leaned toward the accused. The other half claimed the defense didn't have a prayer.

Court reconvened four hours later. The reporters were notified and they bickered and fought with one another for choice seats, or even standing room at the crowded rear of the room. Would the judge allow that first tape? If so, what was on the others? And the big question of the day was, how screwed was John Tromble, director of the FBI? The sense of curiosity was running at fever pitch. The studios were screaming for updates the moment a decision was rendered.

With grim faces, the lawyers marched out and fell into their chairs. Alex was led back to the defense table after four long hours of cooling his heels in a holding cell. He had, however, showered, shaved, trimmed his own hair, and changed into a respectable suit and tie. The time had come, he decided, to present a before-and-after shot for the viewers.

And the contrast between the downtrodden criminal and this towering, clean-cut, handsome man at the table was indeed striking. You saw what they did to me, his old self screamed — now look at what I was before the power of the state fell on my head.

The side door opened. Willis hefted his robes and walked up to his bench. He appeared sad, furious, shaken, and slightly nervous.

Court was brought to order and things

settled down quickly. Willis stared at the ceiling for a long moment, his usual habit before rendering his decisions. A powerfully affecting moment — the former priest searching for guidance and wisdom from on high. Tromble, by contrast, looked perfectly miserable, squirming in his seat, unable to get comfortable.

The eyes came down. "After listening to all the tapes and giving the issue due consideration, I've decided to accept the tapes into evidence."

Alex leaned far back into his chair. Elena actually released a squeal of joy.

But as the court had heard only one tape, the significance of this decision was mysterious. The reporters remained mute.

He looked at Alex. "Sir, will you please stand?"

MP squeezed Alex's arm. The "sir" seemed to be a good sign. He stood.

"Let me begin by expressing my deepest apologies." Willis adjusted his robes and paused briefly. "Let me add a strong personal recommendation. I expect you and your attorney to file a civil suit against the FBI and Department of Justice. You have been wronged, sir. No amount of money will make up for it but it won't hurt, either."

Tromble was seated in his chair, struggling to square the competing demands of appearing confident and powerful while trying also to be completely invisible.

The judge then began addressing the court, speaking quite loudly, and ever so clearly, so that even the farthest reporter in the back wouldn't miss a word or legal nuance. He began with a long summary of everything on the tapes. He had notes, though he referred to them only rarely, primarily when a precise quote was preferred over a generalized summary. There had been a conspiracy of staggering proportions in Moscow; Konevitch was its first victim. His fortune was stolen, his companies taken away, only after he was brutally tortured. The conspiracy reached into the highest offices in the Kremlin; "we have these problems ourselves sometimes," the judge explained, "Teapot Dome, Watergate, Iran-Contra, and so on. This case represents another of those watershed historical embarrassments."

He shared the names of the conspirators, struggling with the Russian names, and outlined their scheme. Next he spent a few moments dwelling on how exactly American law enforcement got duped into being a tool for the conspirators. A good duping requires a gullible dupe, he pointed out; the director of the FBI was that man. A quick description of the quid pro quo: they get Alex, whatever the costs; Tromble gets to sprinkle a few more agents in Moscow. A brief summary of how Tromble violated countless laws and procedures to persecute Alex and Elena Konevitch. There were too many breaches for the judge to count, but a full accounting would be prepared later by competent figures with enough time to wade through all the tapes and other evidence.

In effect, the INS, the FBI, and the Justice Department — the very people represented by the attorneys at the prosecution table — were suddenly branch offices of a cabal of evil people in a foreign land. MP had offered the judge a few pointers back in the chambers, and he threw out some of the more egregious ones: the constant shuffling through increasingly miserable prisons to turn up the heat; punishments inflicted by various wardens under orders from Washington; wiretaps in their apartment; illegal searches; the senseless destruction of their home and property; their money seized by the federal government and their business enterprise shut down and bankrupted.

For ten minutes, not a soul looked bored or even mildly inattentive. Twice the director of the FBI tried to walk out — both times he made a meek retreat back to his position after a stern and angry judge issued a strong warning.

Jason Caldwell sulked in his chair and listened to the bright, shining future he had envisioned collapse in ruins. He could see the evening news that night; him holding forth on the courthouse steps, the picture of brimming confidence promising a quick, punishing victory; then flash to a bunch of mealymouthed legal monkeys dissecting his overwhelming destruction in court. He knew it was going to be horrible — absolutely horrible.

He was right; it was.

Judge Willis ended with another long apology to Alex, then ordered his immediate release from custody.

He grabbed his robes and left.

Tromble dug his heels in and rushed for the door, shoving aside reporters who were bombarding him with questions. He turned to a deputy in the hallway. "Is there a back entrance to this place?"

The deputy smiled. "Sure is."

"Where?"

"Find it yourself, you prick."

The kisses, hugs, and relieved expressions of appreciation at the defense table — along with a round robin of the usual victorious congratulations among Alex, Elena, MP, Matt, and Marvin — lasted five minutes. Marvin eventually lifted a stately arm and quieted them down. The old pro got a strong grip on Alex's arm and solemnly pledged he would personally file and oversee the suits against the FBI, Justice, and INS.

One big suit, a monstrous case for compensatory damages, he promised with a gleam in his eyes.

"What are our chances, and when's the payoff?" asked Alex, ever the businessman.

Marvin smiled and rubbed his hands. "It's not a question of chances or when," he replied. "How much is the only question." He would demand and fight with conviction for ten million; after enough blood was shed, he would give them a break and settle at five million.

"Still pro bono?" Alex asked.

Marvin flashed a ruthless grin. "Not a chance."

Elena said to Marvin, quite firmly, "But you will forget your usual third. You'll take twenty percent or I swear I'll hire another firm tonight."

One look at her and Marvin had absolutely no doubt she meant every word. "Deal."

A mob of reporters descended and was driven off only after MP solemnly vowed he would stand on the courtroom steps all night. They could ask questions to their heart's content and he would bloviate until the moon came out. Before the night was over, he would be booked on five talk shows, and take calls from six book agents and five movie studio chiefs.

Marvin called the lawyers together into a tight huddle. They spent a brief moment trading ideas back and forth, planning what would be a very busy morning of filings.

When they turned around, Alex and Elena were gone.

34

The snow was three feet deep and dry, and though it was only fall, the snow machines were roaring full-blast and tourists in Aspen were at high tide. Neither Alex nor Elena had ever been near skis, much less on them. Both were good athletes, though. After three weeks of mastering the art, they were roaring recklessly down the black slopes like they owned the place.

Elena had argued vigorously for someplace warm. Her preferred option had been a small, pleasant, neglected Caribbean island where the natives were friendly and had no idea who they were, and wouldn't care a whit if they did.

Her preferred option two was one of those private, gated resorts in Florida. A nice one with a thick forest of palm trees, a thousand holes of golf, a well-stocked bar, and a beach where they could drink themselves silly on rum and piña coladas and roast themselves into shriveled prunes.

Alex had experienced enough heat and wouldn't hear of it. A federal prison in Georgia, followed by another in the heart of Chicago, and finally, the worst oven of all, a scorching summer in Yuma.

His Russian roots screamed for someplace where icicles hung off your nose. Exploiting her desire for privacy, he had briefly argued for an Arctic expedition, but Elena did not warm to that idea. The argument shifted slowly southward, working its way through Alaska, then, one by one, through the provinces of Canada, and refused to budge another degree once it hit Colorado.

At the end of the second week, MP called. Elena answered. Alex picked up the other line.

"Have you heard the big news?" MP asked them.

Elena happily informed him, "The only newspaper we've touched all week was the one we used to get a fire started."

"The attorney general quit this morning. Apparently the cows in Montana are calling her back."

"And Tromble?" Alex asked.

"Boy, you are out of touch. Fired, five days ago. He fled to Puerto Rico and is taking no calls."

"And how are you doing, MP?" Elena asked.

"Great. I have an offer right here from

PKR. They're offering a partnership. They don't currently handle immigration law, and they'd like me to set up a new division."

"Will you take it?"

"I don't think so. Terry and I talked it over. It's almost ridiculously generous, but I doubt I'll fit in."

"You won't miss the money?" Alex, the practical one, asked.

"I think I'll be fine. With all the hooplah about you, I've kicked my fee up to three hundred an hour. Nobody's said no yet."

They promised they'd all get together for dinner after Alex and Elena got tired of Aspen, or ran out of money. Truthfully, neither of them was the least bit tired of it. It was such a playground, and the restaurants and bars were great and plentiful.

Bitchy had popped in for a visit two days before. He flew in from Chicago, where he had just closed on a North Shore home. The appellate court that reviewed his case had recently been joined by two new justices: a pair of rabid Giants fans who sincerely enjoyed the misery of their die-hard Jets brethren on the court. Neither was the least bit appalled by Beatty's assault. Besides, his letter to the court sounded so gracious and repentant the judges were all deeply affected. And, after all, it was Bitchy's first offense.

He showed up in a yellow taxi that brought him from Denver International, lumbering out in a three-piece, tailored Brooks Brothers suit, looking like a Wall Street banker — or more like four or five bankers squished into the same suit. He lifted Elena off the ground with one arm and gave her a huge kiss. After months in a cell with Alex, he knew all about her. He hugged Alex and started to kiss him also, but that's where Alex drew the line.

Over a long dinner, Bitchy happily informed them he was now in talks with the Bears, while his lawyers haggled with the football commissioner about having him reinstated in time for spring camp. Bitchy was optimistic. The commish was playing hard to get, but the inside word was that it was all show. Bitchy was a two-year All-Pro, after all, and an ex-con to boot. That combination always did wonders for attendance and TV ratings. He was also confident the Bears would kick in another million on top of his old three million contract. His reputation alone was worth at least that — what team wouldn't think long and hard before taking on a team with Beatty on the roster?

Elena invited Bitchy to join them on the slopes that day, but he demurred and was resting in his hotel room. The truth was, Bitchy wouldn't go near a ski lift. He was terrified of heights.

So Alex and Elena were alone, at the top of the big mountain, staring down at the valley. The sun was out. The snow sparkled and glistened. Hundreds of skiers below them were doing all the silly things people do when balanced on two thin boards — collapsing, racing, struggling to stay upright, occasionally producing bone-crunching collisions.

Alex was in no hurry to get down the hill. He sat down and watched the sun move lethargically through the sky. Elena sat beside him. They held hands. Both knew the time had come for The Talk. It had been put off for weeks while they slept, nearly killed each other with sex, drank too much wine and champagne, ignored work, and remembered why they loved each other so much. But they sensed the differences. More than two years of being chased and hounded, terrorized and threatened, and then the long enforced separation, had changed them. The marriage needed time to adjust.

The year alone had created a more self-reliant, more independent and stubborn Elena. She had lived by herself, started a thriving business, and outsmarted the people who wanted to kill her. It was impossible to shrink back to her former self; nor did she care to.

As for Alex, the vestiges of brutal torture and fourteen months in prison were hard to shake off. Elena wasn't certain he ever would. The smiles came slowly, the eyes never stayed still. He watched strangers with distrust, eyeing their hands first; Elena was sure he was looking for a shank.

"Do you want to stay here?" Alex finally asked.

"You mean America?" Elena replied.

"There are other countries. We could take a chance on Russia again."

"My family's still there. All our friends, too."

"Those are important considerations."

"It wouldn't be good for you, though, would it?"

"I think not. Russia's changing, Elena. The crooks and KGB are taking over again. Yeltsin's a failure, a placeholder until they're ready to make their move."

"And we might have to go through the same thing again?"

"We'll be smarter next time."

"But so will they."

"Yes, they will. You pick. I just need someplace where I can make money."

"That's your problem, Konevitch."

"I didn't know I had a problem."

"You're looking at this backward. Think of it as someplace we can spend money."

"We're not rich yet, dear. Only two and a half million in the bank. It's not enough to live on forever."

"The lawsuit might net another five to ten million."

"The government will fight it to the bitter end. It could take a decade. We might lose."

"MP thinks a book and movie deal might bring in up to ten million."

"A book deal will take at least two years and might amount to very little. Movie deals aren't worth the paper they're written on."

"You're a pessimist."

"I'm a realist."

After a moment, Elena pointed at the small village below. "It's beautiful, isn't it?"

"Very beautiful. Like a small French or German village shipped over and planted in heaven."

"How about a house here?"

"A cramped two-bedroom apartment would cost at least a million. After fourteen months in a cell, I demand space."

She surveyed the town below. She pointed at a cluster of large chalets that climbed up the slopes on the west side. The homes were immense, spaced far apart, pine trees towering over the high roofs, no more than a ten-minute walk to the bottom slope. "How about that neighborhood?"

"At least ten million."

They fell back in the snow, held hands, and stared straight up at the sky. "Alex?" Elena said.

"What?" Alex said.

"I forgot to tell you something."

He squeezed her hand.

"Mikhail had a talk with Golitsin the day before he died."

"I know. Those were his instructions. Give Golitsin a good scare. Fool him into believing Nicky was behind it."

"Well, I told him to talk to Golitsin about something else, too. So Mikhail brought along a few of his friends, and they . . . well, they encouraged Golitsin to chat a little about our money." She paused to admire the sky. "You know how persuasive Mikhail can be."

Alex slowly sat up. "How persuasive was he?"

"Oh . . . enough. Golitsin gave him 225 million reasons to go away and leave him alone."

Alex turned and stared hard at his wife. "Mikhail found our money?"

"I let him keep five million. He more than earned it, you know."

"Where is it now?"

"Switzerland. I don't trust Bermudan banks anymore. Do you?"

Alex stood and spent several minutes staring down on the valley. Elena eventually stood and joined him.

They waited quietly until Alex asked, "Exactly which chalet on that hillside did you buy?"

"The big one almost exactly halfway up the slope." She tried to point it out. "The one with the four big stone chimneys."

"Is it big inside?"

"The neighbors call it the coliseum. The

current owners use walkie-talkies so they don't have to scream at each other all day."

"Is it nice?"

"Crystal chandeliers, six or seven enormous fireplaces, a huge wine cellar, and a twenty-seat movie theater downstairs. If you like that sort of thing, yes, I guess it's nice."

"How many bedrooms?"

"I'm not sure. Six, seven, eight. They're sort of spread all over the place. Hard to count."

"Do they come with children?"

"No. The owner insisted we have to make our own."

"She pushed a hard bargain."

"She was quite tough on that point."

"When do we get one?"

"They're not exactly an impulse buy, dear. They have long delivery dates. Up to nine months, I hear."

After a moment Alex said, "I love you."

"I love you, too."

"Race you to the bottom?"

"You'll eat my dust, Konevitch."

"Snow, dear. You'll eat my snow."

"Oh, shut up, and try to catch me."

AUTHOR'S NOTE

A few years ago, I received an interesting proposal on my Web site from a Russian expat who generously suggested that his adventure might inspire a captivating book. After recently reading my third novel, *Kingmaker,* he thought I had gotten a few things right about modern Russia, and wondered if I might be the right person to attempt a tale about him.

I soon met Alex and his wife, Elena, and quickly became curious, intrigued, and impressed. Not to mention deeply enchanted and enamored. So I dug in more.

The real Alex and Elena Konanykhin became the inspiration for this book and they are its animating force. In real life, they experienced fifteen years I wouldn't wish on my worst enemy — and I pray my worst enemy wouldn't wish upon me. A lovely couple; he, tall and darkly handsome; she, tiny, funny, and vividly, blondely beautiful. Both were strikingly intelligent, deeply in love, and stunned at what they had been forced to endure. Alex in fact wrote a superb nonfictional memoir of his long, amazing trial — a book called *Defiance* — a sad, joyful, engrossing, inspiring, terrifically written account. It's definitely worth reading if you enjoyed this book. My book, after all, is fiction, as are all its characters, except Alex, Elena, and a few historical figures.

Tragically, a year ago, Elena, who had weathered so many dark and bright days with Alex and who battled for his freedom, supported his brilliance, argued his innocence, risked her life, did jail time, and withstood fears and privations most of us could not imagine, died. Two weeks afterward, Alex e-mailed me.

"I am in agony," was all he could say.

As noted on the first page, this book is dedicated to Elena. I am so disappointed in myself that I failed to finish it before she left us.

But also to Alex, whom I am quite pleased to call an American, and a friend.

ABOUT THE AUTHOR

Brian Haig is the *New York Times* bestselling author of six novels featuring JAG attorney Sean Drummond. A former special assistant to the chairman of the Joint Chiefs of Staff, he has also been published in journals ranging from the *New York Times* to *USA Today* to *Details.* He lives in New Jersey with his wife and four children. For more information on the author you can visit his website at www.brianhaig.com.

The employees of Thorndike Press hope you have enjoyed this Large Print book. All our Thorndike, Wheeler, and Kennebec Large Print titles are designed for easy reading, and all our books are made to last. Other Thorndike Press Large Print books are available at your library, through selected bookstores, or directly from us.

For information about titles, please call:

(800) 223-1244

or visit our Web site at:

http://gale.cengage.com/thorndike

To share your comments, please write:

Publisher
Thorndike Press
295 Kennedy Memorial Drive
Waterville, ME 04901